THE SECOND SON

'Perfect for lovers of action-packed crime brimming with heart.' Lyn Yeowart, author of *The Silent Listener*

'Impressive…Loraine Peck gives us a fast-paced gangland thriller…The women are the real strength here.'
Sydney Morning Herald

'A brilliant action-packed crime debut.' Avenue Bookstore

'With overtones of *The Godfather*, these of family dynamics, conflict and expectations are explored with insight and nuance…An exciting new voice on the Australian crime writing landscape.' Good Reading

'Intense. The world building is so detailed and the characters! Looking forward to the sequel already.'
R. W. R. McDonald, author of *The Nancys*

'With twists and turns I didn't see coming, it's got a terrific hook.' Tim Ayliffe, author of *The Enemy Within*

'Fast-paced, great characters, evil plot and a shocking twist right at the end—what more could a crime fan want?'
Herald Sun

'Have you ever read a book and imagined it as a gripping, 10-episode Australian crime drama? *The Second Son* is like that: action-packed, full of surprises, and with enough family tension to keep you hooked with every chapter.'
Readings

'Compelling and gritty, at its heart this crime thriller is also the He says/She says tale of a marriage disintegrating under a Molotov cocktail of toxic masculinity and family honour. Hi-octane, brutal, raw and emotional, this is one striking crime debut.' Greg Woodland, author of *The Night Whistler*

From magician's assistant to crime novelist, it's all about mastering the art of subterfuge for Loraine Peck, whose love of crime fiction propelled her to write the kind of book she loves to read. Loraine and her husband split their time between Sydney and the Gold Coast.

The Second Son won the Australian Crime Writers Association's 2021 Ned Kelly Award for Best Debut Crime Fiction. It was shortlisted for two Davitt Awards by Sisters in Crime and for a Danger Prize by BAD Sydney Crime Writers Festival. The sequel, *The Double Bind* is being published in early 2023.

THE
SECOND
SON

LORAINE PECK

TEXT PUBLISHING MELBOURNE AUSTRALIA

The Text Publishing Company acknowledges the Traditional Owners of the country on which we work, the Wurundjeri people of the Kulin Nation, and pays respect to their Elders past and present.

textpublishing.com.au

The Text Publishing Company
Wurundjeri Country, Level 6, Royal Bank Chambers, 287 Collins Street, Melbourne Victoria 3000 Australia

First published by The Text Publishing Company, 2021
This edition published 2023

Cover design by Jessica Horrocks
Page design by Imogen Stubbs
Cover image by Valentino Sani/Trevillion Images
Typeset in Adobe Garamond by J&M Typesetting

Printed and bound in Australia by Griffin Press, an Accredited ISO AS/NZS 14001:2004 Environmental Management System printer

ISBN: 9781922458971 (paperback)
ISBN: 9781925923841 (ebook)

A catalogue record for this book is available from the National Library of Australia.

The paper in this book is manufactured only from wood grown in sustainable regrowth forests.

For Stead, my very own Croatian.

PROLOGUE

I dream in English now. I know the nightmare is coming when I start dreaming in my own language. This dream is a memory burnt deep into my soul.

My father opens the front door and the soldier raises his shotgun. The blast lifts my father off his feet and hurls him against the wall. More soldiers surge through the front door and my mother starts screaming.

I am fourteen and small for my age; I could pass for twelve. Maybe this is why they don't kill me. Instead, they tie me to a chair and gag me, so I have to watch them rape my mother and sister.

I count them twice. There are always ten soldiers in our tiny house.

My mother pleads with them, 'Leave my Susana alone! Do what you want to me. Don't you touch her!'

But Susana is sixteen. All the boys in school are in love with her. She is both kind and beautiful, impossible to ignore.

My mother's cries for mercy turn to curses. 'You will all die and be sent to hell! You will burn forever! You are weak! You are cowards!'

One of the men steps forward and shoots my mother in the face.

They drink the red wine they find in our cellar and help themselves to the food in the fridge and pantry. They feast as they rape my sister, one after another, all through the night. Until one soldier notices the pools of blood and, with his fingers on her throat, declares her dead.

They catch and kill our chickens and take what is left of the food. They leave me tied to the chair, sitting in my own filth, surrounded by my dead family.

JOHNNY

I blink in the darkness. Someone is pounding on our front door. Amy groans and turns on her bedside lamp: 3.15 a.m.

I roll out of bed, pull on my jeans and head down the hall. The knocking starts up again. Fuck, I'm coming, okay? I check our son on the way past his bedroom. Fast asleep, sheet thrown off, arms flung wide, his blond hair too long for a boy.

I grab the cricket bat I keep in the umbrella stand and check the spyhole. Police. My heart rate cranks up a notch, but I put the bat back in the stand. When I open the door, the wet heat of the night spills in and expensively cooled air swirls out around my ankles.

Two uniforms take up a sizeable chunk of the front patio. They're big bastards, similar in shape, bookends. A tall bloke stands in the shadows a couple of paces back, a glint of red in his hair.

'What's going on?' I'm looking at the suit, trying to place him.

He steps forward. 'Been a while, Johnny.'

3

My shoulders tighten. Detective Inspector Ian MacPherson. The last time we met he was in charge of the Liverpool Narcs. Now he heads up the Western Sydney Organised Crime Task Force. What the fuck? Why is someone this senior at my front door?

MacPherson nods at the two uniforms. 'Constables Bridges and Dyson. Can we come in?'

'Got a warrant?'

'We're not here to search the place. Something's happened.'

Did one of the boys get caught in the middle of a job? But why come to me? Has something happened to Dad? I turn on some lights and gesture towards the living room.

'I'll throw a shirt on.'

By the time I make it back up the hall to our bedroom, Amy is zipping up her dress.

'What's happening?'

'No idea. Two cops and MacPherson.'

'MacPherson? The head of that task force?'

'Yeah.'

'Why would he be here?'

'No idea, Ames.'

I keep my voice down, pull on a T-shirt. Whatever she sees on my face makes her frown.

'I'll put the kettle on,' she says.

Amy walks ahead of me down the hall. My wife is tall, slim and beautiful and I wonder why the hell she fell in love with me. Keeping her and Sasha safe is my number one priority, so I don't let them anywhere near the family business. Amy tucks a strand of blonde hair behind her ear as she peeks into Sasha's room, then closes the door. I can tell by the set of her shoulders

4

that she's anxious. Me too. She disappears into the kitchen and I wish I could follow her, but I keep going, back into the living room.

The cops are looking around. MacPherson is holding a framed photo from the mantelpiece: my brother and me, aged about six and five, sitting cross-legged in Mum's veggie patch, tanned and grinning. Ivan's arm is slung around my shoulders and I'm holding a huge pumpkin like a trophy. MacPherson puts the photo back and avoids my gaze. What the fuck is going on here?

'Amy's making tea, but we can do coffee if you want.'

One of the uniforms gives MacPherson a pleading look.

'That won't be necessary, thank you. Perhaps you could ask her to join us instead?'

Amy must be listening. She comes in and I introduce her.

'Please sit down.' She gestures at the sofa.

Amy perches in one of the armchairs opposite and I take the one beside her. MacPherson sits on the sofa, but the book-ends remain standing, as though they're expecting action. The detective pulls out a pen and one of those black, flip-top note-books. He opens it, looks at his watch and scribbles.

My fingers start drumming on the armrest. Amy reaches over and takes my hand.

MacPherson looks up. 'I'm very sorry, Johnny. There's no easy way to tell you this.' Now his eyes are locked on mine, as if he's searching for something. 'It's your brother, Ivan. He's been shot.'

In two strides I'm out in the hall, snatching up my car keys. My ears are ringing. Why has nobody moved?

'Which hospital?' I shout.

'He didn't make it. Johnny, I'm sorry.'

MacPherson does sound sorry, but I'm back in the living room towering over him. Nothing makes sense. They've fucked this up somehow.

'Bullshit. It's not him.' One of the bookends steps forward and puts his hand on my arm, but I shake him off. 'You've got him mixed up with someone else. Ivan can't be dead.'

MacPherson looks at his notebook again. 'Ivan was shot at the end of his driveway while he was putting out the garbage bins at eleven-forty this evening. A neighbour called it in. Ambos got there before we did, but there was nothing they could do.'

I can't breathe. The keys are digging into my palm. I want to rip that black notebook out of MacPherson's hand and shove it down his throat. I want to rip the world apart. Then Amy's arms are wrapped around me.

'Are you okay, Mummy?'

Sasha is behind us. I can't look at him.

'Oh, God,' Amy groans into my shoulder. I can feel her heart pounding as she hugs me tight. Then she lets go.

'Come on, Sasha. Back to bed.' She bends down and cuddles him, murmuring into his ear as she guides him out of the room. Their voices recede up the hall.

I'm shaking and somehow my face is wet. The cops haven't moved. My knees give way and I slump back down into the armchair. Wiping my face with my hands, I take some deep breaths and, when I can trust my voice, I ask the only question that matters: 'Who did it?'

AMY

I'm amazed and relieved that Sasha doesn't remember waking up last night, seeing me crying, his father unhinged and the living room full of police. I have to explain what happened all over again. I don't want him finding out about Ivan's death by watching some TV report about Croatian–Serbian gang wars. What if a kid at school asks him why his uncle got shot? It's not like Novak is a common surname.

'Something very sad happened last night. Your Uncle Ivan was killed.'

He attacks a fried egg on toast as he tries to grasp what I've said.

'So he won't be here for Christmas?' he asks, as if Ivan's on holiday.

'No, Sash. He's in heaven now.' Sasha goes to a Catholic primary school, where heaven is on the curriculum. But if such a place exists, they sure as hell won't be letting in Johnny's brother.

'Uncle Ivan said he was coming to the Christmas concert.

I'm gonna be a spaceman. He promised.'

Sasha stares up at me, a look of confusion in his blue eyes.

Okay, this will be a process. At ten years old, he's never known anyone who has died.

'He didn't mean to let you down. Sometimes things happen we can't control. You know that, Sash.'

Sasha looks down at the egg, his eyes hidden behind his blond fringe. He needs another haircut. He looks like me, not Johnny, not one little bit Croatian. But he's got his father's temperament. He only speaks when he has something to say and kindness is always just below the surface. He flicks his fringe from his eyes as if he's stepping out of a swimming pool, his expression bewildered. But he reaches across the kitchen bench and pats my hand. My son consoling me; I want to break down and sob. His gesture somehow makes me feel even more alone in this.

We talk about it some more in the car, during the ten-minute drive to All Saints Catholic Primary School, in downtown Liverpool.

'How did Uncle Ivan die, Mum?'

I knew he'd get there eventually. I go with what I think he'll understand.

'He was shot. You know guns are very dangerous, Sash, so it might have been an accident. The police are trying to find out what happened.'

This seems to satisfy him, for now. Let's hope the preparations for the concert in three weeks' time keep him preoccupied.

At the Kiss and Drop area, there's the usual mess, cars arriving and leaving, frustrated parents wrangling children and little kids crying. Sasha is out the door before I can bring the Mini to a complete stop. He weaves around smaller kids, his long legs executing abrupt changes of direction as if he's in a race. Then he stops short and turns back to wave. No smile. Perhaps it's sinking in.

My hands are numb on the steering wheel. I'm outside Johnny's parents' place, and I can't remember getting here. I try to slow my breathing and focus. Every few seconds it hits me again, our new reality looping around in my head—Ivan is dead. Alive one moment, dead the next. Probably didn't feel a thing. I guess there are worse ways to die.

If I could reset the clock, would Ivan still be alive? Ivan, Johnny's hero, not mine. But I didn't want him dead, did I?

Last night, after confirming Johnny was home with me all night, Detective MacPherson asked him to help break the news to his parents, Milan and Branka. MacPherson is no dummy. I'd want Johnny there as a buffer too. There's a reason Milan has a bad reputation. He's ferocious. He hates cops and I bet they don't like him much either. Johnny is still with Branka and Milan and, now that Sasha is at school, I need to be with Johnny. But I make no move to get out of the car. I pull the sun visor down and slide open the mirror. A pale face with red-rimmed blue eyes stares back at me. I snap the visor back into place and look over at Branka's garden instead.

When Branka and Milan arrived in Australia, back in 1980, they bought this single-storey, red, brick-veneer home on the edge of the sprawling suburb of Liverpool. I wonder what the neighbours thought when the Novaks first moved in. My parents would have taken one look at Milan and slapped a For Sale sign on their front fence.

Just before we got married, twelve years ago, Johnny and I bought a house of a similar vintage, three blocks away. Like most of the other houses in this quiet, residential neighbourhood, our place is a triple-fronted brick home with a double lock-up garage. We have a lawn in the front and a backyard shaded by ghost gums. Oh, and a swimming pool.

Ivan's place is three blocks in the other direction. All of us live here in the same area of Liverpool. I know this is normal for most European families, but sometimes I find it claustrophobic.

In contrast to their neighbours, Johnny's parents' house has a knee-high row of Besser blocks, painted white, separating the front garden from the verge. On this side, a big jacaranda throws shade and purple flowers out as far as the street. Inside the fence, staked tomato plants compete for space with brightly coloured vegetables and string beans on trellises. There's no gate, just a gap in the row of blocks. Concrete paving curves through the garden to the three steps leading up to a small verandah and the front door. Apart from a square of grass in the backyard, cultivated the year I was pregnant with Sasha, the whole block is one big vegetable patch. Branka's domain. That square of grass was her gift to me, so Sasha would have a place to crawl, then run around, when we came to visit.

Branka's edible garden is extraordinary. The round face of the woman herself now appears in the kitchen window. I can't stay here any longer. As I get out of the car, the heat hits me like a heavy wet slap.

I let the scents of the garden lull me as I step over the cracks in the concrete path. Just like it always does, the screen

10

door squeaks when I push it open and enter the dim hallway. Branka's bright-yellow kitchen opens up on my left.

Milan and Johnny are slumped at the long timber table, as though they haven't moved for hours. Two huge men, built like front-row forwards, weighed down by grief. Hazel eyes, curly dark hair, Milan's streaked with grey. Their prominent brows bisected by strong, straight noses. They are so similar I know exactly what Johnny will look like in twenty years. Their faces turn as one to acknowledge me. Johnny wears the semblance of a smile, Milan an ugly scowl. He's never liked me. I'm not sure why. Because I'm not a good Croatian girl?

Johnny stands to give me a hug. Milan stays seated and turns his head away slightly as I lean down to give him a kiss. He's still the biggest, scariest man I know. There's a sense of power emanating from him that could fell trees. But he looks diminished this morning. The sunlight pouring through the kitchen window accentuates every line on his broad face.

Branka is wearing a rumpled floral house dress she probably made herself. She'd be horrified to know the hem has come down at the back. After pouring tea into thick white mugs, she stops, transfixed by the large crucifix attached to the wall above the kettle. Jesus looks peaceful enough, considering his plight. Branka's expression shifts from blank to savage before she shuts her eyes and crosses herself.

I make my way around the table and reach out to touch her shoulder. Her eyes are red, her full cheeks shiny and taut from crying. Her chin is trembling. Her face looks broken. I imagine Sasha dying and the thought drives all the breath from my lungs.

Branka is a big woman, but I'm tall, so I manage to get

my arms around her and feel a shudder run through her whole body. We hold each other. She sniffs and breaks away to hand me two milky teas. I place them in front of our men and sit down beside Johnny. Branka turns back to her benchtop and starts mixing flour, eggs and slow, silent tears. Branka's answer to everything is to cook.

When I can't handle the silence any longer, my voice comes out in a squeak.

'Has Detective MacPherson provided any new information?'

Milan looks at me and his face fills with anger. I wish I hadn't spoken. I always seem to say the wrong thing when he's around.

Johnny answers as though he's talking in his sleep. 'A neighbour heard shots and called the police. No one saw anything. Same as when Michael Vucavec was shot last week.'

Stanislav Vucavec and Milan Novak. Two of the biggest gang leaders in Western Sydney. One Serbian, the other Croatian, and sworn enemies. Stanislav lost his eldest son last week. Last night it was Milan's turn.

Johnny sips his tea, then continues. 'MacPherson said the shootings are his biggest priority right now. He doesn't want a turf war. He kept asking if we had any idea who might want Ivan dead.'

Branka moans and Johnny buries his head in his hands. How can I comfort this family, my family now, when they have lost their favourite son? Johnny idolised his brother. Ivan protected Johnny from Milan. He protected Johnny when they were out on jobs. He protected Johnny his whole life, and now he's gone.

Milan stands up, his chair toppling and his whole body

vibrating with fury. He looks as if he wants to kill someone. I flinch, but he marches off down the hall. I hear the back door slam. Branka turns around, sees he's left his tea and hurries after him, holding the mug out in front of her.

I put my hand over Johnny's and squeeze. No response. He stares blankly at the wall.

'Was he working on something…unusual?' Now we're alone I can be more direct. But there's a lot I don't know.

'He was across everything. It could be another crew muscling in. It could be the Serbs. They think we had something to do with Michael's death. Maybe Ivan slept with the wrong man's wife.' Johnny doesn't sound like himself.

'Does your dad have a theory?'

'Dad hasn't said a word since I broke the news.'

'MacPherson made *you* do it?'

'I told them to wait outside, just in case Dad went nuts and pulled out the Bren he's got strapped to the bottom of this table.'

My gut constricts as if the machine gun is pointing right at my belly button. I want to look under the table, but I stop myself. A new fear grips me. Milan will want Johnny to step up. He needs a new second-in-command. I shiver, then squeeze his hand harder and Johnny looks at me at last.

'Milan is going to take you away from me.' I sound like a five-year-old, but the words are out now, hanging in the space between us.

AMY

The funeral goes on forever. Ivan would be rolling his eyes if he wasn't up the front, in the coffin covered in flowers.

More than a hundred people are crammed inside the Sacred Heart Catholic Church, which sits in its own section of Rookwood, the massive cemetery divided by faith. I just heard someone whisper that it's the largest cemetery in the Southern Hemisphere, with over a million people buried here. This city of the dead is like a smaller version of the western suburbs of Sydney.

It's stupidly hot. And it's only November. No seaside breezes for us Westies.

I asked Johnny, why here? Why not Liverpool Cemetery, a five-minute drive from our place.

'Too many Serbs are buried there. The Serbian Orthodox Church is right opposite. We don't go there.'

There are not many places in Liverpool that the men in Johnny's crew avoid.

A big Croatian Catholic contingent is buried here at

Rookwood. Even among the Christians, there are separate sections. Wouldn't want to end up beside a Serb. And of course, Ivan won't, because the Serbs who aren't buried in the Liverpool Cemetery are buried in the Christian Orthodox section here at Rookwood.

All the women are crying, some softly, some sobbing loudly into their praying hands. The men wipe their eyes surreptitiously and cough. I'm still numb. I don't know how I'm supposed to feel. When Johnny stands up to deliver the eulogy, the tears finally begin to slide down my face. He's talking about their childhood, how he grew up knowing Ivan would always be by his side. I feel his pain like a burning ulcer. It's so much more intense than my own very different pain. It makes my pain easier to bury.

I'm glad I'm not Catholic. At least in the Church of England we have the decency to keep our funerals short.

JOHNNY

We walk through Mum and Dad's front door and my vision seems to tunnel. After the funeral, I had to look after some admin shit back at the church, so everyone else is already here. The place smells like cabbage and cigarettes. Home. Sasha runs down the hallway, slams though the screen door at the back and out into the light.

Amy is behind me, whispering. 'We don't have to stay long. Let's just put in an appearance and go home.'

'Yeah, right. Like that's gonna happen.'

I know what's coming and so does Amy. She disappears into the kitchen and I trail after Sasha, past the door to the dining room. I glance in. The senior men are seated around the table, my father at the head. I'm caught in Dad's gaze, a fly in a web. I want to keep walking, but he calls me in and Uncle Baz closes the door behind me.

A white tablecloth covers the big oval table and flowers from the funeral have been arranged in a coloured band down the centre. On the cream walls hang two darkened oil paintings of hayricks and squat women in headscarves bending over to collect what's left of the harvest.

I sit down on Dad's right, where I always sit. Ivan always sat on the left. That way he'd cop the big right hand and I'd cop the slightly weaker left. Dad passes me a bottle of rakia, his home-brewed version of the fruit-brandy firewater. I fill the shot glass in front of me and slide the bottle on.

Twelve men, brutal features, big brows and broken noses. Even with the flowers, it's not a pretty sight. As I look from face to face, it takes me a moment to realise I'm searching for Ivan. My eyes sting with unshed tears.

My cousin Marko is in Ivan's seat. He whispers something to my father, then looks around like he owns the place. Anger flares in my chest. I want to upend the table. I want to grab Marko's smug face and pound it against the floor. My father lays a huge paw over my wrist.

'Pažljiv,' careful, Dad rasps in my ear, then removes his hand and bangs it on the table like a gavel.

'Today we bury my son Ivan. Why?' A low growl begins. My father is finally breaking his silence about Ivan's murder. In his speech at the funeral, Dad spoke about how Ivan could talk his way out of any situation, even as a kid, but he never walked away from a fight. I pick up my glass of rakia and throw the burning liquid down my throat.

'Why we bury my son?' Dad pauses. 'Because Serbian prick shot him, is why!'

Marko is staring right at me during Dad's pronouncement. The rakia hits my empty stomach like a bomb. The warmth gives me confidence.

'We don't know it was the Serbs.' I try to sound reasonable.

17

Marko has a sneer on his face. Dad glares at me as if I've just said something obscene.

'We don't know it was the Serbs? Open your eyes, Johnny! Your big brother was shot in own driveway, killed like dog in street. Killed same way as Michael Vucavec. Michael's father, Stanislav Vucavec, is my enemy. How you not see this? Are you stupid?'

I decide to keep my mouth shut and Dad turns back to the rest of the crew.

'Croats and Serbs kill each other, is normal. We all lost family in last war. I lost my brother, Miroslav, father to our Marko. You think I forget?' Dad's eyes flick to Marko, who shakes his head slowly, his face serious now, fury simmering near the surface.

Dad sucks in a breath as if what he's about to say is a hook caught in his throat. 'Now I lose my Ivan. Stanislav Vucavec, he kill my eldest son.' His hefty right hand slices sideways across his throat. 'Stanislav must die.'

Huge fists bang on the table. This is what these men want. The rakia bottles do the rounds again. I pass on a bottle without refilling my glass. This is the conversation I wanted to avoid. I need to stay sober. And I don't feel like saluting the idea of another man's death. But the rest of the men are eager to raise their glasses.

'*Živjeli!*'

'Ivan!'

'Kill all the fucking Serbs!'

Dad holds up his hand. I can hear my own breathing in the silence. The massive head turns towards me and the bloodshot eyes swivel to search my own. Here it comes.

'It's up to you, Johnny. You pay back Stanislav. For Ivan.'

'If a dog was chewing Johnny's right leg off, he still could not kill the dog.' Marko rocks forward, his face twisted with contempt.

I study my cousin. Even though he speaks English perfectly, his accent is strong. It makes him sound like a robotic version of my father. Marko is prepared to kill to keep Ivan's seat at this table. I should make way for him. Let him kill Stanislav. But Ivan is *my* brother and Dad would never forgive me.

Dad ignores Marko's outburst. He thrusts his chair back and stands up. He yanks a gleaming black semi-automatic from the back of his suit trousers and slams it on the table in front of me. It's Ivan's Beretta, last year's Christmas present from Dad.

'You know what to do with this gun, Johnny?' Dad's tone is almost gentle now, as his gaze shifts from the gun back to me. My mouth is dry, and I wish I'd had another shot of rakia.

I love my brother. Ivan stood up for me. But we have no fucking clue who killed him, or Michael Vucavec. Does Stanislav really think us Croats killed his son? Did he order Ivan killed as payback? It would make sense if he did, but no one saw anything. There's no proof either way. Why reignite this war? Something doesn't smell right. But saying any of this is useless and I'll just look chickenshit.

I wrap my hand around Ivan's Beretta, the metal cool under my fingers, and stand up. I could flip off the safety and end Marko's sneer. Instead, I point the gun towards the floor.

'What you do, Johnny? What you do for Ivan, for family?'

'I'll find out who killed my brother and I promise you there will be retribution.' I speak clearly, raking my gaze around the table, looking every man in the eye. When I get to Marko, I force myself to smile. Then I turn back to Dad. My father has always reserved his pride for Ivan. Right now, there's a question in those hard, brown eyes, but also the warm glow of pride. It fizzes through me like cocaine.

AMY

Turning into the hall from the bathroom, I bump into Marko.

'I am sorry, Amy,' he says in his formal way, moving aside for me, his eyes not quite meeting mine.

Should I say something? But he walks away quickly, heading out the back door to the wake. I make my way back to the kitchen and the women. I've missed my chance.

Heaped platters take up every square inch of bench space and Branka is washing dirt from another mound of potatoes at the sink. The older women, Mary, Ana and Kata, dressed in black, are chatting in Croatian. They could be sisters, plump-faced and portly, but I know they're not related; it's their men who are Novaks.

As I cut up silverbeet and potatoes for another pot of *blitva*, even though there's already way too much food, I curse myself again for not trying harder to learn basic Croatian. But every time I attempt a word or phrase, I'm laughed at. My mouth seems unable to make the short, sharp, yet guttural sounds.

Lexy and Nadya are around my age, in their early thirties,

their black dresses simple but somehow chic. I had to buy a dress for the funeral as I don't usually wear black. I made sure it was conservative. I didn't want to stand out any more than I do already. It's hard to blend into a family of Croatians when you're nearly six feet tall and have long blonde hair and blue eyes. Lexy is like a tiny version of Ana, her mother-in-law. Nadya, Johnny's cousin, is nearly as tall as I am, her glowing olive skin permanently tanned. They look incongruous together, Nadya leaning down next to Lexy as they arrange cured meats and cheeses on plates, talking in English about anything other than Ivan.

I remember the first time I stepped into this kitchen. Branka looked me up and down with a face like stone. Milan came thumping down the hall into the kitchen and I felt the flight response take hold. I remember how much my hand trembled as I held it out to him.

He started laughing. 'Your girlfriend, Johnny, she is shaking. Why she scared?'

I was mortified, but Branka took pity on me. She shooed the two men out of the kitchen, got me peeling potatoes and together we made my first *blitva*.

Getting to know Johnny's family was like arriving on another planet. I was straight out of university, Bachelor of Arts, pretty useless education really, but Mum and Dad insisted. I had just started my first real job, as an HR assistant at our local council, in Strathfield. I was still living at home with Mum and Dad. Growing up in a beautiful old Californian bungalow in Strathfield is probably as good as it gets in the western suburbs. Nothing like the wealthy eastern suburbs, but solid middle-class, respectable. Liverpool did not have the same reputation.

Back then, I didn't really know what I wanted, but I knew what I didn't want. I didn't want a replica of my parents' life, the normalcy, the tedium. I wanted more. I wanted something bigger.

The first time I saw Johnny, Ivan was standing beside him at the bar. I was with some girlfriends at a club in Parramatta, the heart of the west. It was still early in the evening, not crowded yet, and the DJ was playing modern blues and trop rock, Ben Harper and Jack Johnson. My attention kept straying back to the two men at the bar.

To be honest, I was focused on Ivan. Tall and broad-shouldered, he was seriously handsome, with a curly mop of brown hair, dark eyes and those high Slavic cheekbones. Ivan seemed to be teasing his brother, who was even taller.

Johnny was looking at the floor, so I couldn't really see his face. Then he looked up, straight at me. I was thirty feet away, at a table full of girls, but he was looking at me. He blinked, like a lazy cat. I knew I should look away. I wasn't interested in a hook-up, but he smiled at me.

I was twenty-two. A straight one-eighty and essentially clueless.

He waited until a few of the girls got up to dance, then came over and slid into the chair beside me.

'I want to take you out for dinner. Next Saturday night. I'll come by your house, pick you up and take you somewhere special.' His voice was honey and gravel mixed together, his eyes a pistachio-and-toffee colour. He smelled like lemons. He surprised me with his formality, his lack of innuendo. Sydney boys like their innuendo.

'I don't even know your name. Why would I go out to

23

dinner with you?' I was starting to blush, the warmth creeping up my neck to my face.

'I'm Johnny Novak.' He held out his big right hand for me to shake.

I let him envelop my hand. His grip was gentle but firm, and then he let go. Another point in his favour. I hate guys who shake your hand limply just because you're a woman. Or worse, hang on when you've only given them permission to shake your hand, not hold it.

'This is when you tell me *your* name,' he said with a completely straight face, only his eyes smiling.

'Amy Parsons.'

'You're considering my invitation aren't you, Amy Parsons?'

'Yes, Johnny Novak, I'm *considering it.*' I laughed.

'Say yes. We'll get to know each other. No big deal.'

My concern must have shown on my face. Who was this guy? My head was telling me to say no. I sensed danger.

He leaned closer, serious now, intent. 'I promise I'm no trouble at all.'

His body next to mine was making my head spin. I didn't know what else to ask without sounding rude. Where do you live? Now there's a Sydney question for you. You may as well ask 'How much money do you make?' I also didn't want him to leave; I knew I wanted to see him again.

'Okay, why not?' I shrugged. He smiled and everything inside me seemed to liquefy.

He passed me his phone. 'I'll need your number.'

Once I'd added my number to his phone, he stood up, suddenly huge. 'I'll call you on Wednesday night to confirm the time. Okay?'

I was shaking my head and saying 'Okay' at the same time. Like, what just happened?

He turned around, went back to the bar and nodded to his brother. They left and he didn't look back. He took all the light with him.

After three dates, three consecutive Saturday nights, Johnny invited me home to his small, neat flat in Liverpool. The only adornment on the living-room wall was a framed poster of Korcula, a pretty island off the Croatian coast. He lit two scented candles and put on Norah Jones singing 'Come Away With Me', as though he needed to seduce me. I was fanging for it by then, but I knew I had to play by his rules. It was a good kind of torture.

My parents hoped I'd 'grow out of it', continue with my career and marry a doctor or stockbroker. They were careful to be accommodating and agreeable to Johnny, but I heard them talking about him when they thought I was asleep. Right from the start, Dad had an inkling all was not as it seemed with Johnny's family.

'Do we really know what he does for a living?' he asked Mum on more than one occasion.

'They don't expect her to work in one of their fish shops, do they?' Mum worried.

'He's a wog. He probably won't want his wife working. But don't worry, she'll get over him.'

'What if she gets pregnant?' Mum worried some more. I was their only child; all their hopes and dreams were pinned on me like medals.

'We didn't raise a stupid daughter.' Good old Dad, always confident in me.

25

'She's not thinking with her head.'

Mum was right. I was thinking with a whole other part of my anatomy, and Johnny's life, his family, were cream on the strawberries.

The clincher came towards the end of that first year with Johnny. Milan flew us all to Croatia, 'back to the old country', the village, the house they'd left, he and Branka, just after Ivan was born. But the house was long gone, lost in the war; we stayed in five-star hotels instead.

In Split, Milan chartered a one-hundred-foot, big-arsed wooden sloop. There were seven of us, Milan, Branka, Johnny and me, Ivan and his girlfriend at the time, a beautiful, funny chick named Melba, like the toast. Well, really the opera singer, but we called her Toast. And Marko, Johnny and Ivan's cousin. Marko and Ivan were the same age, a year and a bit older than Johnny, seven years older than me. Marko was there on his own; he didn't ever seem to have a steady girlfriend.

When I first caught sight of the boat in Split Harbour, I thought she was a pirate ship.

I lived in a postcard for the next ten days. I'd never been overseas, so it was all insanely over the top to me. As well as the skipper and his wife, who was an amazing cook, there was one other crew member, who was a bit of a perv, but Toast and I ignored him. We knew if we said anything, the boys would beat him up and pitch him overboard.

The Dalmatian Coast was the most beautiful place I'd ever seen. It looked like someone had poured bright-blue dye straight out of a bottle and into the water. It didn't look real.

On the last night, under the stars, Johnny asked me to marry him. We were sitting way out on the bowsprit, our legs dangling over the inky water. I shouted 'Yes!' and flipped myself backwards into the sea.

When I open my eyes, the knife is still in my hand, but I've stopped chopping the potatoes and Branka is looking at me with concern in her dark-brown eyes.

'I'm okay, just thinking about that time we went to Croatia together. Remember?'

'How I forget? I have my boys with me, together in my home country. It was best time of my life.'

She smiles, then her eyes fill with tears. She dashes them away as though angry with herself. I put down the knife and move towards her, and then we are in each other's arms. I hold her tight and she feels nearly as big as Johnny, but much softer. She starts to cry in earnest, long, shuddering sobs. Suddenly we're surrounded, all the women patting and hugging us. It feels good to be one of these women, in this hot kitchen. Maybe I've finally been accepted.

JOHNNY

The men filter out of the dining room. I need to stash Ivan's gun before I join everyone out the back. I'm drawn up the hall to the last door on the left. I can hear the women talking in the kitchen as I step inside the bedroom I used to share with my brother. It smells musty. Closing the door behind me, I head straight to the window to pull up the sash. A light breeze carries the scent of a summer storm.

I'm eight, in my pyjamas, trying to get out of this window to escape my father. I can hear Dad breaking through the solid wooden door with his bare hands. He could just open the door, there's no lock, but where's the fun in that? I struggle to push through the venetians to safety. The drop from the window into the dirt will hurt less than Dad getting hold of me. But I get stuck in the blinds, my back horribly exposed to my father's fury.

I can't remember what I'd done wrong, what test of strength I'd failed, but I remember the fear and I remember Ivan coming home just as Dad burst into the bedroom. He talked Dad round. Afterwards, Mum let us get rid of the blinds to make sure our escape route was clear.

Apart from a few boxes stacked in the corner, the room looks the same. Narrow twin beds. Ivan's old bike against the wall near the window, front wheel missing. Motorbike posters clinging to the walls with brittle, yellowed sticky tape. Why don't they chuck all this shit out and use the room for something else?

I check the gun again to make sure it's not loaded and slide it into a drawer in the bedside table between the two beds. I don't want Sasha seeing it. I'll collect it on my way out.

Remembering Mum's rule about 'No shoes on the bedspreads', I keep my feet on the ground and flop back on Ivan's bed. My eyes seek out the tiny wads of tissue paper stuck to the ceiling, clustered inside and around a stain in the shape of a shark. I can feel the torn square of tissue in my mouth. I'm moulding it into a ball small enough to fit into the empty barrel of a Bic pen. Blowing hard, I shoot it up at the shark. Ivan is faster on the reload, but my aim is infallible.

It's as if Ivan is still here with me.

I wish I was lying in the ground and Ivan was here with the gun.

The door opens slowly and Sasha pokes his head around. The kid hasn't left me alone since we told him about Ivan.

'Are you okay, Daddy? Want to come and play soccer with us? You'll feel better. I always feel better when I'm playing soccer.'

'Okay, Sash, I'm coming.' I get up from my brother's bed, take Sasha's sticky hand and allow him to lead me. The noise of the wake rolls up the hallway to meet us. I step through the

29

screen door and down two concrete steps to the back patio. It's even hotter out here.

Scanning the backyard, I count twenty-five people. More than a hundred came to the church, but only family and crew got invited back. Ivan would be loving it. For him there was nothing better than being surrounded by his family, even though he never married and never had kids. I guess he just didn't get lucky like I did with Amy. He seemed to only ever stick with a girlfriend for a few months. Now he'll never be a dad.

My promise to my father is playing over and over in my head. Amy's eyes meet mine and she knows. But we can't talk about it here.

Dad's younger brother, Josef, is in an apron, barbecuing *ćevapi* and lamb chops. His white shirt is stuck to his back as he works the built-in brick barbecue that runs along one side of the large concrete patio. The smell of the skinless, garlicky sausages competes with the ozone tang of the coming storm. The sausages are winning. Uncle Josef is a smaller, less precise version of my dad. He's not the sharpest, but he's loyal and does whatever Dad wants.

Sasha joins his cousins playing soccer on the square of grass between the citrus trees and the rows of root vegetables. There's a small replica of a goal net at either end. Big men sit on the edge of the patio, hogging the shade of the tin roof, feet planted in the grass, drinking Victoria Bitter straight from the can. Most have ditched their suit jackets and ties, respect taking a back seat to the heat. The women are slamming in and out of the screen door, carrying platters of cured meats, vegetables, salads and bread.

As Mum comes down the steps, I lift a platter of pickles and olives from her hands. She's wrecked. If I held her for too long or too tight, she'd shatter. Her black hair is streaked with grey, her face is lined, and her big shoulders are hunched over her chest, as though she's protecting her heart.

'Are you doing okay, Mum?'

She raises an eyebrow. 'Johnny, take care of your *tata*. Don't let him drink too much.'

We both look over at my dad and then back to each other. She seems to have something else to say, but flaps her hands, sending me off to my father.

He's already a bit glassy-eyed. Those shots of rakia hit hard. But his huge frame is rock solid in his chair at the head of the old formica table set in the middle of the patio, its metal legs leaking rust stains the colour of blood onto the concrete. My parents can afford new outdoor furniture. Hell, they can probably afford to live in a big house in the eastern suburbs, but Dad makes it a rule never to look like he's made any money. You don't call attention to yourself. It only brings trouble. When Ivan turned up recently in a brand-new Range Rover Sport, Dad was disgusted.

'Fancy car. Stupid fuck. Who he think he is?'

I put the platter down on one of the overcrowded trestle tables and glance back at Dad. He's glaring at me, his blood-shot brown eyes the only moving part in his bull-mastiff face. A hand-rolled cigarette dangles from the corner of his mouth, his enormous right hand is curled around a beer and his white shirt is straining across a chest the size of a forty-four-gallon drum.

'Johnny! Come.' He points at the bottle of rakia at his elbow as I make my way towards him.

Uncle Baz vacates the chair to Dad's right. Born Berislav, his name changed to Barry when he migrated to Australia and, thanks to our country's obsession with nicknames, he soon became Baz. He's not really my uncle, he's Dad's best friend. Nothing rattles the man. With his corkscrew hair, open face and easy manner, he's the father I wish I had. He's earned the title of Uncle. He gives me a sympathetic look and a squeeze on the shoulder before moving away. I sit and pour Dad a shot of rakia. He looks at me, then at Baz's abandoned glass. I fill it.

'*Živjeli*, Johnny.'

'*Živjeli*, Dad.' We clink glasses. I down half the shot. I still need to stay sober.

He pats me awkwardly on the back.

'You my only son now. You don't let me down.'

This is not a compliment. From Dad, it's always a threat. But I'm the only one who sees the solitary tear escape his right eye. His thick index finger removes the offending drop. It's like seeing the first crack in a dam wall.

My gaze drifts around the backyard. Sasha has just scored a goal and he's laughing like a maniac, blond hair lit by a last stray sunbeam. Sasha and Amy, the only blonds in a family of dark-haired, olive-skinned Croats. Most of them migrated here in the eighties, before the last war with the Serbs. We got here six months before I was born, thirty-eight years ago. I know plenty of families who came earlier, after the last world war. The men first, then their women and children. The blight on the grapes sent the first wave, communism the next.

I was a teenager in Sydney during the Balkan conflict in the nineties. Ivan and I would take the train six stops towards the city, to Yagoona, where we could brawl outside the local

Yugoslav club. Soccer games started with supporters swapping insults, then turned into riots. Matching my big brother punch for punch, we took on the Serbs. We watched nightly news footage of Yugoslavia disintegrating. The violence there fuelled the hatred here. Back then I had no real idea why it was all happening. I just knew we were supposed to hate the Serbs. It was hard, though. I'd known some of those guys since I was a kid.

In 1996, there were enough Yugoslavs in Australia to start a war, and there are even more here now. But don't go calling a Croatian a Yugoslav, if you want to stay healthy. For many of us Balkans, the war will never end because the losses in Eastern Europe were huge on both sides. The hatred still simmers.

Amy passes me, carrying plates stacked with meat straight off the barbecue. In a simple black dress, she looks incredible. Everyone in the family loves Amy, except my dad. I keep hoping he'll come around. It would probably be different if we'd had more kids; he loves being a *dida,* a grandfather. My beautiful wife is politely directing family and crew towards the trestle tables against the back wall. As the dusk dies around us, everyone seems intent on eating.

Sixteen big men, ranging from early twenties to late fifties, line up to add salads to their plates. My best friend, Anto, Baz and Ana's son, is filling two plates. The man can eat. We've known each other since we were babies. He's shorter than me, but built like a tank and his thick black eyebrows almost meet on the ridge above his nose. Anto is not pretty, but I wouldn't want anyone else beside me in a fight.

There are fewer women than men here, and only five kids. Most of the younger men haven't married yet. Apart from Amy, the women are either tiny like Anto's wife, Lexy, or big-boned like my mum.

'Johnny, you've got to eat.' Amy is standing in front of me holding out a knife and fork wrapped in a paper napkin and a plate packed with all my favourites, *ćevapi, blitva,* cabbage salad and hot chilies. Her clear blue eyes are willing me to eat.

I take the plate. She rewards me with a kiss on the lips, then heads off to get a plate for herself. Sasha is sitting on the edge of the patio, bolting his meal like he's never going to see food again. He says something to Amy and they smile at each other. It's blindingly obvious they are mother and son. He doesn't look like me at all, but we're similar in other ways.

My throat closes up as if I'm choking. They could be taken from me just like Ivan was taken.

At the table, I try to eat, each mouthful hard to chew, harder to swallow. Anto sits down beside me with his two plates. He thumps me on the shoulder, nearly knocking me off my chair, and starts to shovel food into his mouth. I can't help but laugh at him. I start to relax, until I see Marko walking towards us, plate in hand, his shirt dazzling white against his tanned skin. We're all tall, but Marko is tall and lean, like a fucking model. His shirt is finer, the cut of his trousers slimmer. Fucking fashion plate.

Dad calls out to Marko in Croatian and gestures to the seat at his left. Why the fuck does my father want Marko sitting in Ivan's seat?

This time it's Anto who puts a hand on my wrist.

'Mate. Don't let him get to you,' he mumbles, his mouth full of food.

I stop eyeballing Marko and concentrate on eating too.

Marko and Dad yammer away in Croatian.

Anto belches. 'I heard them talking before you got here. Marko's pretty insistent that the order to kill Ivan could only have come from Stanislav. You know how psycho he is about Serbs. Crazy fucker.' Anto speaks more Croatian than I do. He's got a knack for languages.

I grunt in response, but my mind is whirling. What if Marko and Dad are right and the Serbs did shoot Ivan? Then it will be war again, but this time here on the streets of Sydney.

AMY

Lexy is on tiptoes as she stretches across the kitchen table, wiping away crumbs. With her clear green eyes, high cheekbones and red lips, she's like a tiny doll, perfectly formed; at thirty she could pass for sixteen. Anto is still as besotted as he was the day he married her.

Josef's wife, Mary, is brewing Turkish coffee in a copper stovetop pot. She is short and round, her long grey hair piled on top of her head in a messy bun. Branka puts down the saucepan she's scrubbing and with the back of her wet hand wipes the sweat from her forehead.

'I hear Marko and Milan before. They say the Serbs kill my Ivan. Revenge for Michael Vucavec's murder.'

Lexy looks stricken. Her parents are Serbian. She has cousins in the local Serb crew. This is what I was afraid would happen. Milan has always made it plain he hates Serbs. He tolerates Lexy, probably because she's a woman and she's married into his clan, so now she's under his protection. But if Milan thinks the Serbs did it, what will he do? What will he ask

Johnny to do? I need to find out where this line of reasoning might lead. Maybe then I can turn it around.

'Branka, I know Milan lost his brother in the last Balkan War.' I start carefully; this is not the right time to pick at old wounds. 'But none of you ever talk about it. Is that why Milan still hates the Serbs so much? Even though it was twenty-five years ago, and you were here in Sydney?'

'Yes, my Milan lost Miroslav.' Branka's hands plunge back into the sudsy water. She stares out at her garden as though she's seeing a bleak landscape. 'Back in Croatia, we all lost family. And friends. But is also religion. Is politics.'

Mary takes over, with an apologetic look at Lexy. 'The Croatian fascist party make deal with Nazis in Second World War. Together they kill maybe half million Serbs and Jews. Is very bad. Is black mark on our country.'

'But Croatia also have communist party.' Branka continues the story, her chin lifting. 'Our resistance. They work with Allies. Allies win war. Stalin win, so communists win, and they give new country, Yugoslavia, to Tito.'

'Tito is communist. But Tito is also Croatian and good man. Except for being communist,' Mary chimes in.

'We Croats are Roman Catholic,' Branka crosses herself with her dripping right hand, 'but we treat Muslim Bosnians like Croats. Bosnians good people and Croats not racist.'

'Croats never racist. But Serbs…' Mary looks at Lexy and shrugs.

'Hang on, Serbs aren't racists.' Lexy's little chest puffs out and her green eyes flash.

'But Serbs *are* Christian Orthodox.' Branka nods at Lexy as though religion is at fault here, not the Serbs. 'So, they don't like us, they don't like Bosnians. Yugoslavia was six different republics, six different peoples. But Tito, he held us together. And then Tito die.'

Both Branka and Mary cross themselves.

'Then we see bad news everywhere,' Branka continues. 'People are leaving. Ivan is baby. I am pregnant with Johnny. We leave and come to Australia. Johnny born here, but is still Croatian.' She looks at me when she says this, as though daring me to object.

'You're lucky you weren't still in Yugoslavia in the nineties,' I say, and Lexy nods in agreement.

'Was not luck,' Branka declares, banging another clean pot into the dish rack for me to dry. 'Milan, he see war coming.' She points to her own brown eyes. 'I see it. Everybody say Serbs invade Croatia and Bosnia because we have the sea and they stuck inland. They need coast.' She shakes her head. 'When Serbs come, they kill many, many Muslim Bosnians and many, many Catholic Croats. They call it cleansing. Is murder.'

'Like Branka say. Is political, is religious, is for land, but is also for revenge. You see. For what the Nazis do before?' Mary waits for Lexy and me to nod.

'Is not first time Croats must push Serbs back across Danube. Is always the same, over and over, but in the end, we win.' Mary reaches for a tea towel. She turns her friend around and gently dries off Branka's hands, pushing her towards the kitchen table.

'Sit, sit. Drink coffee. Lexy, get Branka some of my *paprenjakc*. She needs to eat sweet.'

I like Mary's way of taking the sting out of her comments about Serbs. Mary clucks her approval as Lexy complies, pouring the biscuits laced with honey and pepper onto a plate. Honey and pepper.

It's like every Croatian I know. Sweet right up until they're dangerous.

AMY

I wake with Johnny's hand cupped around my breast. He's pressed up against me. I can tell he's still asleep from the rhythm of his breath, but his body is awake and searching for pleasure. A shudder runs though me. There is no way I can let him make love to me this morning. But he can't know why.

As I slide away from him, he grunts and reaches for me, but I'm out of bed before he can stop me.

'Where are you going?' He's got one eye open as he throws back the sheet and stretches, his body big and glorious. His desire obvious.

I feel no response inside me. Will I ever come back to normal?

'Bacon and eggs?' I offer, hoping to sidetrack him as I pull on a T-shirt and my favourite yoga pants.

'What's wrong, Ames? I mean, apart from the obvious, Ivan and everything.' He's sitting up now, swinging his legs over the side of the bed, his eyes probing mine.

'You haven't told me what happened while you boys were

all locked away in the dining room yesterday.' I'm pretty sure my diversion will work. 'What's the plan?'

'Marko's been in Dad's ear about the Serbs.' Johnny's face is creased with worry now. He rubs the sleep from his eyes and yawns. 'But I don't think Vucavec is that stupid. Who needs a turf war?'

'A turf war?' I imagine the two gangs fighting it out on the streets, guns blazing, men going down. 'Are you all supposed to retaliate?' My stomach starts to churn. 'Or is it just you?'

He looks guilty. I've hit the nail on the head. My worst fear, he's going to get himself killed. My father-in-law has gone completely crazy.

'How can he ask you? Why would he put you at risk this way? What, does he want to lose *both* sons?'

Johnny hangs his head. 'You know, and Dad knows, I've never killed anyone. Beaten people up, definitely. Intimidated the shit out of people, absolutely. Killed anyone? No. We've got people way more qualified than me.'

The faces of the crew flash through my mind. Who would be more suited to the job? You don't get Milan's reputation by being a nice guy. And Marko was a soldier in the war in Croatia. He's killed before. The thought makes me shudder. The rest of the men may be hard men, but they're unfailingly polite to me. Then it hits me—Ivan's successor has to be feared, so Johnny has to do the deed.

It's as though he's watching these thoughts play out on my face.

'Ames, it has to be me. But I won't get caught, I promise you.'

Every nerve in my body goes into overdrive and my vision

41

is hazy at the edges. Before I can move, Johnny is holding me close.

'You went all pale. Honey, it's fine. I'm here, we'll be okay. There's nothing to worry about.'

His arms are around me and I want to feel safe. But I'm not safe. I will myself to slow down my breathing, hoping my heart will follow suit. Was that some sort of panic attack? I close my eyes, breathe in the smell of Johnny and breathe out the smell of fear. Two more slow deep breaths, and then I push him away with promises of breakfast.

I busy myself in the kitchen. Sooner or later Johnny is going to notice I'm losing it and start wondering why. Splashing water on my face at the kitchen sink, I realise I need to focus on Johnny, not me. He's the one in danger. What's really at stake here is his life, his freedom. How do I stop Milan using my husband to avenge Ivan's murder?

42

JOHNNY

Backing out of the garage, on my way to meet Anto, I notice a souped-up white Calais sitting in front of our house. Over the last twenty-odd years, I've come across enough unmarked police cars to recognise one when I see one. Leaving the Jeep engine running, I walk over to the car.

Detective Ian MacPherson's ginger nut appears as the tinted window slides down.

'How about coming down to the station with me, Johnny?'

'I buried my brother yesterday. Why don't you harass Stanislav Vucavec instead?'

'It's important. Bring your own car if it makes you feel more comfortable.'

'I've told you all I know about Michael Vucavec's murder, which is nothing. I wasn't there. You know that because you've checked my alibi, haven't you?'

'I'll let you into a secret, Johnny. I don't think you shot Vucavec.'

'And I didn't shoot my brother.'

MacPherson sighs. 'You are officially not a person of interest in either case.'

'So I don't need to come down to the station.'

'I want to show you something. Get your reaction.'

I try not to look interested. Visiting the cop shop under your own steam is bad for the image. Then I remember Amy pleading with me this morning—*Use the police,* she said. *Don't become your father's pawn in this stupid game.*

Apart from three months in juvie for stealing a car and a few nights in the cells for drunk and disorderly in my early twenties, my adult record is clean. No priors. But like most of the crew, I'm 'known to police'. If anything big goes down in the local area, I get brought in for questioning, but there's never enough evidence to lay charges. When Michael Vucavec was shot, we were all rounded up. No doubt it's happening again, only this time they're after everyone's whereabouts on Wednesday the twenty-first of November. The night Ivan died.

I stare off into space, over the top of the white roof of the Calais. Across the road, Mr Fellows, our nosy neighbour, is sitting on his front verandah watching us with interest. I should probably call our family lawyer. Nah. I can handle this on my own, might even find out something useful.

'Anytime this year, Johnny.'

'Okay. I'll reorganise my morning and follow you to the station. But I'd better be treated like a bereaved relative, not a suspect.'

'I'll even make you a cup of tea.'

The Liverpool Police Station and Courthouse is an ugly pile of grey boxes halfway down George Street. MacPherson pulls into a bay marked Police Vehicles Only, right out the front. I have to use a credit card at a parking meter across the road. Typical. After texting Anto to delay our meet-up, I cross the street, then trail up the stairs behind MacPherson. The sun pounds on my head like a sledgehammer. The courthouse is in front of me; the police station doors open automatically on my left. Inside, the air-conditioning helps, but the place still smells like pigs.

In the lobby, MacPherson turns around to face me. Well over six foot, nose bent to one side and solid across the shoulders, he looks like an ageing footballer in a badly cut suit. Ginger-blond going grey, permanently burnt face, eyebrows and lashes almost white. Too fair for Australian summers.

This time, the detective actually extends his hand and makes a show of thanking me for my time and says he's sorry for my loss. Almost sounds like he means it. The desk sergeant takes it all in, his arms crossed over his beer gut and a big scowl on his face, seriously unhappy about this little performance. Have I seen this guy before? No bells ring.

I follow MacPherson up a corridor to an interview room and take a seat, while the detective goes off to get me the promised cup of tea. Grey walls, grey linoleum floor, grey desk and a one-way mirror. A camera in the corner and a recording machine on the desk. Trying to remember if I've been in this particular room before helps contain the claustrophobia. I'm not about to be interrogated, though, which makes a nice change.

After depositing two steaming mugs on the desk, MacPherson cues up a laptop, swivels it around to face me and leans over to hit play on a movie file.

Grainy black-and-white CCTV footage. It's dark, except for a time-and-date stamp in the top right corner—1.36 a.m.,

14 November. It looks like Elizabeth Drive, near where it meets the Hume Highway, slicing its way through Liverpool. A black Mercedes SUV appears from the left, an ML63, with after-market chrome rims and low-profile tyres. It's moving fast as it turns onto the Hume, heading east.

MacPherson is watching me. I take a sip of tea and shrug.

'Not sure what you're showing me. A Mercedes ML63. The night Michael Vucavec died.'

'Yes. Now watch this one.' The detective spins the laptop around and cues another file.

On the next bit of footage, the time-and-date stamp is 11.50 p.m., 21 November. My gut contracts as I recognise the date. A black SUV going fast down Bigge Street, past the TAFE. Same non-standard chrome rims. Same car? Is this Mercedes being driven away from Ivan's murder?

Rage explodes in my chest, as I close my eyes, wrestling with the need to hurt someone. Then I look down at my hands, unclench my fists, take a deep breath and sit back. MacPherson is staring at me over the rim of his mug.

'What do you make of what I've just shown you, Johnny?'

'You think this car is connected to the two shootings, Michael Vucavec's and Ivan's?' I manage to keep my voice even, just.

'If a murder happens in the small hours of the morning, we always check CCTV footage. You guys like to kill people in the middle of the night. Sure, you avoid witnesses, but the downside is there aren't many cars on the road then. So if you pass a camera, you end up standing out like proverbials.'

'Not sure what you mean by "you guys", Detective. Should I be taking offence?'

MacPherson raises one white eyebrow and sips his tea again. He sighs with pleasure as he puts his mug down.

'If this same car, with its carefully mud-spattered plates, was involved in both shootings, what does that tell you, Johnny?'

Good question. My brain scrolls through possibilities. 'Could be Stanislav shot Michael and Ivan.'

'How do you know it wasn't someone in your crew?'

'After Michael got shot, my father called a meeting and asked. You can believe it or not, but no one put up their hand.'

'That's hardly proof. It still could have been someone from your crew who shot them both. Maybe they want a leg up the ladder.'

I keep my face in neutral, but my mind swings straight to the image of Marko sitting in Ivan's seat. Nah, no way would Marko kill Ivan, his best mate. Him killing Michael Vucavec was definitely a possibility. But why would he lie about it to Dad?

MacPherson shrugs. 'Or perhaps someone had a grudge. Could be there was one real target, the other hit just a diversion. Could have been the Serb crew.' He's looking at me and I'm giving nothing back. I want to hear all his theories.

Eventually silence works and MacPherson continues. 'Could be someone else entirely, trying to stir up trouble.'

'Was Michael putting out his garbage bins too?' There'd been no mention of it in the media.

'Yes, Johnny, he was. Who knew it was such a dangerous activity?'

'Was the same gun used in both shootings?'

'Not prepared to share that with you.'

'A rifle or a handgun?' I need to know.

47

'No comment.'

This time I raise *my* eyebrow and MacPherson laughs.

'Now you know what "no comment" feels like from the other side of this table.'

'So why am I here?' I'm losing my patience.

'You're here because I've got enough work to do without another shooting. Though I really don't mind if you lot wipe each other out completely. Western Sydney would be better off, but you'll add to my workload. Think about it. Talk to your father. No point going out and shooting someone who had nothing to do with killing your brother, is there?'

'What makes you think I'm about to go shoot someone?'

'Let's call it cop's intuition. Leave it to us. We've got some new leads. Let us follow them up. Just stay out of it.'

As I drive away from the cop shop, my phone rings and my father's ugly mug pops up on the screen. Fuck.

'Hi, Dad.'

'What are you doing talking to police?'

An icy tremor slithers down my back as I look around. How does he know where I am?

'What do you mean? Why would I talk to the police?' I instinctively go for denial.

'What do I mean? Josef call me. He say your car parked outside Liverpool Police Station.'

This is the moment to tell Dad what I've just found out. I wrestle with it for a second and then go with my gut.

'Wasn't my car, Dad. Josef got it wrong. There are plenty of black Jeeps in the western suburbs.'

He hangs up on me as I pull into the potholed car park of

the Commercial Pub, in the centre of Liverpool. I stroll towards the back bar, twenty minutes early for my meeting with Anto, but getting a head start feels like a good idea.

I don't know why I decided to keep the visit to the cop shop to myself, or why MacPherson showed me the CCTV footage in the first place. Maybe I'm getting played. But I trust my instincts, and, for some reason, MacPherson doesn't set off alarms.

The smell of stale beer, the ding of distant poker machines and the coolness of the air-con are instantly soothing. I order a Reschs. The beer on tap here is freezing cold and the staff know how to pull a schooner properly, with a decent head. I have a long swig before I pick up some of my change and head to the tables by the window.

I pick the chair in the corner, so I can see the whole room. My father always sits with his back in a corner, ready to take on the room if necessary. No one is ever going to sneak up behind him. It rubbed off on both me and Ivan. We used to fight over who sat in the safe seat. Whenever I'm alone now, my mind drifts straight to my brother and memories surface like submerged bodies when the right amount of gas has built up in the gut.

Right now, I remember a day like this one, scorching. The tin roof had turned the back patio into an oven. The cicadas pounded their rhythm from the citrus trees along the back fence.

I was about ten, Sasha's age, and crouched on my knees, trying to get the chain back on my bike. Ivan, Dad and Marko were sitting up at the formica table behind me. Suddenly an empty beer can slammed into the back of my head.

'I hear you walk from fight yesterday, Johnny.' Dad's voice filtered through the pain.

'He's crying, Uncle Milan!' Marko was visiting from Croatia. It must have been just before the war, during our summer school holidays. He came every second year. I guess Dad paid his airfare. He always came on his own. When Marko was around, Ivan had no time for me.

'No, Marko, Johnny not cry. Is weak, like piss, but not cry.'

I sent a pleading look to Ivan, hoping for some kind of direction. I could see him wrestle with himself before deciding to help. He stood up, like a lawyer taking his turn to defend his client.

'Dad, the kid was half his size. Johnny did the right thing. He walked away.'

'He walked away. Why I fucking bother? Johnny, you are weak. Next year this boy is big. He come for you because you are coward. If you hurt him now, he knows who is boss. What I tell you?' Dad counted fingers on his huge right hand. 'One. No friends. Two. No feelings. Three. No conscience. Only family. Everyone else is enemy.'

I look down at my glass. Empty. Anto arrives while I'm at the bar buying another beer, so I order one for him and two shots of tequila. Why not? Anto raises his caterpillar eyebrows at the tequila, but he knows better than to comment.

We retreat to the table in the corner and check out the menu we know by heart. We choose the chicken parmigiana, like we always do. I hand Anto a fifty and ask him to order for us both. He slouches his way over to the food counter, musclebound shoulders a little too close to his big, square head. We must have been about eight or nine when Ivan and I used

Mum's food colouring to paint him green. He demolished the side fence pretending to be the Hulk. Even back then, he'd been monstrously strong. His thigh muscles are so big he's developed a bowlegged swagger that would seem comical in most men. Somehow, for Anto, it works.

Unless he's at a funeral or a wedding, he wears cargo pants or cargo shorts, anything with multiple pockets. He likes khaki or grey T-shirts or polos; I tell him he should get a job as a park ranger or join the army. He'd fit right in, he's perfectly comfortable with a chain of command. He likes structure. He's also a tech head and could have ended up in a basement somewhere, hair in a ponytail, massive gut overflowing his cargos, hacking for a living, for whoever paid the most. Instead, he works out daily in his home gym and keeps himself in a perpetual state of readiness for whatever the Novaks need. He can bench-press two hundred kilos. Don't try that at home.

We were born one month apart. He could have idolised Ivan like I did, but for some reason he chose to follow me. He's back at my side as I finish my second beer.

'Mate. Get me another Reschs before you sit down.'

'You on a roll or something, what's the rush, mate?'

'I'm fucking thirsty.'

'Fair enough. Just saying.'

Once the next beer arrives, I finally feel myself relax and smile in what feels like the first time for a long while.

'This was a fucking good idea.' I put my arm around Anto's neck and pull him into headlock. He's my right arm and I want him to know it.

But he pushes me away, red-faced. 'Yeah, cos it's Monday and we've got collections to do and Josef gave me three kilos of

51

skunk to deliver. It's in my car right now, stinking up my boot. I get pulled over and I'm fucked, mate.' He assumes his normal expression—resting grumpy face.

'Anto, you're a worrier. Have I ever told you that? Go get us another couple of shots.'

AMY

Every Monday in summer, I meet my best friend Chaz at the outdoor pool in Memorial Avenue, a few blocks from home. She's here for after-school swimming practice with her daughter, Jenny. Sasha and Jenny are doing laps with their coach, while Chaz and I pretend to do aqua aerobics. But really we're just catching up. Lexy has joined us today; she's more hardcore about exercising, but that doesn't stop her chatting.

Hats and sunglasses on, a pool noodle tucked under our arms, we bicycle our feet underwater; there's an art to staying on the spot as your legs execute frog-like movements. Lexy is in a teeny-weeny red bikini, her olive skin gleaming and her short brown hair tucked behind her ears. Chaz wears a pink rashie to protect her pale skin and her red hair is pinned up under her hat. As usual, I'm wearing my blue Speedo one-piece. Clustered in the corner of the pool, we're as far away from the undercover seating as possible. It's quieter out here.

Charlie Tyler and I met at this pool ten years ago. The idea of my kid drowning in a backyard pool terrified me, so I wanted

Sasha to know how to swim before he could walk. The first time I saw Chaz I thought she was Nicole Kidman. Then I realised she wasn't tall enough and Nicole wouldn't be at a babies' swim class in Liverpool. I am constantly amazed that Chaz doesn't have men swarming all over her, she's so beautiful. But she's also quite standoffish, until you get to know her. Something about her fascinated me, so I wore down her defences. We bonded over our shared fear of killing our children.

'How's Johnny coping?' Chaz asks, her eyes round with sympathy. 'That funeral was horrendous. I can't believe he got through the eulogy without completely breaking down.'

'He's having his moments.' I think back to this morning, finding him standing on the front lawn after breakfast; he was staring at his bare feet, as if the answers were down there, between his toes.

'Anto reckons Johnny will crack up in about a month. It'll take him that long to process Ivan's death,' Lexy adds, her little legs going twice as fast as mine underneath the blue water.

I cop a splash on the back of my head.

'Hey, Mum! Did you see me? My dive was awesome and I was underwater for hours. Jenny saw, didn't you, Jen?'

We all look at Sasha and Jenny, a few lanes over. Tanned and glistening, using his legs and sheer exuberance, Sasha is propelling his torso out of the water, a big grin on his face. I look at Jenny to confirm my son's brilliance. Her pink rashie is a smaller version of her mum's and her curly red hair is woven into long wet plaits on either side of her face. She could be the next Anne of Green Gables, if they filmed an urban Australian version. She's got one hand resting on the end of the pool. No wasted energy. She curls her lip at Sasha as if he's done something detestable. I can't help laughing. They're best mates.

At a shout from the other end of the pool, they both start swimming. Competing as usual. What Jenny lacks in size, she makes up for in determination. Sasha glides through the water with easy grace.

I notice the tear sliding down Lexy's face. Before she can wipe it away, I put my hand out to her, already guessing. 'What's wrong?'

'I got my period again this morning. Another twelve grand down the toilet. I haven't had the heart to tell Anto.' When she finally wrenches her gaze away from the children, she turns her sad eyes up to meet mine. Lexy and Anto have been trying for years. This was their fifth round of IVF.

'You'll get pregnant, Lexy. It will happen. I'm sure of it.' Because what else are you supposed to say?

'Not having a kid might be kind of nice,' says Chaz, her voice so wistful we both frown at her.

'I mean, sometimes I wonder, you know, how much easier my life would be if I hadn't had Jenny. Don't get me wrong, I love her to bits, it's just…' She looks away. 'I could have spent my twenties travelling, like my sister. I wouldn't be stuck in my shitty part-time job at the council. I could have been, I don't know, something.'

It's been hard for Chaz. Her useless boyfriend split back when she was seven months pregnant, no alimony, no family, no help. She does it all on her own.

Lexy looks at Chaz as if she's lost her mind.

'But you're a mum! That's something! That's the most important job in the world.'

'And we don't get enough credit for it,' I add. 'But I've

been thinking about going back to work too, in HR maybe. Or anything, really. Part-time like you, Chaz. I need to feel less dependent on Johnny's family.'

'Why didn't you have more kids?' Lexy asks. 'If I could have one, I'd have six. All I ever wanted was lots of children.'

I've always steered away from this conversation with Lexy, given her own fertility issues, but it's a question I've been asked by many people. It seems when you're young and married, everyone thinks they have the right to interrogate you on this most intimate subject.

'I know…We had Sasha two years in, as soon as we started trying. After he was born, I thought getting pregnant again would be just as easy as the first time. Well, it didn't happen. We got checked out and there's nothing wrong. The doctors said it was just one of those things and we should keep trying.'

'You wanted a girl, didn't you?' Chaz pipes up. 'Remember when you ate all those nuts because you read somewhere that it would help to conceive a girl?'

'Yeah, right, all I got was constipation! But it could still happen. I'm only thirty-two after all. Plenty of time. Wouldn't it be lovely?' I think about all the girls' names I've written down in my notebook over the years. Milan would probably only be happy with more boys. Fuck him.

'Why don't you try IVF?' Lexy asks.

'Sorry, Lex, but after seeing what you've been through, no thanks. If it's meant to be, it will happen. Besides I don't mind being an only child, it's not so bad. Mum and Dad tried for years to have another kid and it didn't happen for them either. It is what it is.'

'So what's stopping you going back to work?' No doubt

Chaz is trying to shift the conversation away from children, for Lexy's sake, but she's giving me a sly look. She knows the answer and I can tell she wants me to air it in front of Lexy, to see her reaction.

'Johnny doesn't want me to work outside the home because Milan thinks it reflects poorly on the Novak family.' This sounds so rehearsed and so lame I try to defend myself. 'I like being home for Sasha, having time to cook and do all the domestic stuff, keep the garden nice, go to yoga classes whenever I want...' I trail off.

Chaz is grinning at me.

'I know, it's ridiculous and I'm bored, and I need to do something about it! But every time I bring it up with Johnny, it's like I've assaulted his masculinity. You're right, okay!'

'I didn't say a word,' Chaz says, her grin even wider.

'I'm not saying I support the patriarchy here,' Lexy's green eyes are serious, 'but as soon as I get pregnant, I'm not working again, like ever. I want to be home and absolutely present for every single second.' She sighs. 'Anyway, it's all useless because I'm not pregnant. Again. And we know the boys are talking about going to war with the Serbs. Imagine how that makes me feel? Why are we being dragged back into this?'

I shoot Lexy a warning glance; this is not something I want to discuss here, or at all really. Just then Sasha bombs us, sending a spray of water over our heads. A welcome distraction. Chaz knows a little about the Novak family business. She couldn't be my best friend and not know. But she doesn't know everything. Some problems you can't share.

JOHNNY

It's a monstrous hangover. My head aches and my mouth feels like wet cement. Anto and I are doing our rounds, catching up on what we missed yesterday. He knows to leave me alone. Every time I get out of the air-conditioned car and walk on the sun-baked streets, I think I'm going to puke.

By the time we pull up outside Bogdan's fish shop, it's late afternoon. I'm wearing my usual work uniform of black jeans and black T-shirt. I like to keep my wardrobe choices uncomplicated. I guess if my life was a cowboy movie, I'd wear a black hat. Right now, I wish I was in board shorts. The air is muggy after a rain-filled night; it's like wading through a swamp. I want this job over and done with fast. I want to go home, fall in the pool, then put my feet up and have a nice cold beer.

Anto gets out of the passenger seat and swaggers down the lane at the side of the shop. He'll position himself near the back door to cut off the other exit. It's an unnecessary precaution but we do it automatically. As I walk in through the front door, the bell jangles. The place smells good—frying fish and hot chips.

I move to the wall on the right-hand side and lean where I can see the whole shop. The colour in Bogdan's face drains away. His wife clocks me, then turns away to concentrate on the deep fryers. Their son is a metre away from me, at one of the tables against the wall; looks like he's doing his homework. He's ten, like Sasha. Sweet kid. He looks up at me and smiles, then back down at a row of maths problems. Somehow, I doubt Sasha's working on his maths homework right now.

Bogdan keeps serving customers, calling out orders. He runs a tight ship. When there's finally a break, I take off my Ray-Bans and raise an eyebrow.

I don't say anything, don't need to, my presence is enough. Bogdan just needs to hand over the money he owes. I don't want a long, drawn-out discussion, not today. I just want to keep moving through the rest of the shops on our list. The smell is making my mouth water. I'll get some of those hot chips before I leave.

Bogdan glances at his son. 'Sorry, Johnny, I don't have money today. Is next week okay?' he whispers.

I get it. He doesn't want to be embarrassed in front of his son, so I move over to the counter and keep my voice down. I've still got a job to do.

'Why would that be okay, Bogdan?'

'Well, I'm asking for my daughter, you know Alexa? She is getting married this weekend and I got a whole lotta extra expenses, you understand?'

'Bogdan, I get it, but how's that *my* problem?'

'Just this once, Johnny.'

'But you're already three weeks late, so if you don't pay me now, you'll be four weeks late. What's going to change between now and next week, apart from you having a married daughter and maybe a smashed shop window?'

I hate this part of the job, but it comes naturally nonetheless. I put one big hand on top of the glass case full of filleted fish. Bogdan watches my hand curl slowly into a fist. He looks back at his wife.

'Pay him,' she says. 'We have less flowers, our guests drink less, we owe the minister instead.' She looks daggers at me. 'He won't put rock through shop window.' She turns abruptly and heads out the back.

Bogdan takes a pile of notes out from under the till. He's a good bloke, so it will be exactly three thousand dollars—fifteen hundred for the house and fifteen hundred for the shop. That's three weeks' rent. I know he and his wife get paid one grand each a week, before tax, because I make out the pay slips. And they both work a sixty-hour week. The store has to be open between 10.30 a.m. and 11.30 p.m. every day except Sunday. Us Novaks are good Catholics.

I could just dock their pay, but Dad wants the families he's 'rescued' to hand over their rent money to me, personally, every week. It's a ridiculous system. We own ten fish shops around the western suburbs, all run by Croatian immigrants. Dad 'sponsors' them, helping with visas and airfares to Australia. Then we set them up in one of our cheap houses. They pay us back their original debt, with interest, plus rent on the house and the shop.

It's all a front for the real Novak business—coercion, various forms of armed robbery and drug trafficking. But there are lines we won't cross. We don't sell heroin or ice—drugs that turn users into ghosts and psychopaths. We stick to party drugs. And I'm the one in charge of laundering the money. On average, I put an extra five to ten grand a week through each shop. Every week. They're the most profitable fish shops in Sydney. Yet here I am threatening to throw a brick through the window of one of our own shops. Bogdan knows I'll do it and he'll have to pay for the new window. How fucked is that?

I give Bogdan back half the money.

'I'll square the books. Think of it as a wedding gift for Alexa. Between us, okay?'

Bogdan is so grateful it's embarrassing. I don't feel like chips anymore.

I call it quits, drop Anto at his place and drive home.

Pointing the remote at our double lock-up garage, I notice the lawn needs mowing. Fuck, the grass grows quickly at this time of year. No doubt I need to clean the pool too. Those ghost gums in our backyard look pretty, but they drop a shitload of leaves in the pool. The lawn and the pool are going to have to wait.

I switch off the ignition and let the quiet of the garage wash over me. Amy's white Mini is where it should be. My family is safe. I lurch out of the car and wince as the movement hurts my head. In this state, only a whisky could make me feel better. A single malt scotch. An Islay single malt. As I open the door connecting the garage to the house and step into the hall, Sasha charges me, rocking me sideways. Not a bad effort for a kid.

'Mate, that was a good tackle.'

'I didn't make you fall down, though, Dad.'

'Yeah, well, it took all my strength to stay upright.'

I pick up my son and give him a cuddle. He smells like sweat and little boy, dirt and lollies mixed together. It's all overlaid with the aroma of something good coming from the kitchen. My mouth waters.

'Come out the front and throw the football, Dad. I'm getting really good at catching.'

'Not tonight, kid. I'm pretty tired.'

Amy comes through the back door and up the hall towards us. Backlit by the sunshine flooding in from the backyard, her dress seems to disappear; all I can see is her shape, like a violin swaying towards me. She looks cross, so I put on my most pathetic expression: a dog desperate for affection. She gives in and kisses me. I wrap my arms around her, Sasha squished in the middle.

'Yuck, you two are gross.' Sasha wriggles out from between us and runs off to his room.

We both start laughing, hanging off each other, laughing like we can't stop. It feels so good. Then her face is buried in my chest and I'm overwhelmed by the need to protect her. I pull her close and I'm in the only place on earth I want to be. We are still, breathing each other in for one long moment, then she lifts her face to mine, and we kiss. I lift her up. Her legs wrap around my waist. Still kissing, I walk us towards the bedroom, but she pulls away, shaking her head, and asks me to put her down. There's a look in her eyes I've never seen before. I could try to find out what's wrong, but now I just feel exhausted. She heads down the hall, calling Sasha for his bath.

Maybe it was just bad timing. If I'm lucky, I might get another chance once Sasha has gone to bed.

I wander into our bedroom. The last of the sun is streaking across our king-size bed. This room is calm and peaceful. It smells like Amy. Out through the windows, I can see the pool.

It's sparkling clean; Amy must have vacuumed it for me. The light bounces off the surface of the water and onto the ceiling. I should have a swim. I can't be fucked.

Slumped on my side of the bed, I unlock the bedside table, where I put Ivan's Beretta after I came home from the wake. I'm not sure why I'm drawn to the gun now. After I've pulled it out, force of habit makes me reach down between my legs to drag out the cleaning kit I keep under the bed. The smell of gun oil pulls me back to my teens.

When we were thirteen and twelve, Dad took Ivan and me out bush for the first time, to teach us how to fire all the handguns and rifles in the family arsenal. Dad was almost gentle as he guided our aim and showed us how to reload quickly. He taught us to clean and care for our weapons. He's pretty obsessive about keeping guns clean.

As we got older, we graduated from hitting bottles propped in trees to shooting roos and wild pigs. First we shot them from the back of the ute, then one-handed from the back of our motorbikes. Every few months we'd head west, out past Bourke and Cobar or down to the Riverina near Cootamundra. Sometimes on our own, sometimes with the crew. Camping and shooting. Eating whatever we shot. Nothing wasted.

When we had the whole crew out bush, we'd rehearse upcoming jobs. We learned how to steal cars the old way, using packing tape or a coat hanger. Dad would pull Ivan, Anto and me aside and give us the night's mission. We had to wait until the last of the crew were snoring in their swags. We'd creep around the camp with knives in our hands, two on guard duty, while the third carefully removed Baz's watch or Josef's gold necklace. The next day, we'd get whacked across the head by the hapless victim as we handed back our haul.

Each time, the job would become more complex; when we were thirteen and fourteen, Dad told us to use our guns.

'Make sure guns not loaded. You not shoot my men because you stupid. Understand? You hold up that petrol station, over there.'

Dad and Baz had marked out the floor plan of a store in the dirt. The big cooler box, full of beer, passed as the counter and our cousins Brick and Blocker would be standing behind it. Josef's sons were still only kids, but at eight and nine years old, they were already built like their nicknames.

Wearing beanies, Ivan, Anto and I had to approach 'the door', eyes down to avoid cameras. At the last minute, we'd pretend to pull our 'balaclavas' over our faces. We burst through the door, yanking the guns from the back of our shorts, yelling, 'Get down! Stay down!' Josef would pretend to be a screaming woman who had to be managed.

In the store, Ivan was boss, so he'd order Blocker off the ground and back to the till to hand over the money. Blocker would pull out a shotgun that was hidden behind the cooler box.

We had several ways of getting that shotgun off Blocker. Sometimes Ivan would grab the end of the barrel, yank it off the kid and whack him on the side of the head so he'd give us the money. Other times, Anto had to grab 'the lady' and threaten her, then she'd plead with Blocker to put down his shotgun. One time, I just launched myself over the cooler box and took him out of the equation. Then we had to get Brick to hand over the money.

After these training sessions, Dad would often get drunk and pick a fight, maybe thump me on the back of the head and tell me I wasn't worth a piece of shit. It didn't matter what I did, I only ever seemed to make it worse. Ivan did his best to talk Dad around when he got mean drunk. My brother had a knack for it. Sometimes he made Dad laugh and everyone would get off easy.

I remember being on my trail bike, in my early twenties, tracking a roo through low scrub, dirt, grass humps and rocks. When I came up close, I ditched the gun, pulled out my knife and leapt off the bike onto the back of that six-foot red. He was so shocked by my sudden weight that I was able to wrestle him to the ground without being gutted by his powerful hind legs. I was about to slit his throat when all the desire to kill drained out of my body. I jumped up and away from him. He kicked to his feet and bounded off. He threw me one backward glance. Nup, not following. I looked around, suddenly paranoid Dad was watching, but I couldn't see a soul. That was the last time I went hunting.

Sasha runs in, fresh from his bath. His eyes light up when he sees the gun.

'Can I touch it, Dad? Let me hold it.' He reaches out his hand, his voice loaded with longing. What the fuck am I doing, sitting on the bed holding a gun?

'No guns until you're twelve. You know that. Family tradition.' I haul myself up, slide the cleaning kit back under the bed with my foot, then return the gun to the bedside drawer, lock it and slip the keys into my pocket. As I look down at my son's disappointed face, I make a decision—I'm going to break that fucking tradition. Sasha will never need to know how to handle a gun.

65

In the kitchen, I drop three blocks of ice into a whisky tumbler and make my way to the sideboard in the living room, where I keep half a dozen bottles of spirits, set up like a bar. I pour myself a large Scotch and take a slug. The smokiness swirls around my parched mouth and down my throat. I sink into my favourite swivel armchair and rotate slowly, taking in the room, the carefully chosen paintings, the furniture that looks expensive but wasn't. My wife has great taste. She's raised my standards. I can't let her down now.

I know I need to call my father. He's called twice today, and I haven't even listened to the messages. He wants my plan of attack and I don't have one. Maybe I should plan on getting drunk again.

Amy comes in and stares pointedly at my glass.

'I would have thought you'd had enough yesterday.'

'Well, I didn't. Stop trying to control me.' My reaction is involuntary and I regret the words as soon as they leave my mouth.

'I'm not trying to control you. I'm trying to help.' She sits down opposite me. 'I'm really upset with Milan. It's crazy. You're not actually going to do anything, are you? Think about the danger it puts Sasha and me in.'

Why doesn't she get it? I have a duty to my family too, and my crew. 'I've got to do something. I don't know what yet, but I don't plan on getting caught.' I get up to refill my glass; the ice hasn't melted, but most of the Scotch is gone.

There's a loud knock on the front door.

Amy looks confused. 'Are you expecting anyone?'

'Nup. I'll get it.'

I head into the hall and check the spyhole. Fuck.

'It's Dad!' I call out.

This is what you get for avoiding a problem like my father—a home visit. By the look on his face, whatever happens next is going to be painful.

AMY

The sight of Milan at the front door makes me shiver. I can't remember the last time he came here. We go to him. He doesn't come to us.

'*Dida! Dida!*' Sasha yells as he runs down the hallway to his grandfather, whom he adores. Just out of the bath, his hair is damp and he's wearing his favourite Spiderman PJs. Milan breaks into a smile, scoops him up and swings him around. The sight of them together should make me happy, but it never fails to unnerve me. Milan crushes Sasha to his chest, kisses the top of his head, then puts him down. He finally looks at me, no smile, just a nod. He pushes Sasha towards me, and I know what's expected. Mother and child must make themselves scarce while the men talk important business.

I want to scream, which would only validate Milan's opinion of me as a useless female. I've had to accept that Johnny was raised in a male chauvinist household, that it affects him in ways he doesn't notice, but I'll make sure Sasha doesn't share the same values.

Once I've shepherded Sasha into the kitchen, I get him plugged into a computer game, earbuds on. Not good parenting, I admit, but I don't want him hearing what I fear will happen between Johnny and his dad. I get started on dinner, making as little noise as possible, so I can eavesdrop.

Our open-plan kitchen dining area is to the right of the front door, off the hallway that runs like a spine down the middle of our home. The floors are all knotty pine or beige-coloured tiles, depending on the function of the room. We had the walls painted a cool white. There is nothing charming about our home, but it's functional, easy to clean, and when Johnny added the small inground pool to the backyard, we felt pretty pleased with ourselves.

Milan and Johnny are in the living room, off the hall to the left. The door is closed, but what I hear of their muffled voices is enough for me to know exactly where this is headed. It's as if no one can see it except me. How can they all be so blind?

Johnny could be way more physically intimidating than Ivan ever was, although he always downplayed his strength, perhaps another reason he was sidelined by Milan and Ivan. But Johnny feels responsible for every one of the Croatian immigrants they set up in the Novak fish shops, and that's something I admire in him.

It took me months to work out Johnny was dyslexic; he hides it so well. Give him a spreadsheet, however, and the man's a savant. That's why he's the one in charge of the money. But when he wanted to cut the fish-shop families in on a profit-share arrangement, Milan and Ivan just laughed.

Ivan didn't have Johnny's sense of responsibility. He lived by their ridiculous family motto—no friends, no feelings, no conscience. What drivel. Ivan never seemed troubled by anything at all. Johnny could not be less like his brother, and for that I've always been grateful. But Milan knows exactly how to pull Johnny's strings.

I can hear my husband defending his right to come up with a plan in which he doesn't get caught. Then the sound of an armchair scraping across the timber floor. Then a slap. Now the low rumble of Milan's voice.

My heart is racing. How dare that bastard slap my husband? Why does Johnny tolerate Milan's bullying? I'm furious and I need to intervene somehow—I'll take a bowl of chips in there and lower the tension. As I reach to open the pantry cupboard, I stop. Milan would be furious. I'll only make things worse. When I first had Sasha, our relationship improved, but any warmth has long since cooled. He wants more grandchildren and I have failed in that area.

Back at the kitchen bench, I drizzle olive oil on the steaks and season them with pepper and salt. The weird thing is, watching Johnny over the last few days, all I can see is Milan. He is so much like his father, way more than Ivan ever was. People listen when Johnny speaks; he has natural gravitas. Whereas Ivan was just good at manipulating people, especially his father. Even when Milan was drunk and in a rage, Ivan could charm him into laughter. Ivan was charming all right, but his smile never reached his eyes. He just took what he wanted.

My fingers start to tremble. The saltshaker slips through my hands and shatters on the floor. Damn. I grab the dustpan and broom from under the sink, clean up the mess and put a stop to any more thoughts about Ivan. Instead, I think about my husband.

70

Johnny doesn't know how smart he is. He could do anything he wants, he's so fucking smart. I know he holds anger inside, but it sits on simmer and I rarely see it boil over. His anger is never directed at me or Sasha. His father can make him mad, though, oh yeah. But Johnny doesn't act on it. His anger seems directed inwards.

Milan is much better at anger than anyone I've ever met. He's *gifted* at anger.

As though on cue, I hear Milan head out the front door. I think about going in to see if Johnny is okay, but that would mean admitting I heard the slap. What we need is a nice normal dinner. After Sasha is in bed, I'm going on the offensive. Johnny needs to be talked out of doing anything stupid. And murdering the leader of the local Serb gang would be right up there with the dumbest idea ever.

AMY

By the time Johnny makes it to the kitchen the next morning, I've already had breakfast with Sasha and put him on the bus to school. It's good for his sense of independence and there are always other kids from his class on the bus. It's too far to walk from our place, and he'd have to cross the Hume Highway, so I usually drop him off and pick him up. It's only a fifteen-minute drive and it's not like I've got too much to do. But this morning I need to talk to my husband, get him to see that things are sliding out of control. He got drunk again last night, so there was no point talking to him after dinner.

Johnny sits at the kitchen bench and hoes into the bacon and eggs I've put in front of him. I may not be as good as Branka in the kitchen, but my scrambled eggs are up there with the best. A sprinkling of dill is the secret. I pour him a black coffee, then sit down beside him, blowing on my cup of tea. Johnny is moaning slightly as he shovels in the food.

'Enjoying that?'

'Seriously the best breakfast I've ever eaten.'

'Nice. Happy for you.'

As he swallows, he glances sideways at me, registering that I'm not happy.

He lowers his head and forks more eggs into his mouth. I bet he's thinking he may as well have this fight on a full stomach. I can wait. I sip my tea and look at him. My big handsome husband. I remember laughing with him last night over nothing, and over Sasha. The way we held each other, the way we kissed. I close my eyes and feel myself soften. Then I remember Milan slapping him, and what he wants Johnny to do to satisfy some warped sense of honour. I sit up straight to give myself more backbone.

As he pushes his plate away, a sigh of pleasure escapes and he wipes his mouth with the back of his hand. Getting him to use a napkin has been an ongoing challenge. He sips his coffee, then swivels his stool to face me.

'What's up, Ames?'

'You know what's up.'

'Honey, I'm under pressure.'

'Well, your coping mechanisms are failing.'

'Don't try and make me feel dumb.' He stands up, towering over me—I know it's unintentional, but it fuels my anger, so I push back my stool and stand too, chest to chest with my husband. Well, not quite, I'm still six inches shorter than Johnny.

'Don't try and intimidate me, Milan,' I growl at him.

'Don't call me Milan!'

'Don't act like Milan then!' I turn my back on him and walk around the bench into the kitchen. I need some distance.

Johnny's shoulders have slumped; he looks sad and frustrated. 'Fuck me, I'm outta here,' he grunts.

From behind the kitchen bench, I can see out into the front garden. As Johnny turns away, I glimpse a black SUV in front of our house. A visitor? A tinted window slides down. In the next instant, Johnny is throwing himself at me, sliding across the kitchen bench, crashing into me. We hit the floor hard, all the breath knocked out of me. There's a sharp crack and an explosion of shattered glass as he holds me down, his body covering me. Another crack. It takes me a second to realise it's a gunshot. I scream, but nothing comes out as I struggle to suck in air.

'Stay here!' Johnny yells.

Terrified, I curl up on the kitchen tiles, surrounded by broken breakfast dishes. I wish he was still covering me, but he's gone. Once I hear the front door open and the sound of his running footsteps outside, I sit up slowly, rubbing the back of my head, then grasp the kitchen bench to haul myself up. Shaking and hugging myself, I pick my way around the broken crockery and edge slowly into the living room. My eyes flit between the shattered plate-glass window and two small holes, high up on the wall, close to the ceiling.

'Fucking hell,' Johnny barks as he joins me, taking in the glass all over the floor. 'Thank God Sasha wasn't here.'

'What, and I don't count?' My voice comes out all wrong.

'Are you okay?' He's right in front of me, grasping me by the shoulders, his wild eyes examining me from head to toe. 'Are you hurt? Did I hurt you?'

I push him away and point up to the two bullet holes.

'What the hell is your stupid war doing in our home?' My legs are shaking and my voice still sounds weird, as if I'm in a tunnel.

74

'Hey, we don't know that was the Serbs.'

'What? You're protecting them now? I thought you were supposed to kill one of them. You haven't done it already, have you?'

'No!'

'So you're telling me someone is shooting at us and you haven't even killed anyone yet?'

'If you really want to know, I'm actually trying to work out how not to kill Stanislav.'

'Really, how very considerate of you. You keep on making your plans, Johnny.' Fear has morphed into rage. I turn on my heel, head for our bedroom and slam the door.

Sitting on the unmade bed, my back to the door, I hear Johnny coming down the hall. He opens the bedroom door carefully.

'I'm sorry, Ames. I'll find out who did this, I promise. They've crossed another fucking line. I'll organise for the window to be fixed today. This morning. Right now. I just need…'

I can hear him shifting the floorboards in our wardrobe and opening the safe. There's only one reason he'd be doing that. I take a peek and, yes, he's checking the safety on his Glock.

In the news, this incident would be referred to as a 'drive-by shooting'. This is our home. When we got married, Johnny assured me there was a code—women and children were out of bounds. But nothing feels normal anymore.

Johnny comes around the side of the bed to face me. The gun is nowhere to be seen.

'Don't touch anything, okay? Just stay in here. And remember, I'll always keep you and Sasha safe.'

I don't bother answering. Safe? Who is he kidding? Nothing like this has ever happened before, but I have to admit to myself that the threat has always been there—hasn't it? Perhaps I need to start facing up to the truth about the family I married into.

He yells into his phone as he heads up the hall. I collapse on our bed and stare out into the backyard at the surface of the pool, smooth in the breezeless heat. My heart is racing. I try to do some deep breathing. At first I beat myself up for being so easily freaked out, then I remind myself that I have every reason to feel afraid.

I'm not sure how much time has passed when I hear hammering from the living room. I stand up shakily and make the bed. By the time I leave the sanctuary of our bedroom, all the glass is gone. Two glaziers are in the front garden, cutting a new window. Surprised there's no sign of police, I walk back into the kitchen to find Johnny cleaning up the last bits of broken crockery.

He leans the broom against the bench and hugs me. I stand mute in his arms, willing him to say he has to leave. I need him out of the house.

'I've got to go to work now, Ames, but all this is sorted. Don't worry about anything. If the police were coming, they'd have shown up by now, so no one reported it.'

I nod. He leans forward to kiss me. I look away, so he has to kiss me on the cheek. He grabs his keys and unlocks the door to the garage. At the sound of the Jeep motor rumbling to life, I head back to our bedroom.

Johnny said another line has been crossed. He also said Sasha could have been here. Normally, I wouldn't have been here either. I'd be driving home from dropping him off. I might be having a coffee with Lexy or heading to a yoga class. I could be at the bookshop or the library, loading up on thrillers to fill the day after my chores are done.

Maybe if I hadn't been here, I wouldn't even know about it. Johnny could have replaced the window and bogged over the bullet holes. A bit of paint and I'd be clueless. But now I'm terrified—I don't know what else he's hiding from me.

I rub my face with my hands. The only part of this drama I can control is to remove Sasha and myself from the field of play.

I need to pack. Enough for a couple of weeks. We'll go to Mum and Dad's. They'll be happy, hoping it spells the end of the marriage they desperately didn't want. I'm not sure I'll be able to bear it, but they do live in one of those secure, gated communities for seniors. How secure, I don't know, but it must be harder for someone to shoot out your front window if they have to drive through a wooden boom gate first.

I wouldn't even be thinking about going to Mum and Dad's if they weren't booked to leave on a European river cruise next week. I think I can handle a week of their not-so-secret gloating. No longer. But how long is it going to take before Johnny either fixes this mess, gets busted or gets killed?

My insides feel like rubber bands pulled in all directions, but I have to stay focused. Whatever happens, Sasha will not be a casualty. If we're not here, we can't be caught in the crossfire. Can we?

JOHNNY

I'm halfway to Anto's when my phone rings. Fuck, it's Dad.

'Come now, we have meeting, here at home.'

'Dad, we just got shot at!'

'Who shoot at you?'

'Don't know.'

'Who get shot? Not Sasha?'

'No one was hurt, but they shot out our front window, scared the crap out of Amy.'

'Front window. Not you, not Sasha, so not change anything. Come here, tell me plan.'

'For fuck's sake, Dad, I haven't got a plan yet. I don't think you get it, someone shot at me and Amy. What if Sasha had been there?'

'Where is bullet hole? You find bullet hole?'

'Yeah, two bullet holes in the living-room wall, high up.'

'So, they not try to kill you. Just scare you. Worked. You scared. Now, pick up Anto, come here. You have ten minutes to think of plan.'

I pull up outside Anto's place as he's walking out the front. His house looks uncannily like ours. Triple-fronted blond brick with brown aluminium window frames. We all live a few streets from each other in subdivisions built in the seventies. Not an inspiring decade for architecture in Liverpool. But the blocks are big enough for a pool and a barbecue out the back and space to kick a footy around out the front. Anto slides his bulk into the passenger seat, a worried look on his face.

'Mate. Got a call from my dad. The boss has called a crew meeting.'

'Yeah, I know. Fuck, I just got shot at!'

Anto stares at me in disbelief as I fill him in.

'Christ, mate! And your dad still won't let you off the hook?'

'No! Why would he put the safety of his only remaining son, his daughter-in-law and his grandchild ahead of his fucked-up need for revenge?'

Anto's eyebrows dip into a V shape; my mate shares my misery. I decide to spill.

'There's something else. MacPherson was waiting outside my place on Monday morning. He took me down to the station and showed me CCTV footage of the night Michael Vucavec died, and the night Ivan died. A black SUV was driving nearby after both shootings. A black Mercedes ML63.'

'Why would he show you that?' Anto doesn't like the police any more than the rest of us in our line of business.

'I think he reckons it was the same offender for both murders. He told me I shouldn't be blaming the Serbs. He doesn't want a gang war.'

'Right. So why not tell your dad? Puts a new spin on things, doesn't it?'

79

'I straight out lied about it when he asked me. I can't back down now. And Dad has to blame someone, so let him blame the Serbs. Maybe it was them anyway. Why do we have to take the police line? I've just got to convince Dad to give me more time to come up with a fucking plan.'

'Did you see the car used in the drive-by this morning?'

'Yep. A black Mercedes ML63.'

'Fuck me.'

'No thanks.'

I pull in behind Marko's gold convertible, which is parked in the only shade under the jacaranda tree outside my parents' place. Resisting the urge to slam the Jeep into his matching gold bumper bar, I wonder why Marko seems to be exempt from Dad's rule against flash cars.

Anto and I make our way through the house and out onto the back patio. The senior members of the crew are already here—Dad's cousins, Mike Novak and his son Boris, AKA Stump and Fibs. Stump lost the top two knuckles of his right index finger during a razor fight in prison, and Fibs never lets the truth get in the way of a good story. Joe and Niko Cetnic are Bigsie and Shrimp because Joe's short and Niko's tall. And, of course, Baz, Josef and Marko. Bigsie, Stump, Josef, Baz and Dad are all getting closer to sixty. Marko has just turned forty and Anto, Fibs, Shrimp, Brick, Blocker and I are in our thirties. The rest of the crew are still in their twenties and have not made the cut today.

'You thin.' Mum is peering at me, pinching my arm. 'Amy not feed you enough? You sit, eat *fritule*.'

She pushes me into my usual seat at the table, next to Dad,

and slides a plate full of little balls of sugar-covered dough towards me. Then she pours two cups of coffee from her urn on the sideboard and plonks them in front of me and Anto.

She doesn't mention the shooting. So Dad hasn't told her. That's probably for the best. She fusses around for a couple more minutes, then makes herself scarce.

We're the last to arrive, which means Dad called everyone else first. The last thing I want is to play whatever humiliating game he's cooked up.

'Okay, Johnny, we are all here. We listen to your plan. You promise.' Dad's eyes are glinting with something that looks a lot like pleasure. I decide to go on the offensive.

'My home was attacked this morning. A drive-by shooting. The front window was shot out. Amy was there and she was pretty upset. Thank God, Sasha was already at school.'

Based on the reaction round the table, Dad hadn't thought to mention it before we arrived. I can't even begin to guess why. To see if I'd bring it up to gain sympathy? To see if I'd still sound scared? Fuck him, I'm going to use it to my advantage, give myself more time.

'Who was it?' Josef asks.

'They shot at your house? This morning? While your wife was home?' This from Baz. The reaction I wanted.

'Yes, while Amy was home, and no, Josef, I don't know who it was. Maybe the Serbs, who knows? All I saw was a black Mercedes SUV. But that means whatever our next move is, it can't be obvious.'

I want everyone round the table to understand that they're involved in this. I take a deep breath and continue, my voice louder now.

'If they know we're behind a payback attack, the Serbs will retaliate for sure, and we don't know who they'll take out next.'

I look around the table and see Anto nodding. Some follow his lead, most keep their faces impassive.

Marko is openly sneering. 'Are you in the planning stage, cousin? Do you plan to grow balls?'

This gets a growl of approval and some laughter, but I know they won't be too disrespectful. I'm the boss's son, after all, and I've just been shot at.

'It's not about my balls, Marko, which are bigger and hairier than yours. It's about brains. Oddly enough, I don't want to get killed or busted. I'm being careful. We don't want this to escalate into a full-scale war, do we?'

I see more agreement around the table now, and my father weighing it up.

'No, Johnny, we don't want war. We want revenge. Is Wednesday and I am patient man. I give you more time. By Sunday you have plan, you tell me plan, I approve plan, or I give job to Marko. Is easy.'

'Give me the job now, boss.' Marko leans back in his chair. 'I will bring you Stanislav's fat Serbian head for your Sunday roast.'

This bit of bravado wins a general murmur of approval and some fist-banging on the table. But I know most of the crew privately think my cousin is psycho.

'You wait for Sunday, Marko. Johnny, you and Anto short on collections last week. I see books too. You fix. And make plan for Sunday.'

I just nod. It could've been worse. I catch Anto's eye, a slight tilt of my head is enough. He follows me out.

We get back in the Jeep and I head towards the Cumberland Highway. We still have another job on our list. Next stop is one of our fish shops in Cabramatta. We're both quiet, letting the tension ebb away. After a few minutes, I sigh and glance over at my best mate. He's looking wistfully at the Krispy Kreme store coming up on our right.

'No Krispies today, mate.' I give him a poke in his rock-hard gut. 'You're getting a little heavy around the middle.'

'Fuck off. I did a hundred squats this morning. I can eat anything I want. I'm blessed with a god-like metabolism.'

'Yeah, right. Listen. We have to make a ton of money and retire early. We need something big and we need it fast, before Dad gets completely out of hand and I end up in jail for murdering Stanislav, the fat fuck.'

'Your dad's just winding you up, and he's using Marko to do it. You could call his bluff and let Marko do the job.' Anto grunts. 'I mean, he's got the right training, hasn't he?'

'Yes, but Ivan was *my* brother.' If I keep repeating this to myself, maybe I can force myself to do what Dad wants. I turn right onto Cabramatta Road.

Anto sits up straight. 'I might have an idea.' He sounds surprised with himself.

'Thank Christ.'

'With Lexy being second cousins with the Vucavecs—'

'Anto,' I interrupt, 'I was the one who got you special dispensation from Dad to marry a Serb!'

'Mate, sometimes I curse you for it.'

'What idea?'

83

'Last night, she told me all her cousins back in Belgrade had just got together for some big family party. She was showing me some photos on Facebook. All these fat fucking Serbs, sitting around drinking and eating, you know?'

'Yeah, so?'

'All the big swinging dicks were there, mate. The Vucavecs, the Milovics and the Novakovs.'

'Really? Interesting…What else did she say?'

'Well, she banged on about it being a shame we couldn't go to all the Serb parties here, because I was a stinking Croat blah, blah, blah. So, I'm being a good bloke, looking through the photos on Facebook with her, saying nice shit about babies, and who do I see pop up in some backyard in Belgrade?'

'Who?'

'Stanislav.'

'What the fuck? Old Stanislav, swanning about in Serbia while I'm over here having my balls busted about how I plan to kill him.'

'I should have thought it through last night.' He mimes giving himself a couple of uppercuts. 'It's got to mean something, doesn't it? Stanislav being there, so soon after Michael's funeral. Maybe something big.'

'Yeah, totally. And maybe that something big involves the Aussie side of the family and that's why Stanislav was there. But what? How do we find out what the Serbs are up to?'

'I reckon we could bug Stanislav's car! I've always wanted to do that.' Anto is grinning.

'Well, we could, or maybe we could snatch one of them, stash him in the warehouse, treat him to a little thumping and see what he tells us. Find out if he knows anything about who killed Ivan and what's on the horizon, job-wise.'

Our warehouse is a freestanding brick building in one of the older industrial areas that ring Liverpool. It's where we rebirth cars, store drugs and keep stolen goods before they get fenced or sold. Dad bought the place years ago. It's secure and the location is a tightly held secret. I smack the steering wheel. I've come up with someone perfect.

'What about Nick Stanic? We know where he lives and he's a weak piece of shit. He'll fold fast.'

'Mate. Hold on.' Anto is grimacing. 'When was the last time you saw him? When we played soccer against him in high school? He's a big bastard now. We'd have to surprise him, and then what's to stop Nick telling Stanislav we grabbed him?'

'He's not that big, and I reckon it might all depend on what we find out. Something really good, we simply hang onto him till it's over. Gives him more motivation to cough up the right info, doesn't it? Otherwise we might not be too happy with him.'

'Sounds risky.' Anto looks worried. 'Can't we just bug Stanislav's car?'

As we pass the red-brick arches of the St George Serbian Orthodox Church, there's a loud bang. I lose control of the Jeep, which swerves straight into oncoming traffic. I put the skids on and yank the steering wheel to the left, away from the front end of the semi-trailer coming right at us.

Time slows down and I seem to stop breathing until I bring the car under control. I turn left into Coventry Street, where I can pull over. We both leap out and see that the left front tyre is blown.

'Was that a gunshot or the tyre?' Anto is examining the fucking great hole in the tyre.

I look back at the church and up and down Cabramatta Road, trying to work out if anyone is paying us a little too much attention. No one I can see.

Then we both spot the bullet-shaped hole in the left front fender, right in front of the tyre.

JOHNNY

By the time I finally get home, after dropping off Anto, it's close to seven o'clock. I'm hungry, I'm tired and I'm hoping Amy has lightened up a bit. As I pull into the driveway, it's a relief to see the living-room window intact and welcoming yellow light spilling onto the front garden. The garage door slides up and I'm surprised by the vacant spot where Amy's Mini should be. A ripple of fear runs through me, but I shake it off. She must have gone to the shops.

After leaving the garage door up for Amy, I unlock the door through to the house. I'm ready for Sasha tonight. I want to make up for the last few days and spend some time with him before bed. It takes a moment before I register that Sasha isn't around. But Amy wouldn't leave him here alone after this morning. There's no smell of food either. Weird. Where the fuck is she?

Then I see the note on the kitchen bench.

Johnny,

I've taken Sasha to Mum and Dad's. I don't think it's safe for us to be at home with you right now. Don't bother calling me or trying to see us. I need time by myself to think.
Amy.

Not 'love Amy', just 'Amy'.

Fuck, fuck, fuck. This is not good. I hit her number on my phone like the screen is an enemy. It rings out. Weird. She's turned her voicemail off. I grab my keys again, jump back in the Jeep and reverse down the drive fast, fishtailing as I take off up the street, anger building in my belly where dinner should be.

Amy's parents' house is only twenty minutes away, but it might as well be on another planet. Each house in this retirement village is slightly different from the next, but they're all somehow the same. The word vanilla springs to mind. The security guard at the boom gate asks me who I'm here to see. He checks his list and shakes his head.

'The Parsons are not accepting visitors tonight, sir.' The last word is added a little too late to be respectful.

He's a big guy, well into his sixties, belly going to fat. I'm thinking how easy it would be to drag him out of his little security cabin and beat him until he cries. Something like fear seeps into the older man's eyes and he starts to reach under the counter. I never find out what he's reaching for because I throw the Jeep into reverse, back up far enough to turn and drive slowly home.

I'm kind of ashamed of myself. The poor bloke was just doing his job.

AMY

At least it isn't my childhood bedroom or something equally demoralising. Instead, I'm lying on a very comfortable, queen-size bed in Mum and Dad's pretty guest room. The decor includes an overstuffed chair, swag curtains and an abundance of scatter cushions in soothing shades of pale green.

I wonder what it would take for Johnny to leave his parents behind and move to another part of the country? If we sold our house, we could start again somewhere else. We could both get jobs. It would be fun. It would be normal. I'd still make sure I was home in time for Sasha after school.

Right now, Sasha is down the hall in 'his room'. With its blue-and-white aeroplane-motif wallpaper, it's out of a feature in *Vogue Living*. He's used to staying here at least once a month, whenever Johnny and I have a date night. He was snoring gently when I checked him before coming to bed.

Slow tears trickle from the corners of my eyes. The curtains are closed, but there's still the vague outline of a ceiling rose to focus on. I've tried yogic breathing. I've tried meditation. I've tried to empty my head, but every time I close my eyes, I see Johnny launching himself across the kitchen bench at me. I feel us crashing to the floor, his weight driving the air from my lungs as he covers me. I hear that second shot crack across the sunny morning and slam into our living-room wall. My eyes spring open again and I try some more deep breathing.

I'd called ahead, so Mum and Dad weren't surprised to see me when I arrived with our suitcases while Sasha was still at school. Mum made me a cup of tea and we sat down at the kitchen table. They looked concerned, but had obviously decided not to ask questions. It would have been so easy to tell them everything, the way I used to, before I married Johnny. Instead, I told them we'd had a fight, several fights, and I needed a few days to myself to think things through. If they had any idea what really happened, they'd call the police and a psychiatrist, and throw me in the loony bin. They'd be so horrified.

But they don't know, and they believe what I tell them. Although Dad can't hide his triumphant expression, he doesn't say a word against Johnny; they both know that would be counterproductive. Mum fills me in on the local gossip. They moved into this seniors' community when Dad retired and immediately started raving about the organised trips to theatres in town and the art classes. They play competitive bridge, golf and tennis here, and they've made a lot of new friends. A bit too much like a cushy school camp for my taste, but they really seem to love it.

Picking Sasha up from school made my day feel a bit more normal. He was thrilled to be headed to Nanna and Grandpa's for the night; he knew he'd get spoiled. When he twigged that

I was staying too, he asked about his dad. Not wanting him to think too far ahead, I'd hidden the suitcases in the garage. I told him Johnny had to go away for work for a few days, and wasn't it nice we could spend some time with his Nanna and Grandpa?

I could ask Mum and Dad for a loan, move up to the North Coast and set up house. Get a part-time job. Johnny would miss us so much he'd walk away from this whole mess and join us. Then I think about the money in the safe under the floorboards in our wardrobe. Last time I counted, there was more than two hundred thousand dollars in there. I don't need a loan; I could simply take half and hit the road, tell Sasha we were heading off on a holiday. Without his father. Hmmmm.

How did Johnny feel when he read my note and discovered we were gone? I don't feel victorious; I feel rotten, as if I've betrayed him. But I will protect my son at all costs.

I also feel safe in a way I haven't since Ivan was shot. My Dad is just down the hall. If I can close my eyes and go to sleep, perhaps it will all be better in the morning.

Music. Loud. Heavy metal. Pounding guitars and someone screaming. I'm being held down. I'm pushing and struggling. Hot breath in my ear and a hand over my mouth. I can't breathe. I push as hard as I can, but I can't get away. I'm going under. Someone help me!

The scream wakes me with a jolt. I'm drenched in sweat, my limbs tangled in the sheets. Moments later the bedroom door bursts open and Mum hurries towards me in her nightie.

'Are you all right, darling? What made you scream?'

91

I need to calm down fast. I can't have Mum derailing their trip because she's worried about me.

'I'm fine.' I force myself to breathe slowly again. 'Just a nightmare.'

'That was some nightmare.'

'Mum, I'm fine. Seriously, go back to bed.'

She's sitting on the bed now, stroking my hair away from my face. Her cool, dry hand is instantly soothing. I feel like a child again and it's so comforting I start to cry.

Why did it have to happen?

The desire to tell my mother is overwhelming. I can't stop crying. She hugs me until I wind down like a broken toy. Eventually I convince her I'm okay and she goes back to bed.

I'm not closing my eyes again. Staying awake until morning seems like a really good idea.

JOHNNY

I park the Jeep in the garage and walk out onto my front lawn. The moon is a tiny sliver. My shoulders sag and my knees buckle under me as I kneel in the grass and let the tears flow. No one is here to see me.

My brother is gone. My wife and child are gone. I have a right to feel this fucked.

Slowly, I stand back up and wipe my face with my hands.

No, I don't have the right to dissolve in the middle of my front garden, and it doesn't matter that no one can see it. I can see it. Ivan can see it.

If he was here right now, he'd grab my shoulders, shake me and tell me to toughen the fuck up. Then he'd put me in a headlock. I smile to myself and the tears start up again.

The last time I saw him was at his place after a big party for the crew. We all got blind drunk celebrating a successful ram-raid on a high-end jewellery store in Mosman. I'd dropped around the next day and found him sitting alone in his living room. The curtains were drawn and his house was a shambles, so I offered to help clean up. He told me to leave it; he seemed distant and wouldn't look me in the eye. One hell of a hangover, I guess, but I wish our final moment together had been different.

Ivan was selfish and manipulative. He could also be a complete arsehole. Like our Dad, he didn't have an off switch. Sometimes I had to drag him away during a fight when I thought he was going to kill someone. He would do anything to get his way. But he'd always had my back.

I wish I'd asked him if there was anything wrong that last time I saw him. I could have helped somehow. Perhaps it was my turn to look out for him. Now I'll never know. Fuck, I miss the bastard.

AMY

While Sasha is at school and Mum and Dad are at an all-day golf tournament, I decide to make myself useful. I pull out Mum's ironing basket, set up the ironing board in the living room and turn on the TV for company.

As I put down the remote, the male newsreader announces: 'Another shooting occurred in Western Sydney last night. The third in the last month, each shooting linked to gang-related activity in our west. Well-known Italian gangland figure Tony Fazzini was shot twice as he was putting out the bins at the end of his driveway.'

I turn around and sink into a chair. We went to Tony Fazzini's wedding. He's the eldest son of Antonio Fazzini, head of one of the big Italian gangs. He's got two little kids.

The footage was taken outside Tony's house last night, less than thirty minutes' drive from where I sit. Crime tape, concerned neighbours, whirling police lights.

'This latest shooting has been linked by police to the deaths of two other known gang members murdered in similar circumstances over the last month,' the news anchor continues. 'Michael Vucavec was shot on the fourteenth of November and Ivan Novak was killed on the twenty-first of November. Is there a vigilante behind this attempt to clean up our streets?'

Mum and Dad will hear about this and freak out. The Croatian and Serbian gangs don't get much media attention, thank God. They don't have the notoriety of the Italians, Lebanese and Somalians. So there was hardly any media attention when Ivan was shot, even though there'd been an identical shooting the week before. I certainly hadn't heard any mention of Ivan being a 'known gang member' until now.

The footage cuts to Detective Inspector MacPherson conducting a press conference on the steps of Liverpool Police Station. We don't get to hear from the policeman because the news anchor keeps talking over the top of him.

'Detective Inspector MacPherson heads up the Western Sydney Organised Crime Task Force. He assured us that these kinds of crimes do not usually endanger members of the general public and that his team is following up several promising leads.

'We are looking at another big bushfire season...'

I switch off the TV.

'When's Dad getting home? Is he coming to watch me play cricket tomorrow?' Sasha asks at dinner.

In Mum and Dad's all-white kitchen, I stare pointedly across at the latest retro-style appliances in matching shades of lemon, on display on the stone benchtops, hoping Mum and Dad will come to my rescue.

'I'll come and watch you, Sash,' says Dad with a complicit glance in my direction. 'Your father has to work.' He leans over the round kitchen table and ruffles Sasha's hair. It's obvious they're related. My dad is tall, still handsome for his age, his blond hair almost white now.

'No offence, Grandpa, but I want Dad to come.'

I find it hard not to smile. I can always rely on my son to tell it the way he sees it. But Dad is a retired lawyer and he's hard to offend.

'Sorry, mate, I'm as good as you're going to get.'

'I'll come too, so that's actually twice as good as only Grandpa,' says Mum, who hates cricket but would watch her grandson staring at the sky for hours. Not that Sasha's likely to stay still for long on a sportsfield.

'I guess that'll be okay.' Sasha considers his options. 'Are you coming too, Mum?'

'As if I'd miss seeing you hit a six! Can you take your plate over to the sink if you've finished, please?'

'What movie do you want to watch, champ?' Dad follows Sasha to the sink. They head out of the kitchen discussing the merits of the DC franchise versus Marvel.

'Thanks for cooking, darling. What a treat.' Mum pops the last spoonful of salmon and spring onion risotto in her mouth. 'You've certainly become a good cook over the last few years.'

'I have plenty of time to perfect my skills.'

She looks at me intently, as if weighing up whether to continue.

'You know, I can help with Sasha, if you want to return to work.'

'Thanks, Mum. Maybe. Let's see what happens. Did you ever want to go back to work after having me?'

'God no. I've always had my charity work and my golf.

And I wanted to be home for you when you walked through the door after school. You had a good childhood, didn't you?' She looks puzzled, as if perhaps my current troubles are somehow her fault.

I stand up and start clearing the plates. 'I had a perfect childhood, Mum. Jumping in the pool after school. Doing my homework with the smell of a delicious dinner wafting down the hall. Just perfect.'

'You've created a very nurturing environment for Sasha. But kids are more resilient than we imagine. He'll deal with change if that's the way you decide to go.'

As I pick up her side plate, she puts her hand on my wrist to stop me, her eyes asking the questions she's been careful not to utter. Perhaps it's something in my expression that makes her drop her hand and bring the conversation back to safer ground.

'Darling, you know that if you're at all bored or at a loose end, you could always come along with me to some charity events. I'm sure I could get you on a few committees.' She beams at me now, as if this is the best idea she's ever had.

I'd rather eat dirt, but I'm careful to keep my expression neutral.

'Thanks, Mum, I'll think about it. Why don't you join Sash and Dad while I finish cleaning up?'

Mum sighs gratefully and heads into the living room. She's put on a few pounds lately, but she's still a stunner, tall and blonde with emerald-green eyes. I remember Johnny telling me that seeing my mum for the first time sealed the deal.

'You've going to be beautiful your whole life, Ames. Your mum is a total MILF.'

I punched him in the arm for being so disgusting.

The memory brings a tiny smile to my face. I miss him.

As I stack the dishwasher, my mind prods at the edges of another, more recent memory, but shies away at the last moment. A shutter comes down with a bang. Don't think about that, Amy—the voice is loud and commanding inside my head. It must be some kind of survival mechanism. I wonder if I should see a counsellor, but how can I tell the truth about what happened?

JOHNNY

I know the reprieve is over when the rakia bottle hits the table. In our house, rakia means 'Now, we talk'. It's only Friday night; I thought I had until Sunday to come up with a plan. Maybe not. Mum has cleared the plates and left us at the dining table. The air-con is on full bore and the fan is making a low *whop, whop* sound as it rotates above our heads. I'm still sweating.

Dad pours three shots and hands one to me and one to Marko.

'*Živjeli!*' we say in unison and knock back the rakia. Dad pours again, then sits back, scowling at me.

'Marko tells me your wife leave you, go back to parents. Explain.'

'How do you know?' I stare at Marko with murder in my eyes, so blindsided I don't even try to deny Dad's accusation. Marko just purses his lips and nods, like he's done me a favour.

'Not my question.' The growl in Dad's voice refocuses my attention. He does not look happy. 'Why I find out from him, not you?'

'I thought she'd only be gone one night, but it's been two. She won't even speak to me on the phone.' I can hear the hurt in my voice and I'm not proud of how I sound.

'She won't even speak to me on the phone.' Dad imitates a child's voice. 'Stop whining!' he barks. 'Tell me why your wife take my only grandson.'

'Because some dickhead shot up our living room!' I shout. I sound like a teenager on the defensive. 'I told you she was scared. But I want to know how Marko knows?' I'm on my feet now. 'You're always sniffing around her, like a rabid fucking dog.'

Marko's expression shifts from smugness to distaste.

Then it all boils out of me, the rage has a focus at last. 'Maybe *you* killed Ivan.' I'm leaning across the table, spitting the words at him. '*You* wanted Ivan out of the way, because you want to be boss someday. Sooner the better. First Ivan, then I guess I'm next. Why? Because you want Amy?'

Marko lunges up to face me, but he's got his hands up.

'You need to calm down, Johnny.'

Out of the corner of my eye, I register that my father is smiling. What the fuck has he got to smile about?

'Ivan was my best friend.' Marko is speaking to me as though I'm a moron, articulating every word slowly in that annoying way he has. 'You already know Stanislav ordered the hit on Ivan. His son is killed, we got the blame. Payback, even though we had nothing to do with Michael Vucavec's death. You know this! You have no right to accuse me of killing my closest friend. Or of having anything to do with your wife.'

Marko sits back down in his chair, as if the effort to explain has exhausted him. He brings his gaze back up to meet mine and all I see is pain.

101

'You should learn respect, Johnny. You should take care of your wife and child.' He shakes his head. 'Nothing bad ever happened to you before. I understand. Ivan always looked after the bad stuff for you. But now you have to grow up.'

My hackles rise again, even though I have a horrible feeling he might be right.

Then Dad's huge spade of a hand slams on the table and the glassware jumps and clinks. He's not smiling anymore.

'Sit down. You still not answer my question, Johnny. You too busy accusing your cousin of killing your brother. You stupid fuck. Why Amy leave? She catch you with another woman?'

I slump back into my chair, exhausted. I'm so tired of my father's anger; I need him to back off.

'For fuck's sake, Dad, I already told you! Getting the front window shot out really spooked her. It would spook anyone! She doesn't feel safe in our house. Her parents live in a retirement village. There's a fucking security guard and a boom gate to get past.'

Dad flicks his hand at me like I'm a fly trying to land in the butter.

'Twelve years she is happy to spend our money. Buy any dress she want. Now she think is good time to leave? What the fuck she doing? Amy liability. Putting my only grandchild in danger if she not under your roof.'

'I just need some time to convince her to come home.'

'*You just need some time.*' Again, he's using a child's voice. 'You act like girl. She respect you when you act like man. She want more money to spend. Here, five hundred dollars, give to Amy. She come back.' Dad shifts in his seat, takes out his wallet and counts out ten fifties. He pushes them across the table at me.

I shove them back at him. Twelve years and he doesn't know her at all. Amy is a good, middle-class girl. I've protected her from the sordid side of the family business. Now she's frightened. She's also the last person likely to be bought off with money. Marko frowns, as if he can't believe what Dad just did either, but it doesn't help.

'This is not about money, Dad. She knew about the promise I made to you. Then our living room got shot up. She's not stupid, and she knows enough about our business to be scared. She's never been exposed to violence of any kind, but she understands that once we act, there will be consequences. We should all be worried. What about Tony Fazzini getting shot putting out the bins on Wednesday night? Same as Ivan and Michael?'

Dad slugs back his rakia and pours himself another. He swings his boots onto the dining table, a sure sign he's on his way, more dangerous by the shot. As for my attempt to bring up Tony Fazzini's murder as a diversion—he just makes more dismissive flicking motions with his fingers.

'You bring Sasha home, leave Amy behind boom gate. Amy, we don't need.' He sips at his drink now, warming to his idea. 'Yes, bring him here, make Branka happy again. Sasha have your old room. We find you good Croatian girl, she give me many grandchildren.'

Now I get it. My son growing up in this house, being trained to intimidate, lie, cheat and steal. Learning to live according to the family motto, as though criminal life is the only life worth having. Fucking hell. I need to tread very carefully here.

'I won't let that happen, Dad. I need time to sort it out. Amy will be back.'

'You look weak, you are weak. I talk to her myself. Or better idea than talking to Amy—me and Marko, we take him from school.'

Marko has his gaze fixed on a spot on the table in front of him, his face like stone. Does he agree with this fucked-up scheme?

I've already run out of time. I need to come up with a plan fast, if only to distract my father. Give him something else to focus on, so he stops thinking that kidnapping Sasha is a good strategy. Then I'll sort out Marko. He must be watching Amy. How else does he know where she is? Has my father told him to watch my wife?

And who the fuck benefits from shooting a local gang member every garbage night?

AMY

Leaning against the bonnet of my car, I watch Sasha walk across the oval towards the rest of the under-elevens cricket team. He moves like Johnny—a bit of a swagger and lot of natural grace. He doesn't look back and wave like he usually does, because he's angry with me. He's never spent this much time away from his father. Even though Mum, Dad and I have told him it's Johnny who's away right now—working, liar-liar-pants-on-fire—he's figured out that I'm somehow to blame.

Johnny has tried calling me over and over. I'm not ready to talk. But when my phone vibrates in my hand and I see Lexy's pretty face, I take the call. I move away from Mum and Dad, who are kicking back in their deckchairs. They love this kind of outing with me and Sasha. I wonder if they wish I'd had more children too.

'Hi, Amy, I'm sorry. I've been meaning to check in with you since Thursday. Anto told me you're having some time out, right? Staying at your Mum and Dad's?'

'Lexy, hi. So good to hear your voice. Yeah, I was pretty

freaked out by the whole drive-by shooting thing.'

'What drive-by shooting?' Lexy's words come out slowly, as if she's misheard. Of course, Anto hasn't told her about it. Don't frighten the children or horses.

I look towards the middle of the field, where Sasha's team is batting first. He's always near the top of the batting order, so I need to keep this call short.

'Someone shot out our living-room window.' I keep my voice down. 'On Wednesday. I figured I had to get Sasha out of there, you know?' Why do I sound as if I'm trying to justify my behaviour, as if I've been weak or something?

'What the fuck? I can't believe Anto didn't tell me.' I hear her yelling. 'Anto! Why the fuck didn't you tell me that Amy and Johnny had their front window shot out?'

A muffled reply, then Lexy's voice again. 'I'll have his balls in a vice. I wonder what else he's not telling me. That's so terrible. Are you all right? Was Sasha there?'

'No, he was at school and I'm fine, thanks. I just needed to get away from Johnny and the Novak family.'

'Where are you now?' she asks.

'With Mum and Dad, watching Sash play cricket.' Sasha's mate Hawken is opening the batting. His great-grandfather was a famous cricketer—the kid has raw talent in his genes. Sasha takes his place down the other end of the pitch.

'At least you can go home to your parents.' Lexy sounds wistful. 'My mum would have me, but, according to my dad, I'm never allowed to darken their door again.'

'This stupid war. Why the hell is it still going? Didn't the Serbs and the Croats live together peacefully for years before the last civil war?'

'Of course we did. Lots of intermarriage. And there is again now, unless you live right where the worst of the fighting happened, near the border.'

'But you were born here, weren't you?' I'm confused. Hawken whacks the first ball out towards the boundary. The two batters start to run, but the umpire yells 'FOUR!' and they retreat to their creases, grinning. Mum and Dad join in the applause.

'Yeah, but Dad went back to Serbia to fight,' explains Lexy.

'You're kidding?' Lexy has my full attention again. 'Why would any sane person leave a peaceful country to go back to a war-torn country—to fight?'

'You're assuming my father is sane. You'd be wrong. And it changed him, of course. He was worse when he came back.' She sighs down the line. 'Before I married Anto, back when we were still talking, my dad told me stuff he'd done that would make your toes curl, stuff he's not proud of. He's a devout Orthodox Christian, so he prays for forgiveness. Perhaps the only way he can forgive himself is to make the enemy seem worse.'

'And you're the devil incarnate for marrying a Catholic Croat?'

'Yeah, exactly. And I guess when you've fought in a war, you never really leave it behind. I mean, look at Marko. He always strikes me as someone who's carrying scars.'

I wonder if I should mention that I saw Marko's gold Mercedes convertible pass me again this morning, when I was busy getting Sasha out of the sulks and out of the car. It's not the first time I've seen his car around over the last couple of days. I hope it's just a coincidence and not something Milan has set up to keep tabs on me.

There's another roar from the crowd. Hawken has put one up that looks like it's going for six, but there's a little kid running out to the boundary.

'Now Tony Fazzini's been shot too, the Serbs and the Croats can't really blame each other anymore, can they?' Lexy continues.

The little kid catches the ball and his whole team runs over and swarms him. Hawken is out and now Sasha is facing.

'Somehow I don't think Milan is going to see it that way, Lexy. Look, I've got to go, Sasha's up. Talk soon, okay?'

Sasha takes up his batting stance, taps his bat on the ground twice. Even from this distance I can see his face is serious, intent. I'm standing beside Mum and Dad when the bowler delivers a bouncer down the pitch at Sasha. There's a loud *thwack* as Sasha hits it high and starts running. Then he thrusts his bat into the air, leaping and whooping as the umpire yells, 'Six!'

JOHNNY

Squinting against a red sun, I turn west onto the Hume Highway towards our warehouse. Anto and I need to get the place prepared for our guest. The afternoon has been hot and dry, the wind blowing out of the north-west, carrying the unmistakable stink of bushfire smoke. Seventy-odd kilometres away, up near Bilpin, Bells Line of Road is on fire. The sky is orange and purple as the sun slides down behind the Blue Mountains. It's the first time I've smelt smoke this fire season and there's a surreal sense of déjà vu in the air. Every summer, Sydney burns.

I remembered too late that Sasha had a cricket game this morning. I tried calling Amy so I could apologise to Sasha, but she didn't answer. As usual. I wonder how she's explained what's happening.

After what Anto told me, I'm convinced Stanislav is planning a big haul—and I want to take it from him. If we find out something solid, Dad will back off and give me more time. He'll choose money first, retribution later. And I'll have time to find the killer. Somehow, I'll track him down.

Amy won't come back unless she and Sasha are no longer in danger and, deep down, I know that's smart. She's always been the smart one in our team. The only way to ensure my family is safe is to neutralise the killer. The idea of Amy gone-for-good turns my knuckles white around the steering wheel. I'll die trying rather than let her go. I gun the engine, feeling the surge as I shift lanes to get around a bus, cutting off some poor bozo in a Honda CRV.

I'm going to find the bastard who's been fucking with my family and deliver his miserable carcass to my dad.

Nick Stanic's house is a small, red-brick box near Liverpool cemetery. We wait until dark before pulling up outside in Anto's Holden GTSR, useful tonight because it has a boot.

I always thought Nick was a bit of a loser, but he's high up in the Serb crew, a trusted lieutenant. Stanislav's dead son, Michael, was Nick's best mate. Nick might not be directly related to the Vucavecs, but there's a better than even chance he'll know if there's a big job coming up.

The lights are on and we can hear his TV blaring as we get out of the car. We're banking on him being alone. The plan doesn't account for a girlfriend or any kind of witness. We creep around the front of the house, but the blinds are down. No cars parked directly out front and no sign of his Ford Ranger ute; let's hope it's in the garage at the end of the driveway.

I've got that hypercharged, indestructible feeling I get before a job. There's no backing down once I set this plan in motion, and I know I haven't fully considered all the possible outcomes. But I'll do anything to get Amy back and this feels like the right first step.

'I still think this is a dumb idea,' Anto whispers. 'We don't know who's in there. Nick could have a couple of mates over.'

'Don't be a pussy. Let's go.'

Anto might not be happy with my strategy, but he's invested in the outcome, so he'll do what he's told. I make my way down the driveway at the side of the house. I still can't see through to the living room, but the other rooms look dark and empty. Anto gives me a minute to get into position, then bangs loudly on Nick's front door, yelling, 'Police! Open up!'

It works a treat. Nick comes flying out his back door, straight into the piece of two-by-four I'm wielding. By the time Anto joins me, I've got Nick on the ground and I'm probably looking pretty pleased with myself. Nick is out cold. We bind his wrists behind him with cable ties, strap gaffer tape round his ankles and gag him. Then I slip a fabric shopping bag over his head. We don't want him knowing the way to the warehouse.

Gun in hand, I walk quietly into his house, checking each room. It's obvious he lives alone. There's a stained mattress on the floor of the biggest bedroom. Wet towels hang off the dirty bath and shower combo. Dishes fill the sink and compete for space on the kitchen bench. The living area is druggie chic. A stained, cigarette-burnt sofa faces a large-screen TV and the coffee table holds a bong, a bowl of mull, empty beer cans and overflowing ashtrays. There's even the obligatory couple of lines racked up on a shaving mirror. A regular little party for one. I'm grateful he wasn't smoking ice as well or he wouldn't have been as easy to bring down.

I turn off the TV. He was carrying his phone and car keys

as he tried to escape. Now I pick up his phone charger and then his house keys, so I can lock the place up. Nick might need to look like he's gone away for a few days.

When I get back outside, Nick is face down in the grass, my best mate sitting on his back. Anto weights 120 kilos, so the Serb is barely able to grunt behind his gag. I pull Anto to his feet with one hand, use my foot to roll Nick over, then crouch down and jam the end of my gun in his ear to keep him still.

Anto brings his car up the driveway. It takes both of us to manhandle Nick into the boot. He's six foot two and built like a refrigerator. In other words, he could pass for a cousin of mine or Anto's. He's wearing tracky daks and a stained T-shirt. He clearly wasn't expecting visitors and it's definitely been more than twenty-four hours since he last had a shower.

Anto takes the backstreets, where there's not much traffic. I follow in Nick's Ford Ranger. Ten minutes later we're pulling up around the back of the warehouse. I unlock, pull the garage door up and Anto drives straight in.

A metal rack full of car parts takes up one wall of the large open space. Nearby is a full mechanic's work area with a pit, hoist and spray booth surrounded by plastic sheeting. On the other side of the warehouse, rolling shelves are stacked with TVs and other stolen goods. There's a small kitchen behind a partition and a bathroom in the corner. One third of the warehouse is overhung by a mezzanine level supported by concrete pillars. Up there is my office and a two-metre-high Commander Bankers Safe. It was a bitch getting it up there, but there's always at least a million in cash in that safe, so we made sure to buy one of the best.

Nick is not happy as we pull him out of the boot, use more gaffer tape to tie him to a chair, then lash the chair to one of the concrete pillars. Once I've pulled the shopping bag off his head, we stand back and have a good look at our catch.

AMY

This afternoon at the airport, I had to practically shove my parents through the international departure gate. Mum looked worried as she disappeared around the corner on her way through to security. By now, they'll be passing over Singapore on route to Dubai and their connecting flight to Amsterdam. I'm relieved, but I also feel more vulnerable. I need my girl-friends more than ever now. So I arranged for Sasha and me to head straight from the airport to meet Chaz and Jenny at the Carnes Hill skateboard plaza in Hoxton Park. The kids love it and it's only ten minutes from home. As usual on a sunny Saturday afternoon, it was crowded, but we found a shady seat, kitted up the kids with knee and elbow pads and fastened on their helmets, before setting them loose with their skateboards.

'Stick to the flat section and make sure we can see you!' I yelled after them. They are still at that age when showing off to their mums is more fun than escaping the leash, so I wasn't worried. Well, not worried about the kids anyway.

'Why are you sitting there with an anxious look on your

face and biting your nails?' Chaz asked. Again, I felt bad that I still hadn't told my best friend anything about staying at Mum and Dad's.

'Can you smell smoke?' I said, looking aroud, trying to divert her attention.

'Yeah, I heard on the radio that there's a fire in the Blue Mountains. God, I hope it's not as bad as last year.'

'We had a pretty wet spring, though.'

'Really, is this what you're worried about?' she asked. She knows me a little too well sometimes.

'Sash and I are staying at Mum and Dad's while they're away.' Might as well put it out there and see her reaction.

'Because you need to look after their non-existent cat or their non-existent dog?'

'Because I need some time away from Johnny and the whole Novak world in general.'

'Okay, now we're getting somewhere. Good for you, if that's what you need. How does Johnny feel about it?'

I was glad she asked; I never wanted Chaz to think my marriage to Johnny was a mistake. They get on well enough, but Chaz has always seemed wary of Johnny.

'Well, I doubt Johnny's happy about the situation, but as I'm not speaking to him, I don't really know.'

'Really? Very mature. What did he do?'

'Nothing. He's done nothing wrong,' I said. That's when it hit me, Johnny hadn't actually done anything wrong. But, again, I felt the need to justify my actions, as much to myself as to Chaz. 'I'm just being protective of Sasha. There've been three deaths so far in what looks a lot like a gang war, and I don't want Sasha anywhere near the Novaks right now.'

'I think that's the most sensible thing I've ever heard you say.' Chaz turned to watch as Jenny executed a perfect nose-bleed, putting her weight on the tail of her board to clear the lip of the kerb, then changing the weight back to her front foot. She balanced herself and the nose of her board on the kerb. We both applauded exuberantly. Jenny jumped off, caught the skateboard in midair and took a bow.

Chaz looked back at me, expectant.

'With Ivan gone, Milan wants Johnny more involved in all aspects of the family business. And sooner or later Sasha is going to start noticing that his father works odd hours. It's time for Johnny to make a choice between his father and us.'

'So you're pushing the point by being elusive?'

'Exactly,' I reply unconvincingly. 'Now, let's talk about something else. You look beautiful in this light. Stay right there. I'm going to take a couple of photos. You've been single long enough, it's time for some online dating.'

Tonight, it's just Sasha and me in the beige-on-beige living room at Mum and Dad's, and it's starting to pall. They don't have Foxtel or Netflix and free-to-air television is not cutting it in the entertainment stakes. The kid went to bed complaining about missing his father, again.

So here I am with a glass of rosé and Facebook. It's always fun at first, liking photos of friends tipsy at end-of-year parties, their kids dressed in outlandish costumes at end-of-year concerts. Friends on holidays in Thailand, the wedding of an old schoolmate in Bali, three friends with new babies, new mothers looking exhausted but happy, new fathers looking happy but terrified. I haven't posted anything for a couple of weeks but that's not unusual for me; no one is going to be worried about my lack of communication. But as I scroll and like, scroll and like, I start to feel bloated and dissatisfied, as if I've eaten too much chocolate.

Back in the green bedroom, I try to sleep. But as soon as I drift off, the sound of that second shot slamming through our living-room window jerks me upright in fear. When I finally fall asleep, I dream I'm being held down. I'm struggling, but I can't break free. I'm screaming and no sound comes out. I wake up sobbing, my hands searching the bed for Johnny. I guess I'm missing him more than I've allowed myself to admit.

It's 2.14 a.m. when I tiptoe to the fridge and pour myself another glass of rosé. What's happening to me? Am I becoming an alcoholic on top of everything else? Slouched at the kitchen table, I try to come up with some answers.

Four days since I left. What needs to happen before I make my next move? What the hell is my next move? I feel like I've backed myself into a corner. If I'm not there with Johnny, how can I effect any kind of change in the outcome of this point-less drama? Is my continued absence enough? At least Sasha is safer here, but what is Johnny doing? Is he safe? He hasn't tried contacting me since just after lunch. He must be up to something. Should I ring him? But that will put me on the back foot. I should call it quits and go home.

Instead, I upend the glass of wine into the sink.

There's no point folding now.

JOHNNY

'Fuck off and die, you Croat cunts.' Nick spits some blood and checks with his tongue for loose teeth. He's still lashed to the chair and wears a bloody grin on his brutish face. We've only been at it for fifteen minutes. Anto has been using Nick as a punching bag and I've been asking questions, but nothing is working. It's amazing how much damage can be inflicted in a short space of time when a man can't defend himself. I just want him to cough up the info and be done with it.

'Come on, Nick. What do you know about Stanislav heading off to Belgrade? What's the big plan? What do you know about Ivan's murder?'

We're getting nowhere.

I don't really mind beating people up; I've been doing it since I was a kid. It was one of the few ways to get any kind of recognition from my father. So I'm pretty fucking good at it. But what Nick needs is to have his predicament sink in a little.

'What the fuck are we gonna do with him?' Anto whispers as we back away.

What the hell have I got us into?

'Come back here, untie me and I'll beat the crap out of you both! Then we'll call it quits and pretend this never happened!' Nick calls after us, his tone of voice oddly reasonable, even friendly, as if this is all just a game.

'I knew we should have bugged Stanislav's car.' Anto, on the other hand, sounds thoroughly pissed off.

It's now one in the morning and Nick still isn't talking, except to swear at us and tell us what he's going to do to us later.

I can't believe he hasn't caved. I feel kind of sick when I look at him trussed up on the chair, head lolling, his eyes swollen shut, blood everywhere, broken fingers sticking out at odd angles.

Anto won't look at me, let alone at Nick's battered face. Nursing a sore fist, he's slumped against the wall near the partially open garage door.

Gazing around the warehouse for inspiration, I catch sight of two petrol containers. Then I glance down at my feet, at the blowtorch I found earlier tonight, but haven't been able to bring myself to use. Making sure Nick can't see me, I creep over to the two petrol cans. I heft one then the other, put the heavier one down and head towards the door with the lighter one.

'Come outside, I've got an idea.' I pitch my voice low as I pass Anto.

At the tap round the back, I pour petrol out of the can onto the ground. The smell is pungent in the night air. When there's only about a tenth left in the can, I fill it with water. Anto just stands there, legs apart, arms crossed, scowling at me.

'What's it smell like?' I bring the can over to him and hold it a few inches from his nose.

'Petrol, peabrain.'

'Exactly what Nick is gonna think when you pour it on him. Then I'll light up the blowtorch and he'll think he's toast.'

Anto is frowning at me now, shaking his head as if I've lost my mind. It's possible.

'Keep up, mate!' I shake my head back at him. 'It's not flammable with all that water in it, but Nick will only smell the petrol, won't he?'

Anto's face clears. 'That's the best idea you've had all night.'

'Yeah, so let's give it a go. Nothing to lose, right?'

'Don't do it! Please! What have I ever done to you? What the fuck!' Nick thinks he's covered in petrol and is completely freaked out.

Lit from behind by a lone light bulb, I'm standing three metres away, holding the blowtorch. Nick has managed to prise one eye open and is staring at me like I've morphed into the devil. Anto is holding the now-empty petrol can as he backs away, genuine pity in his eyes.

'Easy, mate, just tell us what's going on. We know there's a big job about to happen. We know the families met in Belgrade. Fill us in and you walk out of here.' I'm anything but relaxed, but I keep my voice kind of friendly.

Nick finally folds. 'How did you find out?' he squawks. 'Supposed to be this big secret.'

'Well, we know about it, so you may as well save your skin.' I wave the blowtorch and Nick flinches. 'Give us the details.'

'A twenty-million-dollar ecstasy delivery, worth five times that on the street,' Nick delivers through gritted teeth. 'Triple A grade, from Amsterdam, via Belgrade. Supposed to be arriving at the airport on Thursday. That's all I know.' His shoulders slump.

'Who's the delivery addressed to?' I can feel the excitement building inside me. I nearly punch the air, but manage to maintain my relaxed pose, blowtorch flaming.

'Fuck should I know? Stanislav, I guess, or one of his rellies.'

'Okay. How are they clearing it through customs? Have they organised a truck? What's the pick-up time?'

'Jesus, Johnny! I dunno and I'm not about to spill to you.'

Another wave of my blowtorch.

'Look, Stan's got family in parcel-handling, and in customs, in the International Freight building. He's organising clearance. I reckon he'll use one of the vans, drive it himself. Now let me go! You fucking pricks!' He starts thrashing around in the chair.

'Easy, mate. While we've got you, care to shed any light on who shot my brother?'

Nick stops squirming. 'Wasn't us. Stan was pretty sure it must have been one of your crew who offed Michael. He thought one of us must have killed Ivan to get revenge, but no one fessed up. You have to admit, Ivan was a player. It could have been some chick's pissed-off husband.'

I consider giving Nick another whack, but he could be right about Ivan, so I let it go.

Anto grabs a water bottle out of the fridge and holds it over Nick's mouth. The pour bastard guzzles it down. Motioning me to follow him, Anto heads to the far corner of the warehouse, out of Nick's earshot.

'Let's untie him. Let him go. Get out of here.'

'We can't. He'll be straight over to Stanislav's. There'll be a crew at yours and mine within an hour. I'd rather not get shot today, thanks.' I can see what I've said makes sense to Anto, but it also makes him angrier.

'What the fuck have you got us into? What are we gonna do with him if we can't let him go?'

I've been thinking about it and I still don't have an answer.

'I know what my father would say.' I look back at Nick.

'No fucking way.' Anto recoils from me. 'We're not going to off him. He doesn't deserve it. I don't mind beating the shit out of him, but I won't kill him.'

I hold up my hand. 'I know, I know. Me too. I'll come up with a plan.' Why is it always me who has to come up with the fucking plan? I rub my eyes and glance over at Nick again. He hasn't taken his eyes off us.

'Can't believe I let you talk me into this,' Anto croaks. 'What the fuck is wrong with you?'

'A share in twenty million bucks says you'll get over it.'

We sit down with our backs against the wall. Anto's harsh words hang in the air between us. We're both dead-tired, but what we just heard from Nick makes the risks we've taken worthwhile. And Dad is not here in charge, which means we don't have to kill Nick.

'Hey, you still got some of that vitamin K you like so much?' Thank Christ, I have an idea.

In the shower, washing off the stink of petrol and sweat, I feel pretty good about myself. I reckon I've got one piece of my plan in place. Not sure about the other pieces yet, but I'm feeling confident for the first time since Ivan died.

I dry off and flop down on the unmade bed. The early-morning breeze through the open window feels good on my damp skin. I've got time to get a kip in before heading over to Mum and Dad's for Sunday lunch.

The ecstasy is arriving in Sydney in four days' time. There has to be a way to grab it from the Serbs after they've done the hard yards getting it here from Europe and through customs.

I wish Ivan was here so I could talk it through with him, bounce ideas around. The pain of missing him is a knife in the guts. I wonder if Nick is right: was Ivan shot by some chick's pissed-off husband? But how do Michael Vucavec and Tony Fazzini fit into that picture? It doesn't make sense. I groan and rock my head from side to side on the pillow, before forcing my exhausted mind back on track.

Right now, Nick is in la-la land after Anto offered him a beer spiked with enough ketamine to put a horse under. He turned out to be quite talkative until he dozed off. Note to self for future kidnappings—just use ketamine. Now he's safely tied to a bed up at Baz's fishing shack on the Hawkesbury, with Brick and Blocker on guard duty. We can't keep him dosed-up for the next four days, can we? What the fuck will it do to his brain?

But if we let him go, we're saying goodbye to the drug snatch of a lifetime.

If I'm being truthful with myself, I know the most efficient way to fix things for good is to kill Nick. I can almost hear my brother telling me to just get it done. But I don't want it on my conscience. I've made it this far in my life without killing anyone and I want to keep it that way.

I let possibilities swirl around my mind. I'm due at my parents' place in six hours. My brother is dead and my wife has left me, but, finally, I have the beginnings of a plan.

AMY

Sunlight is pouring into Mum and Dad's kitchen and a butcher bird on the doormat is giving us a concert as I dish up fried eggs and bacon. Mum must have been feeding it. I put a piece of bacon aside for later.

'Mum. Why are we still here when Grandpa and Nanna have gone away? When are we going home?'

I knew this question was coming and I still don't have an answer my son is going to believe. As I cast about for inspiration, the phone rings and Lexy's smiling face fills the screen. I snatch it like a lifeline and move away from the breakfast table, but Sasha's eyes follow me.

'Hi, Lexy. How are you?'

'They're definitely up to something.'

'Okay, tell me.'

Sasha now seems focused on his breakfast. I don't care if mine gets cold, I'm not hungry. As I open the glass sliding door, the butcher bird flies off. I step out into the pocket-sized back garden.

'So, Amy, the other night I was on Facebook and saw all these photos of the families back in Belgrade. I showed them to Anto because I wanted him to see my cousin's new baby, but he went really quiet afterwards. At first I thought it was about the baby—you know how much he wants one too—but then, last night, he was out all night with Johnny—at least he told me he was with Johnny. If he lied to me, I'll kill him.'

Now I'm spooked. Even when he's out on a job, Johnny is rarely out all night. So what were they up to? He wouldn't play around on me; I'd stake my life on that. Out partying? Johnny used to enjoy the occasional line, but he gave up drugs when Sasha was born, so that doesn't ring true either.

'Amy? Are you still there?'

'Yeah, just thinking. Did Anto look like he'd been on a bender?'

'Nah, just really tired, like he'd pulled an all-nighter. He did stink of petrol, though.'

'Petrol?' I can't fathom why, unless they needed to torch a car, but they like to rebirth cars rather than torch them, so that doesn't make sense either. Unless the car was involved in a murder or moving a body around. Fear starts to constrict my breathing—I'm letting my imagination get the better of me. I force myself to breathe evenly.

'So did Anto tell you anything else?' I ask.

'Nada. Are you all right? Still at your folks' place?'

'Yeah, still here. Sasha and I are both fine, missing Johnny… You know, because he's away working.'

'Okay, so Sasha is listening. Got it. I'll give you a call if I find out anything else. I will, of course, ask Anto outright what he's been up to, and he will, of course, deny that anything is going on. But I reckon those boys of ours are cooking up something to do with the Serbs. I just don't know what.'

The phone call has only made me miss Johnny more. I know the other women are kept in the dark, but I always thought there were no real secrets between us. I admit it made me feel superior and I'm not proud of it. Now, I'm completely out of the loop.

'Mum?'

I walk back inside and cross the kitchen to Sasha.

'Yes, sweetheart?'

'You look really worried? I heard you crying again last night. And the night before you were screaming. Nanna told me you had a nightmare. Is Dad okay? Has something bad happened to him?'

A fist clenches around my heart as I realise Sasha is seeing and hearing way more than I'm giving him credit for. And he's worried about his dad. I bend over him and fold him into my chest, his head against my shoulder.

'Your dad is fine. He's just working hard, like I said.' I sound lame even to myself.

'Are you mad with him?' Sasha lifts his head, his blue eyes glassy with unshed tears.

Sitting down next to him at the kitchen table, I hold both his hands in mine. I have to tell him something that makes proper sense.

'Sometimes adults need space to sort stuff out. I was mad with your dad, you're right. So I needed a little time away from him.'

'What did he do?'

'He hasn't done anything wrong. He is having to work

126

hard because of what happened to Ivan. He's working two jobs now, his job and Ivan's job.'

I figure this is close enough to the truth and, as far as I know, Johnny hasn't done anything wrong. Yet.

'Okay, so when are you going to stop being mad with him, so we can go home?'

'When he comes back, your dad and I will sit down and talk it through. Then we'll all go away together. That would be nice, wouldn't it?'

'I don't care what we do, Mum, I just want you and Dad to love each other again.'

JOHNNY

This time when I see Marko's car parked in the only shady spot on the street, I don't hesitate. I pull smoothly in behind it, bring my big black bumper up to kiss the gold bumper in front, and nudge the car forward half a metre. The alarm goes off.

By the time Marko rushes out the front door, I'm locking my car. Without a word, he keys off the alarm and starts circling the convertible, looking for damage.

I can't stop smiling as I leave my cousin inspecting his car. 'It's such a sensitive little thing,' I say over my shoulder. When I get to the front door, I lock it behind me. Make the bastard knock to get back in.

Mum must have been watching from the kitchen window. She grabs my face and pulls me down, as though she's going to kiss me, but she gives me a light slap instead. It's only as she steps away that I see she's been crying again, and now I've made her angry. I feel like a dick.

'*Oh moj Boze*. Where are your manners? I bring you up like this? Ivan would be ashamed. Is very hard for Marko to come here.' She hisses at me. 'He say to me, he can't come, he say he's busy. I say to him, you must come, Marko. Ivan would want you to come. But he is sad like the rest of us. Sometimes, he can't look at me, he is so sad.'

Her voice is a whisper now. 'You need to be smarter, Johnny. Can't you see? Your father using Marko to make you angry. Make you more like him, less like you. Don't let Milan do this.' She seems to shudder before flapping me away with her tea towel. 'Unlock door for Marko. Get him beer. Your father waiting.'

Muttering in Croatian and still wiping away tears, she retreats to the stove as I grab a beer for myself and, what the hell, one for Marko. I hand the beer to my cousin at the front door, then head down the hall to the back patio, tailed by Marko, also muttering in Croatian. Sometimes it pays not to understand much of the old language.

What Mum just said makes sense—Dad has been using Marko to get me to step up, to step into Ivan's shoes. But what if I want to wear my own damn shoes?

My father is sitting in his usual seat, waiting.

'Johnny, you have smile on your face. I am thinking you have plan to kill our enemy. Tell your *tata*.'

'The plan is not to kill Stanislav straightaway, but to make him give us twenty million bucks first.'

Marko sits down and sneers. 'Stanislav does not have twenty million dollars to give to us. And why the hell would he hand it over, even if he had it?'

I ignore Marko and stay focused on my father, who is leaning forward, elbows on the table, but otherwise impassive.

After I fill them in on the Belgrade business, and on our

efforts with Nick, I pull a piece of paper out of my pocket and outline my plan for the heist.

Now Marko is also leaning forward, absorbed by my diagrams. Dad doesn't change his expression until I'm finished.

'What you do with Nick?'

'We took him up to Baz's fishing shack on the Hawkesbury.'

'Nick is having nice holiday?'

My confidence starts to dip.

'No, he's tied up and I've got Brick and Blocker on guard duty.'

'You must fix. You know this, don't you, son?'

'We're not going to kill him.'

'Why?' Marko asks. 'We row him out to the middle of the Hawkesbury River. A few rocks to weigh him down. It is easy.'

'Marko is right, is easy. No loose ends, always best plan.'

'I've got an alternative plan. After our little meeting with Stanislav on Thursday night, I'll show Nick a photo. Fifty thousand bucks in a safety deposit box registered in his name, sitting beside Thursday's paper. He gets the key a week after we let him go. The photo goes to Stanislav if there's a leak. Nick will know he's fucked if he spills. He isn't even related to the Vucavecs. He'll bail.'

I'm happy with my plan, but I can still see doubt in their faces.

'Is expensive,' says my dad.

'It'll come out of my share.' I'm digging my heels in and they can both sense it.

Dad flicks his right hand. 'Okay. We leave Nick for now.'

He sits back and contemplates me.

130

'You do all this. You and Anto. On your own. You not come to me for approval?'

My confidence dips even further. 'No, Dad, I did it on my own. Don't blame Anto, he was just following my orders.'

'Anto follow orders. So he get credit or not get credit for helping you?'

Confused now, I just sigh and keep my mouth shut.

Dad bursts out laughing, banging his fist on the table. With his other hand he grabs the rakia bottle and pours three shots.

'*Živjeli!* To my son, Johnny. What you think, Marko? Is my son smart? Smart like Ivan?' Dad pauses and coughs into a curled fist. When he looks back at me, his eyes are sad. 'Not smart like Ivan, but is still smart.'

'Boss, it is hard not to like this plan. No one is as smart as Ivan, but it seems Johnny is not completely stupid. *Živjeli*, Johnny.'

Marko is staring at me as if I've grown another head. Something has shifted. I've always been the younger brother, the pest, tagging along, slowing Ivan and Marko down. Even when I grew bigger than both of them, I was still the kid. It's time for that to change.

'*Živjeli*.' I raise my glass, first to Dad and then to Marko. I can't believe how good I feel. I decide to keep my mouth shut a bit longer, sit back and enjoy the glow. I don't want to jinx it.

'After this is done, you kill Stanislav for family. Okay, Johnny?'

The glow dims a bit.

131

AMY

Blissful views of the ocean compete with lifestyle shots of happy families playing on the beach and dining in seaside cafes. Scrolling through properties for rent on the North Coast is very therapeutic. This is the life I want. I don't want the hot and grimy suburbs of Western Sydney anymore, thank you very much.

Was the frisson of danger I felt when I first met Johnny an omen? His work has never really intruded on our home life before. I've always assumed Sasha was enough of a reason for Johnny to stay away from the most dangerous parts of the family business. How could I have been so blind?

This whole situation has given me a kick up the rear end. I was in cruise mode and now I want to put my foot down and be somewhere else. Anywhere but here. I can't wait around for Johnny to wise up; I need to get Sasha away from his fucked-up family before this whole drama spirals even further out of control.

I look at my watch, 12.30 p.m. Johnny will be on his way

to Branka and Milan's for lunch. We do it *every single Sunday*. I don't mind really, it's kind of nice. Branka is a great cook and I get to load up on a week's supply of veggies. But this week things will be different.

I hit the remote and, as I suspected, there's no black Jeep in the garage. I coast in and Sasha is out of the door before I can get the Mini in park.

'What's the hurry?'

'I wanna see Dad!'

'He's not here, sweetheart, he's still away. I told you. See? His car isn't here either.'

Sasha looks crestfallen.

'Why don't you look through your books and games and see what you want to take on holiday?'

The place smells like Chinese food. In our bedroom, I take in the unmade bed, then pick up a T-shirt off the floor and breathe in the scent of my man. Before I know it, I'm crumpled on the bed, crying silently. After giving myself a moment to wallow, I head to the wardrobe and open the door. The timber boards concealing the floor safe are easy to move aside. I press the numbers on the keypad, holding my breath, certain Johnny has changed the combination. *Ding*, the door pops open. The pile of money looks slightly bigger than it did last time I looked in here. Each bundle of fifties is five thousand dollars, so I grab my beach bag and put twenty bundles of fifties in the bag. One hundred thousand dollars. It doesn't take up that much room and it's not heavy, but it will do nicely. I do a rough count of what's left: at least another one hundred and fifty thousand dollars, if Johnny needs it.

Beside the stack of money is my gun, a Ruger LC9, a small, compact semi-automatic, lightweight and built for fast, accurate shooting. Johnny gave it to me on our first anniversary. I was really upset.

'Why the hell would I need a gun, Johnny? I'm pregnant!' Like that absolved me from the dirty side of life.

'You don't need a gun, Ames. I just thought, you know, I could take you down to the shooting range, have some target practice. It's more fun than bowling.'

Undeterred, he went on. I remember thinking how absurd it was that he was so proud of his gift.

'It's the perfect choice for self-protection, especially for a woman. Not that you'll ever need it, but it's always nice to have. Once you know what you're doing, I'll take you out bush.'

I'd wanted something romantic for our first wedding anniversary. Like jewellery. Like normal people. But it turned out he was right about the shooting range. Even though I'm the last person to be in favour of guns, I have to confess that it was fun and horrifying, all at the same time.

I was six months pregnant when Johnny first took me to the Condell Park Indoor Firearms Range. We rang the bell at the front door and gained entry to a dim corridor leading to a second door. We must have been scrutinised on a monitor and deemed safe. That door opened into a windowless room half-filled by a green counter. A sassy blonde held court, signing us in as I surveyed the display of guns on the wall behind her. I'd wanted to bring my new gun, but Johnny explained that it was way too small. In Australia, you can't own a handgun that's easy to conceal, which is a good thing. Our tough gun laws have made a difference. But I'm married to a man who procured an illegal firearm for our first wedding anniversary.

The blonde manageress turned serious as she explained the rules. I couldn't take my eyes of her long acrylic nails, ballerina-pink shading to magenta, scattered with spider webs and fairies. Nail art and guns, the perfect combination. Johnny was allowed to watch but was not allowed to teach me; instead, their instructor, Allan, would give me my first lesson.

Spare and taciturn, Allan led Johnny and me onto the empty gun range and showed us to our shooting booth. A 9mm CZ Shadow was tethered to a metal bar. Allan adjusted the bar to bring the gun up to the right height. The gun was pointing forward. I could aim it up or down a little, and ever so slightly to the left or right. What I couldn't do was shoot myself or anyone else with it. But I was still nervous. The CZ was much bigger than my little handgun nestled in the safe at home.

Allan showed me how to grip the gun with both hands, keeping my fingers outside the trigger guard, and then how to load the magazine. He told me to rack the slide to chamber the first bullet. I struggled to pull the slide back.

'Don't be gentle, you're not gonna hurt it.'

I don't think he realised I was trying to be gentle with myself.

He held up a paper target with a red circle in the middle, clipped it to the target-holder and pressed a button on the counter, sending the target down a wire to a spot ten metres away.

As we were preparing for my first shot, three men came in behind us, fanning out to shooting booths on either side. Following Allan's instructions, I lined up the rear sight with the sight down the end of the barrel. I put the red circle in the middle of the sights, took a breath and squeezed the trigger. The noise made me jump about a foot in the air and a tiny scream may well have emerged from my mouth. Allan kept a straight face, but Johnny had a bit of a chuckle.

'Did I get it?'

'Can you see the little hole to the right of the red target?' asked Allan.

'Yep.'

'This time don't close your eyes right before you pull the trigger.'

I squeezed off one round at a time, each bullet going through the red target, until the gun clicked. No more bullets. I was holding my breath. I let it out slowly, my whole body shaking. I could feel my baby moving inside me, no doubt performing a somersault.

'Release the magazine into your left hand. Use your right thumb to hit the release button. That's it. Here's the next magazine. Load it.' He pushed a button somewhere and the target moved another five metres down the range.

I tried to shoot, but nothing happened.

'Rack the slide.'

I pulled on the slide, planted my feet a bit wider and took a deep breath. Suddenly, guns on both sides of me started to crack. Despite my ear and eye protectors, the noise juddered through me. I dropped my hands from the gun and around my baby bump, stepping back to look around. The men on either side had their own handguns, untethered. Either one of them could turn around, right now, I thought, and shoot me in the head. The fear must have shown in my face.

Allan motioned me back to my gun. 'Relax.'

I hate it when someone tells me to relax. It's like when you're up on the examination table, about to have a cervical screening test, and the doctor says, 'Relax.' If it's a guy, I always want to tell him to go fuck himself. But I never do. So I swallowed my fear and shot the fuck out of the target instead. Allan sent the target another five metres back up the range. I shot a magazine at every point until, at twenty-five metres, I started missing again. It was over, the air acrid with gun smoke. The sudden silence was broken by the whirring of the target paper coming back to us. Smiling for the first time, Allan unclipped it and handed it to me like a trophy. My hands were shaking as I reached out to take it. The red centre was laced with bullet holes.

'Not bad,' he said.

Then he looked at Johnny.

'Don't get on the wrong side of this one. If she misses your heart, she's gonna clean you up with a head shot.'

But I haven't picked up my gun in years. Small and deadly, it makes me shiver just holding it. I check to see if it's loaded. Empty. I'll stop by the gun range and pick up some ammunition. I slip it into my handbag, even though I know there's no way I would ever use it to shoot someone. But I'm not hiding my head in the sand any longer; I am married to a Novak and I might need to threaten someone with a gun to protect Sasha.

Walking back down the hall, I poke my head into Sasha's room. He's lying on his bed engrossed in a book—*Lizard's Tale* by Weng Wai Chan. The blurb on the back says it's about a boy living in Singapore, surviving on petty theft. I let him choose his own books; it seems the apple hasn't fallen far from the tree. But I'm glad he's reading, glad it's keeping him occupied. I see he's already filled his book bag with more books and games, just like I'd asked him to. I kiss him on the top of his head and leave him alone.

I can't believe what a mess I find in the kitchen. It would be so easy for me to throw the dirty plates into the dishwasher and tidy up. And I could collect all the empty Chinese take-away containers and pizza boxes in the living room while I'm at it. It wouldn't take more than ten minutes. But I resist. I don't want it to be obvious that I've been here. I don't know why. If I'm being sneaky, I don't care. Besides, how hard is it to keep a house vaguely tidy?

I write a note on the shopping-list pad stuck to the fridge, a pen hanging from it on a string.

IOU $100,000. Amy

I don't really owe him the money; it's my money too, but I didn't earn it. I know it's ill-gotten gains, but whatever. My whole marriage has been funded by ill-gotten gains. No point being hypocritical. This cash will get Sasha and me installed in a nice little beach house on the North Coast, while Johnny sorts himself out.

Back in our bedroom, I place the IOU on top of the cash left in the safe and lock it up again, before replacing the boards and closing the wardrobe door. I go to make the bed, then stop myself. Wanting to breathe in my husband again, I hold his pillow to my face. It smells faintly of petrol. What have he and Anto been up to?

138

JOHNNY

It's late afternoon as I stroll down the hall into my parents' living room for the emergency meeting. Marko is already seated, Baz and Anto are in armchairs next to each other and in identical positions—leaning back, relaxed, legs spread. Josef takes a seat two along from my father. As Dad's younger brother, he sees himself as high up the food chain. He'll need to be managed so he doesn't fuck up. Stump, Fibs, Bigsie and Shrimp help themselves to a drink and sit down. Brick and Blocker are still up at Baz's shack, guarding Nick.

The ceiling fan is sending cigarette smoke in lazy circles. Framed posters of Croatian landmarks line the walls and a portrait of Tito hangs in pride of place on the sideboard, a single red rose in a vase beneath—Mum's shrine to Tito, who was born to a Croatian father and a Slovenian mother in a village sixty kilometres north of Zagreb. According to Mum, he was the first and last decent president of Yugoslavia, the man who brought us all together. He may have been a communist dictator, but he was our communist dictator.

We usually meet on the back patio or down at the warehouse. But this is important. All the seats are taken except the one to the right of Dad. My seat.

Ten men, the inner circle only. Cousins and uncles, everyone part of the Novak family regardless of their surnames. Tattooed, scarred, thick brows, high cheekbones, crooked noses and bulked up with muscle. They're not the prettiest, and my father is the biggest and ugliest of the lot.

'First we drink to Ivan,' he growls, leaning back and glaring at everyone.

It's as if we'd all forgotten for a moment; now it feels like Ivan is here with us. My eyes sting as we raise our glasses. Dad clears his throat.

'This not leave room. Understand?'

Nods all round, eyes more focused.

'Stanislav got big shipment coming Thursday, four days from today. A-grade ecstasy from Netherlands via Belgrade. Don't ask how I know.' He taps his nose and earns a chuckle from his men.

'Shipment worth twenty million wholesale.' This gets a less subdued reaction, a bit of backslapping. The men lean forward now, hungry.

'How did they put a deal this size together?' Josef makes sure he sounds curious rather than disbelieving.

'How they put deal together, you want to know, Josef?' Dad watches his brother squirm a little. 'Back in Belgrade, three families come together, get it done. Now I tell you how we take it from them.'

I lean back and let myself drift, thinking about how I'm going to use the money to get Amy and Sasha back. My share will fund us leaving this life behind altogether. But for now I push the thought away. I have to come up with a plan to throw the blame on someone else, not the Novaks. No one in our crew gets hurt and I walk away with more than a million to add to the kitty.

I can't hide the smile on my face. Ten ugly bastards look prettier by the minute. Sometimes I love my job.

When I walk into the empty house again, all my feelings of accomplishment bail on me. No Amy making dinner, no Sasha in pyjamas running to crash-tackle me. I'm startled to find that my eyes are full of tears as I flop into an armchair.

I decide to try calling. She's got to answer sometime, doesn't she? We haven't spoken since Wednesday.

Dialling her number makes my stomach flutter. It feels like back when we first started going out. I can't believe it when she answers straightaway.

'Yes, Johnny, what do you want?' She couldn't sound less interested, but my relief overpowers my anger.

'We need to talk, Ames. How about I take you to that place you want to try in the city, the French place, what's it called again? I'll make a booking for tomorrow night.'

'Hubert,' she pronounces it with a French accent, *Hewbear*, 'and they don't take reservations for tables under six.'

'What the fuck is it about Sydney restaurants? They think they're so fucking good, so much better than their punters. Oh no, we don't take reservations, we are way too popular. Just line up and we'll see if we can fit you in. Fuck that.'

'Well, we won't go then, will we? That was easy.'

It takes me a moment to realise she's hung up.

Fuck! She'd finally answered after days of silence and I let some snooty restaurant's booking policy derail me. It pisses me off, though, the way these popular places call the shots. Fucking toffy attitude.

Something about her, still, after twelve years together, she has me by the balls. I'm grinning. I can't help myself.

A loud thump against the front door boots adrenaline right through me. I lean over and flick off the table lamp, then stand and tiptoe through the darkness to the edge of the living-room window. Peering out, I can't see anyone at the door or in the garden. The street is empty.

I head to the door, pick up my cricket bat and check the spyhole. Nothing. Finally, I open it fast, bat ready. A large pile of blond fur flops into the hallway, blood pooling on the floorboards.

The next-door neighbour's golden labrador, her throat slit like a horrible smile.

JOHNNY

I crouch on my haunches as my head starts to spin. What kind of fucking creep does this to a dog? Molly. A sweetheart of a dog. I can't fucking believe it. I look around more carefully this time. No one. I drag her inside and close the door.

Once she's wrapped in two beach towels, the bright colours seem all wrong. I'll bury her in our backyard and clean up the blood. Amy doesn't need to know.

Then I think about Flynn, the kid next door. He'll be sticking 'lost dog' posters all over the neighbourhood. I have to tell Doug and Kerry, his parents.

It's after nine. Flynn will be asleep. I carry Molly across our front lawn towards Doug and Kerry's front door. The dog feels warm in my arms, as though she's asleep, but there's the metallic smell of blood and a dark stain blooming on one of the beach towels.

This is my fault. I've brought violence to this quiet street. I feel sick. What do I tell them? I put Molly down behind me, pull open the flyscreen and knock on the door. Almost immediately, the TV is turned down and light footsteps approach.

'Hi, Johnny. Everything all right?' Kerry is a curvy brunette, always perfectly put together. She's clearly surprised to see me.

'I've got some bad news for you. Mind if I come in?'

They welcome me into their living room, which is a similar size to ours. Doug sees my face and turns off the TV. I'm relieved he's here. Slim and blond, Doug is a practical man. I'm hoping he'll make this a bit easier for me.

'Mate, do you need a drink? You look a bit peaky.' Doug rests a hand on my shoulder, his concern obvious. 'And ah, you've got some blood on your shirt. Is everyone okay?'

I wonder what he's thinking as he gestures towards an armchair. I sit down and they prop on the sofa, unsettled, leaning forward.

'There's no easy way to tell you this—Molly has been killed.'

Kerry stands up again, hand over her mouth. Doug pulls her gently back down beside him and puts his arm around her.

'Run over?' asks Kerry.

'No, someone killed her. Deliberately.'

'Who on earth would do something like that?' asks Kerry.

'What did they do to her?' asks Doug.

'I don't know who's responsible, but she was left up against my front door, so this is about me, not you. I think it's related to my brother. By the way, thank you for coming to the funeral last week.' I rub my hand across my eyes.

'This must be a very difficult time for you.' Doug sounds like he's placating a dangerous beast that has somehow found its way into their home. 'So you think what's happened to Molly is related?'

'Yeah, I do.' I'm not going to mention the drive-by shooting unless they do.

'Have you called the police?' Doug asks.

'Not yet.' I'm nodding now. 'But I can, if that's what you want me to do.'

'Of course, we have to call the police!' Kerry's voice is shrill now. Doug pulls her in, comforting but also restraining.

'Shh, we don't want to wake Flynn up, do we, love?'

Fuck no. The poor kid.

'I haven't seen Amy or Sasha for a few days. Where are they? Are they all right?' Kerry sounds suspicious.

'Amy and Sasha are staying at her parents' place. She's having a bit of time with her folks.' I can tell how flimsy this sounds, so I move on. 'Obviously, I'll replace Molly as soon as you give me the go-ahead. Sometimes a new puppy is the best way to get over losing a dog.' When I was a kid, I lost my favourite dog to a wild pig out west, on one of Dad's shooting expeditions. It's fucking horrible putting a bullet in a gored dog's head.

'Yeah, thanks, mate. That would be great, but let's not worry about it now.' Doug looks distressed. He seems to be trying to find the right words. 'I heard there was a problem earlier in the week too. Someone shot out your front window?'

'Yeah. Again, related.'

'You're not exactly the safest guy to live next to, are you?'

'Doug, this isn't good, we need to do something. Obviously, we're in danger too!' Kerry is getting hysterical. She shakes off Doug's arm, stands and moves away from the sofa. Now she's pacing.

This is excruciating. I need to put a lid on it.

'I honestly don't think you're in any danger, Kerry. This is a warning directed at me, and only me. Whoever did this must have seen Molly in our front garden, playing with Sasha and Flynn. Look, I'm going to call Detective Inspector Ian MacPherson. He's the cop investigating Ivan's murder, so he'll know what to do. Okay with you two?' More nods. 'Would you like me to take care of Molly?'

Kerry has her back to me, arms folded across her chest. Now she turns around to face me again.

'Can I see her?'

'I don't think that's a good idea.'

'Yeah, Johnny's right, Kez. Leave it with us. Come on, mate, I'll help you. Let's get this done.'

Doug and I carry Molly around the side of the house into their backyard. In the corner, beneath a mulberry tree, we dig a deep hole. Doug finds a stone under the back deck and places it at the head of the grave. After we survey our handiwork, he offers me a beer and I figure it's a gesture I can't refuse. We stand together on the lawn and knock back a Carlton Draught each as fast as we can. Then I call MacPherson in front of him, so Doug knows it's done.

I silently thank God for one small mercy—the lateness of the hour. I couldn't have coped if Flynn had been awake.

I get the hell out of that garden.

AMY

Why did I have to make a fuss about the restaurant? I forced myself to sound like I didn't care he'd called, but I want to see him! I need to see him. Sasha needs to see him. I could scream, I'm so frustrated. Right now I hate Johnny and his whole damn family.

I pull a bottle of rosé out of the fridge, pour myself a glass and take it into the living room. Hoping there's something half decent on TV, I sit down and flick through the channels. Rubbish, rubbish, rubbish. I turn the TV off and start pacing. I have to come up with a solution. Everyone else is pushing Johnny to do something stupid. Why can't Branka see what's going on and put a stop to it? I guess she's never managed to restrain Milan in the past, so why would now be any different?

Johnny has to run away with me and Sasha. Now. Before anything else happens. I have to convince him. But I can't even handle a phone call! I pace some more and finish the glass of rosé. I resolve to call him back tomorrow, when I'm feeling less nervy. I rinse my wine glass out and put it in the drainer. I will not keep drinking. I will go to sleep and deal with all of this in the morning.

It's after eleven by the time I admit to myself that my meditation techniques are failing, again, and I give up trying to sleep. We have to sort this out. I call him back.

Before he has a chance to say anything, I launch in, 'You're right. We need to talk. Having dinner together is a good idea, as long as you don't get any ideas that it means more than it means. We just need to talk, that's all. Mum and Dad have gone to Europe, so I'll see if Chaz can mind Sasha. Okay?'

'Ames, you're making me a very happy man.'

'I'm not promising anything except dinner. How about Frentini's tomorrow night?' Our favourite local Italian. It's not stuffy, they take bookings and it's open on a Monday night.

'Perfect, I'll make a booking and pick you up at seven.'

'No, I'll meet you there.' I'm suddenly convinced I need my own car. I have to remain independent. This time I'm smiling all over as I hang up.

JOHNNY

I take Amy's call as I'm letting myself back in the house, step-ping over the bloody stain, careful to keep any signs of stress out of my voice.

Yes! I get to see my wife tomorrow night. I'll convince her to come home. Yeah, right, and what if she'd been here tonight? Maybe she's better off where she is.

By the time Detective MacPherson pulls up, I've mopped up some of the blood out on the patio and on the floor inside. I've got the front door open before he can knock.

He takes in the remaining bloodstains. 'Looks like you've pissed someone off, big-time.'

'Yeah, seems that way. Come in. It must be after knock-off time—do you want a beer?'

'Can I have a cup of tea instead?'

He follows me down the hall into the kitchen. Though I'd done a quick clean up in the living room, the mess in the kitchen is a bit of a giveaway. I'm not sure why it matters, but I don't want him to know Amy has left me.

'Wife away?'

I sigh and give in.

'Yeah. Amy and Sasha are staying with her parents. She wasn't happy about the front window.'

'What happened to the front window?'

'It was shot out last Wednesday. Same day someone fired at my Jeep. Tonight it was the neighbours' dog, like I said on the phone. Figure it could all be related. Thought you should know. Milk and sugar?'

On the way back into the living room, I point to the bullet holes in the wall.

'You haven't reported any of this?'

'I'm not really the reporting kind.'

'So why am I here now?'

As I sit down, MacPherson undoes a button on his suit, then lowers himself onto the sofa with a sigh. He sips his tea and waits for me to answer.

'My neighbours insisted I call the police. I mean, fair enough, their dog has just been killed. I thought of you, rather than deal with some rookie. Plus, you know about Ivan.'

'You did the right thing calling me. Anything else?'

'The shots that made those holes in the wall came from a black Mercedes ML63, like the one in the CCTV you showed me. I saw the car clearly, in broad daylight. They wanted to be seen.'

'Okay.' MacPherson sits back, glancing up at the bullet holes again. 'I'll get the Crime Scene Investigators here to dig that lead out.'

I guess now I've brought him in I don't have a choice. Fucking hell, cops crawling around my home. The thought of

Dad finding out makes me queasy, but I force myself to stay focused.

'You reckon they're from the same gun that killed Ivan?' I ask, as my eyes stray to the front window and the dark street. When I bring my gaze back to MacPherson, he's staring at me speculatively.

'Could be from the same gun, we'll find out. Was the dog wearing a collar?'

'Yep. The neighbour and I bagged it before we buried her.' I point to the sideboard where a plastic shopping bag holds the bloody leather collar.

'Good. They'll check the fingerprints.' MacPherson pulls out his black notebook, flips it open and starts writing. We go through dates and times for each incident.

'Why do you think this is happening?' he asks, closing the notebook.

'Fucked if I know. Firing at me and Anto, okay. Fair play. A drive-by while my wife is here? Not on. My kid could have been here too. Slitting the throat of the next-door neighbour's lab? That's fucked up. Who does that?'

'Someone who wants to make you angry and provoke a reaction. Made any extra enemies lately? Been stepping on another gang's turf?'

'My family owns a bunch of fish shops.'

'And my family are from Mars. I'm trying to help here, just answer the question.'

But can he really help, I wonder. I guess I've just got to keep using every source at my disposal.

'Not that I'm admitting anything, but what other gang? The Chinese and the Lebs keep to themselves. The bikie gangs are only interested in warring with each other. Out here, it's us, the Serbs and the Italians. Yeah, we've got history with the Serbs, but we've also got one dead on each side.'

'I hope you're not thinking of retaliating, are you?'

I shake my head and keep my eyes directed straight into Detective MacPherson's baby blues.

'Okay. Well, until we know more, I advise you to be careful. Your wife and son should stay with her parents. Why don't you give me the address? I'll make sure patrol keeps an eye out.'

'Mate, it's gated, security guard, the works. Fucking Fort Knox.'

'I might need to find her, Johnny. If something happens to you.'

I give MacPherson the address.

AMY

I'm one of the first to arrive at the yoga studio—shiny timber floors, whitewashed walls and the faint smell of incense. I've been looking forward to my regular vinyasa class; not enough sleep for days on end is taking its toll and my nervous system is shot. I roll out my yoga mat, sit down cross-legged and close my eyes, trying to get centred. I really need this class, especially after my early-morning trip to the Condell Park Firearms Range to get ammunition for my Ruger.

'Hey, Amy.' Kerry is lining up her mat beside me. The weekend over, the kids back at school, it's our time now. This has been our ritual for two years, since she and Doug moved in next door with their cute little boy, Flynn. Our kids go to different schools and we don't really socialise much, but we enjoy our weekly yoga class together. I open one eye and smile weakly at her. Sitting sideways on her mat, facing me, she's obviously dying to tell me something. I open the other eye and swivel to face her.

'You don't know, do you?' she murmurs.

'What am I supposed to know?' My stomach tightens as I notice her puffy eyes.

'Okay. Interesting. Johnny said you were at your parents' place, and I'm guessing you left after your house was shot at?'

I wish the floor would open up and swallow me. I'm embarrassed. One of the reasons I left was so I wouldn't have to deal with our neighbours and their questions. We've taken great pains to ensure no one in our neighbourhood knows what Johnny really does for a living. I look around the room, checking to see if anyone is listening, but most of the others are chatting on their mats too.

'The police didn't show up, so I was hoping no one noticed.'

'We were out, but Mr Fellows told Doug.'

Of course, Mr Fellows, the old guy who lives opposite. Most mornings he sits on his verandah, surveying the street. He walks his dachshund three times a day, checking up on the neighbours. He loves a chat. I should have guessed he'd be spreading the news.

'What hasn't Johnny told me? Has something else happened?'

Kerry's eyes well up with tears. 'Someone killed Molly and left her outside your front door.'

It takes me a moment to realise she's talking about their dog. I gasp and clap my hand over my mouth as I remember Sasha and Flynn playing catch with her on our front lawn only last week after school. Whoever did this must have thought Molly was our dog. Fucking hell, what if Sasha had been there?

'Did Flynn see? Oh my God, Kerry, I'm so sorry. This is all just insane.' My heart constricts as I think of that poor little kid losing his first dog like that.

'He was in bed, thankfully.'

We both start to cry. Kerry reaches for the tissues she has tucked in her bra and hands me one.

Nearly everyone is seated on their mats and quiet now; we're running out of time.

'We haven't told him yet; we pretended she was at the vet. I didn't want him missing school today, so I'll have to tell him when he comes home. How do you explain death to a six-year-old?'

Having confronted the same question with my ten-year-old less than three weeks ago, I understand what she's facing.

'Okay, everyone, eyes front. Deep, slow breaths. One…'

Panic rises in my chest. I have to get out of here.

'Do you want to bail?' My whisper is too loud.

'No, I need to do the class, and you should too. It'll calm us both down. Let's talk afterwards.'

I grab my friend's hand and squeeze it, trying somehow to reassure us both. Turning away, I blow my nose and pretend to join in the first breathing exercise. But my mind is scrambling for purchase. Who would do this, and why hasn't Johnny told me?

JOHNNY

Marko lives in a blond-brick apartment building in the centre of Liverpool, one block back from the Hume Highway. There's a lot of traffic noise. The place looks sad from the outside and even sadder as I walk up the stairs to his apartment on the first floor. Anto is waiting in the Jeep. We have a full day ahead, getting ready for the job, but suspicion is eating away at me. Marko knew Amy had moved out. Either she told him, or he's been following her around.

When Marko opens the door to my knock, he sighs, as if he knew this was coming. He waves me in. The front door opens straight into the small living room. I've never bothered to visit my cousin before; he's always been Ivan's friend, not mine.

The place is neat, posters of the Croatian countryside on the walls, framed family photos displayed on a bookshelf. I'm drawn to a photo of three boys at the beach. Looks like Brighton Le Sands, in southern Sydney. It's me on one side, Marko on the other, Ivan in the middle, all in board shorts with wet hair. We're nine or ten years old and deeply tanned.

I'm the shortest. We look happy.

Next is a photo of Ivan and Marko in tuxedos, their arms draped over each other's shoulders. Then me, Amy, Ivan and Marko on the day Amy and I got married. Ivan's wearing the same tux. There's a photo of Marko as a kid, with his parents, taken somewhere on the Croatian coast. Further along Marko is in full combat gear, rifle in hand, standing with five other soldiers in front of a burned-out barn. Another frame, this time only Amy and Sasha, in Mum's garden. It's a beautiful photo of my wife. My heart starts to race. I turn to Marko and he takes an involuntary step back.

'What do you want, Johnny?'

'I want to know why the fuck you're following my wife around.'

'What do you mean? I am not following anyone around.'

'Yeah, right. Then how did you know she was staying at her parents' place?'

'I think you need help. You need a psychiatrist.'

This is getting me nowhere. I take a deep breath. I have to admit what I've already suspected: Dad ordered him to follow Amy. For Sasha's sake. And there's no way Marko is going to betray Dad. Okay, I need to let this one go. I turn back to the photo of Ivan, Marko and me.

When I've calmed down a bit, I notice Marko's eyes are on the same photo. He looks like a man drowning. Maybe he needs me as much as I need him.

'Look, I know Dad has been pitting us against each other. It's like he thinks if you're undercutting me the whole time, I'll rise to the occasion and suddenly turn into Ivan. It's not going to happen.'

157

'No, you are not your brother.' Marko's eyes meet mine again and there's something in his expression I don't get.

'We need to work together and trust each other, or someone will end up dead.' My voice sounds too loud.

He takes a step forward, his hands curling into fists. 'Is that a threat?'

I put my hands up and let out a big sigh. 'Fuck no! I didn't mean it like that! I mean we have to be a team, or something will go wrong.'

Marko's eyes cut away from mine, his fists unclench and his shoulders relax. He seems to be weighing something up. He points to an armchair and sits down on the sofa opposite. The tension in the air eases.

'Okay, Johnny. You are the boss on this job. I am on your team. Maybe the next job, I am the boss.'

'Thank you.' I reach out and we shake on it. This will be my last job, but he doesn't need to know that. If I'm going to put Marko to best use, I have to put my suspicions about him to bed. And I do need his help. 'If you happen to see Amy in your travels, keep an eye out for a black Mercedes ML63. I saw it right before the drive-by and it might be connected to Ivan's death.'

'How is this car connected?' Marko snarls, as I get up and make for the door.

That's not something I can tell him right now. When I look back, I see a dog ready to be unleashed.

'I've got to go. Be on the lookout. Let me know if you see it. Okay? I'll fill you in later.'

'Okay, Johnny. I will keep my eyes open.'

I walk down the stairs and jump back in the Jeep.

'Sorted?' asks Anto, folding up his newspaper.

'I think Marko was following Amy. He's not admitting anything, but now I've got him on the lookout for the evil fuckers in that black Mercedes SUV.'

AMY

Chaz was happy to take Sasha home to her place after swimming practice. I think he's bored with me now, and he loved the idea of staying over with Jenny, even though it meant spending the night on a blow-up mattress.

I miss Johnny, but I can't let myself get distracted by my emotions. I just have to remember the sound of that second shot slamming into our living-room wall. Or think about Ivan lying in a pool of blood at the bottom of his driveway. After seeing Kerry at yoga this morning, I can add a dead dog to the list of ways to keep myself on track.

Not sure what to wear to dinner with Johnny, I shrug into a red dress, but it feels too try-hard. When I pull on jeans and a T-shirt, I realise I've gone too far in the opposite direction. Besides, it's warm outside and I want to appear cool, calm and collected. If I don't look flustered, maybe I'll be in control and stay on message. A tailored, white linen dress works. I'll pair it with my tan, strappy heels.

I have a cool shower, wash my hair and blow-dry it straight

for maximum length. The white dress calls for a strapless bra and matching undies, both nude lace, so they disappear. Not too much make-up. The mascara wand shakes slightly, but I don't make a mess. I didn't bring any perfume with me, but Mum always has Joy on her dressing table.

I need to have maximum impact on Johnny; I'm hoping his love for me will force him to make the right choice. Lexy is turning out to be a good spy—she rang me this morning to tell me she's now sure there's a big job coming up. I'm convinced for some reason it will be Johnny's last, and not in a good way. Not in an okay, now we've got a decent whack of capital, let's get the hell out of Dodge and make a new life kind of way. No. In a bang, bang, he's dead kind of way.

A growing sense of horror seems to be possessing me, like something really bad is lurching towards me in the night and I can't see it and I can't hear it and I can't run to get out of its way.

The horror has hit me before; I recognise its scent. I don't want it near me again.

I don't know whether it's my instincts telling me to take Sasha and run now, while I still have the chance, or if I'm being delusional. I'm not sleeping well so that can't be helping.

By staying here at my parents' place, taking Sasha to school, shopping, cooking, washing clothes and going to yoga class, I've been trying to convince myself everything will be all right. But I'm still filled with dread, because deep down I'm convinced the worst is coming, no matter what I do.

I've always gone along with what Johnny wants. It's been easy; we've almost always wanted the same things. This time he needs to listen to me, let me be the one to get us out of this nightmare.

I apply a dab of lip gloss and borrow Mum's silver evening bag. It's just big enough for my keys, my phone, my lippy and my gun. I plan on carrying the gun with me everywhere from now on. In the full-length mirror, I straighten my shoulders and tell myself I can make this happen. I'll use everything in my arsenal, even sex. Then I walk out the door to my car.

JOHNNY

Waiting in Frentini's for Amy to show up is like being shot back in time. I brought her here on our third date. I'm light-headed. This is my chance to get her to see reason. If I don't make my case, she'll only pull further away. Amy's not impulsive, she takes an age to make a decision, but once she makes it, fuck, she's stubborn. She's not a risk-taker either; falling in love with me is the only time she's made a risky decision. I guess every marriage comes with risks, though. You could die of boredom.

I can't tell her what's really going on. I'll give her the upside, make her smile, make her want me, like I want her.

Then I see her walk in. Other men glance at her, then stop to take her in, her white dress, high heels accentuating her long legs, blonde hair swaying. No awareness of how her presence has changed the pressure in the room. It's been like this since the first time I saw her. She was spectacular at twenty-two and the years have only made her more beautiful. I stand up and pull out a chair, proud that she walked across the room to my table.

She smiles, but keeps her body away from mine as she kisses me lightly on the lips, then sits down. I sit too, a stupid grin on my face, and soak up the sight of my wife.

The waiter materialises and, with a flourish, reaches into the ice bucket to pull out the champagne I ordered. He makes a big show of popping the cork and pouring, before launching into the specials. I wish he'd piss off, but I can't stop smiling. At last, he leaves us alone and we raise our glasses. Clearly, we have nothing to toast, so we remain silent.

'You look good, Johnny. I've missed your ugly mug.'

'Ames, I will do whatever I need to do to get my family back.'

'Well, I'll be honest. I want it to work. Sasha doesn't like me very much at the moment.'

I sit back and breathe a sigh of relief. I will be the most agreeable man on the planet.

'So, when did your parents go to Europe? I bet they enjoyed having you both to themselves for a while.' Like this was all a planned holiday with the in-laws.

Her eyes slide away from me. 'You know, they've never liked you. They really want me to leave you, for good, and they don't even know what's going on. I just told them we were fighting a lot.'

'I know I'm not the kind of husband they wanted for you.' I grin when she looks back at me, surprised by my response. 'But on the plus side, we actually don't fight a lot, do we? I get why you left, and I know I'm going to have to change things to get you back.'

Our oysters arrive.

'I'm sorry I didn't come to watch Sasha play cricket on

164

Saturday. You were pretty clear about being left alone, but I still felt bad about it. Tell me every single thing he's done since you've been gone.'

Talking about our son is perfect neutral ground. Plus, it makes Amy happy. In her eyes, no other boy is as smart, funny, or good-looking as Sasha. We keep the conversation light until after the osso bucco is cleared away. Now I need to lay out my plan and see how she reacts.

'I talked to Marko. You know, he's such a lonely bloke. I dropped in on him today and, seriously, his little apartment would make you cry.' Sympathy wells in Amy's blue eyes. God, I love this woman. 'I think he's really missing Ivan. I asked him to keep an eye on you, make sure you're okay. It'll give him something to do. All right with you?'

'I've seen his car around more than usual over the last few days. I had a feeling he was checking on me. I actually wondered if you or Milan had put him up to it, but you've never really been friends with Marko. Does this mean the you two are getting on better?'

I knew it! An angry knot forms in my chest. But now that I've asked Marko to help me keep Amy and Sasha safe, I can't really stay twisted about it.

'Yeah. We all have to get along now.'

'Because you've got a big job coming up?'

I splutter into my wine glass. How does she know about that? She's smiling when I look up, happy she's caught me out. So much for my poker face.

'Yeah, I've got some work lined up. We're looking at a really decent pay day. I can cut myself loose from Dad and the rest of the crew. You'd like that, wouldn't you?'

I reach over and take her hand; she allows this for a moment then pulls back.

'I saw Kerry at yoga this morning and she told me what happened to Molly. And my other sources tell me something big is happening. Lots of meetings and phone calls, more than normal. Is this what us women have to do now, make guesses at what you guys are up to? I used to feel like you and I had no secrets.' She sighs and there's an intensity to her gaze that I don't often see. 'I'll admit it, in the past I didn't want to know. But now someone is trying to intimidate us. We're being warned, and I have to stop being clueless. Imagine if Sasha had witnessed any of this?'

'You don't need to know how I'm going to do it, but I will fix it, and then we won't have to worry anymore. I promise.' I still have no idea who's behind all this, but she has to think I've got it all under control.

'I do have to worry, Johnny. You see, that's the problem. The violence has never followed you home before, so I could afford to shut my eyes. But I can't anymore, I have to protect Sasha. Maybe I'm finally growing up.' She pauses, taking slow, deep breaths before continuing. 'When I met you, your life seemed so glamorous. Lately, I've been wondering if I only married you to piss off my parents.' She holds up her hands to stop whatever I'm going to say.

'I don't really mean that, Johnny. I was in love with you, still am, but this life doesn't work for us anymore. I've been researching real estate, up on the North Coast. We can sell our place here, buy a place near the beach, both get real jobs, and be a normal family. We can walk away from your promise to avenge Ivan's death, from this job coming up, from this whole

166

life and the danger we all face. Right now. Your father will forgive you, in time. I know he will. Branka will make him forgive you.'

I take her hand again across the table, and this time she doesn't pull away.

'I love the idea of moving up north, living by the sea, building a new life. But I have to finish things here first.' I squeeze her hand, hoping I've convinced her, but knowing I haven't.

'Don't get involved in this job, Johnny. Stay out of it. I couldn't stand it if you got killed or went to jail. This is all getting way too real.' She looks up at the ceiling and blinks tears away, then brings her gaze back to me. 'I want to go home now. Can we get the bill?'

I walk Amy to her car and draw her in for a kiss. She melts for a moment as our lips meet, then pulls away. If only she'd trust me. She should be coming home with me tonight, but she sees it all in my eyes and turns away.

I know there's no point pushing it, so I open the car door for her. I watch as she pulls out from the kerb, her tail-lights glowing red when she stops at the traffic light down the street. I failed. She knows me too well. She wasn't convinced. It's like a punch in the gut.

A second later, I feel a rush of air as a car streaks by me and pulls up right behind Amy's Mini. Behind the tinted windows three men are silhouetted against the streetlights. It could be anyone driving a black Mercedes SUV, but instinct kicks in before that thought registers. I sprint across the traffic to my car on the other side of the road, then pull an illegal three-point turn in the narrow street. Horns blare. The lights ahead are turning green and there's a little blue Holden Barina, full of teenage girls, between me and the Mercedes.

The vehicles in front move off, but the kid driving the Barina stalls the car. I can't believe her father bought her a manual, what an arsehole. Finally, there's a break in the oncoming traffic. I floor it to get around the stalled Barina and slam the Jeep across the intersection after the lights turn red. Cars to the right and left skid to a stop, more horns blaring.

I keep my foot down. Should I call her? I can't see either car ahead. I know the route Amy will take. I slide around one corner, then another. Her parents' place is around the next left. When I reach the corner, the Mercedes is speeding off as Amy's tail-lights disappear on the other side of the boom gate. The security guard is out of his box, staring after the tail-lights. Thank God her parents chose this place. Thank God for the dickhead security guard. I keep going, trying in vain to catch the Mercedes. But I caught the number plate—IS 007. There's only one James Bond. Who the fuck is this wanker? I want to rip his throat out.

As I'm about to pull into my driveway, I notice the front door is wide open, so I keep driving and park further up the street. My heart hasn't recovered from the chase and now there's more adrenaline pumping through my system. I feel queasy as I open the glove box, a reflex—I know there's no gun there. Ivan's gun is locked inside my bedside table, mine is in the safe under the wardrobe floor. I'm not the kind of guy who takes a gun on a date with his wife. That obviously needs to change.

Easing the car door shut, I walk back down the street,

keeping to the shadows. Behind a bush near the front door, I freeze and listen. Nothing. I force myself to wait five minutes, crouched outside my own front door in the dark, thighs cramping, feeling like an idiot.

I stand and creep inside, grabbing the cricket bat from the umbrella stand. I check each room on my way to the master bedroom at the back of the house. I need my gun, but I stop short in the doorway. The moonlight streaming in through the windows reveals my bedside table lying smashed to pieces against the wall. Ivan's gun is gone.

I lunge across the room, open the wardrobe door, push my clothes back and pull up the boards. The safe is intact. I punch in the combination and the door pops open. The pile of money is significantly smaller than it was and there's a note on top. I sit back on my heels in relief when I see Amy's neat handwriting. I speed-count the rest of the bundles. A hundred grand gone— my lawyer money, my fuck-you money, built slowly over the last ten years, after I finished paying off the mortgage. Her gun is gone too. That's a surprise, but also smart. I'm actually relieved she has her gun. My gun is lying beside the cash. I check it's fully loaded and slide it down the back of my jeans. I won't be going anywhere without it until this is over.

Amy must have decided she needed some fuck-you money too. Fair enough, it's half hers; that's why she has the combination for the safe. But she could have told me over dinner. I close the safe and put the floorboards back in place. As I stand up, my gaze falls on my jewellery tray, where I keep my cufflinks and watches, on the shelf beside my bottle of Eau Savage. My black Gucci watch is gone. Amy bought me that watch. I slide the wardrobe closed with a bang.

Sasha's room is untouched and so is the living room. I pour myself a large Scotch and head to the kitchen for some ice. That's when I see the note. Someone has used the shopping-list notepad stuck to the fridge door by a magnet. A pen usually swings from a piece of string attached to the notepad. The string is broken, the pen is on the floor, but there is a note on the pad. Two words—WHO'S NEXT? And a drawing, two stick figures. One is wearing a dress, a woman, holding hands with a little boy.

AMY

Horns beeping behind me. I check my rear-view mirror, but the commotion is back at the intersection I just crossed. Why do I always assume it's me who's done something wrong? I'm not the most natural driver in the world, but I'm safe. Never had an accident or been caught for speeding. Well, I've had to pretend I was the one driving when Johnny got a speeding ticket—so he wouldn't lose his licence. But that doesn't count.

I'm angry with myself for not talking Johnny into leaving this whole mess behind. I should have tried harder, instead of giving up at the first hurdle. But, really, who am I kidding? How could I have thought it was even possible? As if Johnny would walk away from his father to protect me and Sasha. Not happening. Johnny has only ever worked within the family business. He's been brainwashed to believe it's the only life he can have.

I'm such a hypocrite. During our marriage, I've never once suggested he try something else. We've enjoyed the good life—a nice home, new cars, holidays at the beach, the occasional fancy restaurant. I've been willing to pretend he works unusual hours, rather than face up to what he's really doing.

But he'd never really hurt anyone, would he? So why does he need a gun? And why am I carrying a gun right now?

The real question is: why have I been so obtuse? Was I secretly in love with the threat of drama? What an idiot. My sense of security was already well and truly shattered before Ivan was killed. His death just took my anxiety to a higher level.

As I pull up at the gate, I wave at Darren, the night security guy. He activates the boom gate for me and calls good night as I drive in and turn right past the recreation centre. Is this where I want to end up? Mum is such a snob; she says she likes 'living among like-minded people, enjoying our retirement, without a care in the world'. What she means is everyone is middle-class and conservative, nice, narrow-minded, ordinary people.

Didn't I marry Johnny to escape this kind of life? Perhaps I shouldn't have packed up and left at the first sign of trouble. And why didn't I tell him I took all that money out of the safe? Am I ashamed?

I pull into Mum and Dad's driveway. There's no one to greet me and Sasha is with Chaz. I don't need to be here. During dinner, I imagined going home with Johnny, making up like we used to after a fight, tearing off each other's clothes, hungry for each other. But that would have been the normal me, not this person I've become. I wouldn't have been able to go through with it and that's why I didn't try harder. I'm weak now.

Sitting behind the steering wheel, I'm still imagining Johnny's arms around me. And my heart is breaking at the thought of how much Sasha misses his father. I need to rethink what I'm doing. I could drive home right now! I put the car in reverse.

Then I remember Kerry's tears this morning. What if Sasha had seen Molly? Angry and confused, I park, get out of the car and lock it. I feel like screaming. I feel like driving as fast as I can back to Johnny. I take a deep breath and exhale, stumbling as I let myself in and walk through to the kitchen. I probably shouldn't have driven. I'm drinking too much. I don't care! I don't know what to do. Maybe another glass of rosé will help.

JOHNNY

I crumple the note in my fist, then realise it might be useful, so fold it and put it in my back pocket. My home even smells different, a trace of cheap men's cologne lingering in the kitchen. A slow-boiling fury is working its way through my veins.

It doesn't take long to find the point of entry—the laundry door is splintered near the latch. After closing it as best I can, I bring a chair in from the dining room to wedge under the door handle. Every other window and door is locked tight. At least I hadn't made it easy for them. All the same, the jimmied door is a violation and I'm suddenly ashamed of every time I've broken into someone's home the same way.

With a cardboard box from the garage, I head back to our bedroom and throw all the broken bits of bedside table in, rescuing a few precious drawings by Sasha, and cards addressed to Daddy. Notes and cards from Amy for anniversaries and birthdays. Some animal has touched my special mementos. My hand settles on the gouge in the wall where the bedside table was smashed. Someone will pay for this.

As I walk down the street to collect my car, I feel as if I'm being watched. But why would whoever did this be watching now? They've done what they came to do—make me feel vulnerable.

Why break in? To find a gun. Steal a watch. Leave a note to fuck with my head. Who is IS 007?

It's only ten p.m. and there's no way I'm going to sleep. I pour myself a big fucker of a scotch and queue the next episode of *Mr Inbetween*. I consider ignoring my phone when it rings up on the sideboard, but I haul myself up anyway. It could be Amy. Fuck. It's MacPherson's name on the screen.

'You must be pretty busy right now,' I growl.

'If you lot keep shooting each other, I'll be out of a job, won't I? But the good news is they've beefed up my team and our forensics is getting top priority. We found something interesting.'

'Really? Okay, shoot.'

'Love to, when I catch you in the middle of doing something illegal.' He has a little chortle to himself. 'But for now, I'm just going to tell you we've matched the bullets we dug out of your wall to the rifle used to kill Michael Vucavec and Tony Fazzini.'

What the fuck? Then it dawns on me—there's a name missing.

'But not the same gun used to kill Ivan?'

'I probably shouldn't be telling you this, but a different gun was used to kill your brother.'

I take advantage of my position at the sideboard to top up my Scotch and slug down half of it as I think this through.

'Okay, that's weird. Right? Wasn't Ivan shot while he was putting the bins out? And no one saw anything. Had to be a rifle. Right?'

'Yes. It's exactly the same MO, even the same calibre weapon, but not the same gun.'

'So they could still be linked, but the shooter's got two guns?'

'Yes. We are treating these cases as linked, but there's also the theory that someone took advantage of Vucavec's killing to shoot Ivan.'

'Is that what you think?' I can't help asking. I'm also wondering why he's sharing this with me.

'No. I think it's the same perp with two guns. You heard of Occam's razor?'

'Nup.' I have no idea what he's talking about.

'Basically, it means go with the answer with the fewest assumptions. The simplest answer.'

I'm thinking fast. 'So who do you think is behind these shootings? Some psycho, or a crew?'

'Doesn't feel like a psycho, but I've been wrong before. These shootings feel like hits. So yeah, I've got my suspicions.'

'Care to share them?'

'Not likely. But I can tell you I've got three theories running. Maybe, Johnny, it's you who shot Michael Vucavec first, to throw us off.' I start to sputter my objections into the phone, but MacPherson cuts me off. 'Your intent was always to murder your brother, move further up the ladder in your father's organisation. Fratricide is an ugly crime. It's also pretty convenient the bullets ended up in your wall. You could have even killed the dog to help deflect the blame.'

176

'Seriously? That's your theory? Why the fuck would I call attention to myself with a dead dog and bullets in my wall from the same gun used to kill two men?'

'Yeah, it's not my favourite theory for that very reason.'

'So what's your favourite theory.' Give me a name.

'I think I've already shared enough tonight, Johnny. How about you? This is quid pro quo, remember. What have you heard?'

Only that the car he showed me on CCTV followed my wife home tonight and my house got broken into and a scary note was left on my fridge. Oh, and there's a twenty-million-dollar E shipment coming in via Qantas Freight on Thursday night.

'Johnny?'

'Just thinking. Nah, I've got nothing yet. Sorry.'

I thank the detective and hang up. Much as I love watching Ray Shoesmith juggle life as a father and hitman, he's not going to cut it right now. I need to talk this through with Anto.

Fifteen minutes later Anto is at my front door staring down at what's left of the bloodstain on the patio.

'What the fuck happened here?'

'Long story, come in.'

I pour us both a Scotch and sit down, rubbing my eyes. 'Okay. So, I took Amy out for dinner tonight.'

Anto looks bored. No way does he want to discuss my marital issues at this time of night.

'When she drove away from the restaurant, a black Mercedes ML63 started following her.' Now I've got his attention. 'I managed to catch up as Amy arrived at her parents' place. The Mercedes took off, but I got the number plate.'

I hand him a Post-it Note, IS 007 scrawled on it.

'What a wanker,' he scoffs, then folds the note and puts it in his pocket. 'I'll call Tina tomorrow. We're lucky she still works at Roads and Maritime. She'll find out who the car belongs to.'

'You're still speaking?' I ask. He knows I know he'd started going out with Lexy before he'd actually broken it off with Tina.

'She never knew there was any period of crossover. And neither does Lexy. Okay?'

'I hear you, Romeo. Yeah, call Tina.' A name and address would be key. 'But that's not all.' I slide the note from the fridge door across the coffee table.

'Holy fuck, mate, that's sick.' He picks up the note, his expression both fascinated and horrified. His jaw drops even lower as I bring him up to date on the break-in, Molly's slaying and getting MacPherson involved.

'I can't believe I agreed to it,' I continue, grimacing, 'but he got some CSI techs out here this morning to pull the bullets out of the wall.'

'Your dad is seriously gonna kill you, mate.'

'He's not gonna kill me unless you tell him about it, though, is he?'

'Christ. Who the fuck would kill a dog?' Anto screws up his face, as if he can taste something awful.

'A sub-human prick, that's who.'

He's even less impressed once I fill him in on the latest forensic results on the weapons.

'Hanging around you is fucking dangerous.'

I want to laugh, but he's the second person to say as much

in the last twenty-four hours. Anto looks out the front window, gets up to kill the lights and gropes his way to the sideboard. Scotch bottle in hand, he barks his shin against the coffee table and slumps back on the sofa.

'Why doesn't MacPherson suspect you? The bullets they dug out of your wall, same as the ones they dug out of Vucavec and Fazzini. People we know have gone down for less.' Even in the near darkness, I can see Anto is looking at me funny. All this consorting with the police is not doing much for my reputation.

'He did mention I'm a suspect, but he got it when I asked what I could possibly have to gain by bringing his attention to the bullets in my wall.'

'So who the fuck is it?'

'Why kill one of each crew,' I reply, 'unless you want to start a war? If this prick can kill a dog for no reason other than to fuck with me, then he's evil and deranged. And this evil and deranged nutsack has left me a note threatening Amy and Sasha.'

'Fucking hell, mate. Like we need this at the moment with the job coming up on Thursday.' Anto looks as worried as I am.

I sit back. The job. Maybe the job's the answer. 'The prick who set all this up must want a war between the gangs. Right?'

'He's hoping us Serbs and Croats wipe each other out and take the Italians with us.'

'Exactly. So who stands to benefit?' We sit in the dark, drinking more Scotch, contemplating the question.

'Could be the Chinese.' Anto doesn't sound convinced. 'Could be the Lebs. Yeah, it definitely could be the Lebs.'

'Rashid Sami? What's going on here is all a bit personal,

don't you think? And Rashid Sami's a heavy hitter.'

'Yeah, you're right. But the Lebs have other, smaller gangs. What if it's someone else trying to make a name for himself? And why are *you* being targeted? Why not your dad? Are the Serbs and the Italians getting hassled the same way?'

'I don't know, but that note sure feels personal.'

I refill our glasses and we sit back and think about it some more.

After thirty seconds or so, Anto slams his glass down on the coffee table and looks at me in triumph.

'Why didn't we think of it? The bikies! Ink Slater's bikie gang. Of course we didn't make the connection, because no bikes have been used. If it's them driving around in a Mercedes SUV, it's put us right off the scent.'

'Who?' I'm wondering if I topped his glass up too much.

'Come on, you know, Johnny! Ink Slater.' Anto stands and starts pacing as he lays out his theory. 'His father ran a small crew out of Bankstown, but Ink's dad was better at taking drugs than selling them. He OD'd about three years ago. By then Ink had grown from a skinny kid into a full-on bikie dickhead, still skinny but tatts all over him.' Anto is gesticulating wildly. 'I mean everywhere, even on his face. That's why he's called Ink, but I'm pretty sure his real name's Ian. Ian Slater.'

Anto is a human Who's Who of the Western Sydney gang fraternity. Ink Slater. The name and face slowly come into focus.

'Yeah, I remember him now. Back in the day, when we got rounded up a fair bit, I had to share a cell with him for a couple of hours. The kid must have been in his early twenties and he tried to pick a fight with me. What a stupid piece of shit. So skinny I could have used one fist to nail him through the floor.

180

We were both released after questioning. Amy came to pick me up.' The memory sharpens and my anger rises. 'The arsewipe made a filthy remark to her. You were there. Remember?'

'Yeah, that's him, disgusting mouth on it. Complete fuck-head.'

'I wanted to deck him, but we were still in the police station and they told us to take it outside.'

'Yeah, and he said he had no intention of going outside. He just sat down with that nasty fucking smirk on his face.'

'I was going to follow up on it, but Amy talked me out of it, said she'd heard worse.'

'Ink Slater. IS 007. It all stacks up. He's been building his crew. Sells lots of ice to kids. Fucking prick. He's got a bad reputation for beating up his chicks and generally being an all-round arsehole.'

'He could definitely be our guy. Plus, he benefits from the Croats, Serbs and Italians all being at each other's throats, right?'

'Fuck yeah.' Anto's eyes are blazing now.

'Get Tina to find out where he lives. I think we need to pay Ink Slater a little visit.'

Anto's gone and I can't sleep. Sitting at the kitchen bench with my laptop, I find two news reports straight up. One about Ian 'Ink' Slater getting off a charge of drug supply due to lack of evidence. Then another case of supply; that one went to court, only to have the jury acquit. There he is, on the steps of Bankstown Local Court, smiling. Tall and gangly, long arms sticking out too far from the cuffs of his ill-fitting blue suit. A thug on court day.

This prick has got the obligatory LOVE and HATE tattoos on his knuckles. His face is an unfinished work of art, tatts creeping up from his neck and over his jawline. A seriously anti-social piece of shit. And there's every chance he's been inside my home this evening and written me that nasty note threatening my wife and child.

Pushing back the bar stool, I hunch over my laptop. All I want to do is drive my fist into his smirking face. Instead, I sit down again and find a Facebook page link. He couldn't be that stupid, could he? Sure enough. He doesn't even have his photo settings turned to private. His whole life is open to anyone who cares to look.

I'd been right to insist Amy's Facebook page used her maiden name. No photos of me are ever to be uploaded. No mention of the Novak name. If I googled myself, absolutely nothing would come up. I have zero social-media presence and my busts as an adult were misdemeanours, attracting zero media attention. No newspaper coverage for me. Amy and I check her settings regularly to ensure as much privacy as possible. I could insist she doesn't have a Facebook account at all, but she'd see that as way too controlling. And anyway, it's part of how she communicates with her friends, how they show off their children, keep the grandparents in the loop. I just see it as dangerous. Why give away information? Information means power. Why give someone else power over you? Amy and I differ on that one too.

Ink Slater's cover photo consists of two scantily clad blonde girls draped over a Harley hog. His profile shot is a tattoo of a spider on a bicep. Ink parties with his crew at nightclubs, a beer in his hand and a blonde girl on each knee. Lots and lots of blonde girls. Wild nights, photos of big groups, arms around shoulders, dancing, everyone drunk.

I scroll back through the timeline to a string of birthday messages on the fifteenth of June. 'Happy Twenty-Eighth mate.'

The photos must have been taken early, while everyone was still keeping it together. It looks like the party was in a suburban living room; there's a seriously old lady sitting on a sofa. The rest of the crowd are young, all the guys in their late twenties, early thirties. And there're a lot of them. I count twenty-five different guys who come up repeatedly in the last twelve months. A young crew, everyone immortal.

Fucking hell. Anto was right, Ink has built himself a big crew in a short time. If they're the enemy, we can use their cock-sure attitude to bring them down.

A giant, musclebound bloke appears in a lot of photos. It takes me a moment to work out that there are actually two of them. Twins. Razor-cut hair and wife-beater singlets to show off their muscles. They even have matching scorpion tatts on their left forearms. But no one in the gang comes close to the volume of skin graffiti Ink sports. The guy must own a tattoo parlour. Wouldn't surprise me. I hover over one of the photos of the twins and their names pop up. Mick and Dave Hyde. I check out their Facebook pages and again I'm amazed. There are even photos of them snorting coke from the tanned butts of two dark-haired girls, who aren't twins, but are dressed to look like twins.

Are these guys morons or what?

Google tells me the Hyde twins have both done time for GBH and drug possession. Not as smart as Ink, and that's why he's the boss.

But if it's him behind all this, what's his motivation? Take over the West? And why target me specifically? Is he going after someone in the Serb and Italian crews as well? Threatening their wives and kids? Killing dogs?

All of a sudden I'm exhausted; my face sinks into my hands. What the fuck does Ink Slater want? If he and his twin goons were the ones who broke in earlier, why warn me? Why warn me his next targets are Amy and Sasha?

No way is this inked-up punk getting anywhere near the two most precious people in my life.

AMY

Last night, I promised Chaz I'd do the school run this morning. It's the least I can do, but I hope I'm not still over .05. After dinner with Johnny, I finished off a bottle of rosé, then passed out in Mum and Dad's guest room. I'm hungover, my eyes are all puffy and I look terrible.

I pull into the visitors' parking space outside Chaz's ground-floor flat on Marsden Road. In front of the block next door, an old mattress is propped up against an electricity pole; nearby is a lumpy-looking armchair with a nasty stain on it, both waiting for the next council clean-up. I'm fifteen minutes early, because I want to help her get through the feral stage of breakfast, so she can get ready for work unimpeded. Sometimes I envy Chaz's part-time job as an events assistant at Liverpool Council. Other times, I wonder how difficult I'd find it to get to work every day, even if it's only from nine to three. And after twelve years out of the workforce, how employable am I now anyway?

Chaz lives opposite Marsden Public School. If she hadn't met me, back when the kids were babies, Jenny would walk across the road to school. But by kindergarten, Jenny and Sasha were already joined at the hip. It seemed cruel to split them up.

Johnny wanted Sasha to go to All Saints Catholic College, because that's where he and Ivan went to school. I went to a private school, but there aren't any good private schools out here. Well, except All Saints. Being C of E, I wasn't happy with the idea, until I did the research. The school has a great reputation. The primary school is separate from the high school, but they're part of the same complex. I guess Johnny turned out all right. It was the right choice for Jenny too, because it's a wonderful school, but I know the annual fees nearly break Chaz. I've tried to help, but she's too proud. Or perhaps she doesn't want anything to do with what she sees as my dirty money.

As I get out of the car, I'm horrified to hear Sasha shouting.

'I don't want to go to school! I want to see my dad!' He sounds on the verge of tears as I rush to Chaz's door.

'At least you've got a dad,' Jenny says, as I knock.

'Hey! It's me!' I yell, trying the door and finding it open.

'Thank God.' Chaz looks at me from across the room, shaking her head, her smile strained.

The door opens directly into the main living space. In the small kitchen in the corner, Chaz is at the bench, making sandwiches. Jenny and Sasha are in their school uniforms; Sasha's hair has been combed and Jenny's is in pigtails. Sitting on the other side of the bench from Chaz, they're eating bowls of her homemade muesli. Jenny turns around to give me a little wave, before making a face at Sasha behind his back.

Sasha stares resolutely at his muesli.

I dump my handbag on the sofa, come up behind him and give him a tickle under his ribs. He squirms but doesn't squeal with laughter, his usual reaction. I swivel his stool around to face me. A finger under his chin and I lift his face to mine.

'Are you giving Chaz a hard time about something?'

'He's all right.' Chaz doesn't want him in trouble.

'No. I don't think he is. What do you reckon, Sash? An apology to Chaz and then we'll have a talk about your dad. Sound like a plan?'

Sasha's blue eyes are bright with tears, but the stubborn look is fading. He nods, uses his forearm to wipe his face and swivels around to Chaz.

'Sorry, Chaz.'

'It's all right, sweetie.' Chaz looks adoringly at Sasha. He is hard to resist when he's apologising.

'Well done, mate. Finish your breakfast. It's no good talking on an empty stomach.' I turn to Chaz and mouth *sorry*.

She shakes her head to reassure me and slides the sand-wiches into Ziploc bags.

'I'll finish that. You get ready for work.'

Chaz shoots me a grateful glance and heads to her bedroom.

Both kids have finished their muesli and are looking at me with wide eyes. I think about getting Sasha alone, then decide it's better if Jenny hears this too. That way, they can talk about it later. I pack the dishwasher as I try to explain.

'Sasha, your dad and I had a great talk last night. I think we're making progress.'

'Do you love each other again?' Sasha asks. Jenny looks disgusted.

'We have never not loved each other, but we have some stuff to sort out. And your dad is working really hard. He has a lot on, because he's not only doing his work, he's doing Uncle

Ivan's work too.' I know I've used this excuse before, but I figure I should stick to the same story.

'Dad's looking after all the fish shops?'

'Yes, that's right, and there are a lot of fish shops to look after, right?'

'We've got ten fish shops,' Sasha tells Jenny with more than a little pride.

'I know,' Jenny says. She gives him a cross-eyed stare, pokes her tongue out and slides off her stool. Losing interest, she heads to her room.

'Be patient, Sash. Everything is going to be fine, I promise.' What the hell am I doing making promises like that? Now that I seem to have lost control of my life, there's no guarantee I can keep my word to Sasha. But I have to give him something. 'I'll make sure your dad speaks to you on the phone this afternoon after school. Okay?'

'Okay, Mum.'

How much longer do we have before Sasha stops believing his dad manages ten fish shops for a living? He hasn't believed in Santa, the Easter Bunny or the Tooth Fairy for years. I have a feeling another myth is about to get busted.

JOHNNY

We always use stolen vehicles if we're about to commit armed robbery. It just makes sense to create as much space between the crew and the job as possible. As cars are much harder to steal off the street these days, we find it's easier to break into homes and steal the car keys. People usually keep their keys on a table near the front door, so you can get in and out relatively quickly. It helps if the car is parked on the street.

Last night, Baz and a small crew stole the four vehicles we need for Thursday night, making sure they didn't wake anyone up. They drove the three SUVs and a van a few suburbs away and swapped the number plates with other random cars parked on the side of the road. As an added precaution, we make the number plates hard to read. Can't be too careful. Normally we'd rebirth the vehicles afterwards, but this job is too big, so they'll be broken up for parts.

It's been raining solidly since I woke up this morning. Anto and I are painting mud on the number plates of our four stolen vehicles, while Brick and Blocker jackhammer up

189

another garage pit to match the one on the other side of the warehouse, below the car hoist. I didn't feel bad taking the easy job and giving the younger guys the really fucking hard job. That's what seniority gets you in life.

The new garage pit will be two metres long, one metre wide, one metre deep and lined in concrete. Stump and Fibs are building a false timber floor that will end up twenty centimetres above the bottom of the pit. The false floor will come out in three sections and the space underneath will be our new storage area. It won't fool a police search party for long, but it will slow them down.

Mum arrives with a big box of *fritule* for morning tea, but the rain hammering on the warehouse roof makes conversation impossible. I'm lost in my thoughts, sipping my tea, when a grinning Anto taps me on the shoulder to show me his phone is ringing. On the screen is the pretty face of his ex-girlfriend, Tina. He has to go outside and jump in the Jeep to hear what she's saying. When he returns, he's still grinning: she's come through with a residential address in Bankstown for an Ian Slater linked to the IS 007 number plates. Anto gets the Detective of the Year award.

Seventeen minutes later, we're driving through the guts of downtown Bankstown, one of Sydney's most culturally diverse suburbs. They've even got their own airport. That's where the good news ends. Bankstown's high unemployment means there's an evil twin, a high crime rate. The place is full of crooks and it's also the home base of one of my least favourite rugby league teams, the Bulldogs. They stole the Morris twins off the Dragons and they'll never be forgiven.

Apart from a few new townhouses on Ink Slater's street,

the rest of the dwellings are single-storey, brick-veneer and weatherboard homes, built in the fifties, sixties and seventies. I'm impressed by the general tidiness of the front yards. It looks like a nice neighbourhood, but I know better. We drive slowly past Slater's small, cream weatherboard cottage. Sitting in the driveway is a black Mercedes ML63, IS 007 number plates, chrome rims and low-profile tyres. So out of place. We park halfway down the block and I grab my gun from the glove box. Anto raises both massive eyebrows at me as I stick it down the back of my shorts.

'I'm paranoid at the moment. Okay?'

'Are you sure we shouldn't be waiting until after dark to do this?' he asks.

'Probably, but we'll be careful, and we're running out of time.'

Only two more nights until we pull the job on Stanislav. I need to put some insurance in place.

We're lucky the rain hasn't eased off. There's no one around. We run back towards the house, as if we're trying to get out of the rain. This kind of cottage came with a lawn, a couple of ornamental trees and some rosebushes. Now it's all concrete, with three dead pot plants near the low brick fence running across the front of the property. We stroll as casually as possible up the driveway on the far side of the Mercedes, close to the high, timber fence separating the house from its identical neighbour. Then we crouch down to avoid being seen from the street. The cracked and weedy concrete driveway runs the full length of the house back to an open brick garage, where a black Harley stands in lone splendour. We're definitely in the right place. I head towards the garage in a crouching walk. Anto

191

follows, trying not to slip on the wet driveway.

We take it slowly, popping up to check each room on the way. Closest to the street is the living room with a big-screen TV, a modern corner sofa and a green velvet reclining chair from an entirely different era. There's even a white lace cloth on the headrest. Next is the dining room, an old timber table in pride of place, decked out with a lace table runner and matching green velvet chairs. As we approach the back of the house, we hear voices. In a house this age, they're probably coming from the kitchen. We stop and listen.

'Nanna, ya make the best sangers in the world.' A male voice. A wheedling quality I recognise.

'You're too skinny. If your mother hadn't been a junkie you would have filled out by now.' I picture the little old lady from the Facebook page.

'Don't talk about Mum like that, Nan.' Now there's menace in the male voice and I don't like it. The fucker has no right talking to his grandma that way.

I make a waving motion with my hand, back the way we came. Anto turns and we crouch-walk back down the driveway. Once we're on the street side of the Mercedes we stand up and look around. No one in the street and no twitching blinds. It's still pelting down. Everyone's probably at work. Or maybe no one gives a shit anymore about two blokes creeping around a neighbour's home.

I lead the way across the front yard, up the narrow passage between Slater's house and the one next door. Old garden tools lean against the timber fence. The three chest-high sash windows suggest bedrooms. The first window is open a hands-breadth. I motion to Anto to wait, while I raise my head and take a peek inside. An old lady's room, all crocheted doilies and blankets, old-time photos on the walls.

The next window is also open a few inches and this bedroom hasn't quite made the transition from a teenage boy's room to the lair befitting the leader of a bikie gang. A king-size bed with black sheets takes up most of the real estate, but the walls are covered in posters of Harleys and blonde pin-up girls. In pride of place on the ceiling above Slater's bed is a poster of Gwen Stefani, the rest of No Doubt cut out. A small desk is littered with charging cords, a laptop and bike magazines. At twenty-eight, Ink Slater still lives with his nanna.

Slinking further up the side, I find the third bedroom. This one is empty apart from a single bed and some old timber furniture. Backing out, Anto and I lope across the front of the house and down the street to the Jeep.

An idea has been forming in my mind all morning. I've been moving it around, looking at it from every angle. But the thought of Granny Slater getting caught up in my plan makes me uncomfortable. She'll be there, asleep in her bed, when the cops bust down the door with a battering ram and come through the windows before dawn. She'll be scared out of her wits. Fuck. I hope she doesn't have a heart attack or something. I'll have to make sure she's all right, somehow, after this is all over.

As I walk into Mum's kitchen, the smell hits me and my mouth floods with saliva. She's frying up small fillets of chicken, bashed thin, coated in her homemade breadcrumbs. The sight of them makes me feel about ten years old. Dad is sitting up his end of the kitchen table, looking sour.

'You notice, Branka? You notice our son? Is lunchtime. He

turns up at mealtimes, always.'

'Stop it, Milan.' Mum sweetens her words with a quick smile at my father, then goes back to flipping the chicken pieces in the spitting pan. 'Johnny is young man, needs food only Mama can cook.' She shrugs. 'We always have enough.' She wipes one hand on her apron and reaches up to pat me tenderly on the cheek. Yep, still ten years old.

'Sit, sit, *sjediti, sjediti.*'

Mum pulls potatoes out of the oven, piles the chicken on a plate and sets the food down in the centre of the table next to a big bowl of lettuce, tomato and onion salad. She helps us to serve ourselves, then goes back to the sink to clean up, banging pots and pans around. Only when Dad and I are well into our second helpings does she sit down and start serving herself. I've tried to change this habit of putting herself last, but when we eat in the kitchen, this is how it is. It drives Amy crazy.

'Dad, I need to bring you up to speed on my research into Ivan's death.'

Mum lets out a wail, then slaps a hand over her mouth as though she can't bear the sound. Dad looks as if he wants to lean across the table and strangle me. I feel like a complete shithead.

Mum starts to pray.

'Sorry, Mum, I'll wait until we've finished lunch. Dad and I will talk out the back.'

'No, no, you busy man. You talk, I pray, then eat.'

I look at Dad. He nods his permission, but there's a warning there too.

'So, I've heard something through one of the stoolies we use sometimes. He reckons he was down the cop shop in Liverpool

194

last week and heard two detectives talking about—'

'Ivan,' supplies Dad.

'Yeah. They were saying they had a special task force set up to catch the killer. They reckon whoever shot Ivan, Michael Vucavec and Tony Fazzini was a serial killer.'

'A serial killer. Really. This is what detectives say in front of stool parrot?'

'Is stool pigeon, Milan,' says Mum. She seems to have recovered a bit.

Dad looks at her in disbelief. 'Stool parrot, stool pigeon, all should be dead. Why they say in front of this guy? Is bullshit.'

'Apparently, he was around a corner, couldn't be seen, but he could hear these cops talking. Anyway, he came to me with it, because he knew I'd give him money for the info.'

'You give him money. How much you give?'

'A hundred bucks. Dad, it's not important what I gave him.' Telling him about the two different guns might be too complicated right now. It's time to move him off the stool pigeon fiction. 'Last night a black Mercedes SUV sped by me, right after Amy and I walked out of Frentini's.'

'You see Amy?' Mum breaks in. 'How is my Sasha?'

'Is why we not discuss business in front of women.' Dad pushes his chair back, wipes his mouth with the back of his hand and takes off down the hallway.

'Thanks for lunch, Mum.' I stand up, ready to follow my father.

'Tell me first. Amy and Sasha okay?'

'They're fine, Mum, and they're safe. This will all be over in a couple of days and they'll be back.'

'You have a big job Thursday night. Then you and your *tata*

195

must stop. Is over. We have enough. Then Amy come back.' Her tone is matter-of-fact and I turn to her in surprise. There's no way Dad would have discussed the job with her. But Amy knew too. The women must be talking, but they all know enough to talk only to each other. She grabs my shoulders. Her dark-brown eyes are wet with unshed tears.

'You make peace with Marko?'

'Yeah, Mum, we're fine.'

'*Dobro, dobro.* You be careful. You look after your *tata*. You all come home.'

I nod.

'You promise your mama.' She's got a solid grip on my shoulders.

'I promise, Mum.'

Satisfied, she lets me go and starts clearing plates.

Out in the backyard, the ground is steaming in the sunshine. The humid air is a hot, wet blanket. Sitting at the table under the shade of the tin roof, Dad is rolling a cigarette, his nicotine-stained fingers slow and assured. I sit next to him. As he lights up, I make a decision. If I'm going to protect Amy and Sasha properly, I need his help.

'Okay. So, yes, I had dinner with Amy last night. We're working on getting back together, like I said would happen. But as I watched her drive away, I saw the black Mercedes, three men inside. Same model used during the drive-by. I got a bad feeling, some kind of instinct, you know?'

Dad looks at me like I've lost my mind. Then he makes a circular motion with his hand. Get on with it.

'I caught up with them just as Amy went into her parents' place. Now they know where she lives.'

'*Now they know where she lives!*' he growls, mocking me again. 'You follow them? You shoot them?'

'No, I didn't, Dad.' I struggle to hide my impatience, but I also start to wish I'd done exactly what he's suggesting. I take a couple of deep breaths. The smell of his tobacco calms me.

'I didn't have my gun on me.' I wait while he shakes his head in disgust. 'I went home and discovered someone had broken into our house, stolen Ivan's gun and left me this note.' I pull out the folded note, the words threatening the stick figures.

Dad's expression finally changes to one of concern. Hallelujah.

'Who leave this note? Why he warn us? What he want?'

'I think whoever it is wants the Serbs and the Croats at war again and both crews fighting the Italians. They want me doing something stupid, like killing Stanislav, even though we have no proof he had anything to do with Ivan's death.'

'Maybe. Maybe.' Dad rocks back in his chair and blows perfect smoke rings into the sky. It's one of the things he does when he's figuring out a problem.

He leans forward again, his scowl ferocious. 'We must protect Sasha.'

Bingo. 'You're right, Dad. We need to protect Amy and Sasha. I've already asked Marko to keep an eye on them, but the boys could work in shifts.'

Dad nods, picks up his phone and speed dials, yammering away in Croatian, then hangs up twenty seconds later.

'Josef will be outside school today. He will follow Amy home. You tell Amy she not go anywhere without telling you where. We protect.' He sits back, pleased with himself, and I exhale a sigh of relief.

Dad looks at me again, suspicion blooming in his blood-shot eyes.

'But you not tell me everything. Tell me now.'

'I know who owns the black Mercedes ML63.'

'Who?'

'Ink Slater. He runs a bikie gang out of Bankstown. I reckon he wants us all to kill each other, so he can take over the whole territory.'

Rocking back again, Dad blows a whole lot of smoke rings at the sky.

'He wants to take over whole territory? You go kill this Slater. Crew will protect Amy and Sasha until it is done.'

I consider telling him about the plan forming in my mind, but decide to walk away with this victory. I'll come back and present the idea once I've foolproofed it.

AMY

Although the rain has finally stopped, the road is slippery; I give myself plenty of time to pull up at the stop sign. No more drinking for me. I don't know why I thought that bottle of rosé was a good idea, on top of the champagne at dinner. I've still got a cracking headache. Perhaps I wanted to obliterate myself.

Outside the school, the line of cars is trailing halfway down the block. I barely make it through the stop sign when a little girl runs across the road in front of me, pigtails flying. The car is crawling when I hit the brakes, so I know there's no danger, until I hear a loud bang and I'm shunted forward a metre. Sliding now, my foot jammed hard on the brake, I pull to a stop less than half a metre from the girl.

Frightened, she drops her schoolbag and starts to cry. One of the mothers runs out, scoops her up and gives me a dirty look. I'm shaking. That was too close. I check my rear-view mirror and recognise the man getting out of the white van behind me. Milan's younger brother, Josef. He looks mortified. What's he doing here? He doesn't have any grandkids to pick up.

I wave and point to a space at the kerb ahead where we can both pull over. Then I walk back to meet him.

'Josef?'

He's red-faced and stammering.

'I drive down the street and you stop and wham, I hit you. I'm sorry, Amy. The boys fix for you, good as new. You won't even notice.'

I survey the damage. It's not that bad, a dinged bumper bar. And the little girl is okay. Let's hope she doesn't run out onto the street next time. But I'm still feeling shaky and Josef is acting strangely, as if he's been caught in the act. What act, I don't know. Then it hits me. Johnny told me Marko would be keeping an eye on me; now it's Josef too.

'Are you following me, Josef?'

This has him spluttering excuses about doing some shopping for his wife. I let him off the hook, knowing there's no way that could possibly be true. Mary would never set Josef loose with a shopping trolley. I'll find out what's going on from Johnny instead.

As Josef drives off, Sasha sees me. He climbs in the back of the car, a frown on his face. I reach back to pat his leg, then indicate and move out into the traffic.

'Mum, are you and Dad getting a divorce like Timmy's parents?'

His words are like a sharp blow right under my heart. I pull up again further down the block, so I can turn around and look at him.

'Sasha, sweetheart. It's like I told you this morning, your Dad and I are working through it. You've got to trust me and give me a little more time.'

'I think you're lying to me. Have you done something bad to Dad?'

For a second, I'm gutted by how unfair it feels to have my son blame me for this situation. But I'm also filled with guilt, because I *have* been lying to him. Imagine how he'll react if this separation becomes permanent?

'Would you like to see your dad this afternoon?'

The smile on his face breaks my heart.

'I'll see if I can arrange it, okay?' I jump out of the car.

Johnny answers my call immediately. 'Hi, honey. How you doing?'

'I'm royally pissed off.' I keep my voice down, but Johnny will know I'm angry.

'What's up?' He sounds worried. Good.

'Yesterday it was Marko. Today it's Josef. He just rammed into the back of my car in the school pick-up zone! I nearly hit a little girl!' My voice is a hiss now. I don't want Sasha to hear. 'I agreed to Marko keeping an eye on me, at least he's discreet. I don't even know why I agreed. What's going on? Why do I need to be followed?'

'Okay, calm down, I'll tell you. But you've got to promise you won't get angry.'

'I'm already angry! Haven't you noticed!' This time I can't help raising my voice. I glance behind me: Sasha is staring through the window. I smile at him and take a deep breath.

'I get it,' Johnny says. 'But this is about keeping you and Sasha safe.'

I turn around so Sasha can't see my face. 'Safe from what, Johnny? Spill it. If you lie to me now, it's over. Do. You. Understand? Over.'

'Yeah, Ames, I get it. Okay. I thought I saw someone follow you home last night after you left the restaurant. I might have been imagining it, but I've put the crew onto protection duty, just for the next few days. Just to be on the safe side.'

'Who would be following me, Johnny?' I'm not angry anymore. I'm scared.

'I think someone is trying to stir up trouble between the gangs. But seriously, don't worry about it. It's under control.'

Johnny is trying very hard to sound relaxed, but he's failing.

'Under control, is it?' There's menace in my tone now. 'Your brother was killed in front of his own home. Then we had the drive-by. Our neighbour's dog had her throat slit. Every bin night another "known gang member" gets killed. Now you're saying I'm being followed and it's UNDER CONTROL?'

'Honey, calm down. Trust me. How about I come over there now? Where are you?'

'I'm a block away from the school, where I nearly ran over a little girl because your uncle rear-ended me. I'm standing outside the car, so I can talk to my fucking gangster husband without our son hearing us argue again. Don't you come anywhere near us. Your time is running out, Johnny. You get this shit straightened out right now, or our marriage is over.'

I get back in the car and tell Sasha his father is busy, and he'll have to wait for the weekend. Liar-liar-pants-on-fire.

Sasha cries silently in the back seat as I drive back to Mum and Dad's.

I'm too angry to cry.

JOHNNY

Amy has barely hung up on me when I get a call from Dad. With him it's always best to go on the offensive.

'Hi, Dad. You're not gonna believe this, but Josef rear-ended Amy's car! In front of the school. So much for protection.'

'You plan on telling me truth some day?'

Why would Dad completely ignore what I've just said? His voice has a hard, gloating quality. It makes my skin prickle.

'Not sure what you mean, Dad.'

'After you go, me and Branka, we have visitor. Detective MacPherson. He tell me interesting story.'

My stomach feels like it's dropped through the floor of the Jeep.

'He tell me different story from what you tell your *tata*. Who I believe? You come here now. You tell me everything. Then we see.'

'Okay, Dad.'

I drive on slowly. Right now, I miss Ivan so fiercely it's a searing pain through the centre of my chest. Ivan would know what to do and he'd know how to turn this apparent betrayal of our father's standards into a joke on the police. How the Novaks outwitted the cops again. He'd make Dad laugh about it. After he'd taken the punch to the head. After he'd stepped in front of me to make sure I didn't get hit. But Ivan wouldn't be in this predicament in the first place. He wouldn't have gone down to the cop shop without the family lawyer, and there's no way he would have agreed to CSIs in his home.

But Ivan wouldn't have managed to get any of this information. He'd still be running blind, unaware of this new enemy. Maybe that's exactly why he's dead.

The pain hits again, as strong as when I found out he'd been shot.

I have to pull over. I let my head rest on the steering wheel. I want to punch someone, anyone, a wall. How could Ivan leave me here, alone, dealing with Dad? Tears seep out of my eyes. For a man who doesn't cry, I seem to be doing a lot of it lately.

I rub my face as it dawns on me—Ivan isn't here, so I'll stand up to my father, admit I talked to MacPherson, and tell him why. He has to agree to my new plan. It might not be foolproof, but no plan ever is. Dad needs to accept that I'm putting the family first, as always. Us Novaks have to use everything at our disposal, even the cops, to end up on top. Otherwise, Ink Slater's bikies will crush us.

By the time I pull up in front of my parents' place, I'm furious with MacPherson. What the fuck is he trying to do? Does the guy enjoy interfering or what? I sigh. I guess he figures I'm keeping my old man up to speed. But seriously, what the fuck is his game? Why would MacPherson want to upset Mum with all this?

To top it off, there's fucking Marko's car. In the only shade—again. I nudge it a bit harder this time. No alarm goes off, though, which is a relief. I need time to get myself under control.

I'm determined to convince Dad I haven't fucked up. I reckon it's all working out fine—we have the information we need to put the world right, fuck over Ink Slater and rip off the Serbs. All the risks I've taken will be worthwhile. I take a few more deep breaths, get out of the car, square my shoulders and call on my brother to help me through the next ten minutes, then march into the house.

Mum just kisses me and points towards the back patio. She doesn't even offer me a drink. Shit. Bad sign.

Dad is at the end of the table, a face like thunder and stony-eyed, Marko by his side. Fuck. This moment brings back so many other bad moments. Dad pounds the table once, hard. Marko flinches. The cicadas fall silent.

'Sit here.' Dad points to the chair at his right. 'Close, so I can see your eyes. Tell everything, from beginning.'

I pull the chair out from under the table and move it as far away as I reasonably can, without looking too chickenshit. I glance at Marko, expecting to see triumph in his eyes, but I see confusion instead. Fuck. This is bad.

'MacPherson was there waiting for me, in his car, the morning after the funeral.' Fuck, it feels like forever ago, so much has happened. 'He told me to follow him down to the station. He said he had something he wanted to show me.'

'He had something he want to show you? Why you not call me? Call Sam Dillard?'

No one is supposed to talk to the police without the crew lawyer present. Dad pays him a monthly retainer. His number is on speed dial. I take another deep breath and think of Ivan. The cicadas start up again.

'MacPherson told me he wanted to speak to me as a family member of a murder victim, not as a perp. He wasn't interviewing me, he was showing me something. He told me I didn't need a lawyer.'

'He say you don't need a lawyer. So you believe him? A cop? What I teach? All these years! What I teach?' Dad's eyes are bulging. I can smell my own sweat, but I plough on and tell him about the CCTV footage.

Marko leans forward, engrossed. I can tell he understands the significance of the black Mercedes SUV, the car I warned him about. For once, I'm sort of glad my cousin is here.

After I tell them about Molly's throat being slit, Marko nods, Dad stares.

'The next-door neighbours were pretty rattled. They wanted me to call the police. I figured MacPherson knew the background.'

'Should have buried dog, not let neighbours know our business.' Dad's voice is hard, no sympathy there.

'Yeah. I didn't think of that.' I lie.

'You didn't think at all.' The hand slams down again, jolting me. 'You just invite police into your home?'

'Well, yes, Dad, didn't you invite MacPherson into your home this afternoon?'

Dad reaches out and backhands me across the face. The

206

whole thing so quick he barely moves. I nearly fall out of my chair, but sit back up, my face stinging.

When I glance at Marko, horrified that he's witnessing my embarrassment, again, his face is blank. No help there, but at least he's not adding fuel to the fire. I've got to explain.

'MacPherson said he thought all the shootings were connected and that we should leave it to the police from now on.'

'Leave it to police,' growls Dad. 'He tell me this too. Why should we leave to police? What else you not tell me?'

'I told you about Ink Slater following Amy. I told you about my house being broken into, Ivan's gun stolen, the note they left me. Fucking bikie arseholes.'

I fish the note back out of my back pocket and hand it to Marko. See his eyes go wide. He nods again, which gives me a bit more courage.

'I've been investigating this Slater bastard. I know where he lives. And I've got a plan, Dad.' I lean forward, desperate to get him on side. 'After we steal the ecstasy off the Serbs, we plant some of it on Ink Slater. Then we tip off the cops. Everyone will hear the bikies got busted with a stack of E and we'll be off the hook. Plus, we'll have nuked Ink Slater, who has to be the bastard who killed Ivan. Don't you see, Dad? It's perfect!'

Dad stands, his chair scrapes back and falls with a clatter behind him. Both hands are planted on the table. He towers over me, monstering me. Then he rears back and gives me a thumping great left. I see it coming, but don't try to move. The punch lifts me out of my chair and flings me against the back of the house, where I slide to the floor, gasping through the pain.

'Get out of my house, you rat. Stanislav is my enemy, he

killed Ivan and my son is coward. Want to rat to police, tip off police? GET OUT OF MY HOUSE.'

I stagger up as fast as I can, ears ringing, jaw throbbing. Avoiding Marko and Dad, I stumble down the back stairs, round the side of the house, out to my car.

I drive away fast, desperate to put some distance between myself and my father. The back of my head feels as if it's cracked. I pull my hand away from a tender spot. Not much blood. Ivan always said I had a hard head. At the end of the block, I slow down, calm my breathing, ease my foot off the accelerator.

What do I really want out of all this anyway? Amy's beautiful face appears before me, then Sasha's. The answer is pretty obvious—I want my family back. But is that all I want? Yes, perhaps it's pathetic, but I admit that I still want my father's—and, weirdly, Ivan's—approval. A mix of embarrassment and fury washes over me as I rub my jaw. Dad has no right to react the way he did, let alone hit me.

I know I'm right. Using the police to provide information is something we've been doing for years. Ivan started it, paying a local druggie to tell the police he'd seen something he hadn't. Leading the cops away from us towards someone else. What I've done isn't any different. How can Dad accuse me of being a rat? What the fuck?

I pull up outside my home, park on the street and rest my forehead on the steering wheel.

Right now, I don't know if our plans are going ahead. What if Dad calls the whole thing off? I'm not even sure if Amy and Sasha are still protected. Everything depends on Dad. As usual. And I'm over it.

I know there's a risk Amy won't come back, no matter what I do, but I have to carry on as though she will. I have to believe it's all going to work out. Somehow. If only Amy could accept that this is all about setting up the future for her and Sasha, even if I'm not around to share it.

The house is in Amy's name, mortgage-free, and worth more than $800,000. Sydney real-estate prices are a joke. She could move anywhere other than Sydney and have a bigger place, plus money in the bank. Anyway, it's all hers. If I can fill the safe with at least a mil, their future is sorted. I'll have provided for the two most important people in my life.

Lifting my head from the steering wheel, I notice Mr Fellows sitting on his front verandah, watching me. I feel like flipping him the bird but restrain myself. Sitting up straight again, I try to stare into the future. My new plan is risky, complicated. But it doesn't matter how well everything goes on Thursday night—if we don't throw the Serbs off our scent, the fragile peace between our two gangs will be destroyed. The Serbs will be fucking furious and the retaliation will be swift and brutal.

I still don't get Slater's personal interest in me either. What's that about? Time to find out.

JOHNNY

On my way to Bankstown, the phone rings. Marko. An angry flush spreads up my neck to my face. Is he ringing to gloat?

'What?'

'I want you to know, Johnny, I think Uncle Milan is wrong. I think your plan to fuck up Ink Slater's crew is a good plan. We need to use the police. This is the best way. I tried talking with the boss, but he is still angry. It is not easy always to make him see. He needs to come up with the plan too. You understand?'

I can't believe how good it feels to hear this from Marko. I exhale the anger.

'You really think it's a good idea?'

'Yes. You surprise me again, Johnny. You are smarter than you look. We will see. But I think the boss will change his mind. I will talk to him again tonight. Leave it to me.'

'Thanks, Marko. I appreciate it.' It's an effort to say it.

'We have never liked each other, have we?'

'No.' I'm surprised he's being so direct.

'Maybe we will never like each other, but I said I am on

your team. What I say, I mean. But you fuck up, Johnny, and I am no longer on your team. You hear me?'

'Loud and clear.' I guess I'd rather have Marko with me than against me, so here's hoping I don't fuck up.

I park down the street from Ink Slater's bungalow. There's no sign of the Mercedes and the garage door is shut. No sign of the old lady either. Then I check my wing mirror and see Slater's Mercedes turn into the street and come to a halt halfway up the driveway. There's only one person in the car and he's tall and skinny. Definitely not one of the Hyde twins. I'm not close enough to see any tatts.

As I jump out of the Jeep, I tuck the gun down the back of my jeans and pull my shirt over it, before running across the street behind the back bumper of the Mercedes. I wait until the door opens, then take two strides, my gun at waist height so it can't be seen from the street. Ink Slater's eyes widen as he looks straight into the barrel of the gun, then up at me. Older and uglier, but I know that face.

'What the fuck? Johnny Novak, whaddya want?' His seatbelt still fastened, beads of sweat forming on his forehead, Slater is effectively trapped. The narrow driveway wasn't built for a big SUV with wide doors. His only exit is blocked by me and my gun.

Up close, he's a freak in skinny grey jeans and a black leather vest. Meth-addict thin, the whites of his eyes yellow. He's smirking at me, revealing an ugly mouthful of twisted grey teeth. His hair is black and greasy, short at the sides and long at the top and back. He's got a fucking mullet, for God's sake. Tattoos everywhere, crawling over his pale skin. A

211

new one creeping up from his right jawline, red and angry. A snake's head. Slater still looks amused, but a muscle has started twitching in his cheek.

'You look like you been in a fight.' His eyes are focused on my swelling jaw.

'Why were you following my wife last night?'

'Why would I follow Amy around? You two split up or sumfin?'

'How do you even know my wife's name, you cocksucker?' Without moving the gun, I flick a short sharp left to Slater's nose.

His head snaps sideways and his nose starts bleeding. He brings his face back to upright. Unblinking, he licks the blood from his top lip as if he enjoys the taste.

'I dunno whatcha talkin' about, Johnny.'

'Don't fuck with me, you little prick. I saw you following Amy last night, in this car. You broke into my house, left me a fucked-up note.'

'Bullshit. You got no proof.'

The prick is still smiling and I'm about to lose it. Why not end this now, like Dad said? Kill the bastard who murdered my brother? I flick off the safety.

Slater wipes the blood from under his nose with the back of his hand. His snaggle-toothed grin widens as the rumble of Harleys fills the quiet street and pours into the narrow driveway.

Two giants in black leathers and full-face helmets are propping their bikes behind me. One pulls a sawn-off shotgun from a saddle bag, the other a semiautomatic from a shoulder holster. Without bothering to take off their helmets, they saunter up the driveway towards their leader and me, the guy holding a gun.

212

My lizard brain hits the fight-or-flight button, adrenaline flooding. I keep the gun pointed at Slater.

His eyes on the rear-view mirror, he starts to laugh. He thumps the steering wheel, he's laughing so hard. He finally unbuckles his seatbelt, but makes no move to get out. After all, I still have a gun on him.

'Tell your boys to fuck off or I'll shoot you.'

'I don't fink so, Johnny. No way you're gonna shoot me. Cos if you do, Mick and Dave will kill you. They'll make you suffer for a while first and then they'll kill you.'

The Hyde twins advance slowly and stand shoulder to shoulder at the rear of the Mercedes, both guns pointing at me. As though ruled by a single brain, they slide up their face shields at the same time, to reveal exactly the same face.

A kid on a pushbike rides past, oblivious.

I stand facing Slater, who's still folded up like an insect in the car. I'm a smaller target in profile, but from this distance the twins can't miss. I don't want to die in a driveway in Bankstown. I fucking hate Bankstown. It's full of Bulldogs supporters and I fucking hate the Bulldogs. One of the twins takes another step. I tense up. Slater raises his hand and all movement stops.

'Amy deserves someone smarter than *you*, Johnny. Coming here, on your own. No Ivan to protect you. You're stupid. But today you're also lucky, because you're saving me some time. Got a message for your dad. It's simple. From now on you give us twenty per cent of your take. Not net profit, I want twenty per cent of your gross take, the drugs, the protection, whatever you fence, even some of your take from them fish shops of yours. All of it.'

'I can tell you now, that's never gonna happen.'

213

'Maybe it will, maybe it won't. But right now, this message is the only fing keeping you alive. So, go deliver me message. I'm taking over, Johnny Novak, and not one of you wog cunts is gonna stop me.' He waves his tattooed hand like he's shooing away a dog. I start backing towards the Hyde twins as Slater eases his way out of the car. He motions the twins backwards with his hand.

'Let the stupid fuck go.'

All three guns are lowered, and I turn to walk away.

'And Johnny?' His wheedling voice stops me.

I turn around.

'If you don't deliver me message and I don't start gettin' paid, I'll be visitin' Amy. Yeah. Fuck, she's hot. Don't think that old security guard is gonna stop me neither. And your sweet little boy. Sasha? He could use a new daddy.'

The desire to bring my gun up and end Slater is fierce. But survival wins out. Slater grins at me, as if he can read my mind.

'You got till Friday to deliver the first payment and it better be some serious cashola. That's it. I'm not fuckin around.'

I turn and stride towards my car, trying not to run, horribly aware of my exposed back. I jump in and gun the motor.

I will myself to drive away slowly, still trying to hide my fear. I doubt I fooled Ink Slater and I'm not fooling myself. I can feel the sweat drying on my face and neck as the air-con does its work. I can smell myself. The animal scent of fear. Something I usually smell on others. I should have brought Anto or Marko with me. I had the perfect opportunity when Marko called me. Why did I keep it to myself? What came over me? Am I a liability to everyone, including myself? But what would've happened if I hadn't been alone? A bloodbath in a suburban street, the kid on the bike the only witness. The kid could have ended up a casualty too, taken out by a stray bullet.

Over-dramatising things is not something I normally do. There's enough happening right now, without imagining the worst. I need to stay calm, stay focused, start using my allies more competently, start thinking like a general, not a footsoldier.

As I pull up at a red light, I think about Ink Slater's message for Dad. Not gonna happen. No way will I be taking that proposal to my father. I'm in enough trouble already, without admitting I've come off second best in a face-off with an enemy.

The blood rushes to my head as I remember Slater's evil fucking smile when he talked about Amy. How does he know her name? How long has he been following her? Since he first saw her at the cop shop years ago? My blood rises thick and angry. I'm gonna kill that skinny prick.

AMY

Sasha has been inconsolable. Once I got over being angry, I relented. Besides, I have to convince Johnny to agree to my plan. At the very least, I need to know who the hell is following me and why. So I bought some groceries and took Sasha back home. After a clean-up, the place didn't look too bad. I found an old doormat to cover the bloodstain on the front patio. Johnny's V8 rumbled up our driveway as I started on dinner and he and Sasha had a noisy reunion in the garage.

Now they're wrestling like puppies on the living-room floor, huge smiles on their faces. When he sees me, Johnny disentangles himself, jumps up and wraps me in his arms, nuzzling my neck, breathing me in before kissing me. Sasha has his arms wrapped around our waists, squealing with excitement. I decide to bring things down a notch.

'Why don't you keep Sasha company while he has a bath, and he can fill you in on what he's been doing at school?'

'Anything you want, Ames. Come on, kid.' They head off, Sasha holding his father's hand as if he's afraid to let go.

I've prepared lamb chops with five different veggies. Based on the sheer volume of takeaway-food containers I threw out earlier, there's no way Johnny's been getting enough greens. While it was still daylight, I made sure to take the bins out, too. If I fail to persuade him to leave with us, at least I can try to protect him from getting shot tomorrow night.

We sit around the kitchen table as if nothing strange has been going on in the Novak household. I smile the whole way through dinner; I can't help it. Johnny and Sasha are so pleased to see each other.

Sasha finally gets serious. 'Are you and Mummy getting divorced?'

Johnny stares at me, shocked, as if I've put this thought into his son's head. 'No, we're not getting divorced, Sash,' he says slowly. 'I've had to work really hard since Uncle Ivan went to heaven. But that will all be over in a couple of days. Then the three of us can go away on a holiday together.'

'I miss Uncle Ivan, Dad.' Sasha is so earnest it makes my heart break.

'I miss him too, Sash.' Johnny looks away, trying to keep his own emotions under control.

I'm probably the only person who does not miss Ivan.

'School breaks up on Friday, doesn't it, Mum?'

I nod.

'Dad, are you coming to the school concert on Thursday night? I'm a spaceman.' Sasha is suddenly animated again. 'Mrs Glen gave me a really good part. She reckons I'm a natural. Mum and Nanna made my costume. You should see it, Dad. It's awesome. I look totally like I'm from outta space!'

Johnny eyes cloud over and he silently beseeches me for

217

some sort of guidance. Okay, then, the job is happening on Thursday night. I fold my arms across my chest. Let's see how you get out of this one, Johnny Novak.

'I'm sorry, mate. I'm working on Thursday night. There's no way I'll be able to be there. But Mum will take a video on her phone, so I'll see everything.'

Sasha is so crestfallen that I come to Johnny's rescue.

'Don't worry, Sasha, we'll show Daddy your costume on Saturday. You can put it back on again, use your laser gun on him and then I'll show him the video. Okay?'

Sasha nods bravely, but he's clearly not happy.

'Why do you have to work at night, Dad? Everyone else's dad works in the daytime.'

And this is the reason we have to get out of this life. Right there. Johnny sees it too.

'It's the last time, Sash. I'll be there for the next school play. I promise.'

'Right, Sasha, it's time for bed.' I look at Johnny. 'Why don't you tuck him in and read him a story while I clean up?' It's only seven-thirty and I usually let Sasha stay up until eight, but he's exhausted, and I need some time alone with my husband.

By the time I've turned the dishwasher on for the second time this evening, Johnny is closing the door to Sasha's room.

I follow him into the living room. He folds me into his arms again. I touch the swelling on his jaw and raise my eyebrows. He ignores me and leans down to kiss me. I put my hands on his chest and push him back, just a bit. A month ago, I would have been all over him. We would have tried to stifle our laughter as we ran down the hallway to our bedroom, as mad for each other as we were the first time.

But a lot has happened in the last month and, right now, making love to my husband is not an option. I stare up at the two bullet holes in our living-room wall. They're bigger now. I start to wonder why, but then remember what I came here to do.

'If I say I need space from you, Johnny, that means your whole fucked-up family. I don't want Josef rear-ending me outside the school. I don't want Marko or Anto lurking around outside Mum and Dad's, waiting to escort me to school and back. By the way, it was Anto this evening. But you know that, because he would have been waiting outside in his car when you got home. Right?'

Johnny nods.

'It's driving me insane. You have to stop.' I can't help it, my eyes are filling with tears.

'Okay, I get it. But, Ames, I'm trying to protect you. We just need to get through the next few days and then we'll go away together. Why don't you book something, and we'll leave on the weekend? The three of us, somewhere nice, like Byron. You'd like that, wouldn't you?'

'The job is on Thursday night. Right?'

'It's the last job I'll ever need to do. It's the big one, babe. After this we'll be set.' He tries to pull me back against him, but I spring away like a scared cat. Sitting down on the sofa, I point to an armchair.

'Johnny, you need to listen very carefully. This is the last time I'm telling you. And yes, I am issuing an ultimatum.' Now I've got his full attention. 'We need to leave now. Before the job on Thursday night. You can see Sasha is right on the cusp of understanding his dad is not like other dads. He's not stupid. He looks up to you. He wants to be like you. He'll put it

219

together soon, and what sort of message will you be giving him? Being in a gang is cool?'

He looks devastated, I got him where it hurts. I know there's no way he wants Sasha following in his footsteps.

'We can sell the house remotely,' I continue. 'We've got two hundred and fifty thousand in cash. That's enough to set us up somewhere new, while we both get jobs. Real jobs. Hell, most people never manage to amass that much cash. Don't be greedy.' He has his head in his hands now. This could be working. 'I've got a bad feeling about this job,' I continue. 'And you still haven't told me why I need protecting? Who was following me last night? If you're putting Sasha and me at risk, I will disappear for good. That's what I'll do, Johnny. That's what's at stake for you, right now.'

I've laid it on the line. He needs to understand just how serious I am. I'll put Sasha's welfare before his, every single day of the week.

'Ames, let's talk this through properly, I've got a plan too.'

'The only plan right now is my plan. I mean it. The plan where you agree with me. It's Tuesday night. In the morning you call off the boys. Tell them I'm home and they're all off the hook. We pack up and leave. Tomorrow. I can't tell you how deadly serious I am. You can call your father when we get up north. He'll forgive you, and Branka will be happy. At least you'll be alive.'

Johnny is sitting across from me, poleaxed. He seems older and very tired, but he still doesn't look convinced. I want to punch him. What will it take to get him to change his mind?

'I've told you.' His bloodshot hazel eyes are pleading. 'I can't leave everyone in the lurch. I can't leave Mum and Dad right now. Give me until Friday, Ames. Two days. Can you please just give me two more days?'

I want to relent. I want to walk around the coffee table, sit in his lap and kiss the worry from his face. I want to promise him I will never leave. But I look up at those holes in the wall again and harden my heart.

'Help me load Sasha in the car. I've got to get out of here. I'm going back to Mum and Dad's.'

'Leave him be, he's asleep. I'll stay here on the sofa and you can sleep in our room. You'll have all the space you need tonight, and I'll feel better, knowing you're safe.'

'But I'm not safe here, am I, Johnny? And neither is Sasha. We're leaving. You can help, or you can sit there.'

I march up the hall before I can second-guess myself, and open the door to Sasha's room. He's fast asleep, sprawled across his spaceman sheets, left foot dangling off the bed. Johnny follows me, gently picks up our sleeping son and settles him in the back of my car. Sasha barely stirs.

Johnny holds me by the shoulders. 'Don't you get it, Ames? You're putting yourself and our son at risk, being out there on your own.'

There's such a big part of me wanting to stay, but he has to believe that I'll deliver on my threat to leave him for good. It's the only way I can change his mind.

'You're the one putting us at risk, Johnny. You did this, not me. You want us back? You need to walk away from it all.'

He insists on following us home in the Jeep. It's only as the boom gate closes behind me that I remember he didn't answer my question. Who followed me home last night?

JOHNNY

A loud throbbing roar jolts me awake. After a moment, I work out it's motorbikes. Lots of them. I pull on a pair of jeans and grab my gun from under the pillow. Leaving the lights off, I run to the living room and peer out the window, trying not to be seen. There are at least ten bikies in leathers propped on the lawn in front of the house, revving their engines. I recognise the Hyde twins by their size. I've no idea which one is Slater. They've all got helmets on.

More bikies are driving up and down the street, one of them popping wheelies. What the fuck? The noise is incredible. Lights come on in all the houses I can see from the window. Someone will call the police. I'm going to have to go out and confront these fuckheads. My guts turn to ice as I stick my gun down the back of my jeans and move to the front door. I grab the cricket bat too—it might come in handy if I live long enough to wield it.

Just as I'm about to open the door, the noise changes. I rush back to the living-room window. The bikies are pulling out, one by one, heading away. Damage done. My reputation in this street has gone from bad to worse.

Wide awake, furious and frustrated, I head to the home gym in the back corner of the garage. It's been a couple of weeks since I had a good workout and I might as well make use of the energy coursing through me. My hands are shaking as I bind my wrists and pull on my boxing gloves. I start out with simple combinations on the punching bag hanging from the rafters. Working up the rhythm. I swap over to the speed ball in the corner, right for four, left for four, then alternate hands, over and over, faster and faster. Then back to the bag, dancing around it this time, pounding it with left and right jabs and solid roundhouse hooks, then complicated combinations, until I'm just a punching machine beating the shit out of the hundred-pound bag, sweat flying. Faces appear in front of me, Dad, Marko, MacPherson, Slater. When I finally grind to a halt, I take off the gloves, roll out the mat and give myself one hundred crunches, one hundred squats, then one hundred push-ups.

After a quick shower, I collapse face-first on the bed.

This time, I wake to the sound of my phone ringing. Marko.

'Can you come to your parents' place?'

'Why? Not sure I want to see Dad right now.' My hand goes straight to my jaw as I sit up and check the time—7.30 a.m.

'It is important you come now.' Marko insists. 'You need to talk to the boss, and *Tetka* Branka wants to make you breakfast.'

The thought of my mum's breakfast overrides the memory of how I got my aching jaw.

'Okay. I'll be there in twenty.'

I check myself out in the mirror. Clear-eyed. The midnight work-out did me good. But there's a big purple bruise on my jawline. I have a shower and head over to Mum and Dad's.

The smell of grilling bacon welcomes me. Mum gives me a hug and touches my bruised jaw, before kissing me on both cheeks, a sure sign of a thaw in relations. I hold onto my mama for longer than usual, letting myself relax. I want to unburden myself, let the tears come. She must feel it, because she pats me on the back and pushes me away, handing me a mug of coffee as she points towards the back of the house.

'Your *tata* wait for you. His mood better today. After, you come back here and eat. You too skinny.'

'Thanks, Mum, I'm starving.'

As I walk down the hall, I realise that I don't actually care what my father thinks of me right now; all I care about is Amy and Sasha. I want this over. I want them safe at home.

Dad's in his chair at the end of the table, Marko on his left, as if they haven't moved since I left in disgrace yesterday. I stop a few feet from the table and raise my cup as a salute. Dad and Marko raise theirs in response.

'Sit, son, sit. Marko tell me I owe you apology.'

I sit down slowly, giving myself time to think. I know that cunning look in Dad's eyes—this is a test. Marko looks worried, as though this wasn't the plan.

'I owe *you* an apology, Dad. I should have checked with you first, before I involved the police.'

Dad's face splits into a grin. It's such a rare sight, I can't help but grin back at him. He leans over and slaps me on the shoulder.

'You are right, my son. You are right, you owe me apology

224

and I am big man.' He spreads his arms wide. 'I accept.' His gaze moves away from me to Marko. 'Your cousin, he convince me. This new idea is good idea. Good for us, not for Stanislav. Not for Ink Slater. What you think, son?'

'Right, Dad, you're right, good for us. Bad for everyone else. The way it should be.'

'Marko, look at my son. The way it should be, us here together. Ivan should be here too.' His face falls. 'We take care of that at right time.' He raises his coffee cup again.

Marko mouths *You owe me* and I nod in return.

Dad drains his coffee.

'Marko also tell me Amy and Sasha come back to you last night.'

'Anto told me he followed them to your place after school,' Marko explains, before I get the wrong idea. 'He waited outside until you got home. He told me we could all have the morning off because you would be taking care of it.'

And that's exactly what I thought would happen. I'm not going to admit she didn't stay. Besides, she made me promise— no more tails. She has to be able to trust me, and I have to trust her to be careful.

Dad looks at Marko and then at me. I can almost hear the cogs whirring in his mind as he calculates his next move.

'Now Marko works with you. Wherever you go, Marko goes. Anto as well. You stay together. You protect each other until this is over.' He slaps his palm down on the table and gets up, pronouncement made. Marko and I have already agreed to work together on this job; we exchange wary glances and nod our agreement.

Dad holds up his hand; he's not finished yet.

'You owe Marko big debt, so you treat him with respect. Together we clean up after you.' Dad points a thumb at himself and then rotates it ninety degrees to point at Marko. I'm getting a bad feeling.

'What do you mean, clean up?'

'We clean up your friend Nick. I told you, no loose ends. Now we have all crew onboard for Thursday night.'

My empty stomach flips over.

'Fuck, Dad. Why? That was completely unnecessary.' I shoot a look at Marko, who has the grace to wince as he shrugs. Anto is going to think I was in on it. 'I had a perfectly good plan. I promised Anto. I promised Nick the worst was over. Fuck, fuck, fuck.'

'Grow up, son. You sound like baby. Plans change. Is good for family.' Dad's smile is cruel.

'If it is any consolation to you, Nick was high on the ketamines,' Marko adds, as if it's going to make me feel better. 'He had no idea what was happening, he thought we were going fishing when we took him out to the middle of the river in Baz's boat. I was behind him and used my silencer. He felt no pain. So you owe me for that, too.'

Christ! There's no way Nick had to die. My plan would have worked. What a fucking waste. It's too late to argue about it with my father, or Marko. It's done and I need to let it go. Fuck.

What else will my father decide to change before tomorrow night? There are still all sorts of ways this job could go pear-shaped and we could all end up in jail or dead.

AMY

'What's really going on?' Chaz asks. 'Don't bullshit me this time, it can't just be about you and Johnny fighting.' She sips her rosé.

It's a nice change, relaxing with my best friend under the eucalypts by the school sportsfield. Our reusable bamboo coffee mugs are half-full of wine, but the cooler bag between our deck chairs keeps our nefarious scheme hidden from other parents, who might judge us for drinking on the school grounds. Obviously, my intention never to drink again fled with my hangover. The summer holidays start in two days' time, so there's a sense of anticipation in the air for the kids and parents attending this last athletics session. Jenny is about to start a relay event and Sasha is way over the other side on the high jump.

'Johnny and I do fight, you know,' I answer.

'Stop stalling.'

I sigh and look around. No one can hear us.

'There's some trouble between Johnny's crew and the Serbs.'

'Because of the shootings?'

I nod and Chaz looks puzzled. 'But what about the Italians?'

'Yes, well, the fact that one of the Italians was shot doesn't seem to figure in Milan's plan for getting even with his old enemy Stanislav. He's the head of the Serb crew.'

'And Johnny's supposed to take over Ivan's position in the gang?'

'Something like that.'

'Is it like the mafia, where you have to kill someone to become a "made man"?' Chaz uses her little fingers to make quote signs, so she doesn't have to put her wine down. She's smiling, as if it's all kind of fun and games, but I can also see her frowning behind her sunglasses.

'Johnny's never killed anyone and he's not starting now.'

I can hope.

'I know you left because you want him to choose between the family business and you and Sasha. But there must be a whole lot more to it than you're telling me.'

I've nearly finished my rosé and it's barely touched the sides. I reach down to the cooler bag and position my mug next to the bottle nestled in ice and wait for Chaz to do the same, than I fill them up again. This has to be my last, though. I'm driving.

'Go on, spill. You'll feel better, I promise,' Chaz urges.

I tell her everything—well, almost everything: the drive-by, the ham-fisted protection from the Novak crew, Molly's death…Chaz's free hand is over her mouth, her face a study in shock and horror.

'Last night, I took Sasha home to see his father and told Johnny to cease and desist on the whole protection idea.'

'But why does he think you need to be protected?'

'He thought he saw someone following me home from Frentini's, on Monday night.'

Chaz's hand has gone to her mouth again.

'I've decided it's probably bullshit,' I continue. 'He's over-anxious and wants to keep an eye on me.'

'But why would someone follow you?'

'That's what I've asked him, and he didn't answer. All the more reason for me to think it's bullshit. He's just being over-protective, because we're not under his roof and he has no control over us anymore.'

'Has he ever been controlling like this before?'

'I don't mean controlling like that. He's not usually. At least, I don't think he is.' I sound confused, even to myself. For God's sake, I'm not in one of those abusive relationships.

'But what about you going back to work? Doesn't he always manage to talk you out of it?'

'Yeah, I guess. But I think that's really only a status thing, like "my woman does not need to work because I am a MAN". They're different from us, you know.'

'Who? Men or Croatians?'

'Both! But especially Croatian men!' I laugh. 'He's just paranoid.'

'Well, I suppose he has good reason. Three dead in three weeks. Besides, it must be kind of nice to have a man worry about you.'

'Chaz! You're going to find someone, you know. But you do have to go out on dates for that to happen.'

'Yeah, you're right. One day. But when your guy leaves you when you're pregnant, you kind of give up trusting men.' She puts up a hand. 'I know! I need to get over it.'

'It was ten years ago!'

'I know, I know. E-Harmony, here I come.'

'Those photos I took of you on Saturday afternoon are gorgeous. We'll set up your profile tonight. It'll be fun!' Fun would be good right now.

We clink coffee mugs and look out across the athletics field just as Sasha is running towards the high jump. He leaps and flies over, inches above the bar, landing on a pile of gym mats, then bounces once and lands on his feet, fist-pumping the air as he runs back to the end of the line.

'So what are you going to do next?' Chaz says.

'Seriously? My plan is to get Johnny away from his family and up the coast for a holiday. I told Johnny that if he doesn't leave with me and Sash, we'll go without him.'

'Did you mean it?' Her mouth stays open in dismay.

'Abso-fucking-lutely! I think he understands it's a real ulti-matum, but in terms of inducement, it's been a big fat fail.' I can hear the bitterness in my voice. 'His loyalty to Milan and the rest of the Novaks is proving very hard to shake. But I have to keep trying.'

There's so much more I could tell Chaz, but I think she's had enough shocks for one day.

JOHNNY

Anto waits for a break in the rain before he runs from his front door and jumps into the passenger seat of the Jeep. Marko is already in the back. I pull out and point the car towards the warehouse. I've estimated the time each part of the job will take, but tonight the three of us are doing a run-through to make sure my calculations stack up. We need to be leaving the warehouse and heading to the airport at ten p.m. And we've got fifteen minutes to get into position. Traffic swirls around us, headlights blurring, the squeal of tyres on the wet road.

I glance over at Anto. 'What's wrong?'

'Why would anything be wrong?' Anto stares straight ahead. Maybe he's found out about Nick. I'll try for innocence.

'Well, you might not have noticed, but there's a fucking great scowl on your face. Are you worried or something?'

He finally swings around and glares at me. Pissed off big-time. It takes a lot to get Anto this angry.

'Nah, I'm not worried about the job, Johnny. I'm worried I can't trust you anymore.'

I check Marko's reaction in the rear-view mirror. He's leaning forward, intent. It feels weird having him here when it's usually just me and Anto. Blood rushes to my face.

'What the fuck do you mean?' My turn to get angry.

'I had a little visit from the Hyde boys today.' Anto crosses his arms.

'What the fuck! You're kidding? What did they do?' I turn back to Anto and nearly run up the back of a Toyota Corolla.

'They came up to my front door and knocked on it like a couple of Mormons. But they were in head-to-toe black leathers, with their helmets still on. Twin gimps. Thank God, Lexy was out shopping. Broad fucking daylight. They told me you bailed up their boss Ink Slater yesterday afternoon and threatened to shoot him. On. Your. Own.'

'Yeah, right. Mate, I'm sorry. I should have called you. Pulled you in. I'd just had a big fight with Dad.' I finger the bruise on my jaw, notice I'm doing it and pull my hand away. Marko is frowning at me from the back seat. Looks like he agrees with Anto.

'See, this is what I mean. You're acting fucking crazy. Why the fuck would you go there alone? There's a good chance this meth-head arsehole killed your brother and you decide to just drop in for a chat? What the fuck is wrong with you?'

'I know, it was a completely fucked-up move. I could've been done. Seriously. But they let me go, ordered me to give Dad a message. Slater wants twenty per cent of our take from now on. Like, we pay him for the protection of our activities. Can you believe it?'

Anto nods now, as if it all finally makes sense. Marko sits back, shaking his head.

232

'You did not tell your father or me this morning. Why did you not tell us?'

'As if I could admit to Dad I got beaten in a fight. Didn't even throw a punch. Could have shot Slater and avenged Ivan but got caught out instead. Then I'm gonna tell Dad I got sent home like a dog with a message for him—Hey, Dad, we've got to pay Slater's crew twenty per cent. Yeah, right. Can you even begin to imagine Dad's reaction?'

'Fucking hell.' Anto shakes his head, his anger dissolving.

Marko nods thoughtfully. 'He would not have taken this news well. I understand you not telling him. But what you did? It was stupid.'

'Yeah, yeah. I know. Anyway, I survived. You're the only ones who know and it's gonna stay that way.'

I pull up outside the warehouse and check the time. Five to ten. The traffic conditions won't change in five minutes so we may as well get started on my time check.

'Anto, time us to the airport.'

He fiddles with his phone and gives me the signal. 'Go.'

The rain starts to ease as I head back the way we came, towards the Qantas International Freight building. Sooner or later Anto is going to find out about Nick and it may as well be now.

'While we're in the confessional…Marko, you'd better fill Anto in on what you and Dad got up to last night.'

'We took your friend Nick out into the middle of the Hawkesbury. Now he is with the fishes.'

'Aw, fuck, you didn't? Why? Totally unnecessary. Johnny had the perfect plan!'

Marko shrugs.

'Look, I agree it's completely fucked up, Anto.' I reach over and put my arm around his neck, pull him towards me, then let him go. 'I promised you and I promised Nick. But it's done. Okay? We need to focus now. Get the timing sorted out.' I slap both hands on the steering wheel. 'In twenty-four hours, we'll fuck up the Serbs, plus Slater and his twin gimps. Dad never needs to know about Slater's moronic fucking plan to take over the world.'

AMY

The school hall is packed for the end-of-year concert and the orchestra is making a racket as they tune up at the front. I choose an aisle seat, up the back, in case I have to slip out. Chaz is beside me, the kids in costume waiting in the wings. Thank God Mum has always had a gift for reusing empty paper-towel rolls, cardboard and tinfoil.

Finally, the lights dim and a lone trumpet player stands up and wobbles through three long notes. Next the whole horn section stands, cymbals crash and a kid starts banging on kettle drums—the theme for *2001: A Space Odyssey*. Dressed like astronauts and aliens, children of various ages invade the stage. Sasha and Jenny are front and centre. After a short but dramatic dance sequence, the kids all rush off, leaving the stage littered with tinfoil. The orchestra switches to 'Everything's Alright' and a very young Mary Magdalene flits around the stage, trailed by a bunch of little girls dressed like angels.

'Are they trying to do *Jesus Christ Superstar* in space?' I ask, ten minutes in.

'Either that or *Spacemen Invade Jerusalem, The Musical*,' Chaz replies, sipping on her water bottle. We cover our mouths to stifle our laughter when Sasha loses his cardboard-box helmet during a particularly robust spin.

While I'm videoing, my phone buzzes, a WhatsApp call from Lexy. I slip out into the night to take the call.

'Hi,' Lexy answers. 'They all arrived twenty minutes ago for a poker game I didn't know anything about. So you can imagine how that went down. Anyway, they parked their cars out front and trooped in. I'm talking the whole crew, every last one of them. No one would even accept a drink! Then, a few at a time, they left again through the back garden, out the back gate and into the laneway.'

'Where were they going?'

'I worked out they must have been walking to the warehouse. That's a first. I'm supposed to keep the music on loud until Anto comes home.'

'They're creating an alibi and hoping one of your neighbours complains.'

'Exactly. I took a peek out the front and every spare parking space on our street is taken up by crew cars. Our neighbours will not be happy.'

'Hmmm. Okay. Thanks, Lex.'

'Let's hope they stay safe.'

'That's our role, isn't it? In the dark, hoping they stay safe.' I sound bitter again, not like myself. I fill my lungs and let the breath out with a sigh. 'Anyway. Thanks for keeping me in the loop. Text me again when they get back. Okay?'

'Will do. I can't even watch TV with this bloody music blaring, I'm standing in the backyard so I can speak to you.

Anto's idea of a poker game playlist is Alice in Chains, Red Hot Chili Peppers and a bit of Megadeth thrown in for extra fun. Horrendous. So they better not be too late.'

I thank her, commiserate and say goodbye. Then I call Johnny.

JOHNNY

The warehouse roller doors are closed, but the back door is open and the sound of excited men spills out into the warm night. I feel good as I walk through the crowd, all sixteen of us together for the first time since the funeral. Over in a corner, Dad and Josef are locked in discussion. I ignore them and move between the groups of men. Everyone is dressed in black, white teeth flashing against brown skin. The air seems to crackle with electricity. Jokes are receiving big laughs as the men slap and rib each other, taking the piss or boosting each other, according to who needs what. Fathers, sons and cousins. Everyone related, somehow. Family.

Ammunition loaded, weapons are checked and rechecked. We're using our heaviest arsenal tonight. No reason to leave it here, every reason to take it into the fight. The plan is to threaten and grab, not actually shoot anyone. But if the Serbs fight back, we'll be ready to counterattack.

AMY

'Ames, hang on!' I hear voices, then rustling. Johnny must have his phone pressed to his chest to muffle the sound. I imagine him walking outside the warehouse to take my call. 'Right, that's better.'

He sounds like it's just any old Thursday night. But I know better.

'What are you doing?'

'Sorting a few things out. How's the concert?' When he doesn't want to lie to me, he always answers my question with another question.

'It's a bit weird, but the kids are having fun.' I answer in a monotone, before snapping. 'Seriously, what are you doing?'

Johnny coughs awkwardly. 'So, you're going straight back to your parents' place tonight after the concert, right? I want you to be extra-careful, just for the next day or so, then we can hit the road and head up to Byron, okay? I did what you asked and there's no one tailing you. Everyone's busy, right? Be super-careful.'

239

My skin prickles like a cold wind has sprung up.

'Why? Are you saying we're actually in danger?'

'No Ames, I'm not. But why don't you stay at Chaz's place, tonight? Yeah, that'd be best.'

'I don't think you get it, Johnny. I meant what I said. I don't want this shit in my life anymore!'

He tries to interrupt, but I shout him down.

'You're not listening! I'm done, Johnny. Imagine your life without us. We'll be gone and you won't find us!'

I hang up before he has the chance to reply.

JOHNNY

Back in the warehouse, my confidence is shot and I wish I hadn't answered my phone.

Dad has called the meeting to order. Everyone is seated, all eyes on me. I lever myself up onto a metal bench bolted to the side of the warehouse, keeping my face neutral as I cop a glare from Dad.

'I been talking to Josef.' Dad's voice is deep, slow, deliberate. 'I think we go back to old plan. Is more simple if we leave some drugs in van with Stanislav. After we scram, police find Serbs with drugs. Simple. Easy. No need we involve Ink Slater and his bikies.'

Fuck. Some of the men are nodding amid murmurs of agreement. I need to turn this around. Doesn't Dad remember those stick figures? For fuck's sake—Ink Slater is a threat to Amy and Sasha. And there's the message I was supposed to give Dad. Fuck Josef. I can't believe my father's been swayed by the dumbest member of our crew. The guy may be Dad's younger brother, but he's as thick as a plank. And why this obsession with Stanislav, when he's not the enemy here—he's the opportunity?

Anto sees the panic on my face. He stands up to speak and the group falls silent. 'Boss. What you say goes.' He takes a deep breath. 'But I can't help thinking we should stick to Joh...the new plan. It's not as simple, you're right, but it's gonna be really effective.'

Anto sits back down quickly and looks like he wants to throw up. The men's faces are slack with shock. Anto has never publicly disagreed with my father. Only Baz or Josef, the most senior members of the crew, would dare. Dad's eyes bulge as he glares at Anto and starts to growl, his face turning red. Then Marko stands up.

'Uncle Milan, you are right. You are always right. And I think maybe Anto is right too. If we plant the ecstasy on Ink Slater, then the bikies get the blame. The police will think it was the bikies, the Serbs will think it was the bikies. It is not so simple. But it is better we stick with the new plan.'

'You want we stick with new plan? Anto? Marko? Maybe I not like new plan. I like simple best. Fuck up Stanislav Vucavec. Always best plan.'

The men are confused, all the confidence and camaraderie gone, each one turning to his neighbour. Which plan is best? I'm paralysed, my face frozen. What the fuck would Ivan do right now?

I jump down from the benchtop. My shoes thump on the concrete and I stand tall. All eyes turn to me again.

'You're right, Dad. We need to fuck up Stanislav, and we will. You don't think he's been comped twenty million bucks worth of ecstasy, do you? Every Vucavec, both sides of the pond, will be in hock up to their eyeballs to fund this much dope. And we're about to take it from them. He'll be fucked, all right. The families in Belgrade will probably send a hitman over to make sure Stanislav can't screw them, or anyone else, ever again.' The men are following, liking the story. My father still looks angry.

'So what does setting up Ink Slater's crew achieve? It takes the heat off us from the Serb side, doesn't it? We don't want some hitman from Belgrade coming up behind us in a dark alley, do we?' Heads shake. Nasty thought.

'Plus, plus...' I step forward, wagging a finger. 'Ink Slater gets caught with enough E to ensure he spends the rest of his miserable life in jail, where he will get his skinny, tattooed arse fucked sideways.'

My father is still unconvinced; he couldn't care less about Slater's arse. I have to use my trump card. I let my hands form fists.

'This is not just about money. This is about avenging Ivan's murder.' I growl. 'Michael Vucavec was shot. A week later Ivan was killed. Then it was Tony Fazzini. Who stands to gain the most from pitting the Serbs, Croats and Italians against each other? Ink Slater. Who had the most to gain from murdering my brother? Think about it.' Even my father is nodding now, because what I'm saying makes sense.

'On Monday night, a black Mercedes ML63 belonging to Ink Slater followed Amy to her parents' place. His crew broke into my home and stole Ivan's gun.' The men gasp. 'And they left this behind.' I pull the crumpled note out of my pocket and hand it to Anto, who passes it on. I give every man in the warehouse an opportunity to check out those stick figures and get their heads around the threat.

'Who's next? Is it one of your wives or children?' The men look horrified. Women and children are never brought into this game. I pause then keep going. 'Who's next?' I repeat. 'Don't those words imply there have already been others killed? It's as though he's admitting he shot Michael, Ivan and Tony, and now he's trying to intimidate us by threatening our families.

'We need to fuck up Stanislav and take the E from him, without killing anyone or getting ourselves killed. We need to leave no trace. And we need to plant the seed that this job was all Slater's idea and his crew were behind it. Then we're in the clear and we don't add fuel to *the war*.' Our unimaginative name for the last war between the Croats and the Serbs.

'Slater murdered Ivan.' Saying it makes me realise I'm right. There's no other explanation. 'Now he wants to hurt my wife and child.' I take a breath and growl: 'I promised you revenge—tonight is just the first step, then I will bury Ink Slater.'

The men are on their feet now.

I look over at my father and register his surprise. Dad knows he's been outplayed.

'What do you reckon, Dad? How about we fuck up Stanislav Vucavec and we fuck up Ink Slater?'

'Is good plan, son. We fuck Stanislav and Ink Slater gets blame. We fuck them both. Then you kill the man who murdered my son.'

The men roar their approval.

Outside the warehouse, I gaze up at the stars while the rest of the crew pack the vans and check weapons one last time. I'm worried about Amy. There's pain in the back of my throat as I

244

finger the crudely drawn note in my pocket. What if I did what she wanted and walked away, right now?

Yeah, right.

I have to get the crew safely through this job, then prove once and for all that Slater killed Ivan. As long as he's on the loose, he's a threat to Amy and Sasha.

Sure, I might get captured or killed, but Amy is young and beautiful, she can marry again. Someone with a normal job. She might even be better off without me.

Nah, fuck that. Amy and Sasha will be safe at Chaz's place. After this is all over, she'll come back to me. Everything is going to work out fine.

'Hey, Johnny! You coming or what, mate?'

Everyone is seated in the stolen vehicles. Brick and Blocker are on big black Harleys. The two brothers are the right size— big. Dressed in head-to-toe black leather, black helmets and full-face shields, they look unnervingly like the Hyde twins.

The driver's door to a dark-grey Jeep stands open, waiting. Nice of them to steal me a Jeep. Anto is in the front passenger seat, Marko is in the back, our new formation. I check my watch and climb in. The engine growls. I lead the way down the warehouse driveway, out onto the street, towards the airport. Right on schedule.

At ten p.m. on a Thursday night, traffic is usually light in the western suburbs of Sydney. Tonight is no exception and the convoy stays together. I can feel the adrenaline building, but my movements are slow and deliberate. The Jeep is cruising right on the speed limit, the rest of the crew streaming out behind me.

Anto is drumming his fingers on the armrest. In the

rear-view mirror, Marko is leaning back, eyes half-closed, as though tonight is no more than a ride into town for a few beers.

Our four vehicles and two motorbikes slow as we pass the entrance to the Qantas International Freight building on Link Road. At this time of night, there are plenty of spaces to park opposite the entrance.

I back into my designated spot, closest to the gate. The rest of the crew drive past, then each vehicle backs into a space. Headlights and engines are killed, but the streetlights are bright, CCTV cameras everywhere. We slouch low in our seats, caps pulled down over our faces, no masks yet. With their face shields on, there's no way Brick and Blocker can be ID'd. We have half an hour to wait.

The only one way in or out of the International Freight facility is through the security gate, where ID and freight documents are checked before the boom gate is raised. Parked only twenty metres away, we have a clear view of all vehicles coming in and out.

Anto's binoculars are trained on the gate. We know Stanislav will be driving. We don't know if he'll have any guard vehicles, or if he'll just rely on a few discreetly armed men in the back of his van.

Additional vehicles obviously add complications, especially since they probably won't be allowed into the facility and would have to take up positions in empty spaces along the very rear-to-kerb parking strip we're using.

This part of the plan has the most holes in it. Crew members on both sides went to school together, played soccer together, back in the days when we all came from Yugoslavia. Without masks, the chances of recognition are high. And if a Serb crew car backs into a parking spot and notices that the car next door is full of big blokes wearing balaclavas? It will get ugly, fast.

Now that everyone has their earpieces and mikes on, I check in with the team leader in each car.

'Dad, how's it going over there?'

'How's it going, he asks me. What you think? Is lovely evening.'

'Josef, everything okay?'

'Okay.'

'Baz?'

'All good here.'

'Stump?'

'Yep.'

'Brick?'

'It's a bit fucking hot in all this leather, mate.'

'Keep quiet now—until I confirm Stanislav's van's here.'

My phone vibrates in the centre console. I snatch it up and see Amy's face. There's no way I can talk to her now. Every member of the crew is relying on me. Tonight, I'm in charge. Amy will have to wait until this is over. Her ultimatum rings in my ears and pain shoots through my chest. God, please make her wait.

I clock Stanislav's van approaching from the left, a full fifteen minutes early. The white Econovan pulls up to the boom gate. No attendant cars or bikes. Good choice, mate.

I look over at Anto and answer his grin with a snarl of triumph. I exhale a breath I didn't know I was holding. Marko punches the back of the seat. It's on.

'He's here,' I announce to the crew in a low voice. 'Now, hold still, engines on, but no headlights until you start moving.

He's got to go in and collect the shipment. We don't know how long this will take, but be prepared, it could take a while. As soon as the van reappears on the other side of the exit barrier, I pull out. You know the rest.' Engines rumble back to life in response.

'Yes, we know what we do, son. Is good. Is lovely evening. Don't fuck up.'

'Right. Don't speak Croatian. Don't kill anyone. We do it fast, we're in and out. Does everyone know what they're doing?'

'Does everyone know what they're doing? My son talk too much. Should enjoy evening.'

I draw in another deep breath and let it out. Crank the air-con up a bit; my back is wet with sweat.

Stanislav's van is outside an open warehouse door on the left of the facility. The place is lit up like daylight. It's not hard to keep track, but I check with Anto anyway.

'What can you see, mate?'

'Stanislav got out of the driver's side with some paperwork and walked into the warehouse. Someone else, I think it's Stanislav's cousin, Phil, got out of the passenger seat. He's staying with the van. He's talking to someone in the back. Can't see who or how many, but someone just passed Phil a smoke.'

'Okay, everyone, Anto's confirmed we've got Stanislav as the driver, and he's gone into the warehouse. Looks like Phil Vucavec is in the front passenger seat, and one or more crew are in the back of the van.'

'Not matter how many in back. We crush them,' says Dad.

Ten minutes crawl by, Anto occasionally relaying information.

'He's heading back towards the exit,' Anto says with more

emphasis, his hands rock-steady on the binoculars.

'It's on. Stick to the plan, everyone. Remember, no Croatian!' It's hard to keep the excitement out of my voice.

'*Nemoj se zajebavati!*' Don't fuck up, says Dad.

I ignore my father and guide the Jeep onto Link Road, accelerating towards Airport Drive. In my rear-view mirror, I see Josef pull out and follow. Marko is kneeling on the back seat. He has the best view of what happens next.

'Stanislav is through the exit barrier. He is right behind Josef.'

I slap the steering wheel with an open palm. Yes!

'The boss is now behind Stanislav. Stump is behind the boss.' Even Marko's normally deadpan voice seems to have an edge of excitement as he gives us the update.

I turn left onto Airport Drive, pull down my balaclava and tap the talk button on my mike. 'Masks on now.'

'Stanislav is turning left too. He is coming over the bridge with us. The stupid fuck.'

Our convoy rolls onto the Marsh Street Bridge. A Toyota Prius is driving at an average speed on the opposite side of the bridge, but to me time has slowed to a crawl. The balaclava feels hot but comforting; it's part of my job, a job I've never done without Ivan, but the training has kicked in. My breathing and heart rate have slowed.

I glance out the window. As his car floats past, the guy in the Prius doesn't look over. The road is deserted in front of me. Behind me: Josef's Ford Transit, Stanislav's Econovan, my father's Hilux, then Stump's Explorer. Like ducklings in a pond. I can't see the bikes, but I know they're behind Stump, ready for their part in the show.

Precisely in the middle of the bridge, I jam on the brakes and turn the Jeep to the right, towards the metre-high concrete slab that divides the bridge into east and westbound lanes. Josef hits the skids and turns his van to the left. Now both westbound lanes are blocked. Stanislav has to screech to a stop to avoid slamming into the side of one or the other car. Marko and I are out first, sawn-off and semiautomatic trained on Stanislav and Phil.

I watch Stanislav check his rear-view mirrors. The Hilux and Explorer have pulled the same manoeuvre behind him, blocking his escape. The two bikes come around on either side of the Hilux and Explorer.

Josef's team piles out of the Transit, all guns trained on Stanislav's van.

Anto moves towards Stanislav, motioning him out. He was chosen as our spokesman because he's a good mimic. I asked him to broaden his accent so he could copy Slater's speech patterns.

'Keep your hands where we can see 'em. Get outta the van. Everyone. Now! Hands up!'

Stanislav and Phil do as they're told. There's no movement from the back of the van.

'Tell your mates in the back of the van to gedout or we'll start shootin' fru the door panel. Your call.'

'Get out, boys!' Stanislav shouts, looking around frantically for something, anything, to get him out of this trap.

Anto keeps a safe distance, gun pointed at Stanislav. No movement from the back of the van.

'Make yourself useful. Open the slidin' door. Slowly. Understand? Get your dickhead mates in the back out. Slowly,

Okay? Don't do anyfing stupid.' Anto actually sounds like Slater, and he's all business. I can't help smiling.

Stanislav takes another look behind him. I line myself up to see what he's seeing—a huge bear of a man with a balaclava obscuring his face and a Bren machine gun in his hands. Two guys on Harleys with automatic weapons. Guns everywhere, all trained on him. Stanislav seems to grasp that he has to open the sliding door, but he does it fast.

Three men tumble out of the side of the van. A dark mess of arms and legs, guns drawn, a chorus of safeties clicking off. It's about to turn into a bloodbath.

Stanislav yells at his men. 'Mick, Zoran, Franco! Drop your guns!'

Two guns clatter to the road, but the tall guy in the middle looks like he wants to take us on. Out of the corner of my eye, I see Marko step forward. A shot cracks through the still night and the Serb crumples to the ground.

The other two men take a step away, as though death is contagious.

'Everyone round the other side of the van. Now!' Anto's voice is steely. Our men in balaclavas prod the remaining four Serbs around the other side of the van.

I move forward to check the pulse of the man on the ground. He's been shot in the heart, no exit wound, very little blood. I can't fucking believe it. This was not supposed to happen. Marko stands behind me, staring down at the man. I glance across at him. His eyes are blank, unreadable. I give him the signal to stay put. I'll deal with him later.

In silence, our crew throws eight boxes the size of micro-waves from one set of hands to the next, stowing them in the tray of Dad's Hilux, before securing the tarp. I pull a penknife and Ziploc sandwich bag from my back pocket. With gloved hands, I dig out a small piece of grey carpet from the floor of the van and put it in the plastic bag. Insurance.

I point to Marko and Josef. Then the dead man. Then the van. I move back to my observer position, as Marko and Josef stow the body in the back of Stanislav's Econovan.

'It's Zoran Milovic.' I'm close enough to hear Josef whisper to Marko, who glares at him and puts a finger to his lips.

A small white car is approaching from the airport side of the bridge, heading towards Dad's truck. A woman driver.

Dad motions with his hand, *go back, get out of here*. He brings his machine gun up, so she can see its silhouette in the night. She screeches to a halt twenty metres away and reverses fast in a swerving, panicky motion, until she's well off the bridge. The car disappears around the bend.

The Serbs are now seated against the side of the Econovan, hands and feet bound, gaffer tape slapped across their mouths. I jump in the Jeep and move it forward, out of the way; Marko slides into the back. Dad and his team pile into his Hilux. They drive past the Serbs and head off the bridge. Brick and Blocker rev their Harleys as they pass the bound Serbs. Stump's team follows.

Another car. This time an old Nissan 300ZX, souped up, 'Bohemian Rhapsody' pumping, filled with teenage boys singing as they speed past on the opposite side the bridge. Oblivious.

Backing away from the Econovan, the remaining men in balaclavas jump into Josef's Transit. Anto leaps into the passenger seat beside me and I check my watch. Four minutes since we drove onto the bridge. I pull out first, followed by Josef. In my rear-view mirror, I see Stanislav lurch to his feet. He leans against his van for balance, glaring after us.

The first sirens howl in the distance. Adrenaline throws out one last spike, but I can tell the sirens are coming from behind me, not in front. I stay at the speed limit, off the bridge, down Marsh Street, left onto West Botany, right on Wickham, left on Bellevue. Backstreets, Josef following, all the way back to the warehouse.

AMY

After the concert, we brought the kids back to Chaz's place. They both ran around as if they'd had three glasses of red cordial, before falling asleep in the cubby they built under the kitchen bench.

We set up Chaz's dating profile last night, so we're checking out the men she's been matched with and having a bit of a laugh. But I'm preoccupied, not exactly scintillating company.

'You're in another world, love. What's going on now?' Chaz asks.

'Johnny told me I should keep Sasha home from school tomorrow. He's on a job tonight, and he must be expecting some kind of backlash.'

'Backlash? Holy fuck! Really?' She closes the lid on her laptop and leans over to grab my hands. 'We should go to the police. Stick the kids in the car and drive down to Liverpool Police Station, right now.'

'And tell them what? We think my husband might be murdering the head of the local Serb gang tonight? If you happen to see him around, would you mind bringing him home safely?'

'Do you honestly think that's what he's doing?' She looks horrified.

'No, I don't.' I sigh. 'But he's up to something.'

'We could say you feel like you're in danger.'

'And why do you feel like you're in danger, ma'am?' I affect a deep voice. 'What can I say that won't get Johnny *and* his crew in trouble? I'm willing to leave to protect Sasha, but I'm not throwing Johnny under a bus.'

'So what can we do?' Chaz looks around as if she's working out how to fortify the place.

If someone really has been following me, then just being here puts Chaz and Jenny in danger too. The thought of something bad happening to these two beautiful girls forces me to make up my mind.

'In the morning, I'll tell Sasha he doesn't have to go to school because we're heading up the coast and his dad is going to meet us there. I'll throw our suitcases in the car and leave after peak hour. We'll be in Kempsey by lunchtime. Somewhere near Byron by dinner.'

'How long will you stay there?' Chaz looks like she's trying not to cry.

'I don't know. Until Christmas?' I have no idea.

'Okay, that's less than two weeks away. Hopefully everything will be sorted by then.'

Sasha and I need to leave Chaz's now. I fold back the sheet hiding the two kids and gently pull Sasha to his feet. He leans against me, more asleep than awake.

'Why don't you stay here? I'll blow up the mattress again.

It only takes a minute.' Chaz is blocking me, one hand on my shoulder.

No way. 'We'll be fine.' I look her straight in the eyes. 'Honestly.'

'I wanna stay here, Mum.' Sasha grizzles softly.

'I've got a surprise for you tomorrow, but it means we need to go home now.'

'Is Dad coming home too?'

'Soon. Come on, kid, let's move it so Chaz and Jenny can go to bed.'

Johnny wanted us to stay here, but I'm not putting my best friend in danger. Besides, I want a good night's sleep— impossible on that blow-up mattress. I've got a long drive tomorrow.

I follow Sasha as he sleepwalks out to the Mini, then help him into the back seat and strap him in.

My mind is in overdrive as I set off towards Mum and Dad's. I can't keep procrastinating. If I don't deliver on my ultimatum, how can I expect anything to change? Johnny has to be convinced that I can disappear with Sasha—otherwise he'll never leave his father behind.

I'll pack the suitcases tonight and call Sasha's teacher, Mrs Glen, in the morning. If we drive all day tomorrow, we could be swimming in the cool blue ocean on Saturday.

I pull up at the stop sign one street away from Mum and Dad's. A Harley is coming up the road on my left. I wait for it to go past, but it slows down and comes to a stop in front of me. What the hell? Then a black SUV pulls up beside me on the wrong side of the road. I'm hemmed in. A huge man gets out and bends down to look in at me. A black balaclava. All I can see are two blue eyes staring at me.

It feels as if I'm falling from a great height.

He points a gun at me, taps the window twice, then aims the gun at Sasha in the back seat. Sasha doesn't make a sound. He must be asleep. Dear God, please don't let him wake up and see this man pointing a gun at him.

I'm paralysed. My ears are full of buzzing sounds. The guy with the gun taps the window again. Then he aims the gun back at Sasha. I finally get it.

I open the window.

'Whatever you want, you can have. Please don't hurt my son.' I keep my voice low, desperate not to wake Sasha.

'Both of you, get in the back of the car.' He points to the SUV with his gun. 'Now.'

That line about never, ever getting into a stranger's car flashes through my mind. The worst possible thing you can do. Run. Scream. Anything. But do not get in the back of the car.

I hear Sasha's door open behind me and whip around to tell him to get back in, but the guy from the Harley is unfastening Sasha's seatbelt. With the door open, the inside light has come on, so I can see him. He's tall and skinny. Over his balaclava, he holds a finger to his lips. Tattoos snake out of his black leather gloves, up and around his scrawny arms, and disappear under a black biker vest. An icy fist clamps around my heart. Sasha doesn't stir. The tattooed man has Sasha in his arms. He's carrying my son away from me! I lunge back, but the door closes. He carries Sasha around the back of my car to the open back door of the SUV.

257

A scream burbles up from deep inside me and erupts. Sasha startles awake and instantly freaks out. He starts laying punches on the guy, who throws him in the back seat and closes the door. The windows are tinted. I can't see my son.

The tattooed guy turns to look at me. 'Are you stayin' there or comin' wiv us?'

As if I have a choice.

I open the car door as fast as I can, hoping to wind the first guy, who's still sandwiched between my car and the SUV. It's as if my door has hit a brick wall. He doesn't even flinch. But he does move back to give me more room. I grab my handbag, desperate to get to my phone or better still, my gun. The tattooed man reads my mind.

'Hand it over. Now, Amy.'

He knows my name. I want to vomit. I pass him my bag.

Sticking his hand inside, he pulls out my phone.

'Pincode, Amy?'

I blurt it out in a shaky voice, wishing he wouldn't keep saying my name in that creepy tone.

'Thank you. Now get in the back, Amy. Keep quiet and no one gets hurt. Okay?'

I get in with Sasha, who is huddled in the far corner of the back seat, white-faced and shivering. I slide over and take him in my arms.

In the rear-view mirror another set of blue eyes peers out from the driver's balaclava. This guy looks as big as the first guy. I feel as if we're moving forwards, but it's an illusion—my Mini is being backed up and parked. Must be the guy with the tattoos.

I squeeze Sasha to me, rocking him.

'Don't worry. I'm here. No one is going to hurt you.'

'That's right. All you have to do is put these on.' The first guy is now in the front passenger seat, twisting around to face us, two strips of packing tape in his outstretched hand. 'Use it as a gag. The boy first, then you.'

When I hesitate, he brings the gun up between the two front seats and points it at me. Sasha starts to whimper. I move to comply and the gun disappears. I brush Sasha's hair away from his face and gag him, trying not to sob as I do it. Then I kiss him on the cheek and gag myself. The tape is sticky and hard. It's going to hurt when it comes off.

'Hands out. You first this time.' Black plastic cable ties, like garbage bag ties, only bigger.

I hold out my hands. He zips up the cable, tight.

'Now the boy.'

Sasha has watched the process, his eyes wide with terror. He offers his wrists.

'I'm going to put sacks over your heads and then you're gonna lie down on the back seat.'

As he pulls a black sack over my head, I smell unwashed hair and try not to gag. I can still see some light through the fabric, but not enough. I've got the shakes. I clench my teeth together to stop them chattering.

'Lie down. Now!'

I arrange myself on the back seat, Sasha spooned in front of me, between my bound arms. The seat belt is digging into my back. I squeeze him again, trying to convey reassurance, but he must feel my heart pounding a million beats to the second. He brings up his bound hands to pat me on the shoulder, as if to say, we're okay. He's trembling like a baby bird. The car begins to move.

JOHNNY

Back in the warehouse, the mood's not exactly sombre, but we're all quiet. It turns out Lexy is related by marriage to the dead guy, Zoran Milovic. Marko has said nothing since the shooting. The rest of the crew are keeping their distance.

Anto has used his ecstasy test kit and looks impressed, his eyebrows halfway up his forehead. He gives the haul the thumbs-up as Dad supervises the count. Each of the eight boxes we pulled out of Stanislav's van is full of vacuum-sealed packs of pale-pink pills. Each pack is about the size of a sandwich and holds two thousand pills. Each box carries two hundred bags, or four hundred thousand pills, except for the eighth box, which is only half-full. All up, there are three million ecstasy tabs. Not bad for a Thursday night out with the boys.

The half-full box sits open on a table in the middle of the warehouse. Anto transfers seven sandwich-sized bags to a grey plastic shopping bag destined for under Ink Slater's bed.

Along with the arsenal, Baz and Josef store the drugs under the false floor of our new storage pit. The grey Jeep is up on the hoist, being dismembered by Bigsie, Shrimp and Fibs. The other stolen vehicles wait their turn; the truck out the back will take care of the carcasses.

Once the count is complete and order is restored, Dad motions for everyone to sit down. We all resume our regular seats and benchtops.

'We did good job tonight. Is shame about Zoran Milovic. But he choose to be in this business. Sometimes this happen.' Dad doesn't even glance at Marko. Instead he motions me forward to address the group.

I grow an inch as I take my place standing beside him, my mind occupied with likely outcomes now that Zoran Milovic's death has increased our risk tenfold.

'Stanislav and his crew will probably spend tonight in jail.' I pause to get their full attention. 'Victims or perps, they've got a dead body in their van. It's gonna be pretty obvious to the cops that Zoran was killed by someone else. Obviously, the gun won't be found.' At this point, I stop and look directly at Marko, who nods. But he doesn't look even vaguely guilty. Doesn't he get the jeopardy he's put us all in?

'In New South Wales, when someone gets killed while committing a crime, *everyone* involved gets done for murder if the sentence for the original crime is more than twenty-five years.' I see the faces around me change as they take in what I'm saying. 'And I think we can safely say trafficking three million ecstasy tabs would get us more than twenty-five years apiece.'

Now everyone understands the implications. If we get caught, we could all be facing a murder charge. Not just Marko, all of us. I look back at my cousin and detect the hint of an apology in his eyes. Does he really get it?

'We want the Serbs out of jail as soon as possible. When Stanislav hears about Ink Slater getting caught with a load of ecstasy, we want him in a position to take the law into his own hands. As long as the cops don't find anything else in his van, they should let them all go. And we also have to hope Stanislav is convinced it was the bikies. I reckon Anto did a bloody good job tonight.' I wait and, as I hoped, the men start to clap. Anto scores a couple of back slaps and some gentle ribbing.

'Yeah, mate, you sounded like a complete yobbo,' says Shrimp, and the mood lifts.

'Don't give him a big head, we've still got a job to do.' I point to the shopping bag full of E sitting on the table over to my right.

'Tonight, Ink Slater will end up sleeping on one hundred thousand bucks worth of ecstasy. I know a hundred K seems a lot to use as a decoy, but he needs to go down for a long time.'

I look at Dad, who nods and rotates his hand: keep going.

'Marko, Anto and I will deal with Slater. The boys pulling the cars and bikes apart will stay here and get it done. Those vehicles need to be history by sunrise. Everyone else, go home. Be quiet. Be careful. No talking about tonight on your mobiles. No talking anywhere. Not at the pub, not at home. Stay out of trouble. Dad's got his job cut out for him shifting the E. Give him the space to get it done. Don't come whining to him for your share. You'll get it when you get it.' I glance at my father, who nods and holds up his hand. He'll finish.

'You do what Johnny said. No talk. No collections. No deliveries and no drugs. You do anything to bring attention, I kill you myself.'

•

Just before midnight, Anto, Marko and I walk the three blocks to Anto's place in silence. You never know if someone is following, listening. We hear the music blaring as we turn down his back lane. There may have been complaints, but the police won't be called if we shut down the 'party' now. We stroll through the back gate, then the back door. Anto turns off the music, picks up Lexy and spins her around, before depositing her back on the floor with an exuberant kiss. Marko and I just say thanks and keep walking out the front of the house.

Once we're all in my Jeep, Anto and I start jabbering at once.

'That was awesome!' Anto punches the air.

'We actually pulled it off! Well, Zoran getting whacked wasn't exactly part of the plan.' I glance in the rear-view mirror. Marko is looking out the window.

'Could you work out what the fuck was happening, when they all fell out the back of that van?' Excitement is making Anto's voice higher than usual, a phenomenon that always makes me laugh.

'All I could see was guns,' I reply.

'I know him, this Zoran Milovic, from before.' Marko's voice is flat.

Anto and I look at each other.

'When? During the war?' I ask.

'Yes. I met him once. At the beginning of the war.' He sighs and rubs his eyes. He looks up and catches my eye in the mirror. 'I know it was not our plan. But I recognised him. He had a gun. I killed him. It is done.'

'Yeah, right, mate. Well, it's a complication, but I'm fucking glad it wasn't one of us copping a bullet straight through the

263

heart.' Any anger I felt towards my cousin has ebbed away. I start thinking of places to toss the gun on our way to Bankstown.

'Hey!' Anto sounds excited. 'What if we hide Marko's gun at Slater's place?'

'Fucking brilliant idea.' I slap him on the back. Marko almost smiles. He leans back, relaxed again.

Twenty minutes later, we're driving slowly past Ink Slater's house. No black Mercedes SUV in the driveway. No lights on inside. Wondering if he's out with his mates, I pull over a few houses down and turn the engine off.

After checking our radios are still working, we all get out of the car. Anto walks around the front and jumps into the driver's seat. The night is still balmy, but not stifling. The cooling car engine ticks loudly in the otherwise silent street.

Marko carries the plastic bag full of drugs inside his zipped-up black hoodie. Our guns tucked into the back of our jeans, we move swiftly up the street. When we hit Slater's driveway, we pull on our balaclavas, crouch down and crab across the concrete front yard. Manoeuvring ourselves sideways down the narrow gap between the two houses, we stay below the height of the first window, until we reach the second. Keeping most of my head under the sill, I peer into the dark room.

This time the chest-high sash window is closed, but there's enough light coming from the streetlamp for me to see the lock hasn't been turned. Several layers of paint have gummed up the works. When I point this out to Marko, he nods, pulls a chisel out of his back pocket and slips it between the bottom of the window and the sill, levering the window up an inch.

With my gloved hands in the gap, I slide the panel up.

There's barely a creak of resistance from the grooves holding it in place. Slater must have needed an escape route in the past. To get clear of his drug-fucked father? I feel a pang of empathy. Marko is looking at me expectantly. I cup my hands together to give him a leg-up. There's enough room for him to perch on the sill before ducking his head and swinging around to lower himself gently onto the floor of bedroom. He clicks on his pencil-thin flashlight.

We both hear the Harley approaching, even as our ear-pieces squawk into life.

'Slater's arriving, you'd better get out of there!' Anto's whisper seems unnecessarily loud.

The Harley growls up the driveway. Marko puts the flash-light in his mouth, lies on his back and shimmies under the bed to attach the plastic bag of ecstasy tabs. His legs shift as he pulls out his gun, which receives the same treatment. Marko works quickly, wriggling back out as the bike engine dies.

We hear the garage door being pulled down just as he hauls himself back up onto the windowsill, spins and jumps to the ground like a black cat. A light comes on at the back of the house. We slide the window down, exhaling synchronised breaths when it closes without a sound, then slink around the front of the house. I peer up the driveway as another light comes on down the back. Motioning for Marko to follow me, we run back to the Jeep. Anto has the engine running. Even though no one is chasing us, relief floods my body as we head off into the night. By the time we hit the next corner, we're laughing.

AMY

All I can hear is the blood pounding in my ears. The urge to scream again is coming from deep inside my chest, but the gag means I can only groan. I have to stop shuddering, stay in control. For Sasha.

Unshed tears are blocking my nose. I'm going to suffocate! I need to get my hands up to my mouth and rip off the tape! But they're cable-tied in front of Sasha, my left arm caught underneath him. I blow hard through my nose to clear it, then drag in a lungful of air, filtered through the rancid sack. It still feels like I'm choking, I want to breathe through my mouth! I force myself to breathe out and in again. Slow it down. Slow it down. I pull Sasha closer; he's twitching slightly, but his breathing is steady. He doesn't seem to be panicking, not like me.

All the clues were there, for God's sake! But who are these men? What kind of beef do they have with Johnny? What's he done? It must be the Serbs. Who else could it be? My breathing is speeding up again and I'm getting car sick as we make a left turn and, moments later, a right. Then we stop and I hear the deep growling of a Harley motor revving, right beside my head. The bike accelerates and we move forward fast. I swallow down the bile rising in my throat and try to use my feet against the door to hold us in place on the back seat. My hands are already going numb.

What about the door handle? Can I get it open with my foot? Why? So I can throw Sasha and myself out into moving traffic? I could kick the driver in the back of the head! But what happens if he crashes the car? Do we all die? Get the car door open, that's the best option. But I've got sneakers on and I can't even find the handle. I try to ease one shoe off. The car makes another right and speeds up. We're on a freeway. I can't do anything right now. I concentrate on my breathing, banishing all thought, repeating the word nothing, nothing, nothing. Over and over.

Where are we going? Are they taking us out into the bush to kill us? Sasha is only ten, for Christ's sake! He hasn't even lived yet! Why didn't I just leave town? What was I waiting for? Johnny to wise up and leave with us? I'm such a fucking idiot. I'm the reason Sasha's in danger. I hope the guy with the tattoos locked my car, otherwise someone will have stolen it. Fuck! Who cares about my car? Sasha is quiet now, only an occasional twitch. I think he's falling asleep. Thank God.

We've been going straight and fast for a while now. I hear the sound of an electronic toll connecting to the tag inside the car. Where are we? It feels as if we've been in the back seat for about forty minutes. We're slowing down. I can hear the indicator, then we turn right. The two men haven't said a word.

Sasha is limp in my arms. He must be asleep. I can't feel my hands or my left arm anymore. I hope they didn't tie the cable tie as tight on Sasha. I need to pee. Why didn't I go before I left Chaz's place? How was I supposed to know this would happen? I'm going to have to get their attention. The car slows again, starts to reverse and then stops. What's happening?

'Okay. This is the tricky bit.' It's the first guy, his voice is high-pitched for such a big man. No discernible accent, but he could be a Serb who was born here. 'We'll take your son up first, then you. You need to behave, so no one else gets hurt. Are we clear?'

Up? Up where?

'Nod your head if you understand.'

Distraught and confused, I nod anyway.

The front passenger door opens and the car rises as the man gets out. Now he's behind me, opening the tailgate. I hear tools clanging in the cargo space. Please, don't pick up a shovel. Then the back door opens, near my head. I struggle to sit up.

'No, stay there.'

I lie still again. He lifts my arms and sits Sasha up in the space on the seat in front of me. Sasha wakes and starts thrashing around, elbowing me in the breast. It hurts like hell, but I don't make a sound.

'Sasha. Stop!' barks the man. Then more softly, 'You don't want me to have to hurt your mum, do you?'

Sasha stiffens, I feel him shake his head back and forth. I want to put my arms back around him, but the guy's hold on my arms is like a vice. Pins and needles shoot up my left arm as the blood rushes back. I want to shake it, but I can't. The man is blocking the light, leaning over us, garlic on his breath.

Listen! I can hear distant music, laughter, then two cars beeping at each other. I can smell car fumes through the sack.

Where are we? In the city? At least we're not out in the bush, alone with these horrible men.

The guy gripping my arms releases them. 'Amy, bring your hands back down into your lap now.'

My left arm and both hands don't belong to me anymore, but I force my body to comply as I feel the scratchy texture of wool on my skin. He's wrapping Sasha in a blanket.

'Sasha. Your mum will stay here with my brother. I'm going to carry you upstairs. All you have to do is pretend to be asleep. You won't give me any problems, will you? Otherwise you know what happens? We hurt your mum.'

I can feel Sasha nodding his head slowly. I wish I could tell him to do what the man says. But the tape is stuck fast. I should have tried to scrape it off against the seat under my face! Why did I just lie there like a lump? I can feel his arms between me and Sasha. Then there's a grunt and Sasha is gone.

'Good. Both of you. Lie still, Amy.'

I do what I'm told. The car door shuts. I flinch at the noise. Where are they taking Sasha? Upstairs. Is it an office or an apartment block? If they were going to kill us, we'd be in the bush, not in the city. I can't stand being separated from Sasha. And there's the ever-growing problem of my need to pee. It's quiet, but I know I'm not alone. I can hear small movements from the driver's seat, then the smell of a cigarette.

My hands are still numb, but I bring them under the pillowcase to check the time, then work on getting the tape off my mouth.

'Stop it. Lie still.' From the front seat, the voice from the driver sounds uncannily like the first man. He did say they were brothers.

It seems like an age, but it's probably only five minutes when the front passenger door opens, and I feel the car sink again under the weight of a big body. Heavy breathing. Has he just carried my son up several flights of stairs?

'This is what's about to happen, Amy. I'll take the sack off and you'll keep your eyes closed. Do not open your eyes. If you see my face or my brother's face, you won't be allowed to live. If living is important to you, keep your eyes closed. I'll untie you and pass you a hoodie, which you'll put on. I'll take the tape off your mouth, then I'll open the door for you. You'll get out of the car, you can look down, so you don't fall over, but do not look up, or around. Look at your feet only. Nod if you understand.'

I nod. The threat washes over me. I would do anything to be reunited with Sasha and get to a bathroom.

'If you scream or try to attract attention, I'll shoot you. I've got a hoodie on myself. I'm wearing dark glasses. This car is stolen. My brother will get me out of here before your body hits the ground. We'll dump the car. No one will catch us. Our boss is upstairs with your son. If he hears a shot, he'll kill Sasha, silently, and we'll dispose of his body later. This is all very easy for us. Do you understand?'

I nod more vigorously. This time his words cut through me like a knife.

'Sit up.'

His hand is under the sack, the smell of cigarettes on his fingers. He's working a fingernail under the packing tape covering my mouth. I was right, it hurts like hell when he rips it off. Looking down, I can see big hands with dirty nails and blond hair on his wrists. He cuts the cable tie with a flick-knife.

'Keep your eyes closed and put this on.'

He pulls off the sack and places something fleecy into my hands. I struggle into the hoodie, my numb hands like flippers. He pulls the hood up over my head to help hide my face and opens the door.

'Now you can look down. Do not look at me.'

I stare at the gutter. He pulls me out of the car, then folds my left arm under his and we start walking. I'm tight up against his right side, my eyes fixed on the concrete footpath, old chewing gum, cigarette butts, then two terrazzo steps, rounded at either end, and the bottom section of a pair of dark, timber-framed glass doors. The door on the left opens. He leads me across a terrazzo lobby to a timber staircase. A faded red carpet runner is held at the back of each stair tread by a brass rod. An old building, Art Deco. Silent. It could be offices or apartments. I hope it's an apartment building. More chance of help?

My feet pass through lozenge-shaped patches of coloured light. There must be a stained-glass window. We climb in a curve from the foyer to a landing, where I can see the lower parts of four doors on my right. Then we head up another curving flight and then another, to the third floor. Light spills from an open doorway, the first on the right.

'Keep your eyes down,' whispers the man clasping my arm tightly under his. 'Don't look up!'

He leads me into a dimly lit hallway with an old, honey-coloured parquetry floor, then lets go of me, only to thrust the sack roughly back onto my head as the door slams behind me. Disorientated for a moment, I stumble, but he grabs my arm again to keep me upright. I can still see bit of floor and a closed door on my right. One black biker boot appears near my feet as

271

the man holding my arm comes to a halt.

The bottom of the door to my right opens and I am nudged inside. The room is in near darkness. Now I can't see anything through the sack!

'Where's Sasha?' My voice reedy and frightened.

'He's sitting on the bed. He's fine.'

I stumble forward a couple more steps and bump into Sasha. My hands fly over him, checking. His hands are still tied, the sack on his head.

'I'm here, Sash. Mummy's back with you now.'

Sasha is silent. He must still be gagged under the sack. Animals. But I feel his shoulders sag in relief.

I sit beside my son, pulling him close to me. 'We are going to be all right,' I whisper. 'I'm going to get us out of this. You just need to be patient.'

Through the sack, I make out a silhouette in the doorway. A tall, skinny man, Tattoo Man.

'Here's the deal, Amy. You show us you can be trusted and you get the free run of this bedroom and the barfroom. You act up and try sumfin stupid and you both end up tied and gagged again. Or worse. Understand?'

'Yes, we understand.' I have to cross my legs at the mention of the word bathroom.

'You can't get out of this room, so don't bovver tryin'. The blind on the window is taped down. Don't go to a whole lotta trouble tryin' to peel back the tape and look out. You won't see nuffin except some trees and anovver building. There's nuffin to see that gives away where we are. The window in here and the one in the barfroom are nailed shut. Don't fink you can lift the window and scream for help. Don't fink you can break the window and scream for help. We'll hear you and we'll hurt you. And in this neighbourhood, no one cares. Are you following, Amy?'

'Yes, I understand.' The more he talks, the less convinced I am that he's one of the Serbs. I want him to finish with the threats in front of Sasha and leave, so I can untie my son and comfort him. I can feel him shaking in my arms and his heart is beating too quickly. I need to get him calm. But the instructions continue.

'Keep the pillowcases on until I leave.'

No wonder this sack stinks, he's probably been sleeping on it. The thought makes me dry-heave.

'Okay. Sasha, hold out your hands, I'm gonna cut the cable. Don't do nuffin stupid.'

I feel Sasha's arms straighten, then slump back to his lap as the cable tie is cut.

'Now go to sleep. We'll be checking on you during the night. Like I said, don't do nuffin stupid.'

I shake my head and I can sense Sasha doing the same. We are very obedient. For now.

Once I hear the door close and the lock click, I pull off the stinky pillowcases. Sasha is still trembling and his eyes are bright with tears. As he lifts up his hands and looks at them, I rub them with mine to get the blood circulating, then I reach up to take off his gag. But he stops me and rips the tape off himself, in one motion. He barely flinches.

'I'm gonna kill those men, Mum.'

He isn't trembling in fear at all; he's pulsing with rage.

273

JOHNNY

Waking up on Friday morning, it hits me again. My brother is dead. It's a punch to the gut every morning.

It takes me a few more seconds to realise that I'm alone in the house. When I go to sleep, my unconscious must reset itself to the time before my brother got shot and Amy and Sasha moved out. Each morning, it's as if the pain is brand new. Some mornings, the pain is followed by anger and a sense of betrayal. Other mornings, it's a physical loss, like when you lose an arm or a leg. I've heard about it. Phantom limb pain.

This morning is a phantom-limb-pain morning, made sharper by my sense of triumph. My first job without Ivan by my side. For a moment I let myself fantasise about how I'd be feeling if my brother was still alive and my wife had been in my bed last night when I got home.

It's not as if I would have shared the details of the job with Amy. I would have come home, showered and slipped into bed beside her, woken her up slowly with kisses in her favourite places. I would have shared my sense of achievement. This morning I should be waking up feeling like a king, back from winning the war. I took big risks to put another stack of money in the safe for my family, for our future together.

I roll out of bed and head to the wardrobe. Opening the door, I stick my face into the middle of Amy's side of the hanging space and breathe in her scent, her clothes soft on my skin. I'm glad no one can see me. Then I pull my head out and close the door.

The stack of money will be a while materialising. My brother is dead. Amy and Sasha aren't here. And I need to make my own breakfast. Again.

Screw that, Mum will be happy as a clam to cook me breakfast. And I don't give a fuck what Dad has to say about it.

I take a shower and jump in the Jeep. Once the phone has bluetoothed, I try Amy's number. As usual it rings out, no voicemail. This is getting ridiculous. It's frustrating enough never being able to get through to her, without at least being able to leave a frustrated voicemail. Then I remember she called last night.

'One new message received at 10.05 p.m.,' says the robot voice. There's silence and then the sound of the phone disconnecting. She didn't bother to leave me a message.

Mum has just put a big plate of bacon and eggs in front of me, when we hear the unmistakable sound of a copper's knock. Something about the righteous anger behind the *bang, bang, bang* of the fist on the front door. It's a dead giveaway.

Mum looks at my father for a sign. From the head of the kitchen table, he nods, takes another sip of his coffee and rocks

275

his chair back against the wall. I plough into my food.

It's the same set of burly, uniformed police who came to visit the night Ivan died. The bookends—Bridges and Dyson. They walk single-file into the kitchen after Mum.

'You boys want cup of tea? Bacon and eggs?'

'No thanks, Mrs Novak. We're here to invite the boys down the station for a little chat.'

'I make takeaway, you boys too skinny.'

The younger officer looks at his partner, eyes pleading like a starving dog.

I smile and get on with the job of chowing down my pile of food at record speed.

'No thanks, Mrs Novak, though it's kind of you to ask.'

The senior constable moves forward another step and brings a meaty hand down lightly on my shoulder.

'Yep, right with you, officer.' I shovel in two more mouthfuls, wipe my mouth with the back of my hand and belch, before smiling up at Mum.

'That was truly awesome, Mum.' Only as I swallow the last of my coffee does the hand on my shoulder start to squeeze. I stand up, slowly. No need to spook anyone.

Dad hasn't said a word.

'You too, Mr Novak. We've been told to bring you and Johnny down. We don't have to handcuff you or anything.' The unspoken end of the sentence, *as long as you come quietly*, is understood in the look exchanged between the cop and my dad, who is still leaning back in his chair.

After half a minute, Dad brings the chair back down, slurps some more coffee and lets out an identical belch to mine.

'Branka, ring Sam.'

Mum nods while Dad stands up and follows me and the cops out the front door, down the steps and across the front yard to the waiting police car. At least it isn't a paddy wagon. I feel the younger cop's hand on my head, gently guiding me into the back seat.

After I've waited for fifteen minutes in an interview room at Liverpool Police Station, Sam Dillard walks in. Our lawyer is in his early forties, blond and handsome. He looks like he should be in a toothpaste ad. His accent is pure Eastern Suburbs, private school. He's as Anglo as we are wogs. Dad doesn't trust Croatian lawyers, even those born here. He thinks Skips are better educated. He's a snob or a racist, maybe both. But Sam has proven himself over the years. He's much smarter than he looks. He's wearing a pale-blue suit. As usual. He's a man who loves his job.

'Johnny!' Sam holds out his hand, as if we're meeting at a nice restaurant.

'Hi, Sam, thanks for getting here so fast. I'm up first, hey?'

Detective Inspector Ian MacPherson walks in, turns on the recording device and states his name, Sam Dillard's and the date.

'State your name for the tape, Johnny.'

'John Novak.'

'Thank you. What have you been up to?'

Before Sam can stop me, I launch in.

'Well, I was trying to eat the spectacular breakfast my mum cooked, but that got cut short. Speaking of short, looks like you've had a bit of a haircut since I last saw you.' As MacPherson always sports a ginger buzz cut, this is a safe assumption.

'Nice of you to notice, Johnny. Very nice. So you're saying you don't know what's going on?'

'What do you mean? Have you got a lead on who shot Ivan?' I lean forward, pretending to be curious about what he's got to say. Sam seems pretty curious too, his gaze moving between the big cop and me, as if he's watching a couple of boxers sizing each other up in the ring.

'Last night, we found Stanislav Vucavec's crew, trussed up like chickens, in the middle of the Marsh Street Bridge, one of his boys shot dead and tossed in the back of their van.'

'Get fucked!' I rock back. 'Really?'

This earns me a white eyebrow lift. 'Yeah, Johnny, really.'

'What happened?'

'Well, that's what I was hoping you could tell me.'

Sam puts up his hand. 'Seriously, MacPherson, you're barking up the wrong tree. Obviously, this would have nothing to do with my client.'

I lean forward again. 'Who got shot?'

'One Zoran Milovic.'

'Poor bastard. That's fucking sad. You guys need to do something about this crime wave. It's getting out of hand.'

'Yes, Johnny, it is. I've had to add Milovic to my list of dead gang members here in Western Sydney.' MacPherson sighs and rubs his eyes. 'So what do you reckon happened? Think outside the box, give me your best shot.'

'I've got no idea, mate. Really. Wasn't us, so must have been the bikies, or the Italians, or, and this is a long shot, the Chinese.'

'What do you reckon was in the back of the van, Johnny? What was worth killing for?'

'How do you know there was something in the back of the van?' I ask.

'We got a report from a female driver last night. She drives onto the bridge, sees a few vehicles stopped in the middle of the bridge, surrounded by a bunch of blokes dressed in black, bala-clavas on, waving guns around. She backs off round the corner quick smart and calls triple zero. Our lot arrive and there's only one vehicle left, Stanislav's van. They got hijacked, so there must have been something in the van worth killing for.'

'Sounds like it. Wow! Wonder what he had in the back of his van?' I sit back again, pause for a minute, as if I'm thinking it through. I'm enjoying myself a little too much, so I look at Sam, as if he should have a guess.

'Again, nothing to do with my client, Detective.'

'Did the lady say what kind of vehicles they were?' I pipe up again. 'Did she mention a black Mercedes ML63?'

I can tell Sam wants me to shut up.

'You seem a little too eager to pin this on someone else, Johnny. My gut is telling me you know more than you're letting on.'

Now I keep my mouth shut. Shake my head. Try to look offended.

Sam works out I might really want an answer, so he leaps in.

'It was a good question. Did she recognise any vehicle types?'

'No, she didn't know what kind of vehicles they were. Could have been SUVs. She said there were a couple of big guys on motorbikes too. It was dark and she was scared. You know how it goes.'

'Right, well, that's a bummer, isn't it?' I say.

'Yeah, Johnny, it is. But we're pulling CCTV from around the area, so we'll track those vehicles down. Where were you last night between ten p.m. and eleven p.m.?'

'Playing poker with the boys, round at my mate Anto's place. We do it once a month. No doubt the neighbours will have heard us. We got pretty rowdy.'

And one neighbour did call Lexy to complain.

I avoid eye contact with Sam as the nearly irresistible urge to laugh bubbles up inside me.

MacPherson slaps the table once and stands.

'Johnny, it's been less than illuminating, as usual. All right, you can go. You might want to wait for your dad in the lobby. From past experience, it's going to be a short interview. But listen, Johnny, don't leave town. Okay?'

Just as I settle myself into one of the black metal seats in the lobby, my father appears, Sam trailing behind, talking on his mobile. He breaks off to say he'll call us later and bolts down the stairs.

Dad's face is unreadable. Then he gives me a slow wink. I can't help smiling back. This earns me a frown, so I rearrange my features as we walk towards the exit. The glass doors slide open to the hot summer morning, the sky ridiculously blue. As I reach the top of the stairs, I hear my father grunt beside me.

Directly in front of the station is a cop car. Emerging from the back seat is the skinny, leather-clad figure of Ink Slater. I try to keep the triumph off my face, but don't really succeed and I can see Dad is struggling too.

We head down the stairs with a bit more swagger, as two

uniformed police march Ink Slater towards us. I feel the glow inside me heighten as the gap between us lessens. I have to hand it to him, he seems relaxed. He looks right at me, smiling, his eyes cold. It's as if I'm out in the ocean, a long way from shore, and a sinister black shape is moving underneath me.

There's no way Dad will discuss business in front of a stranger, so the ride home in the cab is silent, which gives me plenty of time to think.

Surely there hasn't been enough time to organise a search warrant for Slater's house? It can't possibly be in response to the hints I dropped during the interview with MacPherson. Only fifteen minutes have elapsed between my first mention of bikies and Slater's appearance, and he wasn't in handcuffs, so he's been dragged in for questioning, just like we were.

There's no way Stanislav would mention his suspicions. Not one of those Serbs would have uttered a peep last night. They're not stupid.

But walking into a police station for questioning, two cops right behind you, is not a situation that calls for a smile. Unless you're psycho or have a serious ace up your sleeve. That look he gave me—it was triumphant. Why? I take a deep breath. Maybe I'm letting my imagination get out of hand. Ink had no reason to smile, other than to fuck with my head.

Next to me, Dad's gaze straight ahead doesn't waver. He looks perfectly calm. He knows about the note threatening Amy and Sasha. He doesn't know about my solo visit to confront Slater. He doesn't know about Slater's very specific threat to visit Amy and Sasha if we don't come up with twenty per cent of our take—today. He's going to be very fucking unhappy if he finds out I kept these threats secret. Especially as Slater and his bikies can now be implicated in the heist. Dad might be feeling proud of me, but that will evaporate if I'm forced to bring him up to speed.

I try calling Amy again. No answer. Maybe she's delivered on her threat and taken Sasha. Yeah, that's why she's not answering. She's in her Mini, heading up the coast. Once she gets to where she's going, she'll let me know she's safe, even if she doesn't tell me where she's gone. I just have to be patient.

AMY

Last night, as soon as we were left alone, we explored our prison. The overhead light bulb in the bedroom had been removed, but a glimmer penetrated the blind on a double sash window. I found the bathroom door and searched for the light switch, my hands still shot through with pins and needles. The sudden, flickering illumination was bright enough to make me squint. The bathroom could have been built in the sixties, but it was clean enough and there was the blessed loo. When I'd finished and washed my hands, I caught myself in the mirror. Pale and sweaty, a red mark across my face where the tape had been yanked off. I looked myself in the eye and told myself to toughen the fuck up, then left the bathroom door ajar to give us some light.

A wailing siren came closer and Sasha ran to the window, frantically pulling the tape off one corner of the blind. The siren's tone slid down an octave as it passed us, not stopping, not coming to rescue us. We took turns looking through the gap he'd made at the bottom of the blind. We were on the corner of a laneway, looking down on two leopard trees, their foliage bright green in the light of the streetlamp. Three storeys up and no passers-by. The building opposite was in darkness, but perhaps we'd see someone in the daylight. We tugged and pushed, but there was no way of opening the window. We carefully stuck the blind back down.

Our bedroom furniture consisted of an old-fashioned timber chest with no drawers and a table with no chairs. No bedside tables, no lamps. Nothing to use as a weapon. The double bed had a sag in the middle, but the sheets were clean and the cream chenille bedspread was unblemished.

Sasha and I tried to sleep, but we were too full of adrenaline. I told him stories and he drifted off. As I began to slide into sleep, he would startle awake in a nightmare, or I'd fall down some stairs in a dream and then we'd both be awake again.

The room was hot and airless. I edged away from Sasha, to give him a better chance of sleeping, and just lay staring at the ceiling. I thought about my childhood, how easy and simple it had been. How would I have coped with being kidnapped when I was ten? How would my mother have coped? The thought was so ludicrous I nearly laughed out loud. As if! My father wasn't some rich entrepreneur, or a career criminal, and we didn't live in a country where that sort of thing happened. But now we do? No. I chose to marry a criminal and this was the result. Angry tears spilled from the corners of my eyes.

Sasha. The name means Defender of Men. That look on his face when he said he wanted to kill the men who had taken us! He is his father's son. I'm proud of the resilience he's shown, but I'm also terrified of what it means. Maybe there's no way he can have a normal life with Novak blood running through his veins. Will nature or nurture win out? As I lay there listening to his even breaths, I promised myself that if I got us out of this mess, I would make it up to him. I would give him a normal life, even if it meant divorcing his father.

We were checked on twice during the night. The key rattled and clicked in the lock, then light streamed in from the hallway. A huge silhouette wearing a balaclava filled the door frame for a few seconds, then the door was closed and locked again.

This morning, one of the two brothers delivered bacon-and-egg toasted sandwiches in white paper bags, along with a takeaway cappuccino and a small bottle of orange juice. He was still wearing a balaclava. I guess I should be grateful, because if we never see their faces, they can let us go.

'Can you tell me what's happening?' I asked, but he didn't even look at me.

'Have you spoken to Johnny, my husband? Is he arranging our release?' I tried again.

This time he looked at me and I thought I saw a glimmer of humanity in his blue eyes, but he turned and walked out, locking the door behind him.

If these men are not part of the Serbian gang, who are they? Who else has Johnny pissed off?

Sasha was ravenous, but I only picked at my sandwich. How long it will take for Johnny to come up with the ransom? It must be about a ransom, surely. Why else would we still be alive?

JOHNNY

I'm out of the cab before it comes to a halt outside my parents' place, leaving Dad to deal with the fare. Calling Amy, I pace up and down the verge, into the shade of the jacaranda tree and out again, crushing the last of the purple petals into the grass. Her phone rings out again. I turn around and Dad is standing in my way, staring at me.

'What is happening? Why that tattooed piece of shit smile at you?' So he'd noticed.

'I don't know, Dad, but something tells me it's got to do with Amy and Sasha. She's not answering her phone. I'm going to drive over to the school now and make sure Sasha turned up this morning.'

'I come with you.' Dad's face tells me that refusing him isn't an option.

I don't pray much. But I'm praying right now, as I make the ten-minute drive between Mum and Dad's place and All Saints. I look over at Dad. His eyes are closed and he's mumbling. Looks like a prayer to me.

The school grounds are quiet. All the kids are in class. Once I've remembered the way to Sasha's classroom, from the last parent–teacher night, I peer through the little square window in the door, scanning the twenty-odd kids inside. I can't see Sasha. I knock on the door anyway and recognise the teacher who looks over, tall and elegant, with wavy, blonde, shoulder-length hair. She speaks to the class, before coming to join us, closing the door behind her. She looks alarmed. My Dad and I can have this effect.

'Hi, Miss…' I start, hoping her name will come to me before I finish the sentence.

'Mrs Glen, Robbie Glen,' she says, after steadying herself. She adjusts her oval, tortoiseshell glasses. 'You seem familiar.' She looks harder at me, taking in my worried expression.

I hold out my hand and shake hers gently.

'Johnny Novak, Sasha's father. We met at a parent–teacher night last year. This is Sasha's grandfather, Milan. We're trying to find Amy and Sasha.' I hold up my phone as though it's evidence. 'Amy's not answering her phone.'

'Sasha isn't here, and we haven't had a phone call from Amy about his absence. I checked with the office during morning tea.'

I know I told Amy to keep Sasha home from school today, but my shoulders tighten as the creeping sense of panic escalates. Where are they?

'Do you want me to ask the class if they have any idea where Sasha might be? You never know, big ears and all that,' she offers kindly.

Dad puts his big meaty paw on my shoulder, which startles me. 'Yes, is a good idea. Please ask the childrens.'

She goes back in, leaving the door ajar.

'His mum and my mum are best friends. We were all together last night after the concert. Mum will know.' A red-haired kid I recognise as Chaz's daughter, Jenny, says this with her arm stuck straight up in the air.

'His father probably stole him because Sasha thinks his parents are getting a divorce, like my parents.' This from a nerdy kid with thick glasses.

'Well, that hasn't happened, Timmy. Sasha's father is this nice man standing right over here.' She points in our direction and the kids turn to look at Dad and me, crowded in the doorway. They don't seem remotely assured. Nervous chatter starts up. Mrs Glen raises her hand for silence and walks back over to us, closing the door behind her again.

'I don't think we'll get anything more out of this lot. Have you tried Charlie Tyler, Jenny's mum? Or Amy's parents?'

I nod as I cast about for anything else to ask.

'Please make sure you let the school know what's going on. Do you think we should call the police?' Mrs Glen looks worried now.

'No, no. I think that would be overreacting, at this stage,' I reply, in a tone that I hope sounds reassuring. 'I'm sure she'll answer my calls very soon and it'll all be fine. And I'll be sure to keep you posted. Thanks very much for your help, Mrs Glen.'

'Well, if you're sure?'

'I'm sure.' I know my sweaty palms will give me away, so I give a dorky wave before turning to leave.

I call Chaz as we're walking back out to the Jeep. 'Chaz, hi, it's Johnny.'

'Good, I was just about to call you. I'm worried about Amy. She's not answering her mobile. You know about her plan to leave, right?'

I rub my eyes. 'Yeah, she told me she was going to disappear on me.'

Dad stops and turns to look at me. I hold up my hand.

'But why wouldn't she be answering your calls, Chaz?'

'That's what's got me worried. Look, there are a few spots between here and Newcastle where the mobile range is a bit dodgy, but I've been calling her every half an hour since eight this morning.'

'She called me just after ten last night.' I try to keep the panic out of my voice.

'That's about when Amy and Sasha left my place.'

'I asked her to stay at your place last night. Why didn't she stay?' Now I sound angry.

There's a beat of silence. 'I asked her to stay too, Johnny, but she wanted to get home and start packing. Do you know something you're not telling me? Is she in danger?' Chaz's voice has taken on a higher pitch.

'No, nothing like that, honestly.' I lie through my teeth. 'I'm sure they're fine. Maybe she's accidentally left her phone on silent or something. You know, from the concert? As soon as she stops for lunch, she'll see all the missed calls.'

'Yeah, I guess.' Chaz sounds like she's considering the idea. 'Let me know the moment you hear from her.'

'Will do, and same with you, okay?'

'Okay, Johnny.'

Dad and I are getting back into the Jeep as my phone starts ringing. It's Amy. Thank God.

'You missin' sumfin, Johnny?' My heart seems to flip in my chest at the sound of that slimy voice and my hand shakes as I put the phone on speaker, but I keep my voice even.

'Shouldn't you be using your "one phone call" for your lawyer, Slater?'

'Don't need me lawyer, done nuffin wrong. I'm back on the streets, mate. But thanks for carin'.'

'So what do you want?' I already know. My whole body feels like it's dissolving. I open the window. I can hardly breathe.

'Seems to me you mighta lost sumfin valuable.'

'I don't know what you're talking about.' Of course, I do. He's using Amy's phone.

'Let me be crystal fuckin' clear then. There's a feelin', down at the cop shop, that me and me boys had sumfin to do with shootin' one of Vucavec's crew last night, in the middle of the Marsh Street Bridge. There's also talk of us makin' off wiv whatever was in the back of the van. What was in the van, Johnny?'

'I don't know what you're talking about.' I repeat myself like a stupid parrot.

'Of course you don't. Always innocent, aren't you, Johnny? Nuffin ever sticks to you. Like that non-stick shit they put on fryin' pans. Doesn't matter. None of this matters. Because I got sumfin you want.'

'What could I possibly want from you?' I know exactly what I want.

Slater's voice drops to a whisper.

'Well, one's got a tiny little mole behind her left ear and smells like some kinda angel. The other one don't smell so good but punches pretty hard for a kid that size.'

I want to reach through the phone and strangle the slithering prick talking about my wife and son. Dad looks like he's about to have a heart attack.

'You evil fucking bastard!' I yell at the phone. 'I'm gonna kill you!'

'Yeah, yeah. I told you this'd happen and you ignored me. I bet you neva even told your Dad what I asked you to tell him. You need to get your arse back to Liverpool cop shop and tell MacPherson you're the one who shot Vucavec's son. Then you had a fight with your bruvver and killed him too, and shot Tony Fazzini to make it all look like some kinda serial killer. I want him off me back. And don't forget whatever you got up to on the bridge last night and the wog you killed there, too. All four deaths need to be on *you*, Johnny Novak.'

My brain is scrambling. I hear the school bell ring. Students carrying lunchboxes pour out of classrooms and into the playground. My eyes search frantically for Sasha—here, safe. But we already know Sasha isn't here.

'And Johnny? After you do all that, I want your dad to deliver to me and me boys whatever you took from Stanislav last night. Had to be drugs, right? A lot of 'em, seeing Stanislav needed a van to carry 'em around.'

The anger inside me is white and hot, igniting my fear.

'I'm gonna find you and rip your heart out with my bare hands.'

'Yeah, yeah. I want you copping to all the killins. I need

291

to see it in the papers. Then Milan delivers me the drugs and I hand over Amy and the kid. It's pretty simple, Johnny.'

'You filthy fucking prick, I'm coming after you.'

'Whatever. Do it or I start sendin' bits of ya kid back to you. Amy, I wanna keep for meself, she's fuckin' hot. And unlike *you*, Johnny, when I promise to do sumfin, I deliver.' Then the evil bastard hangs up.

JOHNNY

It's like the earth has opened up beneath me and my mouth is full of sand. Threatening to cut Sasha up? How did I not recognise Slater as a total psychopath? How could I have been such a colossal fuckwit? Through the Jeep's windows, the noise of children playing is like a soundtrack created specifically to torture me. I turn to face my father, expecting fury, but he looks too stunned and appalled for anger.

'When this Ink Slater say he told you this would happen? What he tell you, but you not tell me?'

Where do I start?

'Start from beginning.' Dad, the mind-reader.

Once I've brought him up to speed, his fists rise and crash down on the dash, The whole car shudders. Then he inhales slowly and lowers his hands back into his lap.

'Okay. Now I see. You stupid, but is past.' His voice is dangerously calm. 'This Slater, he is crazy, yes? Fucking prick thinks he make us pay him for protection, yes? He want war with us?'

'Yes, Dad, I think that sums up what he wanted before, but now he wants a whole lot more.'

'You cannot do as he ask. You know this, right? If you go to police, give yourself up, you give us all up. Police not believe you do job on own. What? You drive four cars, two bikes? Is stupid idea. Forget it. We think of other plan. Drive home. I make calls.'

I go into autopilot, soothed by my father's calls to Marko, Anto and Baz. Keeping the group small.

My mind circles back to Amy and Sasha in the hands of a psychopath. What is he doing to them right now? Despite what my father has just said, I'm going to do what Slater wants and give myself up. But then MacPherson would want to know what was in the van. He'd get a search warrant for my house, the warehouse, my parents' house. Fuck, everyone's houses. The guns and money in my safe, the ecstasy and the arsenal under the floor in the warehouse. My hands are white on the wheel as I concentrate on parking the Jeep outside Mum and Dad's.

Slamming the car door behind me, I follow Dad up the front steps as Marko pulls up. Anto is right behind him, Baz in the passenger seat. Time for a war council.

Who the fuck knows? Someone might actually come up with an idea.

My phone rings again. Unknown number. Fuck. I don't have a choice. I walk down the hallway and slam through the screen door, out onto the back patio.

'What?'

'Detective Ian MacPherson here, Johnny.'

For one crazy moment, I want to tell him everything and

294

get his help to bring Amy and Sasha home. Then I come to my senses.

'Did you miss me?' I ask, in an attempt to bring myself under control.

'Well, your name has been mentioned a lot down here today by a certain someone.'

'Really? Who's been talking about me?' Knowing full well.

'One Ian "Ink" Slater. He's actually been less than polite about you.'

'He's a scumbag, psycho, tatt-covered piece of shit,' I bark, as I pace across the patio, then down the stairs to Sasha's soccer patch.

'Well, well. You don't like him either? Fair enough. Yes, Slater reckons it was your crew up to mischief last night, reckons he has a rock-solid alibi. His alibi has made herself scarce this morning, but no doubt we will track her down in the fullness. Just as we'll be checking your alibi, Johnny.'

The sun drives me back up the stairs into the shade again.

'Have you searched the prick's home? He still lives with his granny, you know.'

'I haven't got enough grounds for that yet, Johnny, but I'm working on it. Should I be getting a search warrant for your premises too?'

I should have made an anonymous tip about the drugs under Slater's bed. They have to act on anonymous tips, don't they? But how would that help me? Amy and Sasha were probably taken just after leaving Chaz's place. That call from Amy's phone while we were waiting for Stanislav to leave the freight facility. No message. It must have been Slater.

'You still there, Johnny?'

'What do you want from me? I told you this morning, I had nothing to do with it. Have you managed to get anything out of Vucavec?'

'I'm not at liberty to talk to you about other people's statements, especially statements from the victim. It pains me to call Stanislav Vucavec a victim, but that's what he is until we can prove otherwise.'

'So why are you calling me?'

'Just letting you know your name has been mentioned. Don't go anywhere, Johnny. Don't leave town. Don't let any of your crew leave town. We found a shell casing at the scene that's the same calibre as the bullet lodged in Zoran Milovic's heart. Good shot, by the way. What's the bet someone loaded that cartridge into the murder weapon without gloves on, never really expecting to fire it?'

'Nothing to do with me, or my crew.'

'We'll soon see, won't we?'

By now Mum has herded everyone into the dining room. She has obviously been cooking ever since we left for the cop shop. A tablecloth has been slung over the big table and the sun is streaming through the window. The fan and air-con are waging a losing battle against the heat.

Mum places steaming bowls of chicken soup in front of each seat; she believes hot liquids cool you down in summer. A cabbage and potato salad sits in the middle of the table, along with a mound of homemade bread, olive oil and lemon wedges. She gives me the side plates, spoons, knives and forks to hand out, before she sits down beside Dad in an unprecedented move. She knows this is business. Dad stares at her, but she just leans back and crosses her arms. Her look says it all—Make me. Just try and make me leave.

For once, Dad bows to her authority.

'Johnny, you tell everyone. Everything,' Dad demands.

After I finish, Baz sums it up: 'So you planned to frame Ink Slater because he was a threat to Amy and Sasha?'

'Is working for you, this plan?' Dad's voice is deceptively even.

I stand. 'We clean up first. Homes, the warehouse, the ecstasy, all the guns. I'll say I was in it alone, hired some blokes I met at the pub, can't remember their names. I've got to do it. I have to get Amy and Sasha away from Slater, even if it means spending the next twenty years in jail.'

'Sit down. You will do nothing.' Mum is as stern as I've ever seen her. I automatically do as I'm told. She raises her right hand and wags her index finger at her husband.

'I already lose one son to your business. I not lose another son. Milan, you need do something. Now.' She reaches across the table for the rakia, pours herself a shot, swallows it and bangs the glass down on the table.

Dad stares at his wife in shock. Speechless.

'How long they been gone?' Her brown eyes bore into mine.

'Last night, about ten p.m., they left Chaz's place. He must have grabbed them on the way home.' Shit, I haven't called Chaz back. She'll be worried. She'll have to stay worried until this is over.

'How you know he has them?' asks Mum. 'Maybe he tell lies.'

'He called on Amy's phone and said Sasha punched hard for someone his size.'

'My Sasha, he is good fighter.' Mum looks proud, then

desolate. She pours herself another shot. She grabs Dad's wrist and hisses at him in Croatian. I don't understand everything she says but register its impact on my father.

'*Tetka* Branka, if Johnny or *Tetak* Milan give themselves up, they give us all to the police. It is the same outcome.' Marko obviously understood Mum's suggestion. His brow is furrowed, an expression I've never seen on his face before. Both Baz and Anto are nodding in agreement.

'Where does he have them?' Mum looks a bit flushed from the rakia.

'I don't know. He's not stupid enough to be keeping them at his place. His alibi for last night's job looks shaky, by the way.'

'How you know this?' Dad looks at me as if I've pulled a turd out of my pocket.

'MacPherson called to tell me Slater was blaming us for the Marsh Street Bridge job and that he has an alibi.' I pause for a moment, thinking it through. 'If Amy left Charlie's place at ten p.m. last night, and got car-jacked on the way home, then Slater's only real alibi is snatching Amy and Sasha.'

'How does this help?' asks Marko.

'Don't know, just trying to think of another way out.'

'Why MacPherson call you?' Dad asks.

'He told me not to leave town. None of us, he said. And he's checking for fingerprints on the shell they found at the scene.'

'Fuck. Marko, why you shoot Zoran and not pick up shell?' Dad gives his nephew a hard look.

'Who is this Zoran?' asks Mum.

'He got in the way of Marko's bullet, Mama. Don't worry about him right now.'

'*O moj Boze.*' Mum crosses herself.

298

'Why haven't the police found the E and the gun we left at Slater's last night?' asks Anto.

'Not enough grounds. Same reason they haven't been here. Right now, it doesn't matter.' I rub my forehead and try to refocus. 'Listen, Slater told me he would start sending me pieces of Sasha if I don't do what he says. We need to get everyone to the warehouse, now. Fill them in, give them time to clean house. Then I've got to go in and give myself up.'

Mum hauls herself up from the table, defeated. She makes her way towards the door, twitching her house dress away from her neck, muttering about the heat and how she'll put the kettle on. Then she stops, turns around slowly, a glint in her eye.

'Who is important to this Ink Slater? Who is important to him like Amy and Sasha be to us?'

'Well, he doesn't seem to have a steady girlfriend. I mean, the guy still lives with his nanna, for God's sake,' Anto pipes up.

I don't get it at first, not until my mother looks at me and lifts an eyebrow at Anto's response.

'Mum, she's an old lady!'

'He steal Sasha and Amy. He break rules first.'

Dad stands now too. He is looking over at Mum with admiration in his eyes.

The rest of us start nodding.

'You're right, Mum. She might even know where he's keeping them.' I can't believe I'm saying it.

'Bring her here. I ask her where is my grandson. She tell me.' Mum's smile is ferocious.

AMY

It is impossible to remain in a heightened state of terror when nothing is happening. The day is passing unbearably slowly, especially given our lack of sleep and the heat. We played I Spy until Sasha started making up imaginary animals hiding in corners, which was fun for a while. But we need a distraction.

I read somewhere that you should get to know your kidnappers, humanise yourself, so it's harder for them to kill you if their demands aren't met. I'm sure Johnny is moving heaven and earth to come up with the ransom, but still, I have to find a way to play this to my advantage. I wonder if any of these men have children. I walk over to the door and knock hard.

'Hey! Is anyone out there?'

Heavy footsteps. A voice on the other side of the door.

'What do you want?' It's one of the big guys. The brothers.

'Can we have a pack of cards or something to read? I've got a bored ten-year-old boy in here.' I smile at Sasha, who looks both insulted and eager to hear the response.

'Okay, I'll see what I can find.'

Five minutes later, the key turns and in comes one of the brothers.

In case it's useful later, I try to memorise anything of significance. This one is wearing jeans and a white T-shirt. The one who delivered breakfast was wearing jeans and a blue T-shirt. Both have black balaclavas, blue eyes and identical tattoos of a scorpion on their left forearms. Apart from the colour of the T-shirt, they are indistinguishable.

'Do you have kids?' I ask the man.

'No' is all I get as he deposits a newspaper on the table. He's back out the door before I can think of anything else to ask him. The key turns in the lock. So much for engaging the enemy.

Under the newspaper is a pack of cards as old as the bathroom. I sit cross-legged on the floor, my back against the bed, Sasha opposite me, lying on his stomach. But it doesn't take many rounds of Go Fish before Sasha sits up.

'Mum, I'm sick of this. Why won't these guys let us go home?' He still expects me to know all the answers.

'I'm sure they're talking to your dad about getting us safely back home.'

'Does he need to pay them a whole lot of money to get us back?'

'Probably.'

'Where's Dad gonna get the money? Do they think we're rich? We're not rich, Mum.' Now he's edgy again. Damn.

'Dad will work it out. You don't have to worry about it.'

He gets up and begins to pace, as though it is his job to worry about it.

'They're not going to kill us, are they?'

301

'Sweetheart, if they were going to kill us, we'd be dead by now, so no, it's about money, I promise.'

'Next time they come in,' he says, 'I'll stand behind the door and tackle the man around the ankles, get him down on the ground.' Sasha is getting excited now. 'You kick him in the head until he falls asleep.' His eyes are blazing, as if he's come up with the best plan ever.

I can't believe it. He may look like me, but right now, he's pure Johnny.

'It'll work, Mum. Me and Dad train on his punching bag all the time. He's been teaching me kickboxing and punching and I'm really good. Dad says I'm a natural fighter.'

Sasha must see the growing look of concern on my face.

'But I think you'll be okay, Mum, even though you're a girl and all that. All you have to do is kick him really hard in the head.' He demonstrates with a roundhouse kick to an imaginary head on the floor. 'If you don't want to do the kicking, you can do the tackling and I'll do the kicking.'

What the hell has Johnny been teaching him in our garage?

'Even if I agreed this was a good plan, Sash, and I'm not agreeing, but even if I did, how many men are out there?'

'Three.' Sasha can see where I'm going with this and his shoulders slump.

'That's right, three. And only two of us. Right?'

'Yeah.'

'So how about I teach you how to play poker instead. It's a grown-up card game and we can place bets. Which means you could win some pocket money.'

'Enough so these guys would let us out?'

'Not enough for that, I'm afraid.'

He sighs and sits down opposite me again, muttering under his breath about tackling and kicking.

As I deal the first hand, I add to my growing list of reasons to divorce Johnny. Not only is he responsible for us being held captive, he's training my beautiful son to be a brawler! I knew they were boxing together, but I had no idea about the philosophy lessons. When did this sense of dominance over women start creeping into my son's world view? If Johnny was here now in this stifling room, he's the one I'd be crash-tackling and kicking in the head.

JOHNNY

It's right on four in the afternoon as I drive Josef's van into Ink Slater's street. We didn't have time to steal a vehicle, so the van has fake number plates. Anto in the front passenger seat, scowling, Marko in the back, whistling softly. Our new normal.

There are no cars in the driveway, but the garage door is down. No way of knowing if Slater or his granny is home. But I'm betting on him being wherever he has Amy and Sasha stashed. Once I start thinking of what he might be doing to my wife and child, my vision blurs. I take a breath and banish all thoughts except the job at hand.

Once in the driveway, I head up to the garage and veer to the left. Anyone looking from the street will be able to see the back of the van, but not an old lady being carted out of her house.

Anto and I stride to the back door, Anto holding his favourite shotgun by his side. I've got my Glock. If Slater comes to the door, he'll get a slug through the heart. Anto takes up a position to the left of the door, so he can't be seen. Marko stays by the van, keeping watch down the driveway. The green paint on Granny Slater's back door is peeling in places. The Glock behind my back, I knock three times. Nothing. I knock again, then glance at Anto as I hear slow steps approaching. I bung a big smile on my face as the door opens on a tiny old lady and a yellow Bakelite kitchen the same vintage as the cottage.

'Hello, Mrs Slater, remember me? Johnny, I'm a friend of Ink's. Is he here?'

'No, he's not here.' She's suspicious. 'I don't know you. What the hell do you want?'

I keep smiling and step in, crowding Granny Slater. She moves back, clearly surprised that I'm entering her house. Surprised too, when the gun appears in my hand and another big bloke with an even bigger gun fills the open doorway. Suddenly she looks stricken, old and weak. She totters back a few steps into the kitchen, putting her hands out to steady herself against the kitchen bench. I feel like a low dog.

'What do you want? You know Ian, my grandson? He'll kill you both for this.' All the colour has drained from her face. I glance at Anto, who also looks sick with shame. I try to appear relatively harmless, which is hard when you have a gun in your hands. So I flick the safety on and stuff it down the back of my jeans. Anto's shotgun is enough.

Anto hands me the plastic bag full of old stockings and scarves that Mum gave us out of concern for the old lady's fragile skin.

'We're not going to hurt you. We just want to take you somewhere quiet, where we can have a little chat about what your grandson has been up to.'

'Why do we need to go anywhere? Ask me whatever you

want. I'm staying here.' She moves stiffly over to the kitchen table and sits down, a stubborn look coming over her face.

I glance at Anto. He shrugs and stays where he is, just inside the back door.

'No, Mrs Slater, we need you to come with us.'

Anto makes a couple of half-hearted motions towards the door with his gun.

'Okay, I'll get my handbag and my keys, so we can lock the door. You can't trust anyone these days. Used to be able to leave the door unlocked when I was a kid.' She mutters to herself as she staggers back up and walks over to an old floral shopping bag lying on the kitchen bench. She picks up a set of keys next to it and puts them into the bag, then spins around and shoots Anto. His shotgun clatters to the floor.

Time stands still. I can't breathe. My best mate is clutching his right shoulder and staring at the old lady with a horrified expression. Then she turns her gun towards me.

I'm as stunned as Anto, but by the time Granny Slater levels her ancient revolver at me, I've got my gun back out. She pulls back the hammer just as Marko appears at the back door, brandishing a Smith & Wesson 9mm. For a split second, Granny Slater wavers, her aim moving from me to Marko, but she is fierce and determined, nothing like the sweet little old lady from moments before.

'Put the gun down, lady, or I will shoot you. It is no problem for me. I have killed old ladies before. It is easy.'

Something in Marko's eyes makes Granny Slater buckle slightly at the knees. Her right hand starts to shake, as if she's having trouble supporting the gun. Closing the distance

306

between us, I prise it from her arthritic fingers and hand the revolver to Marko. I shove my Glock back into my jeans and ease the old lady onto one of the kitchen chairs. She's breathing fast now, her colour bad.

'Anto, sit down. Marko, do something about his arm.'

'She shot me! The old lady shot me!' Anto glares at Granny Slater as if she has turned into some kind of winged demon.

I open cupboards until I find glasses, which I fill at the sink. The heat in this kitchen is crushing. I give a glass each to Anto and Granny Slater, who are now sitting side by side at the kitchen table. I wait while the old lady drinks the glass of water, then I use Mum's old stockings to gently tie her hands together in her lap. The nylon material still smells vaguely of feet, so I use a scarf to gag her. I explain what I'm doing, each step of the way. Her breathing slows as she calms down. She seems to be accepting what's happening.

There's blood everywhere. Anto is pale and the stink of sweat mixes with the acrid tang of discharged gun powder. As I tie up Granny Slater, Marko wraps one of the stockings around Anto's bicep, where there's a neat hole. There must be a bigger one out the back of his arm. Marko grabs a tea towel from the oven rail and uses it to pad the exit wound, before strapping another stocking around it. Then, with another tea towel, he fashions a makeshift sling. Fast and efficient, like he's done it a hundred times.

Now I've got Granny Slater immobilised, I find the bullet in the door frame. With the help of my switchblade, it comes out easily enough. The nose of the bullet is flat. I drop it into my pocket, then grab disinfectant and dishcloths from under the sink and clean up all visible traces of blood. When the police burst in here, they won't be spraying luminol around looking for blood splatter. They'll be searching for a van load of drugs.

'I think we're ready, don't you? You feel okay, Mrs Slater?' The old lady looks resigned, all the fight gone out of her. She manages a nod.

'Anto, go and sit in the front passenger seat. We'll look after Mrs Slater.'

Anto shoots the old lady a nasty look, lurches up and heads out the back door.

Marko puts his hand under Granny Slater's elbow and helps her to her feet.

'Come on, Mrs Slater. *Tetka* Branka, she is waiting for you. She will give you a nice cup of tea.'

Granny Slater looks up at Marko, a frown on her face.

I pick up the old lady's rumpled floral handbag, containing her purse, glasses case, a clean handkerchief and a set of keys. I put her gun back in the bag. There's no point leaving it behind for her to use on me some other time.

Searching for a mobile phone, I find one plugged into its charger on her bedside table. I take the charger as well. The phone is so old it might be the only one of its kind left in existence.

In Slater's bedroom, the ecstasy and the gun are still taped to the underside of the bed, ready for the police when I can work out how to get them here.

Back in the kitchen, I pick up the bag of bloodied tea towels and lock the back door behind me. Through the dusty window of the garage, I spot Slater's Harley. I jiggle the door handle. Locked. One of the keys on Granny Slater's key ring does the trick. Once inside, I bring out my switchblade again and slash

308

both tyres. The Harley lists to starboard, then keels over with a nasty, expensive-sounding crunch that makes me smile.

Back in the driver's seat, I turn around to check on Granny Slater. Marko has her securely stashed in the seat furthest from the door. The tinted rear window is the only window in the back of the van. She looks small and frightened, so I give her my most reassuring smile.

'Don't worry, you'll be back home soon. I promise.'

In the late afternoon on this baking hot day, I reverse down the driveway and pull out onto the street. Not a soul in sight. No concerned neighbours coming over to check out the possible gunshot noise. Doesn't anyone care about what's happening on their street anymore? I drive off in the direction of my parents' place. No one coming to stop three men kidnapping a little old lady. What the fuck is the world coming to.

Dad has the garage door open, his Hilux out on the street. I drive straight in and Dad lowers the garage door behind us. Like the old days when Ivan and I brought home a stolen car. This time it's a stolen granny.

Taking it slowly, I walk Mrs Slater through the house and settle her in a chair at the kitchen table, her hands still tied and resting in her lap. After I remove her gag, Mum makes a fuss, stroking the thin grey hair from the older lady's face and offering her tea.

I turn my attention to Anto. Dad has him in an armchair in the living room, an old towel under the back of his arm. We won't get any stick from Mum about blood on her furniture.

I get my mate a beer and a shot glass, leaving the rakia nice and close to his left hand. I dig some painkillers out of the bathroom cupboard. Dad is on the phone to one of his old buddies, a vet, organising a home visit. Once I'm happy Anto is as comfortable as possible, I pull out the flat-nosed bullet and hand it over.

'You might want to keep a little memento of the first time you got shot…by a little old lady.' We both start laughing, but Anto grimaces when the shaking hurts his arm.

'Fuck you, mate.'

'If I were you, I'd be drinking a fair amount of rakia before the vet gets here to stitch you up.'

Anto pours himself a glass, spilling a bit with his clumsy left hand.

As I walk down the hall towards the garage, I hear Anto toast himself.

'*Živjeli* mate, *živjeli*.'

JOHNNY

It's getting dark as Marko and I use Granny Slater's keys to let ourselves in the back door of her empty house. We figure we can climb out Slater's bedroom window if we hear a car or bike coming up the driveway. We split up, searching the place systematically for any sort of paperwork for another house, a storage unit, a warehouse, a shed. Anywhere it might be possible to hide two people, one of them with a little mole behind her left ear and one who punches really hard.

The idea of my wife and son in a grungy bikie clubhouse makes me so angry I throw my fist through the dining-room wall. Marko comes out of Slater's bedroom tut-tutting when he sees the hole. We don't want the police to twig that the place has been tossed when they finally manage to get a search warrant, but I figure Slater could just as easily have punched a hole in the wall. And I'm wearing gloves.

In Granny Slater's room, there's a display of framed family photos on the mantlepiece above the gas fireplace. Ink is easy to recognise, rail-thin and snaggle-toothed in every photo. But it looks like he has a younger brother, stocky and unsmiling. In the photos of this same stocky kid all grown up, he's as tall as Ink but built as if he's shifted a lot of weights. In one photo, he's in full army commando gear, rappelling out of an army helicopter over water. In another one, taken in a desert somewhere, mountains in the distance, he's standing with some buddies, fully kitted up and carrying Blaser R93 Tactical sniper rifles. I call Marko in.

'Yes, Slater has a little brother.' Marko nods.

'Not so little anymore.'

'Come and see his room.'

I thought the third bedroom was empty. No posters on the walls and nothing to suggest there ever had been. The single bed has an army-issue blanket, tucked in so tight fleas would find it hard to squeeze in. Nothing on the bedside table. But in the dark timber wardrobe, a dress uniform hangs stiffly alongside army fatigues. Dress boots and one pair of everyday army boots have been polished to a mirror finish. Pinned to the inside of the door is a yellowed photo of Ink Slater's brother, aged about five or six, holding hands with a dark-haired woman. This time the kid has a smile on his face.

Marko pulls out the top drawer of a small chest of drawers to reveal three small, black boxes, embossed with the rising sun and crown crest of the Australian Army. He opens each box reverently.

'Three tours of duty in Afghanistan. Ink Slater's brother is a war hero.'

'Shit. Let's hope he doesn't come home to find his granny's been snatched and get in the middle of all this.'

We back out of the pristine room and resume searching. We

come up with exactly nothing. I'm close to punching another wall. I make my way back into the kitchen, where Marko is rummaging through drawers. I feel a vibration in my pocket and a strange ring tone.

I pull out Granny Slater's old phone, noticing it's nearly out of juice. It's a Sydney number, but no contact details come up. I hit answer, but don't say anything.

'Nan?'

'Mrs Slater can't come to the phone right now,' I answer in a posh voice as I sit down at the kitchen table, something like a grin breaking over my face. Marko is watching, bewildered.

'Who's that? Where's Nan?'

'I'm your worst nightmare, Slater.' This is really for Marko's benefit. Clue him in, make him smile for a change. It works, but his smile is kind of scary.

'Johnny Novak, what the fuck are you doin' with me nan's phone?' Slater's voice is venomous.

'We didn't think she should be left all alone, while you're off somewhere being a first-class evil prick.'

'Where's Nan? Is she there? Put her on, you stupid fuck. Do you have any idea what I'll do to *you*?'

'Your nan is very comfortable. All *you* have to do is tell me where Amy and Sasha are, and I'll bring her home, safe and sound.'

'Fuck you!'

'Really, that's what you want to say to me right now? Don't you care about your nan?'

'Nan knows how to look after herself. Besides, you won't hurt her. If you hurt her, I'll kill Amy and Sasha. *You* keep me nan comfortable, *I'll* make sure Amy and Sasha are comfortable.

313

You still need to give yourself up, Johnny. No confession, no wifey.'

My frustration draws me out of the chair.

'What the fuck is wrong with you? I've got your grandmother! It's time this ended. You've had Amy and Sasha since last night. Fucking hand them over, you psychotic little cunt.'

'I tell you what, Johnny. I'll give the kid back to you. If *you* give me nan back to me. That's fair. Amy stays put until you give yourself up, cop to the murders and hand over whatever was in the back of Stanislav's van.' Then the skinny fucker hangs up.

'It makes sense, Ink Slater has two hostages, we have one.' Marko's taking the pragmatic view as he drives us back to my parents' place.

The word 'hostages' makes me disgusted with myself. I dread to think about what Amy and Sasha might be going through right now.

'When I get her out of this situation, Amy will never speak to me again.'

Marko shrugs. 'You are right, you do not deserve her. But Amy knew your family, what you do, before she married you.'

Jesus, that's the most personal Marko's ever been with me. He really picks his moments. 'Thanks for that. But did you ever expect it to get this fucked up?'

Marko ignores my question and comes up with his own. 'Where are we going to hide his granny? Now Slater knows we have her, he will try to rescue her.'

'Will he? Or will he just do the swap, like he said? He knows where I live, so no doubt he knows where Dad lives, but fucking with me and fucking with Dad are two different ball games. Otherwise, why wasn't Dad's house copping the drive-by and Dad's neighbour's dog having its throat slit?'

'Yes. You are right. But it is a good idea to bring in some of the crew.'

We agree to organise it when we get back to Mum and Dad's.

I try calling Slater back to arrange the swap. No answer.

I'm like a character in someone else's movie. The scene in Mum's kitchen does nothing to dispel the feeling that the world has slipped off its axis.

Mum is at the stove, frying veal schnitzels, and Granny Slater is at the kitchen table, mashing potatoes in a saucepan. They're chatting away like old friends. Dad is nowhere to be seen. Marko grabs a beer from the fridge and stalks off down the hall. I hear the back door slam. I know I can rely on him to organise the reinforcements.

This scene of domestic harmony nearly tips me over the edge. I want to take the pot out of Granny Slater's hands and hurl it through the kitchen window. I take a few deep breaths instead, before asking the obvious question.

'Mum, I don't suppose you've found out where Amy and Sasha are being held, have you?'

'Gladys does not know. But she has something to tell you. Sit, sit, we eat in a minute.'

There's no way I can derail dinner. I pull a beer out of the fridge and sit down, repressing the urge to mention Slater's idea of swapping his nan for Sasha. I need Granny Slater to help me free *both* Amy and Sasha.

315

Mum nods encouragement to the old lady. Granny Slater adds some butter and a splash of milk to the mashed potatoes.

'Ian's father, now, he started out okay, but he married a drug addict. That girl was a low-down, dirty whore and she turned my son into a drug addict. Hell, Ian came into this world with the shakes. I admit all those tattoos look terrible, but he's not a drug addict anymore and he can be quite sweet, at times.'

My utter disbelief obviously registers. She puts the masher down and tries to explain.

'I brought up Ian and his younger brother, Jackson. I did it right. Ian has never been to prison, even though the cops tried to fit him up.' Her expression is sad. She must be remembering her poor little grandson being hauled off by corrupt police. 'If he did take your wife and child,' she holds up an arthritic finger, 'and I don't believe it,' she wags her finger back and forth, 'but if he did, it's because he wants something from you. All you need to do is give him what he wants, and he'll give you what you want. Done.' She claps her hands together then leans back in her seat, chin up, arms crossed, satisfied with her pronouncement.

'Mrs Slater, your grandson called me this afternoon, on my wife's phone, and told me he'd taken my wife and my son. So it's definitely something he would do. Okay?'

She heard me but is not hearing me. She looks up at Mum, who has just removed the last piece of veal from the frying pan. Mum turns off the gas and reaches over to pat Granny Slater's shoulder.

'I'm sorry, Gladys, is like I said. Your Ian has our Sasha and our Amy. How do we get them back?'

Granny Slater sags in her chair. She looks old and tired. I'm starting to believe she has no idea where Amy and Sasha are, but she's my best chance. I try again.

'I want this to end peacefully. No one needs to get hurt. If I can talk to Ian, face to face, man to man, we can come up with a solution. Are you sure you don't know of a place he might hang out, his clubhouse maybe? Somewhere else? Somewhere he might be keeping Amy and Sasha?'

She is thinking hard, one hand stroking the other, as though for comfort.

'Sometimes he doesn't come home for days on end,' she says slowly. 'I know they've got a place somewhere. He and his friends work on their bikes together, play pool and drink beer. They don't do drugs, though.'

I remember the photo, on Facebook, of the Hyde twins snorting coke from the pert butts of two girls, but I keep my mouth shut and let the old lady keep talking.

'I don't know where they go. It's best if I don't ask. He wouldn't have taken your wife and child unless you have something he really wants. What does he want from you?'

'It doesn't really matter what he wants, Mrs Slater, he has them, and we've got you. We need to work together now, so we can find Amy and Sasha and take you home.'

Two fat tears slide down the old lady's cheeks.

'Perhaps he'll send you a message?' she says, her voice low and sad. 'Yes, that's it. He'll send you a message.' She nods as if she's finally understood something important. 'Give him what he wants. If he doesn't get what he wants, he can turn nasty.' She is pleading with me now. 'You don't want to make him angry.'

•

Out on the back patio, I try the landline Slater used to call his nan's phone, then the mobile she has listed for him, and finally Amy's phone. No luck. Meanwhile, I've ignored three calls from Chaz.

'Why won't the fucker answer my call? Doesn't he want his grandma back?' My head is in my hands.

Marko grabs my shoulder and shakes it.

'Listen. We need to break a couple of the old lady's fingers. Then she will talk.' Marko is not happy about Mum's soft interrogation technique. 'She shot Anto, she is tough. One finger. We can make sure.'

Dad looks at Marko as though he too is actually considering this as a course of action.

I can't let it happen. 'If I honestly thought it would work, she'd be tied to a chair and we'd have the pliers out. She's got nothing to gain by holding out on us.'

'Okay, what is Ink Slater's weakness?' my cousin asks. 'He does not seem to care enough about his grandma. What does he care about?'

'I have no idea. Ruining my life? Does he want to run the whole western suburbs? Maybe he wants to be the biggest arsehole in Sydney?' I sigh, but the question has refocused my mind. 'He's got a big crew, bigger than ours, and younger. He has at least twenty-five guys to our sixteen. The Hyde twins are his top lieutenants. We know they have no fucking scruples. Everyone's wives and children are at risk.'

'Kill the fucking lot of 'em. Fucking meth-head bikies. Don't deserve to live. Squash 'em like bugs,' Stump pipes up. He and Fibs are on guard duty out the back. Bigsie and Shrimp are around the front.

318

Stump has a point. Just squash the whole gang like so many cockroaches. There's a glimmer of an idea flickering in my mind, but I'm so tired I can barely grasp it. I push the rakia away, pull the coffee pot closer and pour another cup.

'Last night, our plan was to lead Vucavec to believe it was one of the bikie gangs who stole his ecstasy and shot Zoran, right?'

'Yes,' Marko concedes, 'but for Vucavec to be fully convinced, we need the police to find the pills and gun I taped under Ink Slater's bed.'

'Yeah, I need to come up with a way to make that happen. I thought we had a bit of time. Turns out we don't.' I stand up and pace. 'But what if the Serbs find out Slater was responsible for the murders of Michael Vucavec, our Ivan and Tony Fazzini? And they pulled last night's job. How do you think that would go down?'

'Very badly for Slater.'

'And we give the Fazzinis a shot at revenge for Tony's murder, while we're at it.' I'm warming to the idea.

Dad's hand is curling into a fist and uncurling again, as if he's imagining Slater's scrawny neck in his grasp. 'How we prove to Stanislav and Italians that Ink Slater shot their boys and my Ivan?'

'Well, if Slater wants me to cop to the crimes, I need to know about them. Don't I? Otherwise the police won't believe me. Don't get me wrong, MacPherson would love to lock me up, but it will need more than just a confession, otherwise I can say it was given under duress. The prosecution will want evidence, like where I stashed the murder weapons. Two rifles were used. Where are they now? I've got the perfect excuse to

319

ask Ink the question, don't I? If he didn't murder Ivan, Michael and Tony, then he won't be able to tell me anything. Nothing gained, nothing lost. But if he did? I'm absolutely convinced he's responsible, and he'll be motivated to tell me all about it. Then I get him to describe each murder while I record him with a hidden microphone.'

'You think you James Bond?'

I stop pacing and turn to my father.

'I know it doesn't help me get Amy back. But would you admit it could give us some leverage?' My voice cracks in frustration and I turn away to pace again. 'Right now, he's probably letting me stew just to fuck with me. But he has to contact me to arrange the swap—Sasha for his nan. If I can sit him down and get some info out of him and he does tell me something incriminating about the murders, then we can sic the Serbs and the Italians onto him. It would keep his crew busy fighting on a few fronts, wouldn't it? While we rescue Amy. That's Slater's biggest weakness—everyone hates bikies.'

'Fucking oath,' says Stump.

AMY

I taught Sasha poker and we spent hours playing for money we didn't have. We had to keep a tally in our heads, as we don't have a pencil. I did ask but was denied. I guess it could be used as a weapon. Trying to remember who owed what made us forget where we were. For about five minutes.

Chinese takeaway for lunch and pizza for dinner. Sasha has eaten voraciously.

'You're not eating, Mum.'

'Yes, I am!' I tuck into the fried rice with my plastic fork. 'This is delicious! It's so nice not to have to cook. It's like I'm on holiday.'

'Yeah, right. You don't have to pretend like I'm a kid. You have to eat, Mum. We need to stay strong, in case we have to fight our way out of here.'

I eat some more rice before saying, with more assurance than I feel, 'Dad is coming to get us.'

I wonder if Johnny even knows we've been taken. What's the hold-up? What are we doing here? Wherever here is.

By the time we arrived last night, it was close to eleven and there were still lots of people around. Music, nightlife, car fumes. Parramatta CBD would have only taken twenty minutes, not forty-five, so we must be close to Sydney CBD. There were so many sirens during the night—police, ambulance and fire engines. I wonder how anybody sleeps.

Kings Cross is my best guess, or somewhere close by. Which is a good thing. Plenty of people about, night and day. If we do manage to get away, we won't be running down a country road, or a deserted suburban street, or through the bush. All nightmare scenarios.

Whenever I hear them talking, I put my finger to my lips and we lean against the door, straining to hear them. At first, I thought I was listening to one guy talking to himself, until I caught on that there was an argument about who ordered which kind of pizza. The brothers. The one who gives us instructions and the driver. Sasha works it out at the same moment.

'They're the same size and have the same voice, Mum. Like David and Harry at school. I think they're twins.'

Sometimes, we hear the sound of the front door opening and closing, and Tattoo Man's voice. There's something about it niggling at me, as if I've heard it before somewhere, those dropped g's and the lisp, 'f' instead of 'th'…I can't pinpoint where it could have been. God, this isn't Stockholm syndrome, is it? Imagining some kind of connection with my captors?

After those detailed instructions in the car, the first brother, we call him Twin A, hasn't spoken much at all. Of course, it could be Twin B. We have no way of knowing. All my attempts to engage them in conversation have failed.

We have a plastic cup, fork and spoon each and we drink

water out of the tap. There's nothing to hit them with as they come through the door. I can't lift any of the furniture. I could shove the dresser or the bed in front of the door, so they can't get in. But then how do we get fed? And, anyway, the twins are ridiculously big—they'd just smash through the door.

The only weapon I have access to is the mirror in the bathroom. I could smash it, wrap a piece in a towel and use it as a knife. Seven years' bad luck be damned. But I'll need to choose my moment. Then I remember what I told Sasha earlier—there are three of them. I'll need more than a piece of broken mirror.

I keep thinking about the gun in my handbag. I ask myself why I didn't grab it back at the car and shoot Twin A and then Tattoo Man. *Bang. Bang.* I replay it over and over in my mind, as if I could have my chance again, then realise that Sasha may have been shot too. We both could have died out there on the street. Whereas at least we are here, unhurt. So far.

I wonder where my handbag is now. If I can come up with a reason to get out of this room, there might be a chance I could get to my gun. And then what? Shoot all three of them?

I remember watching a TV series about Paul Getty's kidnapping. What if the ransom demands are beyond Johnny's ability to pay and Milan is trying to negotiate the fee down? What if they decide that cutting off my ear, or Sasha's, is the best way to strike a deal?

JOHNNY

Mum and Dad agree to keep babysitting Granny Slater. Mum's doing a good job of bonding with the old woman. There's nothing else I can do until Slater calls me back, so I head home.

As I unlock the garage door leading into the house, I hear a car pulling up out the front, then a loud crash in the living room. A brick smashing through the front window? Fuck! I only just got that window fixed! The smell of petrol hits me as I race up the hall. Fire is spreading in arcs from two broken bottles in the middle of the living-room floor. Through the flames, I see a black SUV pulling away from the kerb. I run back into the kitchen and grab the small fire extinguisher attached to the wall of the pantry. By the time I get back to the living room, the curtains are sheets of flame. Fire everywhere. It's too late.

I turn around and run down the hall to our bedroom, phone out, calling triple zero.

'Hello, what is the nature of your emergency?'

'My house is on fire. Fifty-five Gundibah Street, Liverpool. They need to get here fast.'

I empty my gym bag on the floor, open the safe and throw the cash, our passports, wills and random papers into the bag. My hands are shaking and I'm starting to cough. Smoke is pouring down the hall. Clothes in the bag next. Looking around wildly, I grab a framed photo of the three of us on holiday at the beach last year. What else would Amy want? I empty her jewellery tray into the bag.

I look back up the hall. No way out. When I slide open one of the big windows facing the backyard, the fire rushes towards me. Fast. I push out the flyscreen, throw the bag out the window and hurl myself after it. The pool looks like safety, but I get to my feet and take a few steps back. The whole front of the house is ablaze. As I run up the garage side of the house to the front, sirens are wailing, still streets away. Neighbours in shorts, T-shirts and PJs are milling outside their homes. Someone is yelling but I can't hear anything except the roar of the fire.

Standing a few metres from the garage door, I'm trying to work out how to rescue the Jeep when an explosion blows the garage door out and lifts me off my feet, throwing me backwards towards the street.

Flat on my back, I stare up at the stars. The night seems silent for two beats, before sirens penetrate the ringing in my ears.

Doug helps me to my feet. 'I think that was your Jeep going up, mate.'

Two fire trucks arrive and block the street. An older guy jumps down first, checks out the fire then looks at me.

'Fire Chief Nick Harland. Is this your house?'

'Yes.'

'Anyone else inside?'

'No.'

'Your name, sir?'

'Johnny Novak.'

'Right. Stay there, Mr Novak.'

The fire chief turns back towards the trucks and yells orders. His team is already at work, kitted up in yellow-and-black suits, helmets on, unwinding those big hoses, everyone intent on their part of the job. Fire Chief Harland comes back over, keen to ask me a few more questions.

'Any idea how the fire started?'

Mentioning two petrol bombs will only get the police involved.

'No, I got home, smelt smoke and saw the living room was on fire, so I called triple zero and jumped out the bedroom window, round the back.'

The guy raises an eyebrow, but I hold his gaze and keep my mouth shut. The fire chief seems to catch on. This is the only explanation he's going to get.

'Fair enough. We'll work out how the fire started later. Right now, there's no way to save your house, so my people are focused on ensuring it doesn't spread to the neighbours. Why don't you go and sit down over there while we get this sorted?' The fire chief points across the road.

I hoist my gym bag onto my shoulder and cross the road. Mr Fellows and his dachshund seem to quiver with excitement. He wants to talk, but I ignore him, keeping my face blank, staring at the huge bonfire that used to be my home. The heat is incredible, flames shooting high in the air. It's almost impossible to look away. While everyone's attention is on the fire, I set off down the street. A police car pulls up beside one of the fire trucks. I keep walking.

Halfway down the block, in the shadows, I stop and turn around. The house we bought the year we got married. The house we brought Sasha home to from hospital after he was born. Destroyed.

My wife, my child, my home. Even my fucking car. Gone.

I thought I could protect Amy and Sasha. There are rules you don't break. You don't involve women and children. You don't fucking fire-bomb someone's home. Maybe their car, their warehouse, but not their home. I stand there, out of sight, watching the fire brigade battle to bring the blaze under control.

Granny Slater was right. Her grandson has sent me a message.

Turning my back on the flames, I walk away, my mind a slide-show of images: the living room on fire, the sound of the Jeep exploding. I can smell the smoke on my clothes, but the night air is cool on my face. I could head over to Mum and Dad's, sleep on the sofa or share a bedroom with Granny Slater. That image makes me howl with laughter, which sounds really weird. I pull myself together and keep walking.

What else can go wrong? Maybe I need some kind of divine intervention. I remember going to church with Mum when I was in primary school. Dad stayed home. Ivan and I endured it all: dressing up in our Sunday clothes, standing, on our knees, sitting, standing, on our knees again. It seemed to go on forever. Confession was kind of fun. Ivan and I competed to see who could be sentenced to the most Hail Marys and Our Fathers. Lying in confession didn't seem like a sin to us. And we'd compete to see who could make the wafer last the longest after communion, poking our tongues out to show each other the slowly dissolving wafer, careful Mum didn't see.

Once we hit our teens, Mum gave up attempting to get us to come to church. I try to remember the last time Mum dressed up for church. Then it hits me—Ivan's funeral. We all dressed up.

I think about God and see a scripture card, rays of sun coming out of white fluffy clouds, God in a flowing robe with long hair and a beard. Angels flying around. I might actually still believe in God. Like most religious opportunists, I'm only thinking about God because I'm in trouble.

Imagine going to confession now—'Forgive me, Father, for I have sinned. It's been…' Fuck, how long has it been? 'It's been twenty-seven years since my last confession. This is gonna take a while, Father…'

I can't be fucked going through all the sins I've committed since I was eleven. Besides, I know why all this is all happening— I've fucked up my life.

I need a place to sleep. I could call Anto. Kip over there. But the poor bloke has just been shot. Lexy won't be happy if I add insult to injury and turn up at this time of night, expecting a bed. I could call Marko, but the thought of my cousin's depressing little flat nixes the idea. I don't want to talk to anyone, except Ink Slater, and he isn't answering his phone. Fuck it. I need a drink.

Before I register it, I'm at the bottle shop three streets over, on the main drag. The place is empty, apart from the bloke behind the counter. I stand in front of the single malt shelf, contemplating what kind of night it is. Not as smoky as Ardbeg.

Laphroaig. A smoky whisky to go with a burning house.

'Ah, a man of great taste. A lovely peaty whisky from Islay. One of my favourites.'

A short, plump guy stands behind the counter, his goatee struggling for purchase on a round chin. Skin so pale he looks like he's never seen the sun.

'So what are you celebrating?'

'My house burnt down.' I mentally kick myself. Now the stupid, lonely fuck has a reason to chat.

'Really? Just now?'

I shrug.

'I thought you smelled like a bonfire. You brought the whiff of hell in here with you. Wondered if it was your soul or your body I could smell.'

'What the fuck do you mean by that?' The idea of hitting him is suddenly appealing. The fat little fucker has my full attention now.

'I can see and smell auras, mate. Nothing I'm proud of, mostly I keep it to myself. Comes from my mum's side of the family. Irish.'

'Are you taking the piss?'

'No, seriously, I'm not. I now know you smell like a bonfire because your house just burned down. You have good taste in whisky. You have a very muddy, dark-red aura, which probably means you've very angry right now. So I should shut the fuck up and let you pay for your Scotch and leave.'

'Yeah, I'm not surprised I've got a dark-red aura, mate. I'm pretty fucking dark on the world right now.' I pocket my change, while the man behind the counter puts the bottle in a brown paper bag.

'Can I give you some advice?' There's a fair amount of trepidation in the guy's voice now.

'Why the fuck not?' I half-shrug. Throw it at me.

'You'd be much happier if you had a bright-red aura. That's your natural colour, but it's completely, like, covered up by negative energy. Get rid of the negative people in your life. Surround yourself with positive people. It's time for a bit of a cull.'

'Time for a cull, you reckon?'

'That's what your aura is telling me, mate. Nothing to do with me.'

Yanking the keyring out of my back pocket, I open the side door of the warehouse, switch on one of the lights and throw myself down on the big old sofa. Smells like someone else's sweat and cigarettes. I open my ninety-dollar bottle of Scotch and chug a few mouthfuls straight from the bottle. Probably not how the Scots recommend drinking a fine single malt, but what the fuck. The warmth hits quickly, the smoky taste snaking around my mouth as the liquid slides down my throat.

The first third of the bottle is gone in ten minutes and I feel a little better. When I'm down to the last third of the bottle, I start thinking about my dark-red aura. Who should I cull? Dad would be a good start. I smile at the thought. I can imagine what my father would think of the bottle-o bloke's theory about my aura.

What's Ink Slater doing with Amy right now? My mind veers in a very bad direction, so I pull myself back. I have to keep hoping he's not harming either of them. What the fuck does he want, anyway? To take over my life? He's certainly completely fucked it. He needs to be culled.

What about Amy? What's she thinking? Where's my husband? Why isn't he here rescuing me? Maybe she's come up with an escape plan herself? She probably doesn't even need me. Maybe she's already dead. Wouldn't I feel something if my wife and child were already dead? Wouldn't I know somehow, in my heart?

I'd really be better off culling myself. I can't even keep my wife and child safe. I'm lying on a dirty sofa in a warehouse in Liverpool, surrounded by drugs and guns, getting hammered rather than scouring the streets or torturing an old lady so I can find Ink Slater and grab him by the throat, hold him up against a wall and punch him in the kidneys until he coughs up where Amy and Sasha are being held.

I take another swig.

Who the fuck is Johnny Novak anyway? A petty crim who's been lucky up to now. I've always felt kind of cool, like I'm an outlaw, living by my wits. Not one of those boring drones, working their lives away in office buildings and factories. Did those drones let their wives and children get snatched by some nut job working in the next office? No, because they are the real men, caring for their families. Doing it the hard way.

Maybe I've just been lucky up until now. I always say I like to work smart, not hard. But who the fuck am I to say the ones who work hard are dumb?

I put the bottle down.

I'm not an outlaw living bravely on the edges of society. No way. I use intimidation to bilk money out of hardworking men and women in our own community. My family sells drugs to dealers who sell to high-school kids and kids at rave parties.

They might be called recreational drugs but that doesn't mean they can't kill you. I feel sick. Really sick. I only just make it across the warehouse to the rank dunny in the corner and chunder my guts up, mostly in the bowl. I drink a whole lot of water straight from the tap, then stumble back onto the sofa and into oblivion.

AMY

Earlier this evening, while Sasha and I were lying on the bed, we heard Tattoo Man, his voice loud and commanding as he came through the front door.

'What the fuck you lazy cunts doin'?'

I made a cover-your-ears signal to Sasha, but he shook his head.

'I've heard that word before, Mum.'

'Don't think it means you're allowed to swear, okay? And never use the c-word. It's a terrible word and it's disrespectful to women.'

'What does it mean?' He looked a little shamefaced, like he was supposed to know by the age of ten. Bloody hell.

'It's a nasty name for a woman's vagina.'

He blushed and that was the end of his questions.

A key turned in the lock and the door opened. Sasha and I sat up together and moved to the edge of the bed, facing the door. It was the first time I'd been able to have a good look at Tattoo Man. Tall and thin, he was wearing a black leather vest and raggedy grey jeans, hanging low. Red, green and blue tribal patterns, anchors, snakes, spiders and skulls covered every bit of skin I could see. He wore a grey balaclava and I could smell him as soon as he entered the room and closed the door. Some kind of cheap men's cologne undercut with body odour. In the dim light, his eyes were dark holes.

'How are you doin'? The boys treatin' you right? You got everyfin you need?'

His voice made the hair on my arms stand up, but I realised that his arrival was an opportunity.

'We could do with a fan in here and a change of clothes, but it depends on how long this is going to take.'

'It's gonna take as long as it takes, Amy. But I hear you. I can get that organised for you. No wuckers. What about you, little man? Sasha, any requests?'

'An iPad maybe?' Sasha didn't even have to think about it.

'What, so you can find some fuckwit's unsecured wifi and message your dad for help?'

Sasha looked crestfallen.

'Smart little fucker, aren't you?'

'He didn't mean to cause any trouble,' I jumped in. 'What about a board game? Or some books or magazines? Even a pen and some paper would be helpful.'

'Yeah, yeah. Don'tcha worry, Amy, we'll get you two sorted. Want me guests to be comfortable, don't I?'

'Thank you,' I said, my voice small. I nudged Sasha.

'Thank you.' Sasha's voice was loaded with contempt.

Tattoo Man laughed, a scary, manic sound. After staring at me for what felt like minutes, he left, locking the door. I could still smell him long after he was gone.

Now it's the middle of the night and I'm lying here on the bed, staring at the ceiling again. The memory has finally surfaced: that voice, I've heard it before.

About five years ago, when a local warehouse was burgled, the security guard was killed. Whoever did it, Johnny told me, would have needed a container truck to move such a large shipment of TVs and stereo equipment. And only idiots kill security guards. A few of our crew were rounded up for questioning, Johnny included. It was late morning when I took the call from Sam Dillard.

'Hi, Amy, you can come and get him. And would you mind letting the other wives know? I'm a bit short on time, got to walk straight into court.'

'No problem, Sam. Who's down there?'

'Johnny, Anto, Marko, Stump and Fibs. Took me ten minutes with each of them to convince the police our boys had nothing to do with it.'

I called Lexy; between us we could ferry the guys home. They could have caught cabs, but for some reason they like to be picked up, as if they're VIPs.

I got to the police station first. The automatic doors opened and there were our men, seated in a row, facing the notice-board, all of them fiddling with their phones. They didn't turn around until a voice cut across the foyer.

'Holy fuck! Wanna suck me dick, love? You're fuckin' hot.'

All five heads swivelled as one. Then they stood up and it was like a wall of alpha-male pheromones hit the air. Johnny's glance told me to stay put.

335

The guy who'd insulted me had just come through an interior door into the lobby. Tall and thin, he had half-finished tattoo sleeves crawling up his ropey arms and bloodshot eyes in a sweaty face. He was smiling at me, his yellow teeth like a dog's.

'What the fuck did you just say?' Johnny snarled, as he made his way around the phalanx of seats running through the middle of the room. Within seconds, Johnny was nose to nose with Tattoo Man, his crew spread out behind him. A silent alarm must have gone off. Four hefty uniformed cops barged through the same internal door, surrounding the group.

'Okay, you lot, take it outside. If you start hitting each other, we'll be very happy to charge you with affray,' the oldest of the policemen barked.

'I'll wait here for me ride, fanks, fellas,' Tattoo Man said, as though he was being asked to leave a party.

Johnny held his ground for a couple of seconds and then, still muttering threats, turned towards me and the exit door, the crew behind him. He threw a protective arm around me, almost swooping me up as he drew level.

'Sorry about that, Ames. Stupid little prick.'

Johnny wanted to follow up on his threats, but I talked him out of it. It's not the first time a man has said something disgusting to me, and it probably won't be the last. But I must have repressed the memory and it's taken a couple of days to surface. I still don't know his name, but there's some history there between us. Is that how he knows who I am? Is that why we're here? I probably should have let Johnny do a better job of intimidating the guy. Perhaps then Sasha and I wouldn't be stuck in this airless box, waiting for someone to pay a ransom or rescue us. But why am I blaming myself for this?

My fear has turned to anger and I just want to scream, I feel so frustrated. It's not fair. I've had enough. I'm never going to forgive Johnny for putting Sasha through this. My chest is heaving, I feel sick. Not wanting to wake Sasha, I slide out of bed and try pacing, but it doesn't help, so I sit cross-legged on the dusty timber floor. One deep breath, then another.

My mind does another backflip. Perhaps it really is my fault we're here? Johnny asked me to stay with Chaz. I should have stayed there! It's not like there weren't enough signs. If I was smarter, more perceptive and paid more attention to my intuition, we wouldn't be in this situation.

I've been here before, beating myself up for something I didn't see coming. When am I going to learn?

JOHNNY

Not a great way to wake up—face down on an old sofa, clothes stinking of hellfire, covered in sweat and my tongue stuck to the roof of my mouth. When I try to swallow, it feels like a layer of skin comes loose. As I stretch and rub my eyes, pain shoots through my head. I sit up but can barely move my neck. Staggering to the loo, I can't decide if I need to drink or piss first. The desire to piss wins.

As I drink straight from the tap again, my mind throws out images of the night before. The burning house. The exploding car. The bloke in the bottle-o, something about a dark-red aura. There's still some Scotch in the bottle. The idea of a drink makes me dry-retch. I figure this is a good sign. I can't be a real alkie if the thought of a morning-after shot of single malt makes me queasy.

What would Doug do if Kerry and Flynn had been missing for close to thirty-six hours? What would any decent husband and father do? They would have called the police immediately. The whole neighbourhood would be searching. It would be on national TV and radio. If Amy's parents weren't on a cruise ship in the middle of Europe somewhere, they'd have been all over it. Getting the hunt started. But I've been out snatching old ladies and getting drunk.

I find my phone. The battery is low and I have six missed calls from Chaz. No calls from Slater. I should call Chaz back. But what can I tell her? Sorry, Chazzer, your bestie and our son are in the hands of a homicidal maniac; don't worry, though, I've got it covered.

If I were a normal man, not a criminal, what would I do?

Living with Amy for the last twelve years has changed me. Maybe there's a chance I can become a normal man. But right now, I need help. And, like it or not, I still have to rely on my family. The whole ugly crew.

My phone rings as I'm about to walk into Mum's kitchen. My heart thuds. Ink Slater? No. Detective MacPherson. I turn around and walk back down the hallway, out the front door and sit in the shade on the bottom step under the verandah roof.

'I hear your house burned down last night, Johnny. Anything you want to tell me? And before you come up with any crap about leaving a saucepan on the stove, I've spoken to the fire chief who attended.'

'Right. Well, in that case, you can probably tell *me* what happened.'

'Two Molotov cocktails lobbed through your front window. That's a lot of accelerant. You must have really pissed someone off. Same window that got shot out a few days ago?'

'Yep.' I sigh. There's no point keeping what I know under

wraps. In fact, once I've told the big detective my version of last night, I feel strangely calm.

'Okay, your story tallies with what the fire chief told me. Good thing your wife and child weren't around. Did you see a car? Why don't you come down to the station and fill out a report?'

The idea of sitting down with MacPherson at the station and telling him everything is suddenly overwhelmingly attractive. My legs feel weak. I slump forwards on the steps, phone cradled to my ear, paralysed with grief and indecision. Then Dad opens the front door. I look up at him and his face is one big question.

'Johnny? You still there?'

'Look, I can't come down right now. But I saw a black Mercedes ML63 pulling away. It's Ink Slater. We both know it.'

'He's a piece of work, that Slater, and he seems to have taken a real dislike to you, Johnny. Help me put him away for good. Come in and fill out a statement.'

'Yeah, I'll get to it, but I've got other things I need to focus on right now.'

'Like what? Someone burned your home to the ground, Johnny. Seems to me this gang war of yours is heating up big time. I expect you here at nine a.m. tomorrow. We've already matched the spent cartridge casing to the bullet we pulled out of Zoran Milovic. By then we'll have lifted any fingerprints left behind on that shell. We might even find a match to one of your crew. There's an added incentive for you.'

'Yeah, no problem. Do you know the location of Slater's clubhouse? Bikies always have a clubhouse, don't they? You could search it for evidence—that they made some petrol

340

bombs.' As soon as the words are out of my mouth, I regret them. Dad looks alarmed. The last thing we want is a police shootout with Amy and Sasha caught in the crossfire.

'I tell you what I'll do, Johnny. If we can find some CCTV footage capturing a black Mercedes ML63 out and about in Liverpool near the time of your house fire, I'll see if I can find a judge to issue me a warrant for Slater's home and clubhouse.'

'So you *do* know where it is. Care to share the address?'

'Are you on drugs, Johnny? Of course I know where it is. And I know where your family's warehouse is too. I wonder if there are any petrol containers there. What about whatever was in the back of Stanislav's van?'

Dad walks down the front steps and stands over me. I can tell he wants me to stop talking, but I can't help myself.

'I keep telling you it wasn't us. This is all on Slater. The murders. The job on the Marsh Street Bridge. The shots and the firebombs through my front window. Ink Slater killed my brother and he thinks he's king of the West.'

I'm standing now too, rage boiling through my veins even though I know not all of what I've just said is true. Dad puts his hand on my shoulder, takes the phone from my hand and ends the call.

Once the last crew member slams through the screen door and takes a seat on the back patio, I get straight to the heart of it.

'Ink Slater's snatched Amy and Sasha. Thursday night, while we were otherwise occupied.' Men stand, chairs topple. Josef even pulls a gun out of the back of his shorts.

Dad holds up both hands. 'Calm down. Sit. Everyone listen. Johnny not finished.'

341

Grumbling with outrage, everyone sits back down.

I continue. 'You probably noticed a little old lady in the kitchen with Mum. That's Slater's grandma. Anto, Marko and I picked her up yesterday afternoon. And you probably noticed Anto's sling. He got shot while we were at it.'

An embarrassed grin on his face, Anto gets some back-slapping on his good shoulder and a fair amount of derision.

I bring the crew up to date with my home being fire-bombed, and the vehicle I saw pulling away from the kerb.

'Ink fucking Slater!' Anto growls.

'My thoughts exactly.' I feel myself losing focus. Painkillers would have been a good idea. Rubbing my eyes, I bring myself back on course and fill everyone in on the extent of the ransom, which now includes the stash from the Marsh Street Bridge job.

More outrage. As the voices get louder, Dad stands up again.

'Johnny not finished. Quiet! You all have chance when he finish.'

I can't believe how grateful I am to have my father beside me. Today just keeps on delivering surprises.

After outlining the plan to swap Sasha for Granny Slater, I finish up with MacPherson's promise to get a search warrant for the bikies' warehouse. Everyone understands the importance of rescuing Amy and Sasha before the police carry out the search warrant, fronted by a trigger-happy Special Ops team.

The crew responds immediately.

'Who's Ink's lawyer? You might be able to communicate through him. Pay him a dollar first, though, so he's working for you, client legal privilege, you know?' Stump has actually put up his hand with the missing finger.

'Anyone know?' I ask.

'I'll check with Sam Dillard. He'll be able to find out.' Stump looks pleased to have taken on the task.

Marko leans forward and bangs his fist on the table. 'Everyone has a price. Maybe the Hyde twins can be bought?'

Anto stands up, as if Marko's idea needs room to grow. 'He'll probably arrange for the Hyde twins to do the swap, rather than put his own sorry arse in danger. We bribe them. That fails, we follow them back to Slater and spring Amy.'

The men around the table are nodding.

'Good idea,' I answer. 'Okay. Let's get to work now. Baz and Josef, how about you shift the Es out of the floor safe, up to the shack on the Hawkesbury? Organise two guards on twelve-hour shifts. If this goes bad, the warehouse will be searched very thoroughly.'

Baz and Josef nod. Dad looks like he's waiting to hear the whole plan first.

'Bigsie, Shrimp, Brick and Blocker, stay here on guard duty, Slater could decide to come and get his nan by force.'

Marko leans back in his chair and raises one finger.

'Bring the guns here, in boxes. We will bury the boxes in *Tetka* Branka's vegetable patch. We need them close to hand if this situation escalates.'

'Good idea,' I agree. Bloody Marko's on fire today. 'You're right. Any other ideas, you call me first. Okay? The rest of you clean house.'

'Why we gotta clean house?' asks Fibs.

'If we haven't found them within twenty-four hours, I'm going to the police for help.' I answer.

'You've got to be fucking kidding!' shouts Fibs.

Most of the men are on their feet, again. Dad's face is neutral. He nods to me, go on.

I hold up both hands. 'Hear me out. I don't want to go to the cops, but they have better resources than we do. Have any of us ever found a kidnap victim before? How would you feel if it was your wife and child? Twenty-four hours and then I'm going to the police, and not one of you is going stop me.'

My phone vibrates in my pocket. I check the screen, unknown number. I slap my hand on the table, then bring my index finger to my lips.

'This could be Slater. Everyone, keep quiet.' I let the phone ring three times before I put it to my ear. 'Hello.'

'I'm supposed to organise the swap with you.' At last. My shoulders slump in relief, but the voice doesn't belong to Slater. The accent is less broad, the voice higher.

'What's your name?' I ask.

'I'm not giving you my name.'

'Does your brother look a lot like you?'

There's a pause. 'Yeah.'

'Okay, good. How about you and your brother do yourselves a favour and give me two for the price of one. You'll be well compensated.' I'm looking at Marko, who's nodding. I figure he's right. You don't ask, you don't get. If nothing else, I've planted the seed.

'Fuck off, mate. We're only bringing the small package. You know what you gotta do in return, right?'

'Yeah. Where and when?'

'On the corner of Brandon Avenue and Chapel Road, Bankstown, there's an Ultra Tune. Head down Brandon, next to the Ultra Tune, you'll see a window-tinting place. Next to that, there's a lane. Drive up the lane. There's an old repair place. No one will see us from the road. Got it?'

'Yep.'

'Meet you there, with your package, at one a.m. tonight. Okay?'

'Yeah, but I need to talk to your boss, personally, before the swap.'

'Why?'

'He wants me to cop to the shootings and the job you guys pulled on the Serbs.'

'We didn't pull that job. Wasn't us.'

'Whatever. You understand how this works, if I'm gonna sound convincing to the pigs, I need to know the details. Evidence. Right? You understand? He's got to give me some critical information if he wants this to work. Okay?'

'I get it. I'll talk to him. If he wants to talk to you, he'll call you. Personally.' He loads the last word with sarcasm, before completing his instructions.

'Be there on your own tonight. No one else. No funny business, or you don't get your…package back.'

'Okay. Be gentle with him, he's only ten.'

'You be gentle with the old lady, she's like a hundred.'

He hangs up and relief washes through me. I look up and every eye is on me.

'That was one of the Hyde twins arranging the swap. It's tonight, one a.m. in Bankstown.'

Smiles bloom on ugly faces.

'When they bring Sasha, we kill twins.' Dad glares at me, as though daring me to disagree.

'Well, we could kill them, but apart from Slater himself,

345

who else knows where they've stashed Amy?'

'We make twins tell us where is Amy.' Dad pulls out his switchblade and flicks open the sharp steel.

'Yes, exactly.'

My agreement surprises Dad. He looks satisfied and clicks the knife closed.

'But not during the swap.' I get up and start pacing. 'I have to come with Granny Slater, no one else. I don't know how many of Slater's bikies will be there. We'll put Marko on sniper duty, but I need to hand over Granny Slater and get Sasha out of there, without any bloodshed or drama.' I stop and turn to face the crew. Marko looks pleased, everyone else nods, but Dad doesn't seem convinced.

'I drive you. They are twins. There will be two of us.'

'Okay, Dad, good plan.' I figure it's a waste of my energy arguing. 'In the meantime, Slater will get my message. How can I cop to the shootings if I don't know exactly what happened and where the murder weapons ended up? Follow me?'

'Yeah.'

'Makes sense.'

'And you record him telling you.' This last comment from Anto.

'You've got it.' I smile at my best mate, buoyed by the idea of getting my son back tonight. Within hours. 'That's the first part of the plan. We'll also work out a way to follow the twins after the swap.' Even Dad's nodding now.

'The second part of the plan comes down to us using everything at our disposal to neutralise Ink Slater and his bikies.' I start to pace again as the men lean forward. 'What I want to know is who's put themselves in my shoes and wondered if their wife or child could be next? Taken from their cars, from their homes?'

Some hands go up, everyone nodding. They've all been thinking about it.

'Vucavec and his crew would never pull something like this. The Serbs would never involve women and children, right?'

'Unless the chick was actual crew,' says Fibs.

'Yeah, if she was a soldier,' agrees Bigsie.

'Right.' I'm warming up, hoping to get all the crew on side. 'So there's no exemptions for any active crew member. Fair enough. What about the Italians?'

'No way would they hurt chicks or kids,' answers Brick, whose girlfriend happens to be Italian.

'How about the Chinese?' I'm genuinely curious.

'Who knows what Chinese do. Why it matter?' Dad wants me to get to the point. Now.

'So what's different about the bikies?' I ask. 'Why don't they follow the same rules we all follow? They don't respect women like we do? Is that it?'

'Bikies are meth heads,' pronounces Stump.

'They're scum,' agrees Fibs.

I'm getting exactly the reaction I want from the crew. I'm sure there are a whole lot of bikies out there who respect chicks, but the slur helps my cause. I give them a moment, let the murmuring build.

'What if every garbage night they kill another one of us? There are only sixteen of us and Anto's got a bung arm. And two men will be guarding the shack. Up against twenty-five of Slater's crew, all hopped up on ice. Not a great scenario for us.' Again, I wait for the thought to cut through. Since when did I become a fucking speechmaker? 'So what if I could play Stanislav Vucavec and Antonio Fazzini a recording of Slater admitting to the murder of their sons? Get them to do the work for us to end these fuckers?'

'Johnny, I understand your plan. But I fought against the Serbs back home in Croatia. I cannot be friends with a Serb.' Marko looks like he's in severe pain.

Dad pulls himself to his feet, shaking his head.

'Stanislav my enemy. Is my enemy for a long time. We fight bikies ourselves.'

'We don't have to make our enemies our friends. We don't have to make this coalition last. But we need help, or we lose. The bikies have the numbers on us and they don't play by the rules. Getting Amy back won't be the end. Even if we take the Hyde twins out of the equation, the bikies can burn our houses down and take our wives and children.'

I pause to let them take in that scenario from hell.

'We get the other gangs to do our dirty work for us. Agree to peace, work together to wipe out Ink Slater's crew. The peace lasts as long as we need it to last.'

I look from face to face, letting my fury fuel my last pitch.

'Slater killed my brother and he took my wife and child. His crew burnt my fucking house down. Dad, you and I need to talk to Stanislav and Fazzini and get them on board. We attack as soon as we get Amy back, and we attack with an army.'

Every face turns towards Dad, who keeps shaking his head. Finally, he speaks.

'You get recording, we make calls. We form coalition. After we crush bikies, peace over.' His big right hand slices through the air.

JOHNNY

'Ivan would want you to have his car. You go get it,' Mum says, as we stand in her kitchen and she hands me the keys to Ivan's house and car. 'When Amy and Sasha come back, maybe you all stay in Ivan's house. Or you stay here, I feed everyone.'

'Thanks, Mum.' I give her a hug, because I need one. As I pull out of the embrace, she holds up her hand to stop me.

'Ivan say something to me, the day before he die.' Tears well in her tired eyes. 'He told me he made big mistake. He won't tell me what is mistake. He tell you?'

What mistake? He never admitted to anything. Ever. Now I wonder if his fuck-up had something to do with Ink Slater.

'No, Mum. He didn't tell me, but I knew there was something wrong. I should have asked, and I didn't.'

I let my brother down.

Apart from the guys stationed here on guard duty, the rest of the crew have left. So I walk the three blocks to my brother's place in the blistering heat. Waves of hot air coming off the bitumen create watery mirages up ahead. I stick to the shade, where I can find it, but when I have to cross a street it's tacky under my runners.

I've haven't been to my brother's place since before the shooting. Torn crime-scene tape is snagged on the bushes at the end of his driveway. My eyes skitter away from the dark stain on the concrete where Ivan's life ended.

The place is immaculate—Mum has obviously been here. She probably cleaned up after that last party. The morning after, I just picked up my car and drove home. Ivan didn't want company and I was nursing a killer hangover. I can't even remember how Amy and I got home that night. At least we'd been smart enough not to drive. We were all legless.

And now I'm back here, with another monster hangover. Have I got a problem? Nah, I can cut the fucking amateur psychology. It's two-thirty and there's a lot to do before the swap. Walking through to the garage, I unlock Ivan's brand-new Range Rover Sport. Metallic black. Finally succumbing to his burning desire for a luxury European car, he owned it for less than a month before he was killed. Maybe Dad's right about driving around in a flash car. But Marko is still alive.

It's like a furnace in the garage. Without getting in the car, I stick the key in the ignition, get the engine running and the air-con going full blast, before opening the garage door with the remote. While the car cools down, I open the tailgate to see if Ivan has a towel or something in the back. I'm sweating like a pig and I can smell the alcohol coming out of my pores. I need to wipe some of it off before I slide all over the new leather seats.

Only an old T-shirt. As I lift it to my face to rub away the sweat, the funk of sex hits me, at the same time as my fingers register a dried glue-like substance. I drop the T-shirt as if it was crawling with spiders. Jesus, my brother's cum! And it smells of something else, a familiar scent I can't place. Ivan must have got lucky on the back seat of his swank car and used the T-shirt to wipe off his dick. Go, Ivan.

I start laughing as I walk over to the tap in the front yard and stick my head under it, then shake myself off like a dog. After pulling off my own black T-shirt to dry myself, I climb into the now blessedly cool front seat of my brother's car. As I back out of the garage, my phone rings. Unknown number. I put the Range Rover in park and answer.

'Dave tells me you wanna talk, Johnny.'

Ink Slater's filthy voice makes my right hand curl into a fist on top of the steering wheel. I store away the name. So it was Dave Hyde who called me. The dominant twin?

'We need to meet in person, Slater. You have to show me a photo of Amy and Sasha, safe and sound. And you need to give me some details about the murders, tell me where the guns are, or give them to me as evidence. Otherwise, it won't stick, no matter what I tell the police.'

'Okay, I hear ya, Johnny. We gotta make it stick, don't we? Just the two of us, though. Bring a photo of me nan.' He gives me the name of a cafe on Chapel Road, Bankstown. We arrange to meet at four-thirty.

I allow myself a moment of triumph. By agreeing to meet, he's admitting he ordered the murder of all three men. The evil cunt killed my brother and kidnapped my wife and child. The desire to gut him like a fish fills me with rage and my sense of purpose sharpens to a knife point. Two hours to get organised. First, I call Dad to tell him I now have proof Ink Slater killed

Ivan. Then I call Marko and Anto. No way am I going without backup. Not again.

Anto knows a store specialising in surveillance equipment—to help catch out your cheating spouse—and says they have plenty of recording devices. Slater won't be able to pat me down in a public place. I could just run the voice recorder on my phone, but that might be clumsy, and I want back-up. I need a clear recording of Slater admitting to the shootings.

After I pick out a micro recording device, I take off my T-shirt and ask the girl behind the counter to tape it my chest and show me how it works. She seems to be enjoying herself.

'When you're finished recording, come back here and I'll remove it for you. This tape is really sticky.' Her hand splayed on my chest, she looks up at me and actually flutters her eyelashes, which are long, dark and super-thick. There's no way they can be real.

'I reckon I'll be fine, love.'

As Anto, Marko and I head towards Bankstown in Ivan's Range Rover, we argue about which code has the higher skill level— soccer or rugby league? Anto and I defend league while Marko is solidly pro-soccer. I let the banter distract me, surprised that I'm actually enjoying having my cousin around. Strange times.

We're early and manage to find a parking spot that will provide a clear view of the proceedings. Walking alone to the cafe, the recording device taped to my chest, I feel as if I've got a sign on my forehead: *He's wearing a wire.* I choose a seat at an outside table, my back against the cafe windows, and scan the street. No sign of Slater.

At exactly four-thirty, they saunter up the street. The twins are massive on either side of Ink. Three abreast, they take up the whole footpath. People move out of their way.

I'm sitting at a table for two, but the twins pull over two more chairs and I'm surrounded.

'I thought we agreed it was just gonna be the two of us,' I say, instead of a greeting.

'Don't be a prick, Johnny.' Slater's eyes are predatory, his pupils so dilated his eyes are completely black. My fingers itch. I want to wipe the smirk from the fucker's face.

'Do you have the photo of Amy and Sasha?' I try to keep my voice flat, as if I'm perfectly relaxed, but my state of mind must be pretty damn obvious. He pulls out his phone, swipes and taps, then turns it to face me. As I reach out for the phone, he pulls his hand back out of range. I notice he's shaking slightly. Meth, of course.

'Look, don't touch.'

Amy and Sasha are pale and look frightened, their eyes wide, hands and feet bound. They're sitting on a double bed. I can't make out the rest of the room. No indication of where it might be, but it doesn't look like any kind of bikie clubhouse. Seeing them tied up makes it all seem unbearably real. My wife and child in the hands of a psychopathic meth head. My heart skips a beat and then pumps wildly, my extremities tingling with the need for action.

A small, dark-haired waitress arrives to hand out menus. Her intervention may have stopped me doing something I'd later regret. I have time to calm down as the three men launch into complicated coffee orders. One of the twins actually orders a double-decaf mocha latte. They should just call it a Pointless

Hot Milk. I add a long black to the list and the waitress goes away, only to return moments later with a bottle of water and four glasses. She flips open the top of the bottle and pours four glasses while staring at Slater as if she wants to lick his tattoos. No accounting for taste. Finally, she heads back into the cafe.

'Where's the photo of me nan?' Slater asks.

I hand him my phone with a photo of Granny Slater taken in Mum's kitchen this afternoon. She's baking, flour on her hands and a big smile on her face. Slater can't help it, he shoots a relieved grin at one of the twins, shows them both the photo and returns my phone. Then he sits back and peers at me as if I'm an insect under a microscope. Finally, he shrugs.

'Okay. I'm willin' to share some info wiv you. Stuff you'll need to know for the cops.'

I let a breath out slowly, so it isn't obvious I've been holding it. This might actually work. I lean back, resisting the urge to cross my arms.

'I'm all ears.'

Slater moves his chair forward and talks quietly.

'We didn't kill Ivan. He was on our list, but someone else got to 'im first. We planned do 'im that night, but we got there a bit late and the ambos were tryin' to bring 'im back to life. So we drove off.'

'What? You admit you killed the other two, but not Ivan?'

'Exactly. Don't know who did your bruvver. I've got some ideas, he's got plenty of enemies, but it wasn't us.'

What the fuck? That's got to be bullshit. Why isn't he just admitting they killed Ivan? What has he got to lose?

Slater relaxes back into his chair.

'Are you here to get Amy outta trouble, or to find out who

killed your piece of shit bruvver?'

'Why can't I have both?'

'Let's face it, Johnny, you don't have much bargaining power here, but I'll tell you this for nuffin'. I seen Ivan get up to some pretty out-there shit when he got trollied.'

'Bullshit.' Ivan could get rough when he was drunk, but I was not about to admit that to Slater.

'Let's stick wiv why I agreed to see you.' Slater's eyes are scornful slits.

With some effort I bring my focus back to why I'm here.

'Okay. Take me through each job.'

'We did both jobs pretty much the same way. We spent time clocking their movements. Like everyone, they have a routine. Guys tend to put the bins out on bin night, right? Dave and Mick were there on bin night. Michael Vucavec and Tony Fazzini wheeled out their wheelie bins.' He leans forward again, whispering, 'and they both got shot.'

'Who was the shooter?' I ask, my eyes flicking between the twins. I haven't been introduced, so I still don't know who's who.

'Why does it matter?' Slater raises an eyebrow in amusement.

'I dunno, professional interest.' I shrug.

'Mick's the shooter and Dave's the driver.' Slater looks to his left at one twin, then to his right to the other. Dave has a pierced ear.

'Fair enough. What kind of guns and where are they?'

'The one and only gun used was Mick's Remington 700 hunting rifle.'

'I love my gun.' Mick says in a voice exactly like his brother's.

Slater gives Mick a look that shuts up the bigger man.

'Mick doesn't want to give up his gun, even though I told 'im he has to get rid of it. So you'll need to buy 'im a new one. He'll give you the one he used in the shootins in exchange. We'll do that tonight when you swap Nan for your son.'

'You haven't given me much time to find a replacement gun.' I make a show of checking my watch. Only seven minutes has passed since Slater and the twins arrived.

The waitress returns with a tray of coffees. She distributes them and walks back into the cafe, hips swaying. Slater's eyes follow those hips.

'You should walk into the cop shop with my gun, give 'em a bit of a scare.' Mick can't help himself.

Slater throws him another dark look, takes a sip of his soy-milk cappuccino and stares at me. The snake head curving up over his jaw seems to nod as he speaks.

'Once you've confessed to all three shootins and the job you pulled the ovver night on the Serbs, we'll be ready for the final exchange. But that will be wiv your daddy, because you'll be in jail. We want whatever was in the back of Vucavec's van, plus five million bucks in cash. Then we'll deliver your beautiful wifey back home. Oh, that's right, you don't have a home anymore, do you? No car either, I heard. Why do you keep losin' fings, Johnny?' He leans back again and smiles, as if his world is golden.

I let his jibes about my house and car wash over me. Those things are replaceable.

'So now you're adding five mil to the ransom?'

'Yeah. And I'm feelin' pretty good about it too. Come on, Johnny, she's worth it, you know she is. That wild blonde hair, that beautiful face, those long, long legs. I want 'em wrapped around me shoulders, Johnny.' His smile is a leer now. 'So don't fuck up or she's stayin' wiv me. She'll just have to learn to like it.'

It takes every ounce of self-control I have to stay still, not pick up the glass bottle, smash it on the table and drive the broken end into Slater's rancid throat. I could kill him with what's within reach. This knowledge somehow calms me.

'What do you know about Ivan's murder?' I'm not giving up. 'He was taking out the bins too. The cops reckon it was the same shooter.'

'So you've been talkin' to the cops, have you, Johnny? Good to know. Did they say the same gun was used?' He leans forward again, interested.

'Different gun.'

'Different gun. Different shooter. Not us, like I said. I reckon it was an inside job, using the same MO, so it looked like it was us. But it wasn't us. All you have to do is park somewhere away from the streetlights. Huntin' rifle, good shooter. All you need. But it wasn't us.' Now he's leaning back again, that smug smile on his dial.

I still don't believe him but it's time to move on. 'Okay. Final question. I get the whole war-on-the-West fixation, but it seems like this has become personal and I don't know what I've done to deserve the attention.'

'It's not *you* who got my attention, Johnny Novak. Don't flatter yourself,' he sneers. 'This is all about Amy. I'll never forget the first time I saw 'er, down the cop shop.' His eyes drift, unfocused. 'Fuckin' hot, but classy, you know? Seen 'er lotsa times since. Been keepin' me eye on 'er. Watchin' out for 'er.'

My whole being wants to kill him. Now. But that won't get

357

Amy and Sasha back. I wait. His dark eyes shift back to mine.

'Now fuck off, Johnny. I'm sick of your ugly mug.'

When I get back to the Range Rover, Marko is in the driver's seat. I swing into the passenger side and he pulls out, heading for Liverpool. Shaking with pent-up rage, I rip the recorder from my chest, attach it via an adapter to my phone and hit download. Once the gadget beeps at me, I bluetooth my phone to the car, open the file and hit play.

I let it run and hear a car door slamming, my footsteps on concrete, the sounds of the Saturday-afternoon crowd on Chapel Road. I calm down, amazed at the quality of the audio coming out of the car's speakers. I hit fast-forward, then play again. I hear Slater saying, 'We didn't kill Ivan.'

'Bullshit,' says Anto from the back seat, and I nod, then put my finger to my lips.

When we get to the part about providing a replacement Remington 700 hunting rifle, Marko raises his hand from the steering wheel. I hit pause.

'I have a Remington 700. You can give him mine.'

My initial reaction is relief, one more thing I don't have to worry about. Then I start to wonder. I look at Marko. He's staring straight ahead as he navigates through the peak-hour traffic. He feels my stare.

'What?' His voice is low.

'So you've got a Remington 700?'

'Yes, I do. Along with seven million other people. It has been manufactured by Remington since 1962. It is the most popular bolt-action sports rifle in history. He can have my 700, but he is not getting my scope, sling or bipod.'

'Fair enough.' I say. 'Thanks, mate.' I guess once you've fought in a war, you want your own private arsenal. Whatever makes you feel safe.

'No problem,' Marko continues. 'I give you my old 700. I recently bought a new one. It is an M40A5 Remington 700. It is the best. The US Marine Corps snipers use it. One rifle will be enough.'

Back home...it's pretty tragic that I'm referring to my parents' place as 'home' again, but I guess beggars can't be choosers. Dad is watching rugby league re-runs and Mum is in the kitchen peeling potatoes. Granny Slater is having a nap, Bigsie stationed outside the bedroom door and Brick in the garden, outside the bedroom window.

The Dragons are thrashing the Bulldogs. Nice, appropriate. Definitely worth a second viewing. But Dad takes one look at my face and turns off the TV. Mum comes in and sits down. She's in this now and we won't be leaving her out again.

'You get Ink Slater to admit he kill Ivan? Play me tape.' Dad demands.

I sit down too, put my phone on the coffee table and hit play. No one comments as it plays, but there's bewilderment on both their faces.

'He say he not kill Ivan? If Ivan not killed by Ink Slater, must be Stanislav, he murder my son.'

'I guess it's a possibility, Dad, but my gut still tells me Slater is lying.' Nothing else makes sense. Something nags at my memory, but I can't grab it. Dad is still shaking his head.

'And why he have this, this thing for Amy?'

359

'Obsession, Milan. He have obsession.' Mum comes up with the horrifying word.

'I have no idea,' I answer, but I know why.

'She is very beautiful, our Amy.' Mum knows too.

Dad waves this line of conversation away.

'Ink Slater lying about killing Ivan. We get Sasha back, we kill bastard. You kill, you promise.'

'Dad, believe me, I will have absolutely no problem killing Ink Slater. Anyway, this isn't getting us anywhere. The recording still delivers, and two contracts on Slater and his boys are better than none.'

'Two contracts better than none. We invite Stanislav and Antonio here for lunch tomorrow. Branka cook something nice. I try not kill Stanislav.' Dad nods again, no doubt imagining the scene. Then he shrugs and purses his lips. 'I also have news,' he pronounces, folding his arms and sitting back. He looks especially pleased with himself.

'What news?' Because he wants me to ask.

'Rashid Sami want whole shipment. I organise meeting for after lunch. At Fish Market. You and Marko come. We do deal. Nice afternoon on boat.'

'Really?' Some good news at last. My surprise makes him grin. 'Dad, that's great, how did you organise it?'

'Have many friends you not know.'

'Rashid Sami? Okay, well if the Lebs take the whole shipment off our hands, they must be very good friends.'

'Is good. Yes. Tomorrow, we have the cash. I take twenty per cent. Is normal. You, I give ten per cent, the rest go to crew.'

'What about fifteen per cent each, and we share the rest with the crew? It was my plan.' I keep my voice as emotionless as I can, but I'm not fucking happy. 'Without me and Anto snatching Nick, none of this would have happened.'

'None of this would have happen. Maybe, maybe not. But is my crew. You not boss. I am boss. You take ten per cent and be happy.' Dad turns the TV back on.

As usual, Dad wins. I should have negotiated a better deal up front. I guess whatever I get out of this job will be enough. It has to be enough.

AMY

Our lunch delivery was pasta salad, delivered by Twin A. I know which twin is which now—Twin A has a small gold hoop earring in his left ear. As usual, my attempt to start up a conversation got me nowhere. I loathe pasta salad, but at least there was some greenery mixed in with the soggy spirals. We haven't been getting enough vegetables and I've been feeling bloated and out of sorts. Sasha and I started an exercise program this morning; we took turns choosing which exercise to do next. He wanted to leap off the bed. I wanted to do triangle pose. Our program was never going to last. When he suggested tackling practice, I knew it was time to stop.

After lunch, Tattoo Man delivered a pile of old and yellowed magazines, a few paperbacks and a game of Scrabble, but no pen and no paper. He was full of himself, clearly expecting profuse gratitude. But Sasha wouldn't even say thank you—I was half-embarrassed and half-proud. The kid cannot be bought. Then Tattoo Man called in Twin B to help him bind our hands and feet with cable ties again, before he took a photo of us. It must have something to do with the ransom negotiations, so I was secretly glad.

By the way the light is hitting the blind, I know it's now late afternoon. The last two hours have been really quiet. No signs of life from outside, other than the occasional siren or horn beep. Sasha is reading *National Geographic*s from the eighties. He sniggers when he comes across some bare-breasted women in an article about the Amazon jungle.

A noisy, white pedestal fan moves stale air around our room, almost managing to imitate a breeze. I was so excited about the fan's arrival I didn't notice the Kmart bag until after the twins had left the room. Inside was a pair of board shorts and a T-shirt, Sasha's size, and a yellow sundress for me, again, the right size. But what really threw me was the white lace bra-and-panty set. La Perla, definitely not from Kmart. And 34C. Oh God, Tattoo Man must have bought this lingerie. How did he know my size? What a creep! I shudder and push the lingerie back into the bag.

It's hot as hell. I sniff under my armpits—yep, I stink. I can't believe I've been in the same clothes since Thursday morning and it's now Saturday afternoon. There are towels in the bathroom and now we have clean clothes, but I'm freaked out by the thought of getting naked with those guys right outside the bedroom door. Sasha is pretty stinky too, so I ask him to shower and change. The sound of running water does my head in as I imagine being cool for the first time in days.

Sasha comes out of the bathroom flicking his hair out of his eyes and looking like a new kid in his new clothes.

Fuck it. 'Sasha, I'm going to have a shower too. If anyone opens the door, tell them to come back in ten minutes. Okay?'

'What if it's Dad coming to rescue us?'

What a wonderful thought.

'You can let Dad in.'

'What if it's the police coming to rescue us?'

'You can let them in too, but not those men out there now, not until I'm finished getting dressed. Okay?'

'Yes, Mum.'

I think it does us both good to pretend we have some kind of say over who comes into our room and who stays out.

The water is heavenly. I can't help groaning with pleasure. The body wash, shampoo and conditioner are the same brand I use, which is weird. Have these guys been in our bathroom or is it just a coincidence? Millions of women use these same products; they're not expensive. I talk myself around to the latter conclusion because the former is too hard to handle.

Is that noise the slam of the front door? I finish up, wrapping the towel around my wet hair, then stare at the clean, white-lace bra and panty set, hesitating. It feels safer to put back on my old, sweaty bra and undies, but the desire to feel clean all over wins out, and I rip the tags off the new lingerie and dress quickly. The sundress is cool and comfortable, a welcome change from my smelly jeans and T-shirt. In the mirror, I look almost normal, like a pretend version of myself. Bundling our dirty clothes into the Kmart bag, I emerge from the bathroom just as the key turns in the lock. I dump the bag on the floor and hurry over to join Sasha, who is sitting in the middle of the bed. Perched on the edge, I turn to face the door, the towel still wrapped around my head.

When Tattoo Man walks in, he stops and stares at me. He smells even worse than earlier. His balaclava is riding up on the right side of his neck, revealing a length of green snake and a black spider's web. His thin lips are like a slash in the balaclava, opening to reveal yellow twisted teeth. He's smiling.

'I'm glad you like your new dress.' He sounds pleased with himself. I feel as if I'm going to heave.

'Yes, thank you. We both liked being able to have a shower and get changed.'

'You've got a towel on your head.'

'I washed my hair.' I don't know what else to say.

'You look nice.'

Sasha wriggles closer to me and grabs my hand.

'Stand up. Not *you*, Sasha. Just Amy.'

I do not like the way he just said my name. Why does he want me to stand up? I have goosebumps all over. I don't move.

'I want you to stand up and take the towel off your head, Amy.'

This time I do as I'm told, staring at the floor, so I don't have to look at him and his creepy tattoos. The damp towel is now clutched in my left hand. My lips are trembling. Sasha squeezes my right hand, keeping me anchored.

'Beautiful. Your mum's very beautiful, Sasha.'

Tattoo Man steps forward, reaching out to touch me, even as I recoil from him.

'Stand still, Amy.' His tone is sinister now.

I'm transfixed by his bloodshot eyes, the irises so dark it's hard to tell where the pupils begin, like bottomless pits. Terrified, I look away, over his shoulder, as though I can make him disappear. His rough fingertips are pushing my damp hair back off my forehead and tracing a path down to my chin. The blood seems to rush out of my head and then back in again like a wave hitting the shore. He wouldn't, would he? Not in front of my son. His fingertips trail down my neck, over my collarbone. My whole body is trembling now and I have to clench my legs together to avoid peeing myself. I can't believe this is happening, even though I've been dreading it all along. His fingertips slide further down. He stops at the top of the yellow sundress, then slips one strap off my shoulder. He's checking to see if I've put on the lacy underwear. I knew it—I shouldn't have put it on. He'll see it as an invitation. I'm blushing. I'm going to throw up.

'Don't touch my mummy,' Sasha growls, launching himself off the bed and around Tattoo Man's waist. Tattoo Man staggers back and Sasha lunges again, punching him in the stomach, then kicking him in the shins, before Tattoo Man grasps both Sasha's wrists in one hand. His eyes flashing with fury, he draws back the other arm to unleash a punch of his own.

'Stop! Sasha, he'll hurt you!' I struggle to wrench Sasha back towards me.

'Dave! Get your fat, lazy arse in here!' yells Tattoo Man, slowly lowering his clenched fist.

One of the twins bursts through the door, pulling his balaclava down over his face.

'Get the kid outta here.'

Instinctively, I throw my arms around Sasha, holding on to him, but strong hands prise us apart and Sasha screams.

'Stop! Wait!' I shout, and stop struggling. 'Sasha, go with the man. It will only be for a couple of moments. Then you'll be brought straight back to me. Won't he?' I look up, pleading, into those black eyes.

'Yep, a cupla minutes, kid, then you can come back to your mummy.'

Sasha looks at me, frowning, his eyes bright with unshed tears.

'Go with the man, it's going to be fine. We're just going to talk about getting us home safely. Okay?' Sasha doesn't look convinced, but he has no choice. The Dave twin has a firm grip on his arm and pulls him from the room, closing the door. Now there's no handbrake. I can almost feel the hot breath in my ear. He'll hold me down. No matter how hard I struggle, I mustn't scream. Sasha mustn't hear.

There's a cruel smile on those thin lips as he approaches me again. My legs are pressed hard up against the bed to stop them trembling. I adjust the strap on my dress. Right in front of me now, he reaches out and flicks the strap back off my shoulder. I close my eyes and try to distance myself from my body in a last-ditch effort to protect my mind.

'Okay. Time for business.'

I'm faint with relief as I open my eyes. Thank God. He's moved away from me and is leaning against the dresser, arms crossed. I'm still shaking as I sit back down on the bed, my legs no longer supporting me.

'Amy?'

'Yes?' I take a deep breath, push my terror aside and raise my chin off my chest.

'Sasha will be going home tonight. You need to get him ready, so he doesn't put up a fight. I don't wanna have to hurt the kid, okay?'

Fear shoots though me as I think of being separated from Sasha, but I calm myself with the thought of him safe in his father's arms.

'Okay.' I agree. 'What about me?'

'Johnny is going to give me a whole lot of money for you, and you're worth it. But he's also gotta give himself up for all those murders he committed. He cleaned a few wogs up, I'll give him that, but killing his own bruvver.' He tut-tuts in disbelief. 'Amy, your husband is a bad man, he's gonna end up in jail for a very long time. You'll need someone to look after you. May as well be me.'

All I can do is stare at him as my mind tries to deal with what he's telling me.

'Now, when I let your kid back in, you could tell him what I just said about his dad, but it would be a bad idea. You wanna know why?'

'Why?' I say in a small voice. My ears are buzzing again. My face is hot. I want to scream at him: Johnny didn't kill anyone!

'No kid needs to know his father is a murderin' scumbag. Leave it to me to sort out. I'll make it right for you. I'll even take on the snotty little brat as me own, if you want me to.' His voice and eyes make my skin creep, as though he's touching me again. 'But first I gotta get me nan back and that means handin' Sasha over. If the kid does sumfin stupid, he'll get himself killed. Maybe he and Johnny both get killed. You see? You followin' me, Amy?'

'I understand.' I have no idea what he's saying about his nan. What the hell has Johnny done? I'll say anything to get my son back in here and this disgusting psycho out.

'Good girl. Make sure Sasha understands he's gotta be good too.' He waits for me to nod. 'Johnny is gonna be locked up for a very fuckin' long time. But you and me, Amy, we're gonna have loads of money. We'll fly anywhere we want.'

Two strides and he's back over to the bed, pulling me roughly to my feet, his mouth descending on mine. I try to resist as the rough wool of his balaclava scrapes my cheeks and his hard, thin lips press against mine. His foul breath makes me gag. As he pokes his tongue into my mouth, I twist my face away, once again filled with terror about what he's about to do to me. But he sniggers, shoves me back on the bed and walks to the door.

'You'll learn to like me, Amy. You'll learn.'

I can still feel his tongue in my mouth and his hands on my skin, as though I've been branded. I wipe his saliva from my lips and taste the bile at the back of my throat. Sasha is pushed into the room, the door locked behind him. We rush to hold onto each other.

'He's a bad man, Mum. We're going to have to kill him.'

JOHNNY

We have fifteen minutes before our scheduled meet with the Hyde twins. Dad turns his Hilux into Brandon Avenue, Bankstown, then takes a left into Northam. Marko gets out, reaches into the tray for a small guitar case and heads into the multi-storey public car park. Now alone in the back seat, Granny Slater remains quiet. She knows her part in the plan and seems happy to help her new friend Branka. I'm twitchy, but hopeful our plan will work. Once we get Sasha back in one piece, we'll follow the twins to Amy.

Dad chucks a u-ey and takes another left, back into Brandon, then a right into the laneway by the car window-tinting place. The lane doglegs past dumpsters to an ancient car-repair shop, locked up for the night. There's enough room to turn the car around, so we're pointed back the way we came. There's no other way out. Dad turns off the headlights and leaves the car running. The night is cloudy, no moon, hot and still. No one around. We could easily be blocked in here. Our only backup is Marko.

He'll have taken the stairs to the roof of the car park and be sandwiched between two cars, lying on the ground, his new Remington M40A5 balanced on its bipod. He's got a night-vision scope and a clean line of sight. If this turns out to be a trap, Marko will do what he can to even up the odds.

I gnaw at my thumbnail as I wonder what the last two days have done to my little boy. Sasha's a brave kid. He throws himself into sports like his body doesn't matter. He will have taken his lead from his mother, so it really depends on how Amy's holding up. There's bound to be nightmares. Fuck. I close my eyes for a moment and picture what I am going to do to Ink Slater.

Headlights come round the corner. Time to concentrate on getting Sasha back or kill anyone who gets in my way.

The headlights belong to a black Mercedes SUV. Two identical shapes in the front seats. I can't see a Sasha-sized shape in the back.

'Stay put until I come back there to get you out,' I say to Granny Slater, without taking my eyes off the Mercedes.

'I'll get out when I bloody well want to.' The old lady huffs, but stays put.

Dad raises his sawn-off shotgun, rests the muzzle on the dash and points it at the driver.

I step out of the car slowly, as one of the twins mirrors me from the passenger side of the Mercedes. Instead of coming towards me, either Dave or Mick turns to open the back door of the Mercedes. He pulls something from the back seat. My heart is pounding. The headlights are blinding. I hold up my hand to block the glare.

Yes, it's Sasha, with a black bag over his head.

'Turn off the headlights so I can see!' My voice is just loud enough to be heard above the engines of the two cars. The headlights go off. The result is momentary blackness, but when my night vision returns, I see Sasha's hands are bound and he's pulling away from the man holding him. He's heard my voice. I feel a moment of panic.

'Stay with the man, Sasha! I'll come and get you. You're okay, you're so brave. Stay there.'

As soon as Sasha stops struggling, I turn, open the back door of the Hilux and help Granny Slater out. She has a large Tupperware container of Branka's chicken soup in a plastic shopping bag, along with a loaf of bread and a carton of milk. Branka couldn't bear the idea of the old lady returning home in the middle of the night without fresh food.

Granny Slater also has her handbag, minus the ancient revolver. I take the plastic bag, hold her arm, and start walking towards the twin holding Sasha.

We meet in the middle, between the two cars. I release my hold on Granny Slater's arm.

She takes one step towards the man with the pierced ear and hisses at him. 'Let that poor child go. You should be ashamed of yourself.'

Dave pushes Sasha forward and I gather him to me as I hand over the bag with the food. I can feel Sasha shaking as I hold him against me, his face hidden inside what looks like a pillowcase. He's trying to tell me something, but he must be gagged. All I can hear are distressed mumbles. I curb the over-powering urge to hurt the man standing in front of me. He does have the decency to look ashamed.

'We've slid pretty low here, haven't we?' I say.

'It wouldn't be my choice. But the kid's been well looked after. And Mrs Slater seems happy enough.' Ruefully, he glances at the plastic bag full of food in his hand. Granny Slater takes it from him and walks back towards the Mercedes.

'Goodbye, Johnny, I'm glad Branka has her grandson back. But wait until my grandson gets hold of you. And I'm not talking about Ian,' she says over her shoulder.

I ignore the old lady and focus on the man in front of me. 'Tell me where Amy is. I'll pick her up and this all ends now.'

Dave Hyde shakes his head slowly. 'Ink wouldn't like that. Sorry.' He indicates my father, behind the wheel. 'You were told to come alone.'

'Well, I didn't. What are you gonna do about it?'

Dave sighs. 'Have you got the replacement 700 for Mick?'

I nod, lean down and lift Sasha into my arms, holding him close and telling him how glad I am to have him back. His reply is muffled, as he tries again to speak through the gag. I retrace my steps to the car and place him carefully in the back seat, where Granny Slater had been moments before. Still bending over him, I pull off the pillowcase. The gag is some kind of packing tape. Fucking animals.

'This is gonna hurt.' I rip the tape off.

'I'm sorry, Dad,' he whispers, as I use my switchblade to cut the cable tie from his wrists.

'You did great Sasha. You're so brave. You've got nothing to be sorry about.' I kiss him, my hands on either side of his face.

'Dad, I'm not crying.' His voice is shaking as the tears stream down his face.

'I know you're not crying.' I crush my son to my chest

373

again; it's hard to look at his sad little face. How could I have let this happen to my boy? Dad's big hand is patting Sasha's knee.

'Dida, I couldn't rescue Mummy. I wanted too, but she wouldn't let me.'

The anger in my father's eyes is terrible, 'You very brave. I'm so proud of my Sasha.'

'Now you need to keep being brave, okay?' I keep my voice low. 'Just stay here with Dida and I'll be back in a minute.'

I reach into the ute tray and pull out a gym bag. Inside is Marko's Remington 700, broken down into its constituent pieces. Dave Hyde is walking back towards me with a similar bag. He stops in the middle and waits for me to join him again.

'You know Mick won't swap his gun for anything other than a Remington 700?'

'Don't worry. I have the right gun in here.'

Mick obviously can't contain himself. He gets out of the driver's seat, a shotgun in his hands. I hear Dad respond instantly, getting out of the Hilux. No doubt he's got his shotgun in his hands. This could all go south very quickly, and Sasha will see it all; he might even be a casualty.

Mick stops two metres away, his shotgun aimed at my heart. I don't stand a chance. My heart stops in anticipation of the bullet. In my peripheral vision, I see Dad advance to my right. Marko, for Christ's sake, hold your fire.

'Don't be an idiot, Mick. I'll make sure it's the right gun. Get back in the car.' Dave speaks with absolute authority. Dominant twin all right. Mick grunts and backs up to the Mercedes. Fortunately, Dad backs up too. I start breathing again.

'You'd better open the bag and show me the gun,' Dave says with a sigh.

We both open our bags and look in, a parody of two kids in a schoolyard comparing cut lunches.

Once we're both certain that we've got the same gun in similar gym bags, we swap.

'Now, why don't we stop fucking around and come up with a plan that puts you and your brother in the clear? Why should Slater be the one who benefits here? You two do all the work.'

'Yeah, yeah. Don't think we'll double-cross the boss. Won't happen. Ink's got a major hard-on for your missus, always has. Dunno why. She doesn't have enough meat on her bones for my taste. But he *really* likes her.'

My fingers itch to pull the knife from my back pocket and drive it between his ribs, but I know he's only the messenger.

Dave is staring at me speculatively, maybe the bait I threw out is working. 'We couldn't give her back to you for anything less than, say...the five mil you were going to give Ink. Then we'd seriously have to think about it.'

'Fair enough.' I want the meet to end on a positive note. 'I can arrange that. Put your mobile number in here.' I hand him my phone. Marko was right again. The Hyde twins do have a price.

'Tell me the truth,' I continue. 'You've got nothing to lose.' And I figure there's no harm in asking. 'Did you or your brother shoot Ivan or not?'

'Nup. Like Ink said, we got there too late.'

Dave starts to back away and stops. He's wrestling with something.

'What?' I ask.

'Something the boss said about your wife. He's fucking

obsessed. I don't think he's gonna hand over your wife, no matter how much you give him. You're better off doing business with me.'

'We've got a deal. I'll be in touch tomorrow, as soon as I have the money. Meanwhile, it's your job to keep Amy safe from that evil prick. Okay?'

He nods, but I have no clue if he's taking me seriously.

I take a step towards him. 'If anything happens to her,' I growl, 'I'll find you and kill you.'

'Well, you'd better get a move on with the cash. Without the kid there, there's nothing stopping him anymore, know what I mean?'

'I'll have the money tomorrow. Keep her safe for one more day.'

He nods again and walks away.

Is she alone with Ink Slater right now? What's he doing to her? My blood is surging around my body like a swarm of hornets and my vision starts to narrow. I drag in some deep breaths and hurry back to the front passenger seat of the Hilux. Sasha is on the edge of the rear seat, leaning foward between the two front seats, a determined look on his face.

'Dad, you need to give me a gun. That man? Tattoo Man? We need to kill him and get Mummy back.'

The words make me shudder.

'You make your *dida* proud.' Dad leans back to ruffle Sasha's hair and I see tears in my father's eyes.

'Mummy told me to tell you…'

'Hang on, Sash. I've got to jump out in a sec. Don't worry. Put your seatbelt on. Stay with *Dida*. I'm going to find your Mum and bring her home.'

Dad follows the Mercedes as it backs out of the lane. When we get to the corner, we slow almost to a stop as I grab the bag carrying Mick's rifle and jump out of the car. Staying low, I run to Ivan's Range Rover, which I left parked out of sight near the corner. Dad brakes just long enough to cover my movement, then follows the Mercedes around to the right. I pull the Range Rover away from the kerb and follow.

When we all get to the next traffic light, Dad peels off to the right, as the Mercedes goes straight ahead, towards Bankstown. First, they'll drop off Granny Slater, then I'm hoping they lead me to Amy. All I have to do is follow the twins from a safe distance.

AMY

Sasha did not want to leave, but I convinced him the best way to help me was to deliver a message to his dad.

'Look, you need to stay strong for me, Sasha. These men are not going to hurt either of us. They would rather have the money Daddy will give them. Okay? Does that make sense?'

'Yeah, I guess so. But I think Tattoo Man *is* going to hurt you. He shouldn't touch you or talk to you like that. I still want to tackle the next one who comes in so you can kick him in the head, and then we bust our way out of here.'

'I think you and your dad watch too many westerns together. They have guns and we don't, okay?'

'All right.' Sasha swung again from bravado to tears.

'You just need to tell Dad everything we know. Tell him we think we've been held in an apartment, on the third floor of a building, in Kings Cross or somewhere near the CBD.'

We went over it a few times. He felt better knowing he had a job to do. He stayed silent when they came to take him away.

Now, I'm waiting for the inevitable. With Sasha gone, Tattoo Man has me to himself. He's made no secret of his next step. He's going to walk in that door, lock it behind him and rape me. All I can do is pace around the room like the caged animal I've become, sweating and nauseous. My breathing is out of control. I sink down on my haunches and put my head between my knees so I don't pass out. I'm completely terrified and helpless. And I'm so fucking angry.

I need to be ready. Is this the time to smash the mirror? An improvised homemade knife. But the noise would be a complete giveaway and there goes any element of surprise. A gun beats a knife, anyway.

Once again, I scour the room for a weapon and find nothing. I should have I kept a plastic fork. I can't exactly hit him with a shampoo bottle, can I? Shampoo in the eyes? Yes! That would slow him down for a couple of seconds. I hide the shampoo bottle under a pillow on the bed.

Sitting on the floor in front of the fan, I consider my options. I could wait behind the door with the fan in my hands and whack him over the head with it. But what if it's only one of the twins?

Resistance won't help. If he's going to rape me and I fight back, he'll probably hit me. Shampoo in the eye will only make him mad and then he'll hurt me. I'll focus on the weapon. He could rely on his physical strength to subdue me, but he's pretty skinny. He'll probably use a weapon, in which case I have a chance to take it from him and use it.

Could I bring myself to kill him? The instinctive answer beings a grim smile to my face for the first time since they took Sasha away. Hell, yeah.

JOHNNY

When the Mercedes turns into Slater's street, I keep going, turn right at the next block, right again and find a park a few car lengths from the corner. There's a remote chance they might recognise Ivan's car and I don't want their headlights to hit me if they come this way. Now I can see the red glow of taillights in the driveway of Slater's house. It's all just shadows, but it looks like Granny Slater is being helped from the car by her grandson. If Slater and the twins are here, who's guarding Amy?

My phone vibrates. Dad.

'Sasha, he want to tell you something. Is useful.'

'Okay, Dad, put him on.'

'Dad? I tried to tell you. I'm supposed to deliver a message. Mummy thinks we were in a partment in King Cross.'

'Kings Cross?'

'Yeah, or maybe Ceebeedee. In a partment. It's not like a house, it's up a whole lot of stairs, in an old building. She told me to tell you it was on the third floor and the first door on the right. Everything was really old. And there's three men. Two

380

men who are the same size and have the same voice, so we think they're twins. They took me in the car to meet you. We think the other man is the boss and we call him Tattoo Man.'

'That's really great, Sash. Anything else you remember?'

'They gave us food every day, but we were getting sick of Chinese and pizza. And they gave us some new clothes, some old magazines and a fan. And Tattoo Man really liked Mum in her new dress and then he touched her face and I had to tackle him. I think he's a really bad man and I think he loves Mummy. That's not right. Is it, Dad?'

'No, absolutely. It's not right, Sash. And I'm going to get her back safe and sound. You've done a great job delivering all the messages. Your mum would be proud of you.'

I end the call and sit back, waiting. I'll gouge Ink Slater's eyes out so he can never look at my wife again. Then I'll cut off his hands.

The Mercedes is backing out of Slater's driveway. I sink down low in my seat as the car heads towards me, then turns right and away from me. I follow, leaving the headlights off until we turn onto Marion Street. We're heading into town. I keep three cars between me and the Mercedes, but knowing they're probably heading for the Cross makes it easier to anticipate which route they'll take.

Two-thirty a.m., as Saturday night becomes Sunday morning, the bars of Kings Cross are spilling onto the streets. Nothing like it used to be: Sydney's red-light district is being gentrified, turning into an expensive residential area, full of bankers.

We move at a crawl down the guts of Darlinghurst Road, past the Coke sign. I'm two cars back when the Mercedes turns right. After a couple more turns, they pull up out the front of a three-storey Art Deco building in what is technically Elizabeth Bay. Kings Cross doesn't really exist, it's a locale, not a suburb. One day it'll be just a memory.

I slow down, indicator on, as though searching for a car park. Dave gets out of the car and uses a key to enter the building. I turn left down a laneway, just before the building, so I don't have to cruise past Mick. He's still sitting in the Mercedes, window down, lighting a cigarette.

A car is pulling out, so I snag the parking spot. A bit of luck at last. Grabbing my gun from the glove box, I pull my hoodie up and walk back to the corner, about twenty metres away from the apartment building. In deep shade, under a leopard tree, turned away from the Mercedes, I take out my phone, lean against the wall and pretend I'm listening to someone on the other end. I change the camera around to selfie. All I have to do is lean slightly to my left and the camera screen shows me the parked Mercedes and the footpath between the car and the Art Deco building.

Five minutes later, Dave strides across the footpath and slips into the front passenger seat of the Mercedes. After a brief exchange, Mick pulls out and drives away. I expel all the air in my lungs and feel a sense of exhilaration sizzle through my veins. Sasha was right. Amy is here. I don't know who's up there guarding her, but it's not Slater or the Hyde twins.

Spotting a pizza place further up the street, I walk over and buy the ready-to-go supreme with the lot. I wolf down two slices as I walk back to the building. I'm kind of shocked at myself, but the smell got to me.

I stand on the first of two travertine steps leading up to a pair of timber-and-glass doors. Six names, typed on yellowing paper, beside six buttons. Ink Slater is not on the list. As I'm considering going back to the car to get everything else I need, the door opens and a young professional couple waltz out. In the middle of an argument, they take no notice of me as I catch the door and let myself in. If I wedge the door open now, I can go back to the car and get the gun and the drugs. But someone else might come in or out, remove the wedge, and the opportunity will be lost. Fuck it. My first priority is to rescue Amy. Everything else I have planned is a bonus.

I make my way up the staircase. Stained-glass windows extend up three floors, the colours backlit from the streetlights outside. A faded red carpet runs up the middle of the stairs. I can't imagine living in such a beautiful building. What the fuck is Ink Slater doing here?

On the third floor, 3A is the first door on the right. A Mr Fredrick Handers is supposed to be living here. I knock on the door. Loud footsteps approach.

'Who is it?' A western-suburbs accent, but it's not Slater's.

'Got a pizza delivery here for Dave Hyde.'

The pizza is in my left hand and the Glock in my right.

The door opens on a big, bearded bikie dude, wearing the obligatory jeans and leather vest and displaying an impressive number of tatts on gym-junkie biceps. He doesn't even look at me, his eyes are only for the pizza.

'Nice work, Dave,' he says, as he starts fishing around in his pockets for a tip.

Using the pizza box to push my way inside the door, I punch him hard in the stomach, my fist reinforced by a pistol grip. I close the door with my foot as he plants his face in the pizza box, all the breath rushing out of his lungs. Then I whack him on the back of the head with the barrel of my gun, and he goes down like a sack full of hammers.

Leaving him there in the hallway, I walk further into the apartment. High ceilings, old dark-timber furniture. Even a chandelier. The first door on the right is closed. I don't try the handle. Instead, I check the rest of the apartment, gun cocked. No one else here. Now I try the closed door. It's locked.

'Amy, are you in there?'

AMY

I can't believe what I'm hearing.

'Johnny?'

There's a loud thump, the cracking of wood, and the lock gives way. Johnny flies into the room, only just stopping himself from bowling me over.

I'm standing in the middle of the room, sobbing, and I don't know what gibberish is coming out of my mouth, but he wraps his arms around me. I pull back to look up at him. His eyes are bloodshot, his face pale and drawn. He's aged.

'Is Sasha okay? Did they give him back to you? Is he all right?'

'Yes, love, he's fine, he's with Dad. He's safe.'

Something flickers across his face like a lost memory. Then behind Johnny a big, bearded bikie looms in the doorway, a gun pointed at us.

Johnny must see it in my eyes. He turns around slowly, drawing his gun but keeping it hidden behind his back.

The man is holding one hand to his head. He's wobbling in

his boots, his gun wavering between me and Johnny.

'Keep it pointed at me, mate, I'm the dangerous one,' Johnny says.

As soon as the gun is pointed at Johnny, I launch myself at the bikie's legs, a beautiful, old-fashioned rugby league tackle, down around his knees. Sasha would be proud of me. I bring him down like a falling tree. The gun flies in the air and clatters to the floor somewhere outside the room.

'Well done, Ames!' Johnny sounds amazed, but he's not as amazed as me. The man tries to sit up again but Johnny shoves him down, planting a foot on the guy's chest and aiming a gun at his face.

'What's your name?'

'Pete?' The bikie answers with an upward inflection, like he's not even sure himself. He's younger than I first thought.

'Now, Pete, you're not gonna give us any more trouble, are you?'

Pete doesn't answer but doesn't move either.

'See what you can find to tie him up with, Ames.'

I leave the room for the first time since Thursday night. Near the front door is an open pizza carton and Pete's gun on the floor, a few feet into the living room. A CZ Shadow. Good, I know how to use this one. I pick it up, check the safety and drop the magazine into the palm of my hand. Full. I drive it back home and rack the slide, then look around. The spacious room is full of the same dark-timber furniture as the bedroom. I spot my handbag on the coffee table and head straight to it. No gun.

'How are you going out there, Ames?'

'I've got Pete's gun and I'm looking for some rope or something.'

386

Down the hallway I find a lime-green kitchen straight out of the sixties. It doesn't take me long to locate a packet of black cable ties and a roll of thick packing tape—exactly what was used on Sasha and me.

After tying up and gagging Pete, we use another couple of cable ties to secure him to the old gas radiator in the corner of the bedroom.

'Let's get out of here,' I say, heading back towards the living room for my handbag.

'Look, Ames, the last thing I want to do is leave you here, but I need to get a couple of things out of the car, first. Okay?'

His words send a spike of terror through my chest.

'No. I want to come with you.'

He walks back to me, folds me in his arms again.

'Ames, I need you to get rid of any evidence we've been here. It's important. Wipe down everything you or Sash might have touched. I'll be right back. I promise nothing will happen to you.'

He gives me one last squeeze.

'Keep the gun in your hand. If anyone but me comes through that front door, shoot them.'

JOHNNY

As I made my way back up the stairs to 3A, toting a gym bag, I didn't expect to hear voices.

Fuck. I'd been gone for less than five minutes. Who is it? All three of them? I stop on the second-floor landing, pull on black latex gloves and unzip the gym bag. I reassemble Mick Hyde's rifle with surprisingly steady hands. Thank God for all that training out in the bush. The rifle isn't loaded but two guns are always more impressive than one.

I creep up the last flight of stairs. The door is ajar. Cradling the butt of the rifle in my left shoulder, the handgun in my right hand, I use the rifle to push the door open.

The twins are shoulder to shoulder in the hallway, their backs to me. Only one has a handgun drawn. No earring, Mick. Dave is holding two full plastic shopping bags. At the doorway of the bedroom where she's been held hostage for days, Amy is facing them, Pete's gun held in both hands, eyes and gun pointed at Mick. She doesn't look at me.

Dave holds one of the bags up.

'Put the gun down and we won't have to hurt you. See, I thought you might be sick of bacon and egg sangers, so I brought you some pastries for your breakfast tomorrow.'

I have the rifle pointed at Mick's broad back and my revolver pointed at Dave. Nice big targets. I take another step forward.

'Stay right where you are, Dave. Don't move. Mick drop the gun. NOW!'

Both men freeze. Dave swears under his breath, but Mick doesn't drop his gun, so I take another step forward and nudge him in the back with his own rifle. Mick's handgun clatters to the floor. Dave turns fast and throws a bag full of pastries straight into my face. Amy shoots Dave in the back of the leg and he goes down. Mick reaches for his gun.

'Don't do it, Mick. Look at your brother.'

Dave is sitting on the floor clutching the back of his thigh, eyes locked on mine.

'Hands on your head, Mick.'

The big man straightens up again, his hands moving to his head.

'I'm going to kill you, but first I'll fuck your wife to death in front of you and then I'll kill you.' Mick has a way with words when he's angry.

'Yeah, yeah, like hell you will. Amy, the cable ties.'

That shot was loud. I'm expecting sirens. We have to work fast.

We get both men face down on the living-room floor. Amy holds a gun on them as I get on with the cable ties and packing tape. While Amy guards Dave, I walk Mick into the bedroom with my gun pressed against his kidneys. Mick kicks Pete in the stomach as I manoeuvre him past. What a prick. I manage to cable-tie his wrists to the other side of the radiator, beside Pete, but he keeps kicking, making it impossible to secure his legs. I whack him on the side of the head with my gun, knock him out, then tape his ankles together.

'Dave, you need to get yourself up and over to the other bedroom.' I use my gun to indicate which way I want him to go. Even cable-tied, he manages to lurch to his feet and half-walk, half-hop to the other bedroom, where I secure his wrists to another radiator, then yank his belt from around his waist and use it as tourniquet on his upper leg.

'Don't want you bleeding to death before the cops come, do we?' He telegraphs his next move, so I see the headbutt coming. I tape up his ankles without further injury to either party.

Amy has found some cleaning products and is doing her best to wipe away all traces of our presence in the flat. I hide Mick's rifle and a shoebox full of ecstasy in the wardrobe of the master bedroom. On the bedside table, Amy's little Ruger and Ivan's Beretta sit on either side of my Gucci watch like armed guards.

'Thank you very much,' I say to the world in general.

Now I've got three guns stuck in my waistband and two watches on my wrist. I pull the baggie of carpet fibres from Stanislav's van out of my back pocket. But something stops me. Why throw him under the bus?

'Johnny. I need you out here.' Amy's voice sounds weird; I feel as if a cold hand is clamped on the back of my neck. I should have realised it was all going too well.

I draw the Glock before walking back into the living room, where Slater and Amy are in a stand-off, guns pointed at each other.

'So you came to rescue Amy, did you, Johnny?' Slater keeps his eyes on Amy.

'You better point that gun at me, Slater. I'm the one who's dangerous.' It worked before, so I figure it might work again. He shifts his aim to me, and Amy shoots him. His gun hand drops, his left hand now clutching his right shoulder, his eyes bulging in disbelief, as he staggers towards her, gun pointed at the floor.

'You fuckin' bitch! Why the fuck did you shoot me?'

His left hand slides down to grab the gun from his useless right hand. The gun is coming back up, pointing at Amy. Everything slows down as my finger tightens on the trigger, but Amy reacts first. This time she shoots him in the chest. Slater is already falling when my bullet hits him in the left shoulder, spinning him in midair. He falls to the floor face up, just missing Amy as he goes down. She stands her ground, gun now pointed at Slater's forehead. His eyes are open, disbelieving. He twitches once and lies still. I stare at her in amazement.

Her gaze is still on his face and she's turning green, as if she's about to throw up. I pull her away from the body and sit her down, tucking her head between her knees. Gasping, she hands me the gun without bringing her head up.

'Slow breaths, Amy. Nice and slow.' I grab a cleaning cloth from the coffee table, where Amy must have dropped it, and wipe down the gun, before tossing it on the floor. Then I pocket our three spent bullet casings, wipe my own gun and toss that too. When I run back into the bedroom where Dave Hyde is lashed to a radiator, I find him trying to remove the packing tape over his mouth by rubbing his face against the wall.

'Listen, Dave, pay attention. Your boss is dead. I had to

shoot him; it was self-defence. The police will be here soon. Staying tied up means you can't be blamed for his death. Mention me and you'll end up facing a kidnapping charge. Jurors will take one look at Amy and Sasha and wish hanging was still an option. Just say you had a fight with Ink, he tied you and the others up, and then you heard a voice you didn't recognise, shots were fired and that's all you know. Got it?'

He nods his head slowly.

'Can you keep the other two in line?'

He nods again. Now I have to trust him to be smart.

When I get back into the living room, Amy gives me a weak grin.

'That will teach them to mess with us,' she says.

'You're a fucking firecracker, Ames, but now we really need to get the hell out of here. Four shots—someone will have heard them.'

I look around. We're ready to go. Still no police sirens as I close the door behind us, wiping off any fingerprints I may have left on my first visit to the apartment. Living so close to the Cross, the nice people of Elizabeth Bay are probably used to the sounds of gunshots in the night.

At the top of the stairs, I pull Amy to me—our kiss is long and gentle, almost chaste. I bury my face in her hair and finally grasp what's been nagging at me.

AMY

Casting my eye around the room we'd been held in since Thursday night, I avoided the gaze of the two men tied to the radiator. I tucked the CZ Shadow under my arm as I picked up the Kmart bag filled with our dirty clothes. In my other hand I was clutching the cleaning rag I'd used to wipe down our prison and its ensuite. Back in the living room, I left the Kmart bag on the coffee table, next to my handbag, so I wouldn't forget it. Then I heard the front door open. I was already hyper alert, but it felt as though I'd been given an intravenous shot of ephedrine. As I pulled the gun out from under my arm, my thumb found the safety catch and flicked it off, just as I'd learned to do at the firing range.

Tattoo Man must have seen the blood and pizza near the front door and realised something had gone wrong, because his gun was in his right hand as he slunk out of the hall and into the living area. The man who'd asked me to suck his dick a few years ago at the police station. No balaclava this time and it wasn't an improvement. His black eyes darted around nervously, and his face looked feral as it twitched between amusement and rage. He took another step towards me and the blood started whooshing through my ears. Not a good time to pass out. I forced in a ragged breath.

'Johnny. I need you out here.' My voice sounded as if I was underwater. I was holding the gun in both hands, out in front, trigger finger poised. I let the training dictate my movements and willed my hands to steady.

On my left, Johnny appeared in my peripheral vision, gun pointed at Tattoo Man. He'll give up now, I thought. Two against one. I didn't want to shoot him.

'So you came to rescue Amy, did you, Johnny?' Tattoo Man hissed, his eyes still on me.

Our earlier rehearsal helped. His attention diverted by Johnny, Tattoo Man swung his gun around to point at my husband, his tattoos flexing, fury spitting out of those black eyes. In that instant, all that mattered to me was protecting Johnny. Inhaling, I aimed for Tattoo Man's right shoulder. Exhaling, I pulled the trigger, focused on the impact, prepared for the recoil, and shifted the gun straight back into firing position.

Tattoo Man's eyes swivelled back to me, a look of surprise on his face, his mouth forming words I couldn't hear. I stared at the gun dangling uselessly from his right hand. He took a step towards me. I willed him to stop, but the stupid man grabbed his gun with his left hand and brought it back up to point at me. I had no choice. My belly filled with fire as I pulled the trigger and saw the blood bloom on his chest. Then another shot rang out and he spun around and fell right at my feet, surprise still etched on his face as the light faded from those black pits. The burning in my belly turned to nausea; I was about to throw up, but then Johnny's arms were around me, pulling me to the floor, and pushing my head between my knees.

Now, my heart is racing as I hurtle down the stairs after Johnny. The multi-coloured stained glass reminds me of a cathedral window. Johnny throws open the front door of the building and the night air feels like a kiss.

Holding my hand, he leads me around the corner to a black Range Rover. I recognise Ivan's car and the sweat on my skin turns icy. I back away from the passenger door, swearing under my breath, but my need to see Sasha overrides my terror and I get in, hoping Johnny didn't notice my hesitation.

'Sorry, what did you say?' asks Johnny, as he puts the car in gear and pulls away from the kerb.

'Why are we in Ivan's car? Where's Sasha? Who's looking after him?'

'He's at Mum and Dad's, he's fine,' Johnny says, turning to me. 'Amy, there's a lot we have to talk about.'

He has a strange expression on his face. Everything feels wrong. I'm in shock. I just killed a man. Fucking hell, I can't believe that just happened. The sight of his dead eyes and the bullet holes in his shoulders and chest, it all comes back again like a punch in the face. I'd asked myself if I could kill—turns out I can. I have to hit the window button and stick my head out in case I throw up. When I get myself under control, I look back at Johnny. His eyes are on the road.

'Okay, so can we pick Sash up and go home?'

'No. They fire-bombed our house. It burnt down. My car got destroyed in the fire. We can't go home, honey, I'm sorry.'

There's a terrible sobbing sound. I only know it's me when

I feel the tears on my face.

'How are we going to get out of this, Johnny? This is a war and we're caught in the middle. And I just killed Tattoo Man!' The sound of my wailing fills the car until I choke it back.

'His name was Ink Slater and he deserved to die, Amy. And I shot him too, remember?'

We both know it was my shot that killed the man, but he wouldn't want me shouldering that burden alone.

'Now, I need you to stay quiet while I call MacPherson.'

I slap my hand across my mouth as he punches a number on his phone. The phone has bluetoothed, so the ringing surrounds me.

'MacPherson.' A voice laden with sleep.

'Johnny Novak.'

'What are you doing calling me at this time of night?'

'I've got an address for you, in Elizabeth Bay. You might want to send a team around. And you might also want to check out the black Mercedes ML63 parked around the corner while you're at it.'

'What's the address?'

After the address, the detective wants more.

'What does this address have to do with you, Johnny?'

'Nothing to do with me, mate. Only helping you solve your case.'

'Hmmm, we'll see about that. I still expect you down at the station at nine a.m. or I'll come looking for you.'

'No worries. I'll be there with bells on.'

I killed a man and Johnny is inviting the police over to the crime scene we just left behind. I'm so tired. I might just close my eyes for a minute.

JOHNNY

Amy is still asleep when we get back to Mum and Dad's. She feels fragile in my arms as I carry her into the house. When she crawls into my old single bed with Sasha, the kid wakes up and goes nuts. Seeing them together is confusing. Sasha in Amy's lap, skinny arms around his mum, crying, telling her he's so sorry he couldn't rescue her. It should be the most beautiful sight I've ever seen, but there's that T-shirt in the back of Ivan's car. Why the fuck does a T-shirt in the back of my brother's car smell like sex and also smell like Amy? My mind has been bashing itself up against this horrible question all the way home from the Cross.

Mum and Dad make an appearance and then Mum insists we all eat something. She's making toasted sandwiches as I leave them to it in the kitchen. There's no room inside me for food. Instead, I decide to sit out on the front steps, Ivan's Beretta hidden under a newspaper in my lap, and watch the dark street. Soon enough, Dad brings me a cup of tea.

'Why you out here with gun? I should call boys? Get them back?'

I don't regret sending the men home when we left with Granny Slater. There's no way I'll be sleeping tonight. 'No, Dad, I can keep watch. Just in case.'

'Okay. We are ready if they come.' He retreats inside, only to return with two kitchen chairs, which he carries past me to level ground, positioning them to face the street. He pulls his gun out of the back of his shorts and sits down.

'Is more comfortable.'

I join him on the other kitchen chair and hand him half my paper to hide his gun. He puts his hand on my shoulder, one squeeze, then it's back in his lap. His touch makes my eyes sting.

My mind is on fast-forward.

The twins and young Pete will be in police custody by now. The rest of Slater's crew will learn about their change of fortune soon. They're not likely to retaliate tonight. They might not retaliate at all. I could delay the calls to the Serbs and the Italians. Give the bikies time to scatter. Give them a chance to get out of this life.

Either way, I'm not putting this victory at risk. Not tonight. Instead, I sit, a cup of tea in one hand, a gun and a newspaper in my lap, my father by my side.

I should be euphoric. Ink Slater is dead, no longer a threat. I've outsmarted the twins in ways they don't even know about yet. I rescued my son and my wife. Or did she rescue me? What if she hadn't taken that first shot? If she'd hesitated, would Slater have killed me? I can still see the determined look on Amy's face, her hands steady, as she took that second shot, the one that ended Ink Slater's life. Do I even know my wife at all? I roll my head from side to side to relieve the tension and

398

let the questions go. Sip my tea. Drift.

But my mind snags on a submerged log. The T-shirt in the back of the Range Rover.

The thought I've been trying to avoid is like a sledge-hammer, slamming into first one kneecap then the other. Amy. Ivan. Is that why Ivan couldn't look at me the last time I saw him? A bottomless pit of betrayal is opening up under my feet.

How long had it been going on before he died? I grip the cup of tea so hard I break the handle clean off. I glance at Dad, wondering if he noticed, but his eyes are closed. I drop the handle into the empty cup and put it on the ground beside me.

I must have it all wrong. There's no way. Ivan has always been loyal to me, above all else. Amy, I don't know. Maybe she could betray me. She can kill, that much I do know. How can you ever really know a woman?

No. That's not what happened. I switch my mind onto my other problem.

There's no reason for either Ink Slater or Dave Hyde to lie about killing Ivan. It wasn't the twins waiting in a car with a hunting rifle on the night Ivan died. Stanislav Vucavec could have ordered the hit on his old enemy's son. But that hadn't smelled right from the start, and it doesn't smell right now. What am I missing?

I thought Amy came home to me during that kiss in the stairwell, lit by stained glass—even though we no longer have a home. That was before I knew about her and Ivan. But I don't *know* anything, do I?

I lean the chair back against the house, rubbing my eyes with my thumbs. Think about who killed Ivan, not about Ivan and Amy. What do I really know?

I know Ivan's murder was premeditated. You don't randomly stake out some guy, wait for him to bring his rubbish bins out and shoot him with a rifle. If it wasn't Slater and it wasn't the Serbs, who does that leave? The Italians? Really? Why? Ivan was killed before Tony Fazzini. There's no overlap with the Chinese, so they're out. The Lebs?

It makes sense that whoever murdered Ivan used the prior shooting to cover his tracks. Which makes it an opportunistic, copycat killing. That rules out some random guy finding his wife in bed with Ivan. That kind of killing is done in a moment of passion. He'd have to be a cold fucker to use a prior gang shooting to kill off his wife's latest conquest. So if it wasn't some disgruntled husband and it wasn't one of our enemies, who does that leave?

Was Ivan killed because he was having an affair with Amy? I shut my eyes, trying to see it. Dad has a Remington 303, but he could get a 700. Easy. But it doesn't wash. If Dad found out about an affair, he'd have shot Amy. He wouldn't have killed his own son.

Mum couldn't fire a gun, let alone a rifle. Well, I don't think she can, but the women in my family have surprised me a lot over the last couple of days. The mere thought of Mum killing Ivan is ludicrous.

What about Marko? Up until tonight, he owned a Remington 700. No, he owned two. Plus, he was a sniper in the Croatian army during the war. But there's no way he would have killed his best friend over an affair. Besides, he doesn't even like me, so why would he defend me?

Amy. Amy. Pain shoots up through my chest. Amy is the best suspect. If she *was* having an affair with Ivan, wanted it to end and Ivan wouldn't let her go, she could lash out. Tonight, she proved she can kill a man. I replay the tackle she made on young Pete. She faced down the leader of a bikie gang. She has nerves of steel.

No again. Amy doesn't know how to use a rifle and doesn't have easy access to one either. Besides, she was in bed with me on the night Ivan was killed. Wasn't she? A voice in the back of my head answers the question. Amy always says I can sleep standing up with one leg in an ants' nest. Could I have slept through her getting up and disappearing into the night with a rifle? Could I have slept through her car leaving the garage and coming back again? Or could she have walked six blocks to Ivan's, carrying a rifle? Even at night, it would have been a high-risk strategy.

I let out a long breath. I can't see how it could have been Amy. Or I don't want to. My mind circles around on itself. Nothing makes sense.

The sky in the east is already starting to lighten. I close my eyes and try to focus on my meeting with MacPherson in just a few hours. Everything could still go pear-shaped. Fucking CSIs.

Dad starts to snore and lean to his right. Pulling my chair a little closer, I put my arm around him and let his whopping great head rest on my shoulder. He smells like rollies, beer and Brylcreem. Strangely comforted, I close my eyes just as a local crew of kookaburras let loose. I know their cackles are saluting the dawn, but I can't help thinking they're laughing at me.

JOHNNY

I've had no sleep, but after a shower I feel nearly human. In the daytime, I seem to have more success at stashing dark thoughts under a rock. And with Sasha and Amy back in the fold, breakfast was a festive occasion in the Novak household.

Down at the police station, a Christmas tree has been installed in the lobby. Cheerful. Sam Dillard, in his pale-blue suit, is waiting for me by the front desk. As usual, he's on the phone, but we shake hands warmly.

'Anything I should know?' he asks, leading me away from the desk sergeant after he finishes his call.

'Nah, I think I've got it covered, just need you here so Dad doesn't flip.'

'Okay. I'll follow your lead. I'll only step in if I think it's going to shit.'

Once MacPherson, Dillard and I are installed in an interview room, I bring out my phone and play the recording of Slater admitting to the two murders. Anto has edited out the references to the ecstasy heist and the denial of Ivan's murder.

'How did you get this recording?' asks MacPherson.

'I met with Slater yesterday, took a micro recording device. Smart, hey?'

'Illegal is what it is.' MacPherson scowls at me. 'You do know this recording is not admissible in court, don't you? And why would he tell *you*?'

'Some morons like to skite about their dirty deeds. I don't know if you've noticed this, Detective, but most criminals are pretty dumb.'

MacPherson throws back his head and has a good old belly laugh. I can't help it. I have a bit of a chuckle myself. Sam looks worried.

MacPherson wipes his eyes. 'So I guess you want to know about our raid on the Elizabeth Bay flat last night? How did you know about the place?' He leans forward, serious again. 'Did you kill Ink Slater?'

'Me?' My face is a mask of disbelief. Sam makes a choking sound. 'I've never been anywhere near the place. A little birdie told me you'd be interested, so I called you. So Ink Slater's dead? Best news I've heard in a while.'

'What did the birdie tell you?'

'I seriously don't know more than I told you last night. An address was all I got.' I'm all innocence. 'But you look pretty happy, mate. And I think I've contributed to that. As a law-abiding citizen, trying to help, I think I deserve to know what you found.'

'Do you now?' MacPherson sizes me up, but I can tell he's sitting on something big and wants to spill. I look at Sam and hope he can prod MacPherson to cough up.

'Come on, Detective, surely Mr Novak deserves to know

the outcome of the information he generously imparted to you?'

MacPherson looks from Sam back to me and laughs again.

'Ian "Ink" Slater died at the scene from multiple gunshot wounds.'

'Good riddance,' I snarl. 'The world is a better place without that piece of shit. What else did you find?'

MacPherson hesitates but I'm leaning forward now, so keen that I'm practically willing him to divulge more.

'This will all come out in our press statement later today, so I may as well tell you. Apart from one dead body, our raid yielded a shoebox full of pills, similar to the ones we found a couple of hours ago under Slater's bed. From the markings on the pills, I've no doubt test results will show they come from the same batch.'

I feel bad for Granny Slater; her grandson is dead and that dawn raid I'd hoped for actually happened. I'll go and check on her later today.

'Anything else?'

'All up, we've got a drug haul worth over a million on the street. We also found three other gang members, conveniently tied and gagged. Both the Hyde twins, one of them with a gunshot wound to the leg. And I suspect we have you to thank for all this, don't we, Johnny?'

'No way! Nothing to do with me. As if.'

MacPherson stares at me, probably trying to calculate how he can trip me up somehow. But he must also be dying to boast about the bust because he ploughs on.

'We found two Remington 700 rifles, one inside the flat, the other in that Mercedes SUV parked around the corner, registered to one Ian Slater. More handguns inside the flat. No fingerprints anywhere.' He pauses and fixes his gaze on me for a few seconds, before continuing. 'But we did collect some long blonde hair from one of the shower drains. Doesn't your wife have long blonde hair?'

'The Eastern Suburbs are chock-full of blondes, mate. Why would my wife be there?' But he's got me on the back foot. I'm playing a dangerous game here.

'I don't know, Johnny, but it might be worth investigating at some future date. What we *do* have is a nice clear thumb print on the cartridge casing we found at the scene, and that casing matches the bullet we pulled out of Zoran Milovic. And guess who's profile matches that thumbprint? Your cousin Marko Novak was the last person to touch that casing. Which puts him right in the middle of the job pulled on the Serbs on the Marsh Street Bridge on Thursday night.'

His quick change of tack is a punch to the gut. He must see my reaction. So does Sam, who puts a hand up to intervene. But I'd prepared for this scenario.

'Marko left his gun at my place a couple of weeks ago. He had some friends with little kids staying from Croatia. He thought he'd be extra careful. I had it locked up in the gun safe, of course, right where it was supposed to be, but when those bastard Hyde brothers burgled my place last week they took it.'

'How convenient. You didn't report the theft, Johnny, and you had the perfect opportunity when I was sitting in your living room, going through the other incidents.'

This earns me a surprised look from Sam, but he doesn't interrupt.

'Yeah, but you saw the bullets in the wall from when they shot out my front window. You saw what they did to my next-door neighbours' dog. They burgled me the very next night. I could have rung you up again and told you, but I figured you had enough on your plate. And your team hadn't exactly set the world on fire solving my brother's murder.'

MacPherson chooses to ignore the dig. 'Perhaps the reason you didn't call was because the gun was an illegal firearm, purchased on the black market, serial number filed off.'

'Really? I had no idea.'

'Yeah, right. Well, the gun that created the rifling marks on the bullet that killed Milovic was also conveniently found taped under Ink Slater's bed, and he's not around to refute your story.' MacPherson sits back and sighs, but there's still a smile playing around the corners of his mouth.

'Look, Johnny, my gut is telling me you masterminded this whole thing. You pulled the job on Stanislav Vucavec and his crew, framed Ink Slater and set up the whole scene at the Cross last night.'

'Not me, Detective MacPherson. Seriously, I'm dyslexic. I'm not that bright.'

AMY

Last night, while I was cleaning up in the Kings Cross flat, I found my phone in the kitchen, sticky with fingerprints. Because I'd had to give Tattoo Man the pincode so he could use it to call Johnny, I wondered if he'd spent time looking through my photos. Disgusted, I threw it in the sink, sprayed it with bleach and wiped it down.

This morning, while Johnny is down at the police station and Branka is getting lunch organised, I leave Milan and Sasha watching footy re-runs. I find myself a spot in the corner of the backyard, under the shade of a couple of banana trees. As I press Chaz's number, I can still detect a whiff of bleach on my phone.

'Oh, thank God, Amy! Where the hell have you been? Why haven't you called me back?' Chaz sounds totally pissed off.

'I'm really sorry, Chaz. It's been…out of control.' I have no idea what to tell her.

'Where are you?'

'Milan and Branka's.'

'You're back from the North Coast already?'

'We never made it up there.'

'What happened? Johnny was supposed to call me the moment he heard from you. I called him over and over and he didn't call me back! I'm so mad with you both for making me worry like this!'

'I'm so sorry, love.' I make a decision. 'You can't tell anyone what I'm about to tell you. Are you alone?'

'Amy, you know me. It's in the vault. Jenny's out the back, she can't hear me. Tell me!'

'So, what happened is this guy, the head of the local bikie gang, kidnapped me and Sasha, just after we left your place on Thursday night.'

'What the actual fuck?' Chaz sucks in a big breath. 'You're kidding? Are you both all right?'

'We're fine. Well, sort of. Johnny organised for Sasha to be released and then busted me out.'

'Busted you out?' Chaz sounds as if she's hyperventilating. 'What do you mean? Was anyone hurt?'

'No, no, nothing like that. He used his persuasive powers. Now we're back here at Milan and Branka's, safe and sound.'

'You know your house burned down, don't you? I drove over there last night, to see if I could get some news out of Johnny, because he wasn't answering my calls. There's a smoking ruin where your house used to be. And crime tape across the front. I thought you'd been burned alive. I actually called Liverpool police to find out if there had been any casualties.' Chaz's anger finally gives way to tears.

'Oh God. I'm so sorry, sweetie. Really I am. I feel terrible,

I should have called you when I woke up this morning. But Johnny brought me home late last night and this is the first chance I've had. I think I'm still in shock.'

Chaz blows her nose loudly. 'It's okay, I understand. I'm just so relieved you and Sasha are both okay. So you're at the in-laws? I'd have thought that was the last place you'd want to be. I guess you can always move into Ivan's place.'

I swallow. 'Yeah, not sure that's a good idea. We might stay in an Airbnb until we sort something out. Anyway, don't worry about it, okay?'

'I think I actually need to see you to believe you're okay. Did those bikie thugs…you know…interfere with you in any way?'

'No, they treated us pretty well, considering. But the leader of the gang was covered in tattoos and seriously creepy.' The memory of his fingers on my face sends a deep shudder through me. 'But Johnny got me out in time.'

'Fucking hell, how hideous for you. How's Sasha holding up?'

'He'll be fine, I hope. We've got stuff on today, but we'll have a proper catch-up with the kids tomorrow. Okay?'

'Amy, I'm going to have to be honest here. Have you considered that being part of the Novak family might just be too dangerous?'

'I've got a plan, Chaz. I'll tell you tomorrow. I need to help Branka now. We've got people coming over for lunch.' Chaz would die if she knew who.

I hang up and wonder if I'll ever have the guts to tell my best friend the truth.

•

Branka is running around like a mad woman, preparing a late lunch for her husband's sworn enemy, Stanislav Vucavec, and the head of the Italian crew, Antonio Fazzini. The dining table is set with Johnny's grandmother's handmade linen from Dubrovnik. The room is flooded with the heady perfume of gardenias, masses of them sitting in a shallow, blood-red vase in the middle of the table. For me, it's the smell of Christmas.

Johnny managed to get in touch with both gang leaders early this morning, and wasn't surprised that they were available and very curious.

At the front door, Johnny greets Stanislav and his cousin Phil with an outstretched hand and brings them through to the living room, where Milan and Sasha have set up the bar on the sideboard. Both Vucavecs are tall, blue-eyed, dark-haired and lean. Dressed nicely in tailored trousers and linen shirts, their only concession to the heat is their rolled-up sleeves. Their expressions are serious as they shake hands with an equally solemn Milan, but they break into delighted smiles when introduced to Sasha.

'Hello, Mr Vucavec and Mr Vucavec, I'm Sasha.' Looking earnest in a crisp pair of blue shorts and a white shirt, Sasha holds out his hand to Stanislav, then Phil, just as he's been taught. Branka retrieved the new clothes from under the Christmas tree this morning. No doubt there will be more presents for her grandson under the tree in time for Christmas Day, only two weeks away now.

Branka had a new outfit stashed under the tree for me too—I'm in a conservative navy frock. There's no other way to describe it, but it beats the hell out of that yellow sundress. Johnny introduces Branka, in her Sunday best, then me.

Stanislav bends over Branka's hand, as though he's going to kiss it, and then does the same to me, with a wink. I find the gallantry strangely endearing.

The four men settle into armchairs with glasses of beer, no drinking from the bottle today. Branka retreats to the kitchen and I stand by the sideboard with Sasha, taking it all in. Regardless of the differences in eye colour and body shape, these men could be cousins. They share the same brutish ridge across the eyebrows, the same wide faces and olive skin. Looking at them seated together making polite conversation, I'm struck again by the stupidity of this ongoing nationalistic animosity.

Antonio Fazzini arrives with his brother Alonzo, both short, dark, hairy men in beautifully tailored suits and polished leather shoes, the flash of gold cufflinks and chains nestled at the throats of open-necked shirts. I'm almost surprised when they don't speak with New Jersey accents.

The awkward civility dissolves over lunch, Branka serving but not sitting with us, until I get up and pull the chair out for her myself. She blushes as she sits down next to Milan. Stanislav is on her left, then Phil, Antonio and Alonzo. I'm between Johnny and Sasha, who is on his best behaviour; he seems to understand his role implicitly. He asks the men about where they grew up, what their favourite games were when they were his age. Conversation becomes easier.

The fish soup is excellent, followed by a variety of roasted meats, served with *blitva* and carrots. Fresh bread. Good red wine from Korcula. Simple food cooked to perfection, each platter presented by Branka with a delighted thump on the table and an admonishment to eat.

When the final course is cleared away, I help serve coffee

411

and Branka brings in a plate of sweet, doughy *fritule*.

'Okay, Sasha, come with me. *Dodi brzo*, now. I need your help.' Branka stands in the doorway, ushering Sasha out. She glances at me, expecting me to follow. In the past, I would have been happy to escape, but not this time. She raises an eyebrow and closes the door behind her.

Milan offers us all a shot of rakia. As the wine has already dulled my senses a little, I sip the strong black coffee instead.

Johnny retrieves his phone from the sideboard and holds up his hand for quiet, before tapping the screen. A loud click, a bit of static, then Johnny's voice: 'Okay. Take me through each job.'

When Tattoo Man speaks, it's as though I'm back in that room with his fingers trailing down my throat. My lunch moves uneasily in my stomach. I killed him. I shot one man and killed another. The shock hits me again, waves of stress pounding over me. I want to run out of the room, but I have to stay and hear this through.

No one moves, all eyes focused on Johnny. Beneath the table his hand finds mine; he squeezes it once, then lets go. When he stops the recording, the room has turned chilly.

'Who were you talking to?' Stanislav is sitting very straight in his chair, eyes burning. Phil looks like he's ready to kill in an instant.

'Why would he tell you about whacking our boys?' Antonio is angry and confused, both hands clenched in fists on the table. His brother mirrors him.

'You know Ink Slater, the head of a Bankstown bikie crew?' Johnny receives disbelieving nods round the table in response. 'I met with him yesterday. He kidnapped Amy and Sasha.'

All eyes swing to me in horror. Luckily, I've regained some semblance of control, though I can feel a bead of sweat working its way down the side of my face.

'He car-jacked me on Thursday night.' I'm a bit pleased with myself for coming up with the right term. My breathing is returning to normal.

'He wanted me to confess to the murder of your two sons and my brother Ivan,' Johnny explains, 'as part of the ransom for Amy and Sasha.'

'But they are free again?' Antonio is even more confused.

'I negotiated the release of my son.' Johnny leans back in his chair and fails to mention the negotiation involved handing back Ink's nanna. 'Then I followed Slater's men to the Cross, where I found Amy.'

'These men must all die!' Stanislav is looking around, as if this is the natural next step and everyone will agree.

'Well,' says Johnny, 'we may have already taken care of most of the problem. Slater's dead.' He pauses for emphasis, glances at me as if he still doesn't believe it. 'His lieutenants have been picked up by the police, along with a significant amount of ecstasy, apparently.'

Johnny averts his gaze from Stanislav when he mentions the ecstasy. I admire my husband's performance as he stares into his empty shot glass. Milan uses this as a cue to refill all the glasses. This time I push my shot glass forward to be filled. Why not? I guess I'm now officially Johnny's partner in crime. I didn't ask for it, but I have certainly received my initiation into the family.

'He killed my son. I need to know how this Ink Slater died,' Stanislav demands. I can tell the other men are just as interested in Johnny's answer. But it's Milan who takes up the story.

'Ink Slater kill my son Ivan. He kill your sons. He take Amy and my grandson. On Friday night he burn down my Johnny's home. His car. Gone. Everything gone. My Johnny shoot him and now he is dead, but must still pay.' Milan boils it all down to the bones.

'So you invited us here to help you make him pay? But you're telling us he's already dead.' Stanislav is still confused.

I sip my rakia, which tastes bloody awful, and lean forward. Now it's my turn.

'We don't know how the rest of Slater's crew will react. They're bikies, they're probably all on ice.' The men all nod at me, no doubt agreeing with my description of the bikies, but perhaps also curious that I'm speaking up again. 'Who knows what they'll do next?' I continue. 'Will they take your wives and grandchildren too?' I'm gratified by the looks of terror I see on the faces of these big scary men. After all, I'm speaking from experience, from a place of terror they will never know.

'I will put a contract on every one of them,' says Stanislav.

Antonio competes: 'They are all gonna get whacked.'

Johnny smiles as if a weight has been lifted from his shoulders. 'We'd be pretty happy about that, wouldn't we, Dad?'

Milan gives a half-nod, half-shrug, a purely European gesture, a show of grudging respect.

'Thank you, gentlemen,' I say as I stand. 'I need to help Branka in the kitchen.' I add this purely for Milan's benefit, concerned I may have overstepped, but he stands too, his eyes unusually warm as they meet mine. Our guests follow me down the hallway, stopping to pay their respects to Branka on their way out.

414

JOHNNY

Under Anzac Bridge in Sydney's inner west, Fisherman's Wharf is heaving with tourists and Sydneysiders. Wondering why Dad and Rashid Sami chose a location guaranteed to be this busy on a sunny Sunday afternoon, I follow Marko and Dad onto a dock running perpendicular to the car park. Each of us carries a large duffle bag full of pills. The choice of venue becomes clearer when I notice a sixty-five-foot, red-hulled Azimut motor yacht backing into a berth towards the end of the dock, its mirrored, tear-shaped windows reflecting water and sky. The back of the boat is still two metres away from the dock when I recognise the muscular Lebanese man at the stern of the boat—Rashid Sami's brother, Hakim. He yells out to us.

'We're not supposed to stop here! Tourist boats only. You gotta jump when the skipper brings the boat to within a metre.' He's smiling, as though he's going to enjoy the show. One of his front teeth glints gold in the afternoon sunshine.

Dad doesn't like the idea of jumping onto a moving boat one bit. He never really learned to swim. He's also convinced

415

that the whole continent of Australia is surrounded by man-eating sharks. I've seen him dog-paddling in the Adriatic but, even then, he held onto a rope tethering him to the back of the boat. He's turned pale now, so I time my jump to get onto the duckboard first, reaching out an encouraging hand to Dad. He glares at me, then jumps, nearly knocking me into the drink with his duffle bag. Marko is the last across.

'I suggest you hold onto something,' Hakim Sami says, before yelling up towards the fly bridge to an unseen skipper: 'All aboard!' The motor yacht jerks away from the wharf, then cruises out into Blackwattle Bay.

We make our way from the duckboard onto the aft deck, where Hakim greets us with his left hand extended. The three middle fingers are missing. He laughs at the look on Dad's face, then sticks out his right hand to shake.

'Milan, you're looking good!' he says with a modicum of respect, now that Dad is grasping his hand and towering above him.

'Hakim Sami. Is nice to see you. You know my nephew, Marko? My son, Johnny?'

'Yeah, Milan, I think we've bumped into each other a few times down the cop shop over the years, haven't we, boys? And then there was that little dispute we had about who should really own north of Parramatta Road, right?'

I can tell by Dad's scowl that he's still unhappy about the outcome of that skirmish, but he's not going to react to the dig and jeopardise what we're here to do.

Now we can see into the main saloon of the boat: like a luxurious living room, all pale wood and cream upholstery. Two more stocky Lebanese guys stand like sentinels on either side of the glass sliding door between the aft deck and the saloon. Even in board shorts and T-shirts, they're clearly hard men, one with a livid scar where his right eye should be, the other handsome in comparison. Those three working eyes are roaming over every inch of us Croats.

A tall, tanned, big-bottomed girl in a tiny bikini opens the glass sliding door. Another almost identical girl, wearing an even tinier bikini, appears with a tray bearing three frosty bottles of Peroni. Behind her emerges Rashid Sami, small, muscular and deeply tanned, his hand outstretched.

'Milan Novak. How are you?'

Dad drops his duffle bag, shakes the hand of his counterpart and takes one of the proffered beers.

I haven't seen Rashid Sami for a few years. Although the head of the Lebanese crew is only a couple of years older than me, he's too high up the food chain for the usual round-ups. He has some serious gold jewellery going on. Looking up at me, he shakes my hand, a big smile on his face, capped teeth, blinding white. Brown eyes, deadly cold.

He clicks his fingers. 'Girls, up on the bow and don't come down until I tell you.' The girls scamper up the side of the boat.

'Now the deck garnish has cleared off, let's sit inside and enjoy those beers while we discuss business. I apologise, but my men will frisk you first. It's just routine, you know, to make sure this isn't some kind of set-up. The Feds are getting pretty creative these days. And you can leave your bags out here.'

I'm glad our crew only has to worry about the Western Suburbs Organised Crime Unit. Snaring the interest of the Federal Police must be a whole different ball game.

I kind of figured we'd get searched, so I'm not carrying,

but I know both Dad and Marko will be armed to the teeth. I offer them both a diplomatic way out by suggesting they leave all weapons on the white leather seat running along the stern of the boat.

There's a bit of grumbling in Croatian between Dad and Marko as they pull an impressive range of hardware out from under their shorts and linen shirts. Then we're all frisked gently by either One Eye or Handsome. Hakim has disappeared inside, which concerns me a little, but I decide to go with the flow and hope for the best. Just for a change.

Dad makes it through the frisking test with Handsome. But Marko fails his test with One Eye, who finds a small knife strapped to his leg, right below his ball sack. Marko and One Eye square off against each other. We all back away. Things are about to get ugly, when Rashid Sami speaks sharply in Lebanese. One Eye smiles and extends his hand to Marko and they shake. Seriously, sometimes it feels like I'm the only sane person in the world. I need to get away from this life.

Soon the three of us are seated in armchairs facing Rashid Sami, who is lounging on a curved sofa across the saloon.

'I'm hoping you've brought along something useful.' Sami gestures languidly to the bags lying abandoned on the aft deck.

'We have two million, nine hundred and seventy-two thousand pills,' I reply. 'Not the three million my father promised. I had to use twenty-eight thousand pills to set something up. You might hear about it on the news. It's good for both of us.'

'I did hear that young Ink Slater was found dead and that his crew were caught with a load of pills. That was you?' Rashid Sami is staring at me with new-found respect I don't feel that happy about earning.

'All I can say is the world is a better place without Slater.' I'm not admitting anything. 'Our price is seven dollars a pill. Now, this is triple A-grade MDMA, nothing backyard about the quality. You should get anywhere between the Australian average of thirty-two to fifty bucks a pill. It's a premium product.' I pull out the small baggie of pale-pink pills that had passed the frisk test, each pill stamped with a lightning bolt. I hand them over to Rashid, as Hakim comes up the stairs with a testing kit.

Hakim sits down beside his brother, brings out a test tube and litmus paper. It doesn't take long before he nods, clearly impressed.

'These are as close to pure MDMA as I've ever seen,' he tells Rashid, who seems mildly annoyed. His brother has clearly taken away some bargaining power.

Rashid turns his attention to Dad. 'I meant to say, I am sorry for your loss. Ivan was a great bloke. Did you find out who killed him?'

'Ink Slater killed Michael Vucavec, Tony Fazzini and my Ivan.' Dad has decided to go with Occam's razor. I wish I could, but it's still not sitting right.

Rashid nods. 'And now Ink Slater is dead. Good. May Ivan rest in peace. So, we will pay your asking price of seven dollars a pill, which means we need twenty million, eight hundred and four thousand dollars.'

Now it's my turn to be impressed—pretty good mental arithmetic.

'Twenty mil is good.' Dad waves away nearly a million dollars with a magnanimous smile.

I glare at him; it's not his to give away.

'What?' He shrugs. 'Always leave change on table. Is good.'

'I like this rule, Milan,' says Sami. 'Thank you.'

Rashid raises his beer bottle. We clink, say cheers and drink our beers.

'Hakim!' barks Sami.

His brother nods, collects his testing equipment and heads below to get the cash.

A large, black, Nike duffle bag sails up the stairs to land with a thud, followed by another, then another, until there are four duffle bags in a heap at the top of the stairs. Hakim reappears, grinning, holding a fifth bag.

'Here you go, boys!' Unzipping each bag in turn, he opens them wide to reveal the contents, chock-full of cash. 'Four mil in each bag. All fifties.' Hakim throws a five-thousand-dollar bundle of fifties to each of us, so we can see the cash up close. I reciprocate by heading out to the aft deck to retrieve one of our duffle bags. I show the Samis the sandwich bags packed with pills. There's no longer a lot of room to manoeuvre in the saloon full of bags of cash and drugs.

'Now!' Rashid snaps his fingers again. 'We can all sit here on my lovely boat, counting money and pills, or we can trust each other. What do you think we should do, Milan?'

Dad looks intently into the eyes of the small Lebanese man and appears to see something there he likes. He smiles and stands up. The rest of us follow suit. Everyone shakes hands again.

Hakim walks out onto the aft deck and yells in Lebanese to the skipper. The boat makes her way back to the dock. Dad is positively graceful as he leaps across the gap between the duckboard and the dock, clutching his Nike duffle bag full of money.

JOHNNY

I leave Marko and Dad back at the warehouse, counting money. Josef and Baz have been called in to help and the mood is upbeat. Until I learn who killed Ivan and why, I can't join in the celebrations. My mind keeps taking the dark path, back to that T-shirt in Ivan's car.

Sasha's hysterical laughter greets me as I walk through Mum and Dad's front door and find him chasing Amy up the hall with a water pistol. When Amy takes refuge behind me, I cop a squirt in the face. I can't help smiling as I run after my kid and scoop him up when he tries to escape out the screen door. Holding him in my arms, I never want to let him go. But he thrashes around, yelling, 'Put me down, Dad! Put me down!' Amy is doubled over with laughter.

I look from her face to my son's and sigh. I release Sasha and give him a gentle push towards the kitchen.

'Go and talk to your *baba*, but don't squirt her. Treat our Branka with respect. Okay, Sasha?'

'Okay, Dad.' Sasha gives me a huge grin, then runs full

pelt towards the kitchen, only slowing down to give his mum a quick squirt in passing.

'Looks like he's going to be okay.' I'm surprised and relieved.

'He had a nightmare last night.' Amy's expression changes instantly. She stares anxiously at me. 'But I went straight to him. I woke him up and held him,' she continues. 'It probably won't be the last nightmare. But he's young.' She sighs. 'He just needs time.'

'What about you? Will you be okay?'

Her hand flies to her face, covering her eyes as if there's something she can't bear to see.

'That creep told me you had to confess to all the murders and that you would do something stupid and get yourself killed.' Her voice is a rasping whisper. 'No matter what you did or how much you paid him, I don't think he was ever going to let me go, Johnny.' She pauses, inhales deeply, then drops her hand and stares straight at me. 'But did I have to kill him?'

'We both shot him, Ames. We did the right thing. You know that, don't you?'

The look in her eyes is so bleak, I want to put my fist through the wall. Ink Slater had better be burning in hell right now.

'Did we have to kill him?' she whispers.

'You gave him fair warning. If you hadn't winged him, he would have shot me. He didn't have to die, but he aimed his gun right back at you. He was pretty unhappy, Ames. He was going to kill you.' I almost smile. 'He messed with the wrong girl.'

This is when I should take my wife into my arms. I don't move. As she stands in the hallway, the sun streaming in, Amy's hair is a halo. She's wearing her own jeans, rescued from the Kmart bag and freshly washed. Mum must have helped her find an old T-shirt. Metallica, one of Ivan's favourites. Part of me dies.

'We need to talk.' I incline my head towards my old bedroom.

Amy nods, but there's something in her eyes I can't read. Is it guilt? It's time to find out what's been happening behind my back.

AMY

Johnny is staring out the window as if he wants to escape through it, rather than have this conversation. He turns and sits on the end of his old single bed, beside a pile of Sasha's washing.

'Why don't we drive over and pick up our suitcases from Mum and Dad's? We can see if my car is still there, where Slater parked it.' If I distract him with mundane tasks, I might never have to tell my husband about Ivan and me.

He doesn't answer, he doesn't look at me. I sit opposite him, on the end of Ivan's bed, our knees nearly touching. When he brings his gaze back to mine, his eyes are full of pain.

'Were you having an affair with Ivan?'

The question really should surprise me, but somehow, just like everything else, I knew it was coming.

'No.' My voice is small, not the vehement denial he's probably expecting.

'So what was going on between the two of you?'

'Why do you think there was something going on between Ivan and me?' I'm not avoiding his eyes like a guilty person, but

424

there's a terrible sadness flowing through me, making it hard to breathe and hard to hold his gaze. And I do feel guilty.

He seems to be willing himself to stay calm. His hand is shaking as he brushes a few dark curls from his face. He knows. He's found out somehow. But what exactly does he know?

'I found a T-shirt in the back of Ivan's Range Rover. It smelled like sex, like he'd wiped himself after fucking someone in the back of his car. The T-shirt also smelled like you, Amy. Your scent.'

I raise my gaze to the ceiling as my eyes fill with tears. I do not want to cry. I blink the tears away and take a deep breath, sitting up straight. Finally, I bring myself to look directly at my husband.

'Remember the night, right before Ivan died, when he had that party at his place? He made us all drink tequila shots?'

Johnny nods, but there's a grimace there too, no doubt he also remembers the hangover the next day. All the younger members of the crew were there, wives too, and we alternated between margaritas and shots. We were all completely plastered.

'Right. Well, because Chaz was looking after Sasha, I had the night off and I got pretty drunk. We were all trolleyed, remember?'

He just nods.

My eyes become unfocused as my mind replays what happened next.

'Ivan asked me to come into the garage to check out his new car. He made me get in the back seat, so I could hear the surround sound and smell the leather.' I take another deep breath and look down at my hands, as if they don't belong to me. Don't say it.

'What happened, Amy?'

'Ivan climbed in the back seat too…' I force myself to look up again, pleading with him to understand. 'It all happened so fast. I kept pushing him away and yelling *No*, but it was like he couldn't hear me. Maybe I gave him the wrong idea… somehow.' I can't believe I'm blaming myself, again, for what Ivan did to me. It's not my fault, but I don't want to be a victim either.

'He held me down, his forearm was across my neck.' My hand is at my throat. 'I couldn't breathe. He pulled up my dress, he ripped my undies.' My eyes are closed and I'm back there, the smell of the new car, the alcohol on his breath, the thumping music, so loud it feels as if it's inside my head. That big forearm pressing into my throat, closing my windpipe, the knee between my legs, forcing them apart. I think I lost consciousness for a moment. When I could breathe again, the forearm was gone. Then his hand was over my mouth as he thrust himself inside me. His breath hot and loud in my ear.

'What are you saying, Amy? What the fuck are you saying?'

I open my eyes. Johnny is turning purple. He springs up, storms over to the window, opens it as far as he can and leans out, away from what he's just been told about the brother he's always idolised.

'When he'd finished,' I continue dully, 'he took his T-shirt off, wiped himself and threw it in the back.' I take a deep breath. 'Then he went back inside to the party, left me in the car.' My voice seems to fade out.

Johnny has his back to me. I can feel the anger coming off him in waves. He blames me, just like I've been blaming myself. Is this when I finally get to see my husband lose control?.

JOHNNY

I unclench my fists, trying to contain the boiling black rage. What kind of bullshit is this? There's no way Ivan would do this to me. Ivan was a player, and sometimes he played rough. But to go for Amy? How was that even possible? How could I not know? I turn away from the window, back to Amy, but I keep my distance.

'Amy...' I don't know what to think. I can't look at her. Closing my eyes, I try to block out the images she's loaded into my mind. I rub my hand back and forth across my forehead, taking myself back to that night.

'I don't even remember getting home. Fuck, that's bad.' If what she's saying is true, then I'd been too drunk to help when she really needed me. 'How did we get home?'

'Marko found me in the back of Ivan's car. I was crying. He guessed what happened. I didn't tell him. All I wanted was to get out of there. Desperately. I could hardly walk, so I let him drive me home. He told me he hadn't been drinking, but to be honest, I didn't care. He told me not to tell anyone. He kept saying he'd fix it.' Amy is talking fast now, as if she wants to get it all out.

'He was very determined. He kept saying that if I told anyone, it would destroy the whole family. He explained it to me and, even though I was drunk, it made sense. He said, "Johnny will never forgive Ivan. Uncle Milan will never forgive you, Amy. And *Tetka* Branka will not believe it even happened."'

Marko was right, that's exactly how it would have played out. I'm starting to believe her. She's waiting for me to catch up. I nod.

'On the way home, Marko told me he still has nightmares. The same nightmare every time, seared into his memory. The Serbian soldiers shot his father as he opened the door. There were ten soldiers. They raped his mother and his sister. They shot his mother when they grew tired of her. They raped his sister over and over and over. She died while they were raping her. And Marko was forced to watch.'

I suddenly feel terribly weak, and terribly tired. I let her talk. My anger slowly dying. She must see it in my eyes. She takes a long breath, lets it out, continues.

'He told me if I wanted my marriage to survive, I had to leave it to him to fix…He told me I wasn't to blame. He kept saying that it wasn't my fault. That I had to put it behind me and pretend it never happened. I had no idea what he was planning to do, Johnny. If I'd known, I promise you I would've stopped him. You have to believe me. I would've stopped him.'

My phone rings. I pull it out of my pocket, intent on ignoring it. I need to console my wife, but I feel dead inside. Glancing down, I see it's MacPherson. I show Amy the phone.

'I've got to take this.' I'd rather be hit by a train.

'It's fine, Johnny, we can talk later. Okay?' Amy gets up and walks out, clearly relieved to take a break from our conversation.

'Yes, Detective, what's going on?' I couldn't give a fuck. I want to kill my cousin. I want to dig Ivan up and make sure he's really dead.

'Interesting developments, Johnny. It appears the flat we raided last night, in Elizabeth Bay, belongs to an elderly gentleman named Fredrick Handers. Heard of him?'

There's never any upside to admitting anything.

'No, never heard of him.' Is he trying to establish that I've been to the flat and knew the owner? I don't care. I turn to face the window again and see thunderheads above the trees.

'Neighbours say they haven't seen Mr Handers in months. Looks like Slater may have knocked him off and taken over his flat. Someone's been helping themselves to his savings, but there's no sign of him anywhere, poor old codger. But the twenty-eight thousand pills we found wouldn't fill up the back of a van.' He pauses and I can almost hear him change gear. 'So I wondered if you might be able to tell me how it all links to the job pulled on Stanislav's crew?'

'I have no fucking idea. Nothing to do with us.' I'm on autopilot, staring out the window. Deny, deny, deny. The wind picks up, as images of Ivan holding Amy down on the back seat of his Range Rover ravage my mind.

MacPherson ploughs on. 'But Slater's alibi for that night has fallen through, so it could well have been him.'

I know I should feel triumphant, but I'm numb. And I can tell he hasn't finished.

'The other thing that doesn't fit,' MacPherson pauses,

letting the moment build, 'the other thing that doesn't fit, Johnny Novak, is your cousin Marko's fingerprint on the casing that held the bullet that killed Zoran Milovic.'

Time to say nothing. Let the silence stretch. I'm not helping him reach whatever conclusion he's going to reach. Right now, I couldn't give two fucks about any of it.

'So I've decided to believe your little fairy tale about the Hyde twins stealing the gun from you,' MacPherson finally concedes.

'Ink Slater was a psychopath and the twins are scum and you've cleaned them off the streets.' My voice is so flat it's robotic. I try to inject a more positive reaction. 'I'm happy for you, Detective. Well done. Just shows what a well-led task force can achieve.'

'Don't piss in my pocket, Johnny.'

'Seriously, I mean it. Any news on who killed my brother?' I know who killed my brother.

'I was keeping the best till last. The Remington 700 we found in Fredrick Handers' flat was the same gun used to kill Tony Fazzini and Michael Vucavec. We found another Remington 700 in pieces in a gym bag in the back of the Ink Slater's car. It's the gun used to kill your brother, Ivan Novak. It looks like I was right all along—Slater's gang was behind all three murders.'

I have what I wanted. Our crew cashed up and free, my wife and child safe. I even know why my brother was murdered. I want to cry, but I keep my voice light.

'Sounds like you can expect a promotion, Detective.'

'Yeah, maybe. And perhaps you should join the police force, Johnny.' The detective starts laughing, then stops. 'Seriously, son, get away from your father. Go put that brain of yours to good use. I hope I never have to talk to you again.'

The sky is darkening, thunder cracks close by. Turning away from the window, I put my phone down on the pine table between the two beds and flop on my back, scowling up at the ceiling. I could be sixteen again, waiting for Ivan to come home. When it's dark, Ivan will drive us to Burwood or Strathfield, and we'll burgle someone's house.

My hands laced behind my head, I focus on the damp patch on the ceiling in the shape of a shark. I'm not sixteen and Ivan is not coming home. Ivan is dead, shot by his best friend, our cousin Marko. Shot because he got drunk at his own party and raped his brother's wife in the back seat of his new Range Rover. Shot because he raped Amy. My brother, Ivan, raped my wife, Amy.

My eyes fill with tears. It's impossible to believe. Ivan always found it so easy to pull chicks. He was tall, funny, good-looking, much better looking than me. I worshipped him. What the fuck happened to him? How could the brother who always protected me hurt me this way?

But Ivan didn't do this to me. He did it to Amy. Raped her. Raped her while I was getting pissed no more than twenty metres away. How can she ever forgive me? Marko was the one there to comfort her, drive her home, tell her not to say anything to anyone. He would fix it…

I want to snap Marko's neck. I want to hug the bastard for being there for Amy when it counted. And Jesus, that story about watching his mother being raped, his sister raped to death and his whole family killed. What a fucked-up memory to carry around. It would eat at you like cancer.

431

I had no idea. I remember, back near the beginning of the war, Dad was like a powder keg we had to tiptoe around. I was eleven when Mum told us Dad had lost his big brother, Miroslav, in the war. But no one spoke about it, no details. I remember asking if that meant Marko would come and live with us. But Marko decided to stay there and fight. For the next five years. I was relieved; I didn't want to share Ivan with Marko. What a selfish brat I was. Still am.

Marko has never talked about the war in front of me, and neither has Dad. The subject is off-limits. I've never known anything about the brutal reality of that war. No wonder they both hate Serbs.

Since Ivan's death, I've been confused, running in circles. Only now can I fit together the pieces of the puzzle. Mum having to convince Marko to come over for a meal. The guilt he must have felt trying to look her in the eye. All those moments when I couldn't work out what was going on for him, expressions on his face that I didn't understand.

Amy distant and avoiding sex. Angry when she found out about my promise to avenge Ivan's murder. I thought she was just scared, but she's a fierce woman who was forced into silence. And she must have realised that to break her silence after Ivan was killed would only deliver more death. I would have killed Marko. I'd be in jail right now. She's been protecting me all along, when I should have been protecting her. I feel sick with shame.

Now I understand Marko's willingness to hand over his Remington 700 to use in the swap. He figured it could end up implicating Slater's crew, and that was a risk worth taking. But did he factor in the chance that MacPherson would tell me the gun had been used to kill Ivan? Does Marko want me to know?

I rub my eyes. What am I going to do? I promised to bring retribution for Ivan's murder. Retribution! Like some kind of superhero. What a fucking joke. I was forced to take a stand to avoid shaming my father in front of our crew. All the while Marko knew who had pulled the trigger. Fucking hell.

So am I going to lie here and cry? Or call MacPherson back and tell him what really happened? Or go around to Marko's place and shoot him? Or tell Dad and let him sort it out.

Maybe, for a change, I should ask Amy what she wants?

I stand up, two steps and I'm back at the window. The first fat drops of rain are falling on hot earth and it smells like childhood. I perch on the sill, duck my head and swing my legs out, then drop into the yard. As I step out from under the eaves, the rain hits me, falling harder now, in a hurry to wet the ground.

Tipping my head back, I silently ask the sky for some answers. A sense of calm descends on me as the rain runs down my face, soaking through my shirt, warm and heavy.

My mind is suddenly surprisingly clear. I finally understand how right Amy was all along: my first priority is to get her and Sasha away from here and build a new life somewhere else. It isn't a dream anymore. It's up to me to make it reality. If Amy agrees, we can leave after Christmas. Somehow I know Amy will agree.

I can keep my brother's secret. Ivan paid with his life.

I could hurt Marko, but what's the point? Marko was a sniper in a dirty war. He saw his mother and father shot and his sister gang-raped to death. He'll carry the guilt for the rest of his life. When Marko killed his best friend, he was avenging his sister's honour, as well as Amy's.

Standing in the rain between the house and the side fence, I realise I have to accept that sometimes people are driven to do things they don't understand, driven by needs they don't want to acknowledge. Ivan was brought up in a household where violence was always the solution. He sheltered me from a lot of it. So is it all really Dad's fault? I never got to meet my father's parents, but Dad's stories about his childhood in the old country were scary, awful.

I know I'm programmed for violence too. I snatched a man from his home and threatened to burn him alive. I'm ultimately responsible for his death, and I know the pain and regret I've been ignoring will catch up with me. And there's Ink Slater. I don't ever want to take another life.

And now I've got close to three million in walking money, my enemies are behind bars and our crew is free. Our whole crew, free to make different choices.

The rain stops as abruptly as it started. The storm has moved on.

We are all products of our past to a greater or lesser degree. But we do get to choose our own future. I want a different future.

Ivan is gone, but Amy and Sasha are here, and I need to get them away from this life, so Sasha will never need to know how to use a gun.

AMY

Branka couldn't understand why I didn't want to move straight into Ivan's house.

'I change the sheets on his bed. Is all ready for you two. You can leave Sasha with me if you want.'

Sasha has been clingy, so I don't think I'll be leaving him anywhere for a while, and I certainly don't want to set foot in Ivan's house, let alone sleep in his bed. The thought makes me gag. Johnny gets it immediately.

'We need a break, Mum,' he explains. 'We'll go into town. We can afford to splash out for a couple of weeks.'

On Airbnb, I find a three-bedroom apartment at the end of Macquarie Street, near the Opera House, and book it until the first of January. We'll have Christmas and New Year's Eve overlooking Sydney Harbour.

Very conveniently, Ink Slater left my car keys in my handbag. After collecting our suitcases from Mum and Dad's, we drive into town in the Mini. At least Sasha and I now have clothes, and I can replenish Johnny's wardrobe while we're in town.

By the time we get to Macquarie Street, it's dusk. The bats are wheeling above our heads. We walk along the harbour fore-shore, Sasha between us, holding our hands as if he can tie us together himself. Over dinner in a Thai restaurant, Johnny and I pretend that everything is okay again—for our boy.

When we finally tuck him up in bed, in his own room, we wander back out to the balcony. The Bridge is lit up like a like a giant Christmas decoration. Ferries and hydrofoils make busy trails in and out of Circular Quay. Straight ahead, the Opera House is poised at an angle I've never seen before, as if it's about to take flight or sail away, those impossible curves all lit up. The air coming off the harbour is salty and strong. Over to my right, the twinkling lights of harbourside suburbs dance on the water.

'It must be amazing to live here, or in one of those mansions by the water,' Johnny says, as he hands me a glass of rosé and takes a sip of his beer.

'Too rich for our blood, though, right?'

'Does that mean you still want to move up north, Ames?'

'Do I have a choice?' Our eyes meet.

'It's your choice what happens next. What do you want?'

'Peace.' I sigh and lift my glass.

'Peace.' He clinks his beer bottle against my wine glass.

'And no Novaks in the same neighbourhood,' I continue, while I've got the chance. 'Or bikies, or gangs of any descrip-tion. And no more crime. You've got to go straight.' I study his face, trying to gauge if it's sunk in just how serious I am.

'Fair enough. I think I'm ready. North Coast?'

'Yeah, that should be far enough away.'

We talk long into the night. Johnny makes me go through everything one more time, and then we agree to pack it away.

That dark night, when Ivan raped me, is no longer a secret between us, no longer something I have to hide. But the pain is still just under my skin. Johnny says he understands, but he doesn't. How can he? He's dragging around his own demons.

We lie beside each other, but don't touch, the sounds of the harbour slowly lulling us to sleep.

JOHNNY

Looking around the warehouse, I know I'm going to miss these big, ugly men. Dad is sitting at a card table. Josef hands him grey plastic shopping bags full of cash, one for each man, as they step forward to collect their share. Dad dispenses the cash like a king. King of the Croats. I smile to myself. Fuck, yeah, I'll miss this lot.

Beers are passed around and it starts to feel like a party. Anto still has his arm in a sling, but otherwise seems fine. He's kicking back on the sofa, a beer in his good hand, a shopping bag of cash in his lap.

Once everyone is paid, Dad stands up and clears his throat. It sounds like an elephant coughing. The men settle and turn towards the boss.

'You all be careful. No new car, new boat. Not be stupid fucks. Okay?' Dad glares around at the group of men, one face at a time, until he gets to me.

'This was Johnny's plan. Was good plan. His Amy and Sasha taken, but he bring them home. His house burned, but he can build new house. Ordinary house. Not stupid, big house. Ink Slater is dead and Hyde fuckers pay for long time. The rest of bikies? They run. Is good. I say thank you to my son.' Dad raises his beer, then sits down to a round of applause.

This is my opportunity, no better time will come, so I stand up and wait for quiet.

'Thanks, Dad. It was a wild ride, wasn't it?'

'Luna fucking Park, mate,' says Bigsie, and everyone laughs.

'I promised you I'd find Ivan's killer. Ink Slater denied it, but the gun used to kill my brother was found in his possession. I think we got our man.'

This brings a round of applause. I take care not to look at Marko and I have to hope Dad never works it out.

'I've been doing some thinking,' I continue. 'I reckon we've all got some choices now that we didn't have before. Money gives you choices, doesn't it?' Everyone is nodding; there's even a slight tilt of the head from my father.

'I've been talking to Amy and we've decided to move up to the North Coast. We'll try a nice little town called Hallows Head, south of Byron, see if we like it. I'm going to start a security company, installing burglar alarms.'

'So you can go back later and get in easy?' asks Stump, a confused frown on his face.

'No, really. I figure if I don't know how to protect people from criminals like us, who does?'

Everyone is quiet for a second. Do they think I'm having them on? Or are they wondering whether to take offence at being called criminals? Not likely.

'Reckon you'll need any help?' Anto speaks up. 'I want out, I'm over it. I don't want to get shot again, like ever. Lexy and I have been talking about getting out of Sydney. We drove up to the North Coast on our honeymoon. Fucking gorgeous.'

'Why not?' A grin breaks out on my face at the thought of Anto and Lexy coming too. 'Awesome. Amy will be stoked to have Lexy close by.'

'I'm not going anywhere. Sydney is home,' says Baz, as if someone is telling him he has to leave.

I glance at Dad, wondering what's going on behind his massive forehead.

He stands up again, and everyone shuts up.

'This not good idea.' Dad's face is impassive. I have no idea what's coming next, but I'm curious about my body's reaction—and there isn't one. Maybe I don't care what my father thinks anymore.

'Who will look after fish shops?' he asks, going straight for my weak point. He knows I've always tried to protect those families.

'I'm settling their accounts with you.' I hand him a manila folder and he sits back down to open it. One page, ten names next to ten loan amounts, all under $20,000 but all impossible to pay off on the wage we give them. A total of $157,570. I hand him the cash in a brown-paper bag. 'They can stay in our rental properties, work in our fish shops and survive on the rent we charge and the wages we give them. But if they want something different, you have to let them go. Okay, Dad?'

He looks pissed off with me but then his mouth curls into a begrudging smile. 'If they want, I let them go. Agreed. You have any other surprises for me, my son?'

'I've been training Blocker on the books. He's dyslexic too, so I figured he might have the knack for it.' Blocker grins as faces around the circle turn towards him in surprise. 'Looks like I was right. But I'll keep an eye on things for the next few months, until he's confident.'

'I still don't like your plan,' Dad says, then he shrugs. 'But is your plan, my son. So maybe is better plan than I think.' This is a big admission from him, and he seems a bit startled by it as he leans back in his chair.

My surprise must be showing on my face, because Dad starts laughing. A rare raucous sound, contagious. It makes me smile.

'No worry, Johnny. I not come visit and burgle your new customers. I have plenty of money.'

Marko is looking at me. He appears relaxed, but there's a coiled quality in the set of his shoulders and a question in his sad brown eyes. This is my last chance to expose him.

'I want to thank you all for helping me protect my family.' I deliver the line straight to Marko and his question is answered.

He raises his beer bottle.

'*Živjeli*, Johnny! *Živjeli*, Anto! *Živjeli!*' The crew drink to our health.

With Doug and Kerry's permission, Flynn will wake up to a golden labrador pup on Christmas morning. I've already made sure Granny Slater is okay and Mum has been dropping around to see her. I feel like I've fulfilled my obligations. I'm free to go.

I relax at last and raise my beer in salute.

AMY

The view from the balcony is like a postcard—a wide expanse of blue ocean and the sun sending an orange glow down to the surf club and the houses along the beach.

Johnny is manning his new barbecue, pork chops and *ćevapi* sizzling on the grill. Branka is in the kitchen, giving Lexy instructions on the art of cooking Croatian *blitva*, as opposed to Serbian *blitva*. It's all silverbeet and potatoes to me.

As I gaze out towards the water, Johnny catches my eye and raises his beer bottle. I spread my arms to encompass it all and smile. Drifting to the edge of the balcony, I give thanks for the view I can't believe I own. We bought this place the moment we saw it, only two months ago. It already feels like home.

Sasha still has nightmares. So do I.

I had to force myself to make love to Johnny the first time since the rape. It was hard, but each time it gets easier to forget his brother on top of me. I'm healing. We're all healing.

After turning the sausages again, Johnny joins me and we look down on our front garden, ringed by red and pink hibiscus bushes in full bloom, palm trees swaying in the blessedly cool sea breeze. Milan is sitting on a bench under the shade of a big old frangipani, a carpet of yellow and white flowers on the bright green lawn around him. He and Branka are visiting for a week. Driving through town yesterday, I spotted Branka checking out real-estate shop windows. Please, God, no. Maybe a holiday place, but if they retire up here, I will lose it, or worse. Lexy and Anto bought a place three blocks away and I'm happy about that, in a guarded way.

I'm waiting to see if Johnny is able to give up the adrenaline rush of his old job and live an ordinary life.

Milan is smoking a hand-rolled cigarette, his boots planted in the grass, his bottle of beer glistening on the bench beside him as he watches a heroic game of soccer. Anto takes a flying leap but misses the ball and Sasha scores again, straight into the net Johnny set up yesterday. My gorgeous boy dances around as if he's just won the World Cup, blond hair burnished gold by the setting sun.

Johnny is standing behind me. He kisses me on the back of the neck and places a business card on the balcony railing in front of me.

NOVAK AND SON
SECURITY SYSTEMS. NO JOB TOO SMALL.

Novak and Son, hey? I haven't told him yet.

I pull his hand down onto my belly and wonder if it's a boy or a girl growing inside me.

JOHNNY

My arms are around Amy, my face buried in her hair, when I feel my phone vibrate in the back pocket of my board shorts. Strolling back to the grill, I pull out the phone. Antonio Fazzini. What does he want?

'Johnny?' The voice is like gravel in my ear.

'Yeah.' I don't say his name. I don't want to bring the old life onto my new balcony.

'I got good news and bad news. We've been cleaning up that problem we discussed over lunch at your dad's place.'

'Okay...' I'm not admitting to anything on the phone.

'But we can't get to the twins. The screws are keeping 'em in protective custody, till after the trial. They know they've made some serious enemies, so they won't be talking to the pigs. Doesn't matter, we'll take care of them sooner or later. No problem.'

'Okay,' I say again. I've got a nasty feeling I'm about to find out the bad news.

Fazzini coughs once, then continues.

'You probably knew Ink Slater had a younger brother. Jackson. I hear they let him visit the Hyde twins, cos he's some kinda Special Ops war hero. Just got back from Afghanistan. He knows what happened to his brother. That piece of scum deserved to die, but you know how it is with family. The word is out. He's coming after you and Amy. Thought you oughta know.'

I end the call and look across at my beautiful wife as she stares out to sea.

ACKNOWLEDGEMENTS

It is an unbelievable joy to see *The Second Son* in bookstores and in the hands of readers. Thank you to everyone who reached out to tell me how much they enjoyed this book and what it meant to them. I took a writing course hoping to realise a dream: to write books after a lifetime of reading. There are many people involved in bringing that dream to life.

Penny Hueston and Michael Heyward, you are by turns talented, patient, kind, supportive, positive and funny. Thank you for your continued faith. Penny, I lay my Ned Kelly Award at your feet like a cat bringing home a lizard.

Kate, Ems, Imogen, Julia, Sophie, Maddie and all my Texters, thank you for your talent and hard work and for managing me with such grace. Onwards!

Alice Lutyens, Pippa Masson, Benjamin Paz, Caitlyn Cooper-Trent and all at Curtis Brown. I hope to do you proud.

Zahid, Rufus, Marina, The September Tribe, especially Tina, Paul, Emma, Veena, Charlie and Robbie, thanks for your insight, friendship and laughter.

My thanks to the Australian crime-writing and book-selling fraternity and sisterhood—you're a weird and wonderful bunch and I love you. Megan Norris and Karina Kilmore, it's a delight to belong to Sisters in Crime and to the Australian Crime Writers Association. Thank you Sue Turnbull, Andy Muir and Catherine du Peloux Menagé for including me in the BAD Sydney Crime Writers Festival.

My writing mates: Anna, Candice, Tim, Andy, Pip, Petronella, Rae, Nicola, Allie, Emily and Lyn, you're a mixed bag of sweeties.

My coaches, cheerleaders, and glamazons: Sharon Elliott Dunne and Maz Farrelly, and the friends who never forget to ask, 'How's the next book going?', thank you. The Denton-Pensa-Cetnic clan for letting me in, and Barry 'Baz' Bandur, in memoriam. Our crazy Croat who died too young. *Živjeli!*

Marilyn Peck and Colin Peck, my darling parents, your endless encouragement has always been my greatest strength. And Stead Denton, my husband, my inspiration, the one I love and try to entertain. Thank you for your endless patience and support and for sending me upstairs to write.

If you enjoyed *The Second Son*, please read the sequel, *The Double Bind*, and get in touch via Loraine Peck Author on Facebook, Instagram or at lorainepeck.com.

READ ON FOR AN EXCLUSIVE EXTRACT
FROM LORAINE PECK'S SEQUEL

THE DOUBLE BIND

COMING 4 APRIL

AMY

There's very little packing to do when your house and car have been firebombed.

We had the keys to a brand-new Range Rover Sports to replace Johnny's burnt-out Jeep, but sliding behind the wheel of his dead brother's car gave my husband the creeps, and I simply wouldn't get in it. I was raped in that car by the brother Johnny idolised. We considered torching it. I even bought a jerry can of petrol, but sanity prevailed, and we sold it. With all we owned in the back of Johnny's new Jeep, we left the blackened shell of our home in western Sydney and moved up here to the north coast of New South Wales.

I picked Hallows Head because of a blissful summer holiday I'd spent here as a kid. A village of six-thousand souls gathered around a famous surf break. Seven-hundred kilometres north of Sydney. I thought it would be far enough away to leave that mess behind, to build a life without secrets. I was wrong.

I fell hard for this house. The owners had already bought

elsewhere so we arranged a quick settlement and moved straight in. Our new home is all clean lines and open spaces with an incredible view across town to the surf club, the beach curving around to the headland, the sea a vast palette of ever-changing blue. Timber, stone and glass, set over three storeys: I never imagined I'd live in a place like this.

Four bedrooms, a three-car garage, a pool room for God's sake. The living area opens out onto a big balcony and there's a 'master retreat' on the top floor. Imagine! We're just a few streets up the hill from the beach and everything is within walking distance.

We can afford a beautiful home with an ocean view in Hallows Head because Johnny made a ton of money on his last big job, the one I thought would get him killed. But he survived, we all did. I still can't believe we've left Sydney behind, even though I know you can never escape your family.

I found rustic and beachy pieces in Byron, Ballina and Bangalow and this big house nearly felt like home by the time our eleven-year-old son Sasha started his last year in primary. I'm glad he didn't have to start high school in a new town; in a year's time, he'll have friends. Well, that's what I'm hoping.

He was quiet as I walked him to the local Catholic school that first day at the end of January, the sea breeze in our faces. Sasha has never been one to chatter; he's like his father that way, only opens his mouth if he has something important to say. But now he's much more guarded, aware of every car going past, every man who gives me a second look. At the school gates, Sasha told me he didn't need me to walk him to and from school anymore. Okay. But he still needs the light on and his bedroom door open when he goes to sleep.

It took me a while to realise he was sleepwalking. I should take him to a therapist, but how do I explain the original trauma? Yes, well he was kidnapped by the head of a bikie gang, but I was right there holding his hand. Actually, counsellor, he was holding mine.

Give me a woman who says she always listens to her intuition, and I'll give you a liar. Three months ago, I tried to convince Johnny to cut and run, but he wouldn't abandon his family, his crew. I should have left, taken our son to safety. I still beat myself up for staying when I could sense the darkness rolling towards us like flood waters in the night.

Johnny Novak was brought up to be a criminal; he's genetically engineered to lie. I'm not sure what he's hiding this time, but I recognise his tells: hyper-vigilance coupled with a certain distance. His face dissolves into a thousand-yard stare when he forgets I'm watching.

I want him out in the open, away from the shadows, but if there's one thing I've learnt over the last few months it's that it doesn't matter where we are, Novak blood runs thick through Johnny's veins.

The naive girl who married a man from the wrong side of the law thirteen years ago is still inside me, but she's scared, pregnant and holding that secret close. I'm not ready to acknowledge that this child could be the product of rape, and I'm afraid to tell my husband. I don't want to see the light die in his eyes.

Sasha is no longer the happy kid he was before his Uncle Ivan was gunned down in the street. Now I wake up and find him standing over me, his hand on my shoulder, his eyes open

3

and terrified even though he's still asleep. During the day, he's prone to anger over the mildest inconvenience. A ticking bomb with the timer in the red zone.

I'm a mother, daughter and wife with a deeply held belief that I will be held accountable for my actions. I killed a man to protect my family and every night I'm visited by his shade asking me to aim my gun at his kneecap rather than his heart.

No court of law will ever hear my side of the story; my husband muddied the waters too well. But there are times when I want to absolve myself: stand in front of a judge and jury, make them understand what Ink Slater did to me and my family. I'd tell them how Slater held me down, his rank breath hot in my ear as he described exactly what he wanted to do to me. I'd tell them my son was tied up and gagged like an animal, his innocence stolen.

The tall, thin man covered with tattoos didn't get to rape me; that dubious and dreadful honour belongs to Johnny's brother, Ivan. In my dreams the two men are interchangeable, the violent echo of the earlier rape shudders through me regardless of who is holding me down.

Some nights I will both Ink and Ivan to come to me in my nightmares, so I can fantasise about killing them over and over again. What does that make me?

JOHNNY

'Nice house,' Anto says.

'Try not to look like you're casing the joint,' I tell my best friend, as I grab a clipboard from the back seat.

Mountainside Drive is the dress circle of Hallows Head. Each home on the curve around the hill has a spectacular view of the sea. An ad for our new security business appeared in the local rag for the first time yesterday and today we're putting together a quote. Old-school advertising still works in this town.

Chatting with Carl Carrera on the phone this morning, I noticed a strong American accent and a sense that he wanted to impress me with his wealth. So far, it's working.

Backing into the bush behind the town and made of huge concrete slabs, Carl Carrera's house is one of the biggest in Hallows. Floor-to-ceiling windows reflect the sky and the ocean. The gravel driveway widens out to three double-width garage doors. Anto and I have to cross a timber boardwalk suspended over a large pond full of carp to get to the front door.

We're both wearing our new white polo shirts—Novak and Sons Security embroidered on the chest instead of a polo player. I only have one son, but I figure the name will create a sense of trust. Permanence. Amy seemed to like it when I showed her the business card. She had a goofy look on her face as she slid the card into the back pocket of her cut-off jeans.

Turning up for work in shorts and polo shirts…Christ, the rest of the crew would take the piss if they could see us. Of course, Anto's shorts are cargoes with the maximum number of pockets, so some things never change. I haven't run a security business before, but how hard can it be? We know the other side of the industry; surely, it's just about reversing our tactics.

The front door is painted with so many layers of gloss black I could check out my nasal hairs in the reflection. I bang the gold doorknocker—a howling wolf—three times. Anto and I grin at each other, weirdly nervous. This may be the first time we've sought entry to a stranger's property with the view of protecting rather than exploiting it.

A woman wearing a see-through pink dress and a skimpy, yellow bikini opens the door and gives us a big grin. She raises the glass she's holding in greeting.

'You must be the security guys.' She has an Australian accent with a slight American twang, short dark hair, big diamonds in her ears and is built like a swimwear model.

'Nice to meet you, Mrs Carrera. I'm Johnny Novak and this is Anto Kovacic.'

I hand over one of our new business cards because what else am I supposed to do with them?

'Oh. Thank you.' She studies the card for a moment. 'Come in. And call me Layla. Everyone calls me Layla.'

6

I try not to stare as she turns and walks down the wide, stone-flagged hallway, swaying slightly. It's only 11 a.m. and she appears to be nicely toasted. We pass several closed doors and then the hall opens out to a large living space. The walls are pale render, and the high ceilings bear the indents of the timber scaffold used to hold up the cement pour. Layla turns around to address us.

'Carl is out. He told me to let you guys measure up, or whatever you need to do so you can put together a quote. Okay?'

'Thanks Layla. We can give you a quote, no problem, but there are several options to explore.' I check the cheat-sheet on my clipboard. 'Do you need to access video from each room remotely? Or is it just external security you're looking for? Your husband wasn't very specific.'

This could be a waste of time, but we have to start somewhere. Going straight was never meant to be easy.

'Carl wants the works. Top-of-the-line, inside and out.' As she waves her free hand around to illustrate her point, I spot another whopping great diamond on her ring finger. 'Is that helpful enough for you, Johnny Novak?'

Smiling up at me with big brown eyes, she takes another sip of her drink then licks her lips. Anto is watching us and he seems to be enjoying himself a little too much.

'Absolutely Mrs Carrera...I mean, Layla. Right, mate. Let's start outside with a perimeter check.'

As soon as we're safely back outside, Anto does a great impression of a double-door refrigerator laughing its head off.

'Layla likes Johnny,' he singsongs.

'Fuck off.'

A three-metre cement-slab fence runs around the sides

and back of the property, enclosing tropical gardens on four terraces. The pool is surrounded by yellow-and-white sun lounges and matching umbrellas. No fence across the front, but the external passageways on either side of the house are planted with spiky-looking succulents and end in tall, deadbolted gates. You could climb over the gates, but you'd be in full view of the street. Not an easy home to break into, but that's not why we're here.

We get to work taking photos and measuring, first outside then inside. Every now and then, Layla turns up with glasses of cold water and flirts with us. Things could be worse.

Anto and I have already installed state-of-the-art security systems in our own new homes, but Amy drew the line at cameras in the bedrooms or bathrooms. She doesn't know anything about Jackson Slater's vow to avenge his older brother's death, and that's the way I want to keep it. No use adding to the burden she's carrying. My wife accepted that the security system installation was a practice run for our new business, but I was really trying to ease my increasing paranoia.

Amy picked this town, said it had a good school and was small enough to still be a village, a community. She said we'd probably get most of our work in Ballina and Byron but Hallows is convenient to both and still a sleepy seaside town. Maybe too sleepy.

Sometimes, it takes me a moment to realise I'm still moving at a different pace from the locals. When I'm buying a newspaper, the guy across the counter wants a chat. Coming from the city, we don't chat. We're too busy for casual conversation, and anyway I don't surf. Yet. Might need to learn if I ever want to fit in here. Why not? Anto and I could be out the back on our boards in the middle of the morning. That's what half the locals seem to do.

I don't want to stand out in our new town, but it's hard to blend in when I walk down the street with Amy. Everyone looks, she has that kind of beauty. She and Sasha go swimming down the beach a few afternoons a week, after school. They're both tanned and their blond hair is nearly white. Sometimes I let them walk ahead of me just so I can look at them. I nearly lost them both to Ink Slater. Evil, obsessed prick.

'Mate, where the fuck are you?' Anto clicks his fingers in front of my face and hands me the end of the tape measure. 'Go and stand at the end of the driveway so we can see what range camera we need.'

The crunch of the gravel under my feet sounds expensive and brings me back to the job. Top of the range, hey? Maybe going straight will work.

Who am I kidding? It's been two weeks since I heard that Slater's brother was coming for us. I feel exposed here without the rest of my family nearby, Dad, Marko, Baz... the whole crew ready to pile on if needed. Up here, it's just me and Anto and I'm waiting for my world to shatter. It helps to have my best friend on the look-out, but neither of us is a match for a Special Opera-tions soldier fresh from his third tour-of-duty. We may both be big, strong and handy with guns, but we're not Special Ops and that imbalance makes it hard to sleep at night.

AMY

After dropping Sasha off at school that first day, I decided to find a job, one that ensured I could still be home for my son after school. The only work that seemed to fit was waitressing. At first, Johnny wasn't happy about it.

'You don't need a job. We don't need the money. Why do you want to wait tables?'

It's extraordinary that a wife having a job could be seen as a problem—but that's what this family is like. Now Johnny is away from his father, Milan, he's more flexible, but male chauvinism has been part of his upbringing. Women are to be respected and protected. Until they're not. Whatever, I'm trying to reawaken my sense of independence in the hope it will heal me. Getting a job is a step towards that.

'It will get me out of the house,' I said, frowning at Johnny. 'I'll meet people. We need to make some new friends. Much as I love Lexy and Anto, we need some newbies too.'

Anto and Johnny have been friends since they were kids and Anto's elfin wife, Lexy, is like a sister to me. As a Serbian, she's also an outsider in this tight-knit Croatian clan.

A couple of weeks ago I started working for Veena Sankar, who was born in Hallows after her parents migrated from the Punjab. Veena is nearly as tall as I am, with an understated beauty, a ruby nose stud and a dozen small silver hoops around the cuffs of her ears. A trained anaesthetist, she ran away from the pressure of a top job in a Sydney hospital to come home and open a cafe. Wearing colourful dresses and a cowboy hat, she works the till and passes orders through to the kitchen. She has a core of steel beneath her warm and friendly exterior.

Veena's Cafe sits on the ocean side of the Esplanade and the tables on the veranda have an unobstructed view of the beach. Sometimes I get stuck, hands stacked with dirty plates, bug-eyed by the sight of the sea.

Today, I'm working my usual shift, eleven 'til three: the perfect shift for a working mum. The other lunch waitress, Amelie, also has a kid in school. We started on the same day, so learned the ropes together. She has long dark-blonde hair, pale skin and blue-green eyes and makes me think of that fairy tale about the mermaid trapped here on land by an evil queen. There's a wariness to her movements and dark circles under her eyes. She looks lost, but I don't know her well enough to dig deeper. We all have secrets.

Amelie and I have eight tables each. Veena jumps in when things get busy, deals with the till and take-away orders while cranking away at the big, hissing coffee machine. Veena's husband, Brett, produces exceptional food from the cramped kitchen.

I hand the menu to three guys from the local real-estate agency who come in often. Wearing short-sleeve shirts and ties, they stand out in this town. Casual dressing is taken to a whole new level when you work in a beachside cafe.

'I'll have my usual thanks, darl,' says the older man, staring at my breasts.

'BLT?' I ask, even though it's what he always orders.

'Yep, and an orange juice.'

I accidentally step on his leather-clad foot as I take the menu from his outstretched hand and have the pleasure of seeing him wince. When I turn around, there's a big guy taking a seat inside rather than outside, where everyone else wants to sit. He's looking at me, so I grab a water bottle, a glass and a menu.

'Hi. Here's the menu. We're just serving lunch now, breakfast is over.' I say with my waitress smile.

He doesn't look down at the menu. He's still staring at me and doesn't return my smile. Dressed in a grey T-shirt and cargoes tucked into combat boots, he's clearly not in Hallows for the surf. There's something about the way he's staring that has the hairs on my arms standing to attention. I tell myself to get a grip. Men stare at me. It's been happening since I was Sasha's age. As long as he keeps his gaze above my breasts I won't need to tread on his foot.

'What's good?' he asks, his voice deep and raspy, as though it doesn't get used very often.

'The Big Aussie Beef Burger.'

'I'll have it.'

'Do you want the pineapple ring?' I don't think pineapple has any place near a burger but, apparently, I'm in the minority.

'No.'

Good for you. 'Chips or salad?'

'Salad.'

12

'Anything to drink?'

'No.'

A man of few words.

'Coming up.' I say as I write the order on my pad and turn away, stopping at another table to pick up some dirty dishes. When I look back, the guy is still staring at me and because he's caught me looking, I feel heat rise up my neck.

Then I hear a shot. I drop the plates and throw myself down on the floor with my hands over my head. Silence. I turn over and sit up. My vision blurs and then everything goes dark.

I wake up propped against the counter, Veena fanning my face with a menu and Amelie holding a glass of water to my lips. I try to scramble to my feet, but gentle hands keep me where I am, sitting on the floor with my legs stuck out in front of me like a child. I'm beetroot with embarrassment.

'What happened?' I ask.

'A car backfired, you hit the deck and then you fainted.' Veena looks concerned.

Everyone in the cafe is staring at me, conversations suspended. I wave away Amelie and Veena and get to my feet.

'I'm fine now. Seriously.'

They both look at me dubiously, but it's busy, there are broken plates to be cleaned up, the kitchen bell keeps ringing, and the servery window is full of steaming meals awaiting delivery. We get back to work. What the hell just happened?

Even though I'm studiously avoiding looking in the direction of the big guy, I can feel his eyes following me around the room. He's taking his time with his burger.

'That bloke in combat boots likes you,' whispers Veena as

I hand her a saucer full of cash from the real-estate guys. She checks the bill, adds most of the cash to the till and slides the change into our tip jar. 'Ever seen him before?'

'No.'

'He obviously hasn't met your husband!' Veena laughs, but when I don't join in, she hands me another saucer. 'Let's get him out of here. Take him his bill.'

Although the man is leaning back in his chair as I walk towards him, he looks uncomfortable, like he'd rather be somewhere else.

'Here you go.' I put the saucer down on the table rather than hand it to him.

He pulls a twenty dollar note from his wallet, the rising sun emblem stamped into the brown leather. The Australian Army's crest. Maybe he's just been away on duty. God knows what he's seen and had to do.

'Thank you for your service.' I say, just as my father taught me.

He seems surprised, then glances at the crest on his wallet, looks back up at me and nods.

'Keep the change.'

He stands. He's as big as Johnny. He hesitates for a moment as if wanting to say something, then turns and walks out.

When things quieten down a bit, one of our regular customers waves me over. Willow comes in most days for a cup of Earl Grey and the salad special. She has long dark hair and wears silky, flowing clothing in shades of cream and cafe au lait. She likes to sit inside at a corner table.

She points to the chair opposite. 'Just for a minute. Veena won't mind.'

I sit obediently, unsure about what's coming.

Willow leans forward and continues quietly, 'I think you may have had a panic attack.'

I don't want to be a person who has panic attacks.

'Has it happened before?' she asks, big brown eyes searching my face.

'Not really.'

'What does "not really" mean?'

Last week when Anto and Johnny were installing the new security system, I was in the kitchen when one of them set off the alarm. The sudden screeching noise had me flat on the floor with my hands over my head. I didn't faint, but it took me a while to get my breathing back under control and stand up. No one saw it happen, so I pushed it to the back of my mind. Loud, sudden noises startle everyone don't they? Willow is waiting, so I take a deep breath and answer.

'Last week, after a sudden loud noise, I ended up on the floor like today.'

'Did you faint?'

'No.'

Her eyes are dark pools; it's as if she can see inside me. She pulls her shoulder bag from the back of her chair, rummages around in it then hands me a business card.

—

Willow Brant
Life Coach and Healer.

—

'Come and see me and we'll get to the bottom of it.'

I thank her, take the card, stick it in my pocket and get back to work. I already know what's at the bottom of it. I hear a loud bang and I hit the floor because my body is getting me away from gunfire.

AMY

Johnny is still asleep as I close the door to our ensuite and make it to the loo just before throwing up. It's been the same every morning for a month. Good thing Johnny sleeps like he's been clubbed in the head; he still has no idea I'm pregnant. I can't work out when I had my last period. It shouldn't make any difference, but it does. If I'm more than twelve weeks pregnant, the baby is Ivan's and the product of rape. If I'm eight weeks pregnant, all is good in the world, I'm carrying my husband's baby. I sit on the loo and pray for that outcome.

The week before I was raped, nothing physical was happening between me and Johnny because I had a bad case of the flu. Sasha brought it home from school and I could barely get out of bed. Ivan's party was my first night out in a fortnight. God, I wish I'd still been too sick to go. Either way, it's not the baby's fault. But I don't know how Johnny is going to feel about it. I don't even know how I feel about it.